The Sandpit

Nicholas Shakespeare

The Sandpit

Harvill *Secker*
LONDON

1 3 5 7 9 10 8 6 4 2

Harvill Secker, an imprint of Vintage,
20 Vauxhall Bridge Road,
London SW1V 2SA

Harvill Secker is part of the Penguin Random House group of companies
whose addresses can be found at global.penguinrandomhouse.com

Penguin
Random House
UK

First published by Harvill Secker in 2020

A CIP catalogue record for this book is available from the British Library

penguin.co.uk/vintage

ISBN 9781787301764 (hardback)
ISBN 9781787301771 (trade paperback)

Typeset in 13.25/18.5 pt Arno Pro
by Integra Software Services Pvt. Ltd, Pondicherry

Printed and bound in Great Britain by Clays Ltd, Elcograf S.p.A.

Penguin Random House is committed to a sustainable future
for our business, our readers and our planet. This book is
made from Forest Stewardship Council® certified paper.

MIX
Paper from
responsible sources
FSC
www.fsc.org   FSC® C018179

To Roger and Ian Kellas

The essential self is innocent, and when it tastes its own innocence knows that it lives forever.

JOHN UPDIKE, AFTER WILLIAM BLAKE

Prologue

Shula read his text message, and the air thinned around her. Why was he sending her this? It was exactly what they had agreed he must never do.

Her instinct was to call him. In that void between dialling his number and the distinctive British ringtone, she caught herself. Foolish. Foolish. Abruptly, she rang off. Her need to hear Rustum's voice ran deeper than her common sense.

The baby was still asleep, no one else in the bedroom, yet she had the sensation that eyes were tracking her.

She turned off the phone and slapped it, face down, on the small chest of drawers. Her movements were self-conscious, disembodied even, the actions of a young woman who had just woken up and was watching herself being watched. She knew implicitly that even the most neutral gesture, like unpinning her hair, would become data.

It was early Saturday morning and he was supposed to have telephoned last night. She had dozed off, waiting. This reckless text of his, so out of character, added to her foreboding.

She picked up her brush and pulled it through her hair. She hadn't had time to wash it, although the baby took pleasure in the smell and in grabbing hold and hiding in the black weight of it. Her son Samir, too, had loved to tangle himself like that. With his departure, she had had to cut herself off from the physicality that she had shared with her first-born, as well as rechannel the longing which prickled her skin whenever she thought of her husband. It was an acute missing, and she had struggled. But that was the deal.

And now this text.

She tried to conjure her more robust self, and view it as a bit of a game, as in the beginning she had treated their Friday-night telephone calls. But the surveillance had changed the way her mind worked. It had reached such a deep invasion of privacy. The men in the car parked permanently outside knew what books she read, what radio stations she tuned in to, the food she ate.

With a deliberate gesture, she put down her hairbrush, fighting off a sick feeling that they could even hear her thinking. The baby was her only relief, swaddled on the bed. When the baby was crying was the best time to have her most subversive thoughts. She couldn't believe that they would want to listen to those sharp, obliterating shrieks.

The building was silent. It would be after midnight in Oxford. In the city outside, dawn was breaking.

She stepped to the window to feel the early morning's breath on her neck, her shoulders.

Stars in the clear sky. Smell of hot seeds. The small maple tree below has a red kite trapped in its branches. Between the leaves, the black roof of the Paykan glints in the street light. A second vehicle is drawn up beside it, newer, larger, also without number plates.

Suddenly, footsteps on the roof, a rattling of shutters, someone beating on the door downstairs.

The baby stirs.

A separate hammering on the door at the back.

PART ONE

Chapter One

THE PLAYGROUND WAS DESERTED. THE only adults in sight on that chill afternoon were a couple studying the glass-fronted noticeboard outside the school building known as 'the Rink'. A short, thickset man in a brown leather bomber jacket and a long blue-and-white striped scarf wrapped ostentatiously around his neck, and a woman in jeans, slender, taller, wearing a fur hat and ear muffs.

Dyer's heart started to race. Gennady and Katya. They must have finished their meeting, and were waiting for their son to reappear.

To avoid Katya and her husband, but also out of habit, Dyer turned left at the gate and walked towards the sandpit.

This square enclosure, three metres by three, was one of the few remnants of the school as Dyer remembered it. Framed by a low brick wall next to the boundary fence, the box of sand was a continent away from the rush-hour traffic on Banbury Road. Its view over the grass playing fields took in the granite war memorial, the cricket pavilion, and the Cherwell, invisible but indicated by a line of leafless elms. In Dyer's time, a blue barge nestled on the riverbank, its lower deck doubling during swimming competitions as a changing room. But the barge was gone. Ditto the tuck shop and the woodwork shed where Dyer had learned to cut out a plywood shape which he could almost pretend was a machine gun. Yet Dyer would only have to raise his eyes to the circular Gents clock on the wall outside 'Slimy' Prentice's study, like a cold winter sun, with its hands at 4.03, for his eleven-year-old self to have recognised in an instant where he was. That and the sandpit.

To Dyer's irritation, another father occupied the spot where, since early February, he had taken to waiting for Leandro. A big, overweight man in his late thirties, hunched over, pale brown face, spectacles, with a sparse beard and thick unbrushed dark hair, and enveloped in a long unbuttoned coat. Dyer didn't know him, but he recognised the camel-coloured overcoat: exactly what he coveted for himself in this climate, where the cold still caught him unawares. Dyer had envied the coat from a distance during the match against Summer Fields, a fortnight before – he retained a vague image of the person wearing it suddenly producing a notebook, and tucking this away after making a quick entry. When Dyer next glanced across the pitch, the coat had gone.

The man hadn't seen him. Knees apart, feet in the sandpit, where at Leandro's age Dyer had sat on a sunny day with a magnifying glass and scored his initials onto a tennis ball, he leaned forward, and with his index finger sketched something in the sand. He looked at this, whatever it was, and muttered to himself in an animated way, finger hovering.

'Are you Samir's father?' said Dyer.

The man's arm froze. He raised his head. His face tightened when he saw Dyer advancing.

With his palm, he very rapidly erased the marks that he had made. 'That's right.'

'We haven't met. John Dyer. Leandro's dad,' and held out his hand.

The man stood up at the second attempt. He stamped his shoes, once, twice, three times. Then he stared at his hand, covered in moist sand, and wiped it on his coat, before shaking Dyer's.

'Rustum Marvar.'

Dyer glanced down. 'I'm interrupting you.'

'No, no, I was working something out.'

Dyer craned. 'Something interesting?'

Before Dyer could determine what this might have been, Marvar kicked out his foot and scuffed away the last traces.

'Just a problem,' he said and sat heavily down and stared out, arms folded, over the deserted playing fields.

Dyer, left standing, gazed at this big, grave, wood-sawed man with his matted brown hair.

'A problem you've solved?'

Marvar took his time to answer, as if he was choosing a wine. 'Nearly,' he said. 'Nearly.'

The quondam reporter in Dyer recognised the tension in Marvar's response. A long time ago in Belém, he had heard the same suppressed note in Colonel Rejas's voice. The tone of someone who wanted to share his excitement, but did not dare to – until Dyer triggered a way to earn his confidence. Not that Rejas's subsequent confession had advanced Dyer's career. There came back to Dyer the deranged eye of one Phoenix School mother who, swivelling to peck him with tiny questions about South America, had enquired what his greatest scoop was, and he started to explain that it was a story he had decided not to publish.

Dyer was used to sizing people up. He was quick to see that he and Marvar might like each other. 'I haven't noticed you much on the touchline,' and sat down beside him.

The remark detonated something in Marvar. His eyes returned to the sandpit, his bulky frame trembling inside its loose-fitting coat. 'And I have chastised myself,' his hand finding a forehead to clap. He hadn't been able to watch Samir play as often as he would have liked because of his work. On top of that, he had a new boss, a difficult man. Things were going on at work which had made it impossible to get away. Otherwise, he would have noticed how Samir had been victimised. He looked up at Dyer, mild brown expressive eyes magnified by round wire-framed lenses.

Marvar was agitated, but Dyer sensed that it wasn't merely what had happened to Samir that was brewing inside him.

'You mustn't blame yourself,' Dyer said in a reasonable tone. 'I didn't notice – and I was there.'

Whether Marvar took comfort from this was impossible to say. He spoke between large breaths as though he had been running. 'When Samir told me ... what *this boy* ... Vasily Petroshenko ... did to him ... *and* to your son. I did come here. Immediately! I spoke to ... Mr Tanner, is it? And now he's talking to our two boys, with *the other one*, together. But is that enough? Will it stop these tantrums? This boy should go and see a clinical psychologist, not Mr Tanner! People who bully have issues. I know bullies – *you* must know bullies.' He returned to where he'd started: he had not forgotten his rancour with himself. 'No, no, I should have been there. That is to say, I should have been watching Samir. But I will take him away somewhere soon, somewhere nice, maybe the next long weekend, and I will make up for it. I will make up for my negligence,' as though also voicing a promise to someone else.

Dyer thought of asking where Samir's mother was, but it seemed wiser not to. Perhaps Marvar was in the same boat as Dyer. People in Rio had not batted an eye, but in Oxford Nissa's absence was noticed. The older crowd were surprised to learn that she was still alive, and their eyebrows rose higher to discover that she had gone on to have twins with someone else. He felt their instant reassessment

– there must be something wrong with Dyer that she had left him. Marvar might be another single father with a turbulent romantic past.

On the low wall beside him, Marvar gave a shiver and sat back, buttoning up his coat. The city lights glittered through the naked trees. He stared at them. The sky was not yet black. Dark clouds moved in the distance.

'In my day,' Dyer felt obliged to point out, 'parents never came to watch their children play football.'

Marvar turned his head. 'You were at this school?'

'Yes, but a while ago.'

'Then you must have liked it to bring your son here.'

'Liked it?' said Dyer. He paused, thinking back. 'It's more complicated than that.'

There was the plunk of rubber soles on concrete. Marvar glanced nervously around. On the other side of the fence, a jogger ran by, breathing heavily.

Marvar looked back at him. 'Explain to me the complications. No, no, I'm interested.' He held up his hands and fluttered his fingers. 'You see, I worry about Samir ... he has so many things he has to deal with.'

Until now, Dyer had kept to himself his motives for sending Leandro to the Phoenix. The expression in Marvar's eyes – a compound of anger, excitement, fear, self-control – made him open up.

Chapter Two

DYER HAD ARRIVED AT THE school gates at four o'clock on that bracing cold February afternoon, fed up. He had been back in England seventeen months. His research was leading down a blind alley. The Oxford weather, the conversation of parents, oppressed him.

On top of everything, this bullying incident with his son.

It brought Brazil back; the heat, the silver foil of the sea, his years as a foreign correspondent...

A journalist has to be at home with everyone, a terrorist or the policeman who hunts him down. But these middle-class rich, who were far from being idiots, were surprisingly indecipherable to Dyer. They conversed in his language. A good many of them shared his background and education: once upon a time they might have been his readers. But their take on the world dismayed him.

For the sake of his son, Dyer had curbed his instinct to judge and to flee. He was going to try, for once, to be uncomplicated about this; play hard, work hard, become a committed Phoenix parent. He would blind his inner eye, and gag his natural tendency to say what he thought.

Dyer reasoned to himself that he felt this way because he was older, having come relatively late to fatherhood. Plus in Oxford he was the native, as it were – it would have amazed him if half of his fellow parents at the Phoenix School were in possession of a British passport, unlike in what he shrank to call 'his day'; as for the rest, although younger, they united in being much better employed than he was, and immeasurably better off. They worked in the City, the Far East, Asia, Africa, North America, for global corporations and governments. They jetted in from the earth's round corners, from places which, at his son's age, Dyer had known about only through his stamp collection. One or two even had bodyguards.

That afternoon, Dyer had finished work at the Taylorian at 3.30. Before leaving the library, he ordered up a book on Portugal's accidental discovery of Brazil in 1500. Then out of habit he checked the BBC news on his laptop.

The big drama of the moment – relegating to second place a UN report on global warming – was a speech by the new incumbent in the White House. The American president had made it his mission to dismantle one by one each of the treaties signed by his predecessor. His latest target: the nuclear deal with Iran, more than four years old now. His shrill accusations that Iran was not abiding by its international agreement had scalded the government in Tehran to threaten to restart its nuclear programme. Israel was promising in that case to retaliate, as was Saudi Arabia.

Dyer spooled back to the offer made by his editor two decades before: 'You're the doyen of Latin American correspondents – everyone knows that. But the accountants have decreed: "Shut Latin America. Full stop." You can have either Moscow or the Middle East. Which is it to be?' After hesitating for a week, Dyer had chosen neither: South America was the fount of his stories, the world he cared about.

But sometimes you regret your choices. In moments of private commotion, Dyer couldn't help speculating about the life he might have led. Maybe it wasn't too late to pull Leandro out of the Phoenix and take him to Tehran, Dyer thought ruefully, on realising that he had walked past Bardwell Road.

He turned right into Linton Road, hopping over a crack in the pavement, and headed in brisk steps back towards the school.

On the corner, he waited beside an old-fashioned red pillar box for a large black Lexus to dislodge itself from the kerb. Dyer had been a boarder in the house behind, brick and stucco, the colours of cold sores and sticking plasters. On how many Sunday mornings after the service in Hall had he sat astride this lopsided Edwardian postbox, waiting for his parents' mauve Singer Gazelle to chunter into sight? He preferred not to go there.

The wild-looking mother at the wheel of the Lexus scrambled out to assist her daughter with her cello. Once the vehicle had lurched off, Dyer crossed.

When the newspaper closed down the bureau in Rio, he had stayed on to finish his book about the cultural and social history of the Amazon basin. Published at an exorbitant price by the Oxford University Press, this was carefully reviewed in the *TLS* and in one or two anthropological quarterlies, and forgotten. Dyer had been kicking his heels when his aunt Vivien telephoned from her house in Lima and begged him to go and see a friend of hers who worked for a children's charity in Rio.

Dyer never could resist his aunt, a former prima ballerina, married to a retired Peruvian diplomat, who had devoted the last quarter of her life to improving the conditions of street kids in Lima. The upshot was that he went and met Vivien's friend, and by and by accepted a job with Ibeji, working in a *favela* perched on an emerald crevasse beneath the outstretched arms of Christ.

He continued to have inappropriate love affairs. His aunt had suggested that he needed someone 'much rounder' after Astrud. Dyer took his girlfriends to Lima to stay with Vivien in order that she might vet them over her home-baked gingerbread biscuits. But not, for some reason, Nissa.

They had met at a party in the Museum of Tomorrow in Guanabara Bay. The blurry glaze of her eyes. The sheen of her voice. Nissa could begin a sentence in Brazilian and end it in French or English, and flirt in all of them. Undefended, Dyer went home with her after they ran into each other again at a photo exhibition of Peru's Sendero years. Within weeks they were living together in his rented flat off Ipanema.

She gave birth to Leandro fifteen months later. After what had happened to Astrud, Dyer had folded himself tight, refusing to invest in a miracle, until one eyelid quivered open, then another, and two bottomless pupils of midnight blue stared out for the first time, and, appearing to focus, saw a middle-aged man who had started to sob.

Yet the arrival of Leandro did not fulfil Nissa.

Nissa had a short attention span if it didn't involve her. A baby was a competitor. Leandro was four when she left Dyer for an English lawyer, Nigel Trenchpain.

Dyer's despair was transparent, colourless.

'I thought she was different,' he told Vivien.

'Hardly anyone is, my dear.'

'Oh, Vivien,' he said. 'Oh, Vivien.'

'It's OK,' she held his head. 'It's OK.'

Following a brief and unexpectedly straightforward tussle, he gained custody of his son.

Leandro had his mother's deep laugh and *mameluco* eyes, like antique glass, and his father's unsettling persistence.

Weaned off the quick fix of journalism, Dyer flexed his stubborn streak to safeguard his independence. The BBC and then *The Economist* approached him to be their stringer, but he declined. Dyer's life concentrated on his son.

His days freed up once Leandro began attending the nursery school opposite. While hysterical presidents battled with impeachment, Dyer spent his mornings giving English lessons to wealthy clients; his afternoons teaching glue-sniffing orphans how to read and write.

At what point did it dawn on Dyer that God might have been Brazilian once – as Dyer had believed on arriving in Rio thirty-three years earlier – but had since changed nationality? It was a culmination of separate incidents more than any abrupt revelation, and stole up on him like the subject for his next book. Beneath the art-deco arms of Christ the Redeemer, a street kid was being killed every other week in Dyer's *favela*. Drugs and flick knives were discovered in two satchels at Leandro's new school. Even the beaches had started to stink.

Rio. It had become true for him. A great city – a great solitude.

Over a cold and suddenly tasteless lager in his local bar on Joaquim Nabuco, Dyer was ambushed by an occult feeling that he needed to get Leandro out of Brazil before his son got a blade in his abdomen, or Dyer did. In the five years since she had walked out, Nissa's new life had left her no space for Leandro, and so it was up to Dyer to act.

It was lucky that Dyer had saved for a rainy day, of which Oxford proved to be drearily full. With what remained of his severance package from the newspaper, a small inheritance from his father, and a larger, unanticipated one from Vivien, he would educate his son as he had been educated.

In his late fifties, Dyer had no property to pass on, but he could give to his only child the indisputable kick-start of a middle-class British education – which was all that England had to offer these days, as Vivien reminded him in one of their final telephone conversations; she would die in her bed at the age of eighty-eight in her clifftop house in Barranco, a blazing torch to the morning of her last breath. 'Why not take Leandro to Oxford?' was her question that Dyer had repeated to himself in a moment of beer-fuelled desperation. Both Vivien and his mother, Vivien's older sister, had been at the Phoenix, and the memories of their schooldays were unusually positive. Going to Oxford would be a good decision, Vivien said. Plus, he could research his next book there. 'And think of the fly fishing – you're always grousing there aren't chalk streams in Brazil.'

Once vocalised, the idea stuck, impossible to pour back into the frosted glass. Nigel was all for it. He had been at Summer Fields up the road, was even thinking of putting the twins down … Nissa was renovating their weekend bungalow in Búzios, and too distracted to worry about her son moving so far away. 'As long as you write to me every term what he has been doing. I used to love getting your letters.'

She had come across a bundle of them recently, inside a large envelope with 'João' on it. 'I see that spidery handwriting and immediately I know why we're not together.' But she had been happy to find them, she didn't want the letters not there, she said.

A week after Brazil lost 7–1 to Germany in the World Cup, Dyer booked two flights to London. In early September, having found a small house to rent in Jericho behind St Barnabas church, overlooking a deserted boatyard and the canal, he brought Leandro to Oxford. His main worry when he carried their four suitcases inside and thought about the quiet life that he had signed up for by making this move was that he might get bored.

Oxford was not a place to go barefoot. The huge wide unfriendly streets, the cold wind that whipped at his ankles, the food which tasted like his aunt's leftovers, the language. 'Daddy, what's a bosom?' asked Leandro after they had been there a fortnight, hoping for a reaction. Compared with Rio, there were not many pressing invitations to Dyer's gaze or touch.

The tempo of the city was rushed. People walked or cycled to lectures, to dinners that began punctually with a Latin grace. To dawdle was for tourists or dropouts, or for people who were lost. Almost from the first morning, Dyer felt lost.

The adjustment was harder for him, oddly, than for Leandro, whom he had lured to England with a prospectus woollier even than one of Viven's tea cosies. They'd get a dog, he'd take Leandro fly fishing, they'd live in a brick house. Plus, by going to the Phoenix, Leandro was continuing a family tradition.

Except that the school had changed, Dyer had changed. He was a different person, thicker in body, his eyes less blue, with grey streaks in his thinning brown hair, and his ideals battered; and yet in various ways he was not. It added to his sense of double vision when he walked through the new security gates, as if his boyhood Instamatic had jammed and he had continued clicking away, regardless, on the same negative. At his son's age, Dyer had believed that he had innumerable chances, as many takes as he wanted – like Leandro's digital camera, given by Nissa as a parting gift. In returning to Oxford, Dyer felt that he had lost his contours; he did not see the path ahead, the windscreen obscured by reflections, of dashboard clutter, the detritus of exile, of homecoming. He felt on a different road, as if his steering wheel was on the left-hand side, like the 'continental drive' green Beetle that he had bought second-hand from a garage in Cassington, mainly because it reminded him of Brazil.

On this Siberian afternoon, five birds migrated overhead, slicing west through a listless grey sky. Dyer punched in the code and pushed open the gate, glancing up at the clock. Mr Tanner had asked to see Leandro and Vasily together at 4 p.m.

Chapter Three

THE BULLYING HAD STARTED THAT term, after Leandro was catapulted into the school football XI two years prematurely. The new coach had telephoned Dyer on the eve of the announcement to explain how he wanted 'to shake things up'. He considered Leandro mature enough to make the leap; as well, Leandro would have company – Samir Marvar, another talented player from Leandro's year was joining the team. ('He's a "ledge",' said Leandro, having to explain that this meant a legend. 'He can kick the ball fifty-four times on his toes.')

'I shouldn't say this,' the coach went on, 'but they've both got it in them to play for the Oxford Schools team.' He laughed when Dyer said that he himself had never advanced beyond the second XI in cricket. 'A dad's greatest kick is to watch his son surpass him.'

Afterwards, Dyer felt that he deserved a far greater kicking for not having acted against Vasily Petroshenko straight away.

Striking to look at, with blond, almost white hair, and red-rimmed grey eyes, Vasily was a large-limbed Russian boy in his final year at the Phoenix. Tall for his age – he was thirteen – and with a disconcerting self-confidence, Vasily had put it about that he was a shoo-in for captain of the football team, having played two matches for them the previous season. To then see his name asterisked in the second XI for the match against Summer Fields was a humiliating shock for which he was ill-prepared, and it goaded Vasily to blame not himself or the coach, but whoever had usurped him. When Vasily scanned the team list, where his name should have been, his bulging glance read 'Dyer, L.' and 'Marvar, S.'

426,938

On their own, the incidents were small. Dealt with one by one, Vasily's tantrums would have been manageable. By not addressing them, a damaging relationship became normalised; and Dyer, to his shame, in not helping his son to navigate the waters with Vasily, had assisted.

Vasily's reaction on discovering that he had been replaced by an eleven-year-old boy was to take Leandro into the playground and demand that he climb the flagpole in front of the others. No, refused Leandro, flushing, it was out of bounds, he would get in trouble with the teachers. But Vasily insisted in a menacing voice. It was a Phoenix tradition, anyone who got into the first XI two years early had to climb the pole. If Leandro didn't climb it, he would be locked in the loo by the rest of the team and stripped.

When the inevitable happened, and Leandro crumpled to the tarmac, scraping his knee, a teacher ran up and demanded to know what he thought he was doing.

Vasily stood there, grey eyes blinking. Leandro, blood trickling, said nothing.

The attempted scaling of the flagpole had resulted in a visit to the school nurse, and in Leandro receiving his first Minus.

Dyer held back from making it a national incident. This was a stand-alone episode. Impatient of all kinds of bullying, he was indignant on Leandro's behalf, but he made provision for Vasily's resentment. Boys will be boys. Leandro had to learn to tough it out. No one had been tougher than the kids on the beach where Leandro had sharpened his football skills. It would make his son stronger. It had nothing to do with Vasily's mother.

Leandro kept to himself what really was going on: that what Dyer hoped was merely an ad-hoc moment was the beginning of a concerted campaign to destroy his self-worth with a peer group of which Vasily was overlord.

It was Leandro's history teacher who alerted Dyer. She suddenly turned to him and said: 'Is Leandro OK?'

'He's had an earache.'

'No, no, not that.'

Dyer gave her a quick look. 'Why?'

'He doesn't seem very happy right now. I've noticed he's withdrawn a lot. He was far friendlier to begin with, and he's not a shy boy.'

Leandro had been flailing a bit in his work, it was true. The peeling away of academic kids at the start of the second year had left him in a lower class. Supremely fluent on his feet, uninhibited, with a quick intelligence, he fumbled, however, with Wordsworth and the Napoleonic Wars. Dyer wondered if the malaise was due to that.

'Leandro, is there anything you'd like me to help you with?'

'No.'

'You're sure?'

Silence.

His son, although diligent, had always been temperamental. He shared Dyer's tendency to be moody, which expressed itself when he was hungry or tired, or was asked a question that he didn't want to answer.

'Leandro?'

'Dad . . .' he said, on a warning note.

If it unsettled Dyer to see Leandro exhibiting characteristics he shared, then it also blinded him. He attributed his son's subdued behaviour to longer days at school, to Leandro's flu which had given him a painful ear infection, and to his own malaise at the sound of winter slamming against the panes, the chill dark afternoons – weather for reading and taking notes, and not much else.

Dyer did not uncover what was going on until, arriving to collect his son one afternoon, and unable to prevent his glance sweeping the playground for Katya, he came upon a stricken-looking boy who reeled towards him. At first, he failed to recognise the disconsolate figure, then the faded uniform began to register. Exactly as his parents had done, Dyer had purchased this second-hand, from a room behind School House which opened at odd hours and was staffed by vultures who volunteered in order to pick through the best stuff. The stacks had shrunk to a few items by the time Dyer turned up. Almost all new boys wore pristine dark blue corduroys; Leandro's were weathered, greyish, the colour of the February sky.

'Leandro!'

He was biting down on his lip and his eyes were shining. Behind him, a group continued to kick a football around with exaggerated concentration. A tall, fair-haired boy, who seemed to be their leader, turned and smiled at Dyer. A knowing, mocking smile, emanating a malicious energy that escorted Dyer back to the *favelas*.

Leandro's nose was still running by the time they returned to Jericho. It was alien to his nature to snitch, but in trickles and half-sentences he choked out what had happened in the instant before Dyer appeared. How the other boys had looked to Vasily, saying, 'Can Leandro join us?' How Vasily, shining with self-satisfaction, replied sneeringly, 'Not today, sorry. You're rubbish at football. Come back when you're better.'

That night they sat up late. Dyer yielded to no one in his ability to extract information. Leandro's story was followed by another. And another. Until Dyer had a vision of his son like a prisoner of the Tupi Indians, suffering in silence the punishment that they reserved for their bitterest enemies, wrapped in a writhing coil of poisonous toads which had started to shrink around his neck.

Dyer learned how Vasily had tried to drown Leandro in the swimming pool. 'He pushed my head under and didn't let me out. His mother was sitting right in front and thought it was just a joke.' How, arriving for training practice, Leandro had stepped over the rope barrier beside the pitch, 'and he whipped it up and hit me between the legs.' How, incited to new heights of malice, Vasily had shut Leandro in a locker ten minutes before his training session with the first team, and started banging on the lockers on either side, not stopping until it was time to go. 'You'd taken me to the doctor for my earache and it really hurt my ears.'

Leandro wasn't Vasily's only victim. 'He does it to Samir too.' In his jealous turmoil, Vasily had only to see Samir bouncing a football on his toes for him to march over and kick the ball away as far as he could. He had also posted insinuating comments on a group chat, speculating whether Leandro and Samir might be gay.

Dyer felt sick that he had downplayed Vasily's behaviour. A surge of guilt overwhelmed him that he had failed to protect his son. Since Leandro's mother lived 5,700 miles away, and had never displayed much maternal interest, it fell once again to Dyer to do something, even if Leandro himself didn't want his father to do anything. 'Please, please, no.' But this also was part of bullying, Dyer recalled.

Between discovery and action, Dyer lay awake, eyes closed. The smell that she had left in the air. Like wheat. '*But you don't have a choice, dear,*' came his aunt's voice, as if on a crackling old radio. In the *favelas*, the bullies were the ones you had to neutralise.

Dyer telephoned the school in the morning and was put through to Mr Tanner, head of day children, and a blackbelt stickler for rules. He responded with super-efficiency. 'I want you to write it all down.'

'It's reached a point,' Dyer added, 'where I feel it has to be dealt with.'

'And so it shall,' said Mr Tanner, a boyish-looking man known as a good rugby player. 'And so it shall.'

Bullying, he hardly needed to remind Dyer, had absolutely zero place at the Phoenix. He knew 'young Vasily', considered him 'quite free range' in a tone that suggested 'cocky little shit'. The rapidity of Mr Tanner's reaction on receiving Dyer's email hinted that this was not an isolated incident, something that he felt at liberty to vouchsafe during a follow-up telephone conversation in respect of another boy whose father had also registered a complaint. Dyer deduced that he was referring to Samir Marvar.

'What I'd like to suggest is the following,' Mr Tanner said. 'I'm going to get the boys together to talk about it, but first I will meet with Vasily and his parents.'

*

The street lights switched on. Dyer closed the gate behind him, and stood for a moment looking back down Bardwell Road. This was the start, this was the gate from where he had set out, the portal to the world beyond. He had hoped that he would find there the excitement and fulfilment he pictured for himself when he read the passing of Arthur or *Treasure Island* or *Greenmantle*. He would meet his Guinevere. In real life, she would touch his shoulder. You. At last.

He turned – and that was when he saw Vasily's parents waiting by the Rink.

Chapter Four

A LARGE PART OF DYER'S guilt had to do with his eye being not on Vasily, but on Vasily's mother. Most of the Russian mothers were boarding mums who lived in Moscow or St Petersburg and visited Oxford once a term; Katya Petroshenko, by contrast, based herself during term-time in a gated community off Jamaica Road. Little was known about her. A former Murmansk beauty queen with an idiosyncratic command of English was the story going round. 'Vut zer fuck iss *bum-break?*' was one phrase that had been attributed to her, but this may have been the registrar's touch.

Dyer had met Katya the previous autumn. He was standing outside the Rink when a light hand stopped him. He turned and saw a very beautiful woman. His height, slim. Her straight blonde hair was tied up. She seemed to recognise Dyer.

'Are you Leandro's father?' The voice is deep, but feminine.

Dyer cracks a smile.

She is wearing flat shoes and no make-up. Her face looks as if it has been washed in a cold stream. She has high cheekbones and a faint gossamer moustache, like peach fur.

'Katya Petroshenko,' she says. 'My son Vasily is in A block.'

He meets her gaze without conceding much curiosity. After Nissa, he has resisted beautiful faces. Her eyes are the grey of an Arctic wolf. They look like eyes that can see a long way in the dark.

Katya compliments Dyer on Leandro's running achievements on Sports Day, back in July.

He feels himself relaxing at once. Having a son who runs fast – that gives him a gravitas he can take pride in.

Their conversation over the next ten minutes touches on Leandro, who had jogged every morning on Ipanema; on Vasily, also a keen runner with an obsession for football – 'He is hoping next term to be school captain'; on Katya's absent husband Gennady, a Ukrainian oil executive. As she begins to explain his job, Dyer realises that he has met Gennady already, at the headmaster's annual Fathers' Breakfast beside the Cherwell; Dyer had recognised him in a flash as one of those noticeably short men who pack out first class in long-haul flights, with a wide black moustache, large square teeth, and tinted glasses, although it was overcast.

As to Katya, Dyer formed the impression of a nice, evasive, professional wife, who was aware that she stood out because of her natural good looks.

The composition of the teams had long been settled by the time of their next encounter, after the February half-term. Katya bustled and smiled when she collided into Dyer on the Woodstock Road. It had rained for two days; now the sun was out. She was dressed well, expensively. Pearl-grey jacket, a bit early for spring, brown cashmere jersey. Her pleated blue skirt was the colour of the airmail envelopes that Dyer would post his father from Brazil.

Dyer was awkwardly relieved that she did not bring up the subject of football. Both of them heading in that direction, the Phoenix School was what she wanted to discuss. Dyer seemed to fascinate Katya when she discovered that he had been a pupil there.

She was light-hearted in her attitude towards him. 'Excuse me, but why are all female teachers called Ma?'

The school's customs and rules perplexed her. What was this thing Minus? What did it mean, 'out of bounds'? And why, unvarnished nails on slender hips, did she have to make an emergency taxi-drive to Boswell's to buy her son a diabolo!

Sex. The furnace which smelts mud into gold. With no effort, she made him giddy. He felt his hardness, and tried to diffuse it by very earnestly answering her questions.

Dyer knew what it was to be a foreigner. Prey to a potent blend of obligation and history, he untangled for Katya the expressions and traditions of which the ultra-spin diabolo was but the latest phenomenon – and already being superseded by gel pens that smelled of apples.

When she looked at his lips as he spoke, as if it would help her to follow, his groin tingled.

So they walked together down Canterbury Road, through Park Town towards the Phoenix School, with Dyer telling her in his most contraceptive voice about marbles, jacks, conkers ('I like the way you say conkers'), Airfix kits, Action Men, stilts, superballs, Frisbees, fidget-spinners – all trends requiring stock, with pressure to purchase from shopkeepers who knew exactly how to supply Phoenix mothers like Katya with the appropriate currency.

'I'm heading over there,' said Dyer, on their arrival at the school gates. He gestured towards where the first XI were limbering up, although he couldn't spot Leandro.

Her grey eyes lingered on him. 'Thank you,' was all she said. Her teeth white as mint.

Dyer had done most of the talking. About Katya, he had learned nothing, except that her husband was away quite a lot. Her face was luminous, but her depth uncertain. His eye fell helplessly to her upper lip.

'I live just round the corner. Would you like to go to the Bookbinders one night?'

'What, for "a pint of bitter"?' She was regarding him.

'Or if it's vodka you prefer, there's that cocktail bar on Walton Street.' In heels she would be taller. In her flat red shoes, he could look her straight in the eye.

'I prefer to try English beer.'

'It would be a pint and a half at the most. While our sons do their homework.'

She gave him a slow, reluctant smile. Not the smile of a free woman, but the broadening smile of someone who wanted to be free, perhaps. 'All right.'

Diaries were consulted, telephone numbers exchanged. A plan was hatched for the following Tuesday, even as her son was thumping on the sides of a football locker with Leandro trapped inside.

... the women exposed their parts with such innocence there was no shame. They laughed and enjoyed themselves greatly.

He thought of Katya next day in the Taylorian while transcribing the encounter of Pedro Álvares Cabral's sailors with the Tupi Indians on the Brazilian coast. Her grey eyes twisting to look up at him. The faint golden down on her upper lip. She was married, but he had a fantasy of possessing her. Her fingers were gripping the pillow, he was soaring, the whalebone of her naked back, hoarse sounds coming from his throat, her throat.

This was before he went to collect Leandro and encountered him in tears bolting from the Hard Court, and discovered how Katya's son had been victimising him.

There are things you cannot say to someone face to face. You are a coward. You have taken the wrong path. Your son is a bully.

Katya telephoned Dyer after he had sent his email to Mr Tanner. Not at all warmly she said: 'It sounds like the boys are having problems.'

'I know they're going to be meeting – let's see how everything evolves.'

Inevitably, she was no longer free on Tuesday to join Dyer at the Bookbinders. Her husband was flying in from Moscow to discuss the situation with Mr Tanner. He would be staying on in Oxford for a few days.

Chapter Five

SEATED BY THE SANDPIT NEXT to Marvar, Dyer did not mention Vasily's mother. He talked, instead, of the difficulty of explaining Brazil to North Oxford; the uncertainty of life in Rio; Vivien's legacy – barely enough to cover Leandro's time at the Phoenix; and how, as a christening present, Dyer's father had paid Leandro's enrolment fee, or else Leandro might not have gained a place.

'Has the school changed much?' Marvar wanted to know.

'It's the same, and yet not the same.'

'How is it different?'

Dyer thought. 'We swam in the river. There was no security. We didn't have telephones – we wrote home once a week.' He still made Leandro write thank-you letters, he said. 'And it wasn't nearly so international.'

At the time, Dyer had felt unusually secure. He had a sense of fellowship with his peers, a feeling that because his mother and aunt had been through the school, it was some-how to be trusted. Yet after his parents died, taking away the answers they could have given, Dyer had come across his own letters home and was struck by a sadness that never found words, the bleakness of the weekly reporting of film titles and sporting outcomes and I-hope-you-are-wells. He had suddenly felt sorry for that boy waiting on the red pillar box, the wartime wounds and imperial aspiration which meant that his teachers and his parents could only ever supply their inadequate best ... leaving him to muddle through with some sort of grace, delighting in marbles and conkers and crazes to make do.

'What about the education?'

'There were some decent values,' said Dyer, with his tongue a little bit in his cheek.

'Yes, but what did you really *learn*? What were you taught that helps you in your life today?'

There was a strange quality to Marvar's probing. It stimu-lated Dyer to take more care in how he answered. It was as if Marvar was struggling to resolve a parallel issue, and Dyer could help him.

'We were taught that everyone has a talent,' realising even as he said this how banal it sounded. 'It may be hidden to the world, but dig deep enough – you'll find it.'

'What is *your* talent?'

'Oh, I'm still digging.'

'Seriously.'

Dyer had not spoken to anyone else in Oxford like this. He hadn't had a drink. This was coming from an earnest place, and looking down on himself he didn't entirely trust it. He continued with a half-smile, not wishing to be overheard, not wanting to sound like his old headmaster making a sales pitch. 'In my case, it was probably more of an instinct that I discovered than a talent. I learned that every action is a decision between good and bad. What it's about is living as good a life as you can. I left here wanting, every time I was faced with a choice, to do the right thing – if that were possible. But don't we all?'

'I don't know, do we?' asked Marvar, and answered his own question with another, as if afraid of the answer. 'What about now, what is the lesson our boys are getting *now*, would you say?'

Dyer's reply had taken seventeen months to mature. How the school had changed was a source of unavoidable fascination. As the father of a day boy there – a third-generation Phoenician – he had, on this topic, a long perspective.

The modern tribe of Phoenix parent belonged, in Dyer's view, to a powerful and pervasive freemasonry which extended into the deepest crannies of international finance, law and politics. Invariably, these parents were buying into an old-fashioned luxury brand like Burberry. If you put on a Burberry mac, you wore it – and immediately you were times ten. Plus, what it enabled you to cover up was limitless. In this respect, the school, despite reputation, had evolved to offer a highly efficient detergent service. It dangled the unspoken lure of rinsing away where you came from – impurities which lurked in your background and wealth – to emerge, rebranded, as wholesome exemplars of the Phoenix's three much-trumpeted rules: 'Be considerate, be considerate, be considerate.' People were never suddenly rich, any more than they were suddenly good. For a number of foreign parents in possession of what Balzac had called 'great fortunes without apparent cause', the Phoenix was where they laundered their children.

In Dyer's time, a majority of the boys, and the dozen or so girls, had not travelled outside the Midlands, let alone beyond the United Kingdom. They were the sons and daughters of the professional middle classes, the children of doctors, teachers, civil servants, diplomats, stockbrokers, solicitors. A small number took their summer holidays in France. But Abroad was as foreign a concept to most of them as modern notions of wealth would have been; it was not the catchment area it since had become.

'My headmaster used to teach geography,' Dyer recalled. 'This one never sees inside a classroom.'

Mr Crotty was busy criss-crossing the globe to entice pupils from the very countries which Dyer had been taught were once Britain's most steadfast enemies, or else which Britain had cut down the middle. Dyer counted them out on his fingers. Germany, Russia, China, Japan, Italy, France, Holland, Spain, Turkey, Argentina, India ...

'And Iran,' Marvar said, with smiling deliberation. 'You have forgotten Iran.'

So it was out of the bottle. 'You are Iranian?' He nearly added: the Axis of Evil.

Marvar made a speechless gesture, not denying it.

Dyer had thought he might have been from Morocco or the Lebanon.

'You say that Summertown knows nothing of Brazil,' reflected Marvar, his mouth compressing. 'Try telling these people you are from Tehran!'

Dyer sat up. Iran. He had been reading about it only an hour earlier. He was intrigued to find out more, but there was a dispersive quality to Marvar's conversation which made him hard to follow.

From the few details that Marvar divulged, Dyer gathered that he worked at the Clarendon laboratory as a junior physicist. He was indeed a single father like Dyer. His ex-wife lived in Tehran, where he had studied. Dyer heard the longing in his voice as he spoke of Tehran. But when Dyer asked about the current situation there, he looked detached, diminished.

He glanced up with impatience at the clock.

'Four-forty. They are taking their time.' He reached down to brush some grains of sand from his shoe.

'Then they may be treating our complaint seriously,' said Dyer.

'They have followed protocol. They have been too literal. They do not realise it's a systemic problem. It's not going to get fixed *without a lot of work*.'

'They'll keep an eye on him, though.'

Marvar said nothing. He sat staring at the sand that he had disturbed as though he was still working out his problem.

At last, he turned to Dyer. 'Was there bullying when you were here?'

'Christ, yes.'

'Were you bullied?'

Dyer had not thought about it until the moment Marvar asked, and had not prepared his answer.

'I suppose so.'

He was aware of Marvar's brown, nervous eyes measuring him. Once more, he felt a chemistry between them; two single fathers sitting here, on this cold February afternoon, waiting beside the school sandpit for sons who had been bullied, who kept asking themselves: *'Why didn't I see it earlier?'*

Dyer's turn to stare over the darkening fields. The football pitch had disappeared, replaced by a black screen speckled with a few orange lights.

Funny how the mind was good at pocketing some things while keeping the glow on others. He thought that he had left his childhood behind him, but it was there in the dusk.

*

It had happened towards the end of his second year. Then, the craze was not diabolos or apple-scented gel pens, but model aeroplanes from World War Two – a memory still relatively fresh. The words that Dyer assembled to salvage the incident were impregnated with astringent smells, of Araldite, turpentine, paints in miniature tin pots.

For his eleventh birthday, he told Marvar, his parents had given him, at his whining insistence, an Airfix kit. The cardboard box contained three rails of grey plastic components which had to be twisted off, painstakingly glued together, then painted with appropriate camouflage and markings to denote whether the aircraft belonged to the Allied or Axis forces. When he stuck on the last transfer, it filled Dyer with a sense of accomplishment that he could conjure even now, to balance on his fingertips this three-dimensional object, the first which he had created all by himself. He hangared the plane in his bedside locker on top of his stamp album, to bring out and dive, handheld, through the air – bursting from the clouds on an unsuspecting, imaginary enemy.

One morning he opened the locker and found the plane gone.

For the next forty-eight hours, nothing seemed emptier. He kept coming back to look inside. Distraught, he challenged the other boys in his dorm – Finnock, Garridge, Trundle, Stook, Croach – and was met with blank or smirking denials. The matter of a missing model aircraft was too minor to take up with his housemaster, a remote and preoccupied figure who had been held prisoner by the Japanese in Singapore. Dyer's parents were far away. He tried to cry himself to sleep without making a noise.

Two nights later, he stood in the bathroom brushing his teeth when a boy entered wearing a red tartan dressing gown. In the mirror there appeared the freckled rather pale face of Rougetel, a shy 'newbug' from the dorm on the next landing. An unusually gifted pupil, and already 'a ledge', in Leandro's word, for completing his maths prep in minutes, Rougetel had suffered terribly in his first term from homesickness – his parents lived abroad – and Dyer had gone out of his way to comfort him after he ran away one day. This had developed into a friendship. Rougetel helped Dyer to solve Slimy's more difficult fractions. When Dyer's grandmother took him to the Mitre for lunch, Dyer invited Rougetel along. During the last hols they had independently sent each other polite Christmas cards.

Swallowing hard, Rougetel stepped up to the basin. After a furtive glance around, he bent forward with his face nearly touching the mirror, like Dyer's mother, so close that Dyer could see the indentation in his chin, as if a pencil had been pressed to it – and he whispered to Dyer's reflection: 'Look in the sandpit.' The need to keep his voice down made it sound like the putter of a distant propeller.

Dyer told Marvar: 'I waited until everyone was asleep. Then I sneaked out in my pyjamas, down the road – the doors weren't locked – and I dug around for a bit.'

Marvar, captive, said: 'You mean here? In this pit?'

'Somewhere here.'

'And – did you find it?'

Dyer remembered the night, a little faded maybe, like a restaurant bill in an old blazer. The cool freshness of the air after the bathroom – the tiled floor had reeked of disinfectant. The dark deserted street, the low fence, the sandpit. And the moment when his fingers encountered a hard outline and, brushing away the sand, exposed the curved tip of a plastic wing coloured with Dark Green and Dark Earth markings.

'It might even have been there,' pointing to where Marvar had rubbed out his marks. He gazed at the mounds and furrows emphasised in the street light. 'But as I said, this is many years ago.'

One digs up the past to pay for the future. Climbing the fence to look for something precious in a place where he wasn't supposed to be – hadn't this been his initiation as a foreign correspondent?

Marvar watched him with a curious smile. 'What was the plane?'

Dyer heard himself recite, like a long-forgotten verse learned by heart: 'An Australian fighter called a Boomerang, made by the Commonwealth Aircraft Corporation between 1942 and 1945.'

'A Boomerang!' said Marvar, with another smile, full of irony and humour. 'After the stick you throw and it comes back? Oh, I like that,' and he repeated the word with feeling. 'Boomerang ...'

Just at that moment a light went off in a window. There was a movement in the playground, and three figures emerged from the doorway to Mr Tanner's office.

Vasily, the tallest, peeled off when he caught sight of his parents. Katya detached herself from her husband, running forward to place an arm across Vasily's shoulder.

Leandro walked on towards the Rink with Samir, a slim, good-looking, dark-haired boy who skirted around the embracing mother and son with the loose grace of a young deer.

Marvar, waving, heaved his big body up. 'Samir! Over here!'

If he hadn't stayed in neon-lit labs in a cold unyielding climate, and not gone hunchbacked and plump thanks to years of sitting on a stool, this is what he would have looked like, thought Dyer, following.

Under the Rink light, their two sons wore the expressions of boys who had taken an important step. They exuded the sense of being grown up that only children can feel.

Dyer smiled at Leandro. 'Got all your prep?'

Katya came by, holding Vasily to her. Gripping his son's other arm, Vasily's father talked to him urgently, in Russian. He lifted his head, and his face hardened when he saw Dyer. Katya's eyes turned, finding his. She looked at him and then looked away.

*

Mr Tanner telephoned that evening. 'They've had a smashing meeting. In fact, Vasily doesn't dislike Leandro. He thinks he's a very good footballer.'

'I'm glad to see he's well-trained,' said Dyer in his driest voice.

Fluently, Mr Tanner continued: 'I'll keep a watchful eye on things. I'm grateful you drew it to our attention. Accounts like this are very troubling to us and need to be addressed.'

Not for one second had his son believed Vasily, it was plain to Dyer. Leandro knew that he'd been bullshitted, and he would go along with it. Still, secretly he seemed relieved that it was now out in the open. To hear Vasily utter the words 'Oh, I've always admired you' in front of Mr Tanner and Samir, it lanced something. It got his father off his back about being bullied, it got the bully off his back, and the experience served to bond him with Samir. By the time of the match on Saturday, Leandro's ear had cleared up, he was talking as he used to, he looked like himself again.

Chapter Six

THE END OF FEBRUARY. THE days short and cold and dark. The low grey light of winter.

Dyer went to the Taylorian early. In life you need something to do and something to undo, in his case a Brazilian way of existing that had obeyed no hours or rules. He now had a project which forced his days into a new routine and took him to the same corner of a reading room overlooking the Randolph Hotel. Silk-shaded lamps like pith helmets. Long tables of bleached oak. On the wall opposite, above shelves of red-bound French bibliographies, an unrestored painting of two figures in a classical landscape. He liked the silence and the jungly smell of old books, the undergraduates who hungered to learn, young women who lived in digs in St Clement's with clothes on the floor and the poster of the Cézanne exhibition.

Sometimes, coming down the stone staircase, the glance of an attractive face met his and he could tell what she was thinking. A middle-aged man on his own. Not someone who paid attention to his clothes – jeans, trainers, a pima cotton shirt beneath the pullover. Experienced. Fit. Reasonably intelligent, but not an academic. Distracted, imbalanced, intense, possibly interesting. In the cold air his skin was pale. He was always forgetting his gloves.

'You look so glum.' In a surprising exchange early on, a single Phoenix mother, whose novel Dyer had agreed to read, said to him with cappuccino foam on her lips: 'Tell me three things that have made you happy.'

'When my son laughs—'

'Oh, you're such a sop.'

After he left the Bon Croissant, he thought of two others.

The euphoria that ambushed him when one of his street children read for the first time. The twisting face of a woman, the tanned legs spread wide on the sheet, the hand in his hair. It counted for something.

The last woman he had slept with, eighteen months before, was a divorced teacher from Leme with braided black hair and a passion for the novels of Clarice Lispector; they had tumbled into bed in the knowledge that his departure from Brazil was imminent. In Jericho, Dyer intuited that Leandro would welcome a fond maternal presence, after observing his father's daily struggles with a clothes hanger, the washing, the cooking, but also with trying to make their quiet evenings together more fun. But when Dyer tried to conjure that female Other who might share their home, he couldn't.

Several times, he saw a face in profile or caught an outline from behind, a laugh, a smile, a movement that promised to unlock his stasis, and felt that he had found her. He wasn't aiming for a mythical creature, but for a positive, straightforward woman whose contours might fit, without abrasions, into the life that he had built for himself and his son. He might as well have been looking for a goddess. He had searched a thousand faces, there was never an answering gleam.

But he knew that he didn't want a repetition of Nissa. Each time, it was what held him back. His fear of marking one more decent person through his feelings for someone else, like the impressions left scratched on a writing pad beneath a letter to another woman.

Above all, he didn't want the recriminations. The twist in his gut as she sought to justify her behaviour with Nigel, who had been every bit as helpless in his desire for Nissa as Dyer. The tremolo in her voice as she told Dyer: 'That's why I loved you, your sensitivity, your wish to make me understand what you felt, your wish to explain, the way you moved your hands, the way you looked at me and held my hands, so that if I couldn't believe what you said, I could believe the way you held me.'

Even a casual affair was hard to envisage. In Oxford, the enemy of carnality was the bicycle in the hall. In the sawdusty Portuguese prose of Sergio Madrugada, associate professor of colonial history at the University of Coimbra, he suppressed his lascivious thoughts of Katya Petroshenko.

Dyer's life in Oxford had developed into a ramshackle structure based on the Taylorian. At the fringes was the Café Bon Croissant on Oakthorpe Road, watering hole of the polished-marble-worktop Summertown brigade. But there was also the traditional, self-absorbed Oxford of the Turl and Ducker's shoe shop, which had closed down in Leandro's first term; and, at the end of the lane, the Mitre, where Dyer's grandmother from Clitheroe would treat him to a roast beef Sunday lunch when he was Leandro's age.

Dyer inhabited this Oxford like a well-cut old suit. He was at school and university here, and he had his goat paths. He took his son to the Phoenix along the same wide streets, on foot or in the Beetle; at other times, Leandro bicycled on his own. At nine, Dyer had a cup of tea and a rice cake at the Café Lisboa before heading to the library. At twelve-thirty, a bowl of soup and a bread roll in the King's Arms. In the afternoon, before collecting Leandro, a quick shop for dinner in the Covered Market. The pheasants hanging, the white plastic buckets of whelks, the smell of fresh ground coffee. There was an aroma about Cardew's that he loved best in the world. Then later on, he had to be at home to prepare a meal for Leandro and to help with his homework, if that was demanded. In the evening, sometimes, at a dinner party in Summertown or at High Table – Merton, Trinity, Exeter – as the guest of academics who toiled in esoteric fields not so dissimilar from Dyer's.

You feel your ugliness when you walk past beautiful buildings, how quick your life is, and insignificant, and sometimes you feel uplifted. His was a rarefied Oxford, its chapels and halls each like a caravel in its own dock; an impoverished, friendless city lay outside, its pavements home to people who had nothing, as in the *favela*. Gradually, he had re-ascended to a panorama of it all, from windows, college rooms, church towers – he climbed the staircases, worn stone and creaking wood, to rooftop terraces. Oxford lay below in its quads and separatenesses, cordoned off. The afternoon is over and he stands looking down at the faces beginning to stream home.

The home match on Saturday against Horris Hill took place on an afternoon of cold sunshine.

Dyer was late in leaving the Taylorian. Until now, he had found his research a slog, and never much minded breaking off to watch Leandro play: it compensated for the matches that his parents had missed. All at once engrossed in Professor Madrugada's recently published monograph on the 'accidental arrival' in Brazil by the Calicut-bound fleet of Pedro Cabral, Dyer reached the Phoenix shortly before 2.30 p.m. The game had begun.

Horris Hill were racing forward. There was a long kick.

The air was split with cries, cheers, the muted beat of gloved hands clapping.

He passed behind men in Barbours and scarves, women in ski jackets and woollen hats, until he found a gap.

The parents stood around the pitch, Phoenix on one side, Horris Hill on the other.

Impatient to know the score, Dyer noticed, standing on his own, the father of the Phoenix striker, a Namibian-based bullion dealer whom he had talked to at the Summer Fields game, and walked over to him.

Dyer looked forward to his touchline chats. Somewhat to his amazement, the edge of the pitch had turned out to be an incomparable forum for discovering what was going on in the world.

Leandro's promotion to the first XI had introduced Dyer to a higher level of achieving parent. The Hong Kong-based mother of the centre forward was heiress to a chain of clothes factories in Cambodia; not only that, her second husband owned a large uranium mine in Niger. The left winger's father was foreign secretary of his West African republic. As for the father of the full back, he was No. 2 in the Chechen parliament, and, according to Leandro, wanted by Interpol – a fact that emerged after Ma Crotty requested a routine criminal record check so that Mr Abdurashid might join his son on the school skiing trip to Davos ...

Dyer had gained through Leandro not merely entrance to a number of arenas where entry in ordinary circumstances was thrillingly forbidden, but a ringside seat.

He had no illusion that what he picked up were titbits. Plutonium grade. But titbits. All the same, it was in his blood to tease these stories out, with their entrails.

It never ceased to fascinate Dyer, how indiscreet people can be when they don't think you are going to use the information. Everybody loves to talk about what they do, who they are. Phoenix parents who would cross the world twice to avoid publicity behaved incautiously out of character when removed from their security staff and safe bases. Relegated to the touchline – often at a time, if the game was midweek, when most other parents were at work – they became uncalculated, porous. Finding it suddenly intolerable to be standing on a drizzly afternoon beside a prep-school football pitch next to someone who had no idea who they were, they snatched the slightest opportunity to tell him, on the presumption that he was bound to be like them.

Saturday's match against Horris Hill is a textbook example.

'How are they doing?' Dyer asks.

'They're losing,' grumps the striker's father. 'Two nil.'

He follows the game with a dutiful expression, no longer like a person expecting to be recognised, until he cannot hide that the score is of far less moment to him than his responsibilities as the proprietor of an open-pit gold mine near Windhoek.

Breathing on his fingertips, he starts to tell Dyer in a confiding tone how not long ago he was approached by the Iranian government to smelt an immense quantity of bullion.

'I sent out one of my people. He came back. It was gold all right – the bars were stacked to the rafters of a warehouse in Tehran. Only one problem, though.'

Dyer encouraged him to go on. His gathering of information was instinctive, what he had been trained to do, even if there was no outlet. It was another compensatory act, a deflection from his hitherto unexciting research. Now and then he might experience a transitory pang that he wasn't any longer a journalist, but to date not one of the stories that he heard while watching Leandro play football had made him wish to pick up a pen. Fourteen years since he had last filed an article, and he was perversely content for his storytelling muscle to remain dormant.

'On each and every bar was the stamp of the Central Bank of Kuwait. These were the Kuwaiti gold reserves, stolen by Saddam Hussein!'

'So what did you do?' he prompted, reminded suddenly of Marvar.

'The CIA were keen for me to go ahead, but the Iranians never returned my calls.'

Dyer nodded, poker-faced, as fifteen minutes later he nodded out of the same continuing habit when the father of the Phoenix goalkeeper, a French-Canadian hedge-fund manager who for some obscure reason had developed what his wife teasingly called 'a man crush' on Dyer, used the half-time interval to tell him the background to a story that had seized the headlines.

Days earlier, the runaway favourite to be the next head of FIFA had been arrested in Switzerland for assaulting a chambermaid. Intense speculation in the world's media revealed no one to be in possession of the facts – save, that is, for Gilles Asselin, whose company, he let slip to Dyer, as their sons changed ends, owned the hotel in Geneva where the assault allegedly had taken place.

'It's a story, nobody can prove it except me, but I'm telling you the story.'

Gilles Asselin, thinning grey hair with a jutting bony nose and an amused slur to his accent, was forty-one, but looked older. He was a former speed-skate champion who was known to jog five miles every day – Dyer might benefit from copying his regime, Leandro felt. Gilles had worked for Goldman's and then for Paribas until he decided to create his own company. He owned a chateau near Liège, and kept a private jet at Kidlington and his long white athlete's fingers in an awful lot of pies.

Impermeable when it came to business, Gilles was gleeful in relaying to Dyer the genuine reason behind the arrest. 'It was a case of mistaken identity!'

The FIFA candidate, 'a connoisseur of rough sex', had called up his madame to request his favourite girl, who not being available, it was arranged to have her place taken by someone *au fait* with Monsieur's forceful tastes. So the madame assured.

'Am I going too fast?' Gilles says, at Dyer's expression.

'Not at all.' Dyer's care to conceal his curiosity has only made Gilles more confessional. 'So what went wrong?'

Gilles grins. 'Ding-dong. Enter Sudanese room-cleaner. Monsieur is nonplussed. Not what he expected, quite. Nonetheless … he pounces. She resists. The harder she resists, the more he assumes this is part of the game. He gets more violent. He chokes her, slaps her. She hits back. This excites him further, *naturellement* … Moments later, ding-dong. Standing there, white leather boots to her thighs – the correct woman …!'

'How do you know all this?'

Gilles taps his watch. 'Same thing that allows Apple to monitor my step count.' And when Dyer goes on looking blank: 'Data sniffers, bots, cameras. They know exactly where he's been, what he's done … If you have the money, you can buy a history of anyone. You can buy a history of yourself! A good Moldavian techie will call up the data for you. Where you were at dinner last night, your conversation, text messages, images of you walking home. He could piece together your life better than you ever could. Oh, *bien fait*, Phoenix!'

The ball had curved in a high, unlikely arc from the half-way line, over the players' heads, into the Horris Hill goal. Dyer, still absorbing Gilles's information – a history of himself, nothing appealed less – had failed to register the scorer.

'Did you see that?' said Gilles, turning. 'Did you see what your son just did?'

'Well done, Leandro!' Dyer shouted.

It was why he was in the team. He had the soccer style of Brazil: surprise, craftiness, balance, spontaneity.

'That was some kick,' said Gilles. He couldn't let it go. 'I hope those bloody scouts are watching.' It was no secret – Gilles's fierce ambition that amounted almost to an obsession for his son Pierre to be selected for the Oxford Schools XI.

'Your boy is devastating,' observed Gilles's wife Silvi, joining them.

'All from his mother,' Dyer assured her. He was accustomed to joking that Leandro had Nissa's eyes, but her legs, too.

'And from you?' Gilles was curious to know.

Dyer considered it. 'His obtuseness.'

'Are you obtuse?' asked Silvi. 'I don't think of you as obtuse.' She was still looking at Leandro.

'Oh, yes.' Dyer was stubbornly saving himself for something. What, he did not know. Perhaps it was why he gravitated towards parents like Gilles and Silvi. Their stories were beads for a rosary that he elaborated while he waited for it to show itself, as he performed his daily circuit from Jericho to the Taylorian and back.

'He's so alive,' she murmured, 'so himself,' and turned her pale face to Dyer.

Silvi Asselin – she was born Silvi Kareva in Estonia – has a squint, not unattractive. She comes from a small town west of Tartu, but speaks of it little. Her father was a Stalinist who killed himself when the Communists lost power. Her narrow green eyes give the impression of being always slightly trained on the road out of town, to the world beyond Lake Võrtsjärv and its broken-down carriages, the stained brick, the three-legged cat; possibly beyond Oxford, even.

Having caught her husband, Silvi stands on permanent vigil against anyone who might resemble herself. Those careless enough to treat Silvi as a mere conduit to Gilles are not invited to their impressive house in Ward Road, with its malachite bathrooms, butler called Brian, large modern paintings hung next to smaller old masters. ('Sometimes upside down,' bitched one football dad.) Here, Silvi is chief executive, not Gilles.

Silvi likes Dyer because he listens, and because the small-town Estonian girl in her responds to the notion of playing patroness and matchmaker to impoverished single artists.

Dyer likes Silvi because she likes his son, and because there is something generous in her that has nothing to do with her husband's wealth.

Shapely in her expensive grey latex, like the smooth rubber handle on a hammer, Silvi flashes Dyer a smile. Long white face, short hair, reddish, as the breast of a robin, she looks at him in the way of a woman who needs to be played, not approached head on.

'Has his mother been in touch recently?' she asks.

'Hardly at all.'

Angry to justify herself, Nissa had cast Dyer as the Devil: 'He's addicted to everyone's stories but mine. He's nicer to people on buses than he is to my family. He's a cold Englishman. He's a ... he's a ... *é um narcisista maligno.*'

'Where's Leandro going to go after the Phoenix?' Gilles meanwhile was wanting to know.

'It's still up in the air.'

'Eton, he should go to Eton,' decided Gilles. 'Or Wellington. They do the IB programme. Where were you?'

Dyer told him.

'That's a good school. Why doesn't he go there?'

'He might,' said Dyer, reluctant to admit that a fee-paying school was unlikely. Not saying, I can only just about cover the Phoenix's astronomical fees.

Brushing past Dyer, a curly-haired brown dog lunged after a flock of pigeons that had landed on the grass, and was shouted back.

The whistle for the second half reverted their attention to the game.

Silvi touched his arm before she moved off. 'See you tonight. You're coming to dinner, remember? There's a woman I want you to meet ...'

Dyer was about to reply when a male voice stopped him: 'How's that boy of yours? Still winning every race?'

Chapter Seven

THE SPEAKER HAD APPROACHED FROM behind, unannounced. It shocked Dyer to recognise the dog-owner, who walked right past him and snapped on a lead. Beneath thick dark hair combed back and jetty eyebrows, his handsome face was blotched as though from eczema or sunburn.

Dyer had last seen Lionel Updark on a January evening six weeks before, at a cocktail party thrown to mark his return to England. Dyer didn't recall his cheeks and forehead looking like a stickered trunk then.

The man with the shiny disturbances on his skin was a diplomat, based until December in Rabat, and currently awaiting news of his next posting in an oat-coloured manor house near Woodeaton. At the Phoenix, they had sat in the same class. Forty or more years went by before their next encounter, at Updark's party: an occasion when the host did not hide that he had pulled away in the race which mattered.

Dyer couldn't remember who that evening had told him that Updark had been promised Paris. Feeling patronised and a failure, Dyer had drunk too much duty-free claret and flirted unsuccessfully with Updark's over-perfumed wife.

This is the first time he has noticed Updark at a football match. That Updark might have chosen to avoid public appearances was understandable. Closer to, his mottled face looked as though red chilli had been pounded into it. The unwholesome effect was emphasised by the neatness of his clothes. Polished brogues, blue corduroy trousers sharply creased, well-fitting tweed jacket with a burgundy V-neck jersey beneath.

The ends of a faded yellow-and-blue scarf trail down over his padded coat, and it takes Dyer a further second to register that the scarf is striped in the Phoenix colours.

'Hello, Lionel. I didn't know you were a football dad.'

An autumn father like Dyer, Updark has a daughter at the school who does not, to Dyer's knowledge, play team sports.

'Oh, I always like to see who's in the first eleven.'

He stands scrutinising the Phoenix players. 'Dyer, L. And Marvar, S. to boot. I say, they've done well to be in the team. You, I recall, were captain of the second cricket eleven.'

Dyer can't put his finger on it, but there is something artificial in Updark's behaviour, like a man pretending to have a limp.

'Who's winning?' asks Updark, distracted. He was late because his dog had run off.

'Horris Hill.'

'By how much?' scratching his maculate cheek, his attention no longer on the players but on the parents congregated beside the touchline.

'Two–one.'

Dyer is tempted to ask Updark about his ugly rash, but his wait-I'm-watching-the-football expression puts him off.

This smartly dressed Updark is at odds with the plump, ungainly boy who sat in Slimy Prentice's Latin class flawlessly translating Horace. The mismatch is disturbing and it gets in the way of Dyer's memory. They were not especially close at the Phoenix. Updark had been academic-minded, aloof, interested in the classics and cricket – he was scorer for the first XI. Highest tally of Cothill wickets taken by a Phoenix bowler? Most number of runs against the Dragon? Ask Updark. His knowledge allowed him to participate, to be a player himself.

Hard to recreate that studious introverted character from this compact man. Only the thick dark hair was the same. He could have been a farmer with his dog and corduroys, the sort of ruddy-face you'd see behind the wheel of a Range Rover, or unfolding a shooting stick at a point-to-point, not at a prep-school football match.

'You must find this weather tedious,' Dyer said to him, for something to say, 'after Morocco.'

'No more so than you,' and spun around.

His dog now was barking at some swans.

'Come here!' Updark yanked at the turquoise lead. He wore an open-necked shirt, but moved up and down the touchline like a man in a tie.

'What's he called?'

'Spassky,' in the tone of someone who had not chosen the name.

He was a dog like a poodle with tight clumps of brown fur, the same tan colour as Marvar's coat, and a white streak on the belly.

'Hello, Spassky,' bending down to tickle his chin.

Two eyes partially hidden beneath long brows seemed to take him in. Leandro was always asking for a dog. From the day of their arrival.

A wet tongue licked his fingers.

'We've only just got him,' said Updark, his face reddening all over at the effort to restrain him. When he reached out his hand, Spassky shunned it. 'He's a cockadoodle.'

Cockadoodles made good bird-dogs, Updark explained, and they didn't shed hair. His daughter had allergies.

Did that explain the fiery patches on Updark's cheeks which made Dyer think of the lobster on the Pitu bottle? Was it genetic?

Dyer stood up. 'How is …' He had forgotten the name as he had forgotten the name of her mother, and then remembered. ' … Beatrice enjoying the Phoenix?'

Updark's daughter – Leandro thought her odd – was in the year above Leandro.

The school was perfect for her, said Updark, enumerating why: she was captain of the chess team and head of the debating society. In all the top sets, too, with the exception of biology.

'Have you decided where she's going afterwards?' was Dyer's inevitable next question.

'She's set her heart on Wycombe Abbey,' said Updark. 'But she's got to get in first,' adding in an indulgent tone: 'She wants to be a diplomat.'

'Is that what you'd like?'

'Oh, I think so. She'd be the fourth generation Updark in the Service.'

There was something touching in Updark's inherited loyalty to Queen and Country, even if the pride that he took in his daughter impeded him from enquiring after Leandro. Had Updark asked, 'What do you wish for *your* child?', Dyer would have replied that he wanted Leandro to connect with something he cared about and to lead the life that suited him, and neither wealth nor climate should have anything to do with it. 'Be considerate' was cockadoodle as far as it went, but the Phoenix motto left out too much. In place of the name of another school, Dyer had hoped by now to have come across one unseen line or story that he could give his son; like in a Borges parable, it would encompass and answer everything, it would be the pin number to the universe's vault. He was still in the process of searching for it.

Dyer nodded. 'And you? Have you heard what your next post will be?' The rumour in the Bon Croissant was that Updark's Paris Embassy was on hold, suddenly, for something more hush-hush.

'Not yet,' said Updark. 'Not yet.'

As a journalist, Dyer had come across diplomats like Updark, and in general he got along well with them. The majority were civilised merchants of high-class gossip. They shared a professional interest, immortalised by the poet Flecker, at whose college Dyer had been, as the '*lust of knowing what should not be known*'. Only, in Dyer's case this forbidden knowledge was tailored for public consumption.

'You know where would be interesting?' reflected Dyer. 'Iran.'

Updark's alert hazel eyes fixed him. 'What do you know about Iran?'

His expression was hard to read. He looked combative, as though ready to thrust his crimson face into a scrum.

'Not much more than I learn from the news,' said Dyer. 'But I was nearly posted there. One always has a tender spot for the things one didn't do.'

'The problem is, which Iran are you talking about?' There were two Irans, Updark went on, a little over-eager, like a teacher, to share his superior knowledge on the subject. 'The nice, democratic, charming face to the world, which we would all like to believe in, ancient, sunny, Paris-educated

– or Scottish, in the case of the current president.' Then there was the Iran of the hard shadows, the Revolutionary Guard, the judiciary, the nuclear commission—

The dog was chewing the end of his scarf. 'Stop that!' Updark jerked his scarf away and coiled it tighter around his neck.

Spassky watched Dyer, then barked. The whirr of the docked tail. Pigeons scattering like applause into the sky.

'Come on, Phoenix ... move it!' Other shouts returned Dyer to the pitch.

'Good pass, Leandro!' The game had ten minutes left to go when Dyer heard the shout.

Updark had vanished in the same disarming manner as he had materialised. In his place stood Rustum Marvar.

He was in his gangsterish coat, unbuttoned, the pale green lining the colour of dry grass. Dyer had seen him the day before, on a bicycle racing through traffic lights. Marvar was so deep in thought that he had failed to register Dyer waving.

He had only just arrived. 'Please,' dropping his voice to a dramatic whisper, 'who is winning?'

Dyer told him.

Marvar nodded, then bent to do up his laces. He still had sand on his shoes.

'Can Phoenix rise from the ashes?' Marvar said sonorously, standing up.

'Possibly,' smiled Dyer, glad to see him. 'They don't like to lose to Horris Hill.'

With some people you could feel friends straight away. A bond had sprung up between them beside the sandpit.

But this Marvar was not the subdued person Dyer recalled talking to on Tuesday evening. He was excited, carefree, drunk – except that he was sober. 'Go on, Samir!' he flung in a loud, almost hysterical voice, after Samir received a pass from Leandro through the legs of the Horris Hill striker.

His father's shout burned through Samir like a thrill. He straightened his back, lifted his elbows like wings in the cold air. In an electrifying sequence of quick, deft moves, he trapped the ball with his left foot, dribbled it past one defender, then another, flicked it onto his right foot and booted it between the goalkeeper's outstretched hands into the back of the net.

Instinctively, Marvar and Dyer embraced. A dog was barking. Unfamiliar with touchline protocol, Marvar was punching the air and emitting loud whoops.

Dyer did not remember afterwards what he thought of at that moment, but he was aware that Marvar radiated with an extraordinary energy. He was having a moment in the sun.

'See what happens when you come and support him!' laughed Dyer.

His earlier conversation with Updark had filled Dyer with a powerful desire for Phoenix not to lose this match against Horris Hill. It was important in a way that he had not felt before. Not merely to justify Leandro's position in the team – and to have his talent recognised alongside the achievements of Beatrice bleeding Updark – but to justify Dyer's belated defence of his son against Vasily.

He almost wished Katya was watching. His eyes kept sliding to the second XI pitch, until someone told him they were playing away; that was the third XI.

It hadn't gone anywhere. Not even a drink.

The whistle again. One of the Horris Hill players was down. The play paused while both teams stood in a circle around the boy, and the referee checked that he was unhurt.

Over Marvar's shoulder, Dyer saw Gilles Asselin glancing in his direction. He had the furtive look of a man who wanted to slip away and make a call. He lifted a hand on noticing that Dyer was staring at him.

Dyer was relieved when Gilles resumed his discussion with the person he'd been talking to, a short fleshy man of about forty, with curly orange hair and the hint of a moustache, and wearing a peaked blue baseball cap with 'Cal' stitched on to it in gold letters. As Silvi had reminded him, Dyer would anyway be seeing Gilles later. Better to keep dry till then what remained of their conversational powder.

Marvar, brimming, turned to Dyer: 'Hey, I wanted to ask you something.'

Dyer waited, curious. Phoenix parents seldom asked him anything.

'Ullswater, do you know it?'

'In the Lake District?'

'Tell me, what is it like?'

Dyer had once fished with his father near Pooley Bridge. 'Extremely beautiful and surprisingly wild,' and remembered his first trek in the Peruvian Andes. How the peaks and clear blue lakes above Huaraz carried him back to Cumbria.

When Marvar said that he had decided for the upcoming exeat to take Samir climbing in the mountains around Ullswater – a poem that Samir had had to learn by heart, composed there, had given Marvar the idea – Dyer looked at him in his long thick enveloping coat, and almost laughed.

'But keep this to yourself. Please. I haven't told anyone.'

'Of course,' said Dyer. Although why anyone should be interested in Marvar's excursion to the Lake District, he couldn't fathom.

'I know I can trust you not to say anything.'

'Really?' said Dyer, amused. 'And how can you be sure?'

'Samir told me. About that policeman in Peru. You got this story out of him. This incredible, incredible story, and you didn't tell it.'

Dyer gave an inward groan. Leandro. Shooting his mouth off.

'Is it always so important to say everything? You never told me about *your* problem.'

'Touché. But really. Why didn't you tell it?'

'Oh, lots of reasons.'

'Give me one.'

'It was too personal, too unhistorical to use as journalism.'

'You only wanted to write historical stories?'

'If you like.'

'Another reason. Please …' He wanted more, like some-one holding out a glass to be refilled.

'There was a woman.'

'There's always a woman.'

'It was a great love. If I told his story, he was likely never to see her again.'

Marvar looked carefully at him. 'And did he see her again?'

Dyer smiled, as back, back went his mind to the bargain that Rejas had forged with his government. Yolanda had been arrested for protecting the revolutionary leader Ezequiel in an apartment above her dance studio. Rejas had agreed not to stand for president, in a campaign he was favoured to win, on condition that she was given a quiet release after two or three years.

'*Quién sabe?* After that, I stopped being a journalist.'

Serious all of a sudden, Marvar said: 'I have a story … not a love story exactly,' and paused, as though meaning to go on, a comma not a full stop. But he was interrupted by the whistle for play to continue. After that, conversation was pointless. It was all about the match, which ended, with no further goals scored, in a draw.

The players shook hands and gave three cheers. The parents started to dribble off to the match tea before the scones were all devoured. Inside the Phoenix goal, Spassky lay on his back, rolling in the mud.

Chapter Eight

LEANDRO ASKS DYER TO CARRY the games bag with his dirty clothes. Leandro's arms are full already with his satchel that's bulging with textbooks and notes on the Battle of Trafalgar; he is to be tested on this in a few days.

They step through the gates and set off down Bardwell Road.

It always depressed Dyer on their walks back to Jericho to notice what Oxford had become: it seemed to have mimicked London, with 4×4s on the pavements, and scaffolding, which did not tally with his idea of it. This feeling extended to the dinner parties to which, as a single father, Dyer received plenty of invitations – at least early on.

He had never forgotten his first dinner party, in Summertown. The hostess was a Phoenix parent. A husband found at INSEAD, two children raised to be considerate, a kitchen that spilled out over white marble tops into the living room. The refurbished home of many a brittle, unattended North Oxford mother. Conversation, like a blurring fan, went round and round the same subjects; where you were going on holiday, where your child was going to school next, how very lucky everyone was to be living here, in Summertown.

Summertown. It could have been Luton, save for the prices of the pinched red-brick houses, the M & S food hall – said to boast the highest turnover of any branch in England – and the coffee shop, started up by a Phoenix father and his new organic girlfriend; everybody rolled their eyes about it, but you saw them in the queue, spending their £8 per 'change your life' latte. Smuggertown, its detractors called it.

The Smuggertown mothers reminded him of Nissa. They behaved like characters from the Globo soaps. He was familiar with their bickerings, the little piranha bites that stripped a marriage of its flesh. Had Dyer married one of them he might have lived here, in Stratfield Road or South Parade, an insider, calm in the eye of a storm that was blind to its own rampages. Watching life jog by from the windows of the Bon Croissant. Working out at the St Edwards Sports Club. Dying day by grey cold day of tumeric chai lattes and artichoke ice cream.

In Smuggertown, you did things *para inglês ver* – for the English to see; above board, in full view, keeping up appearances, and politically correct. Meanwhile, the real business was going on down the coast, in the quiet deserted streets off Norham Gardens.

Tonight, it was a dinner party in Ward Road. Guests from London. 'You must come for a meal' had been repeated many times over, and finally a date was given. Dyer had accepted weeks before, hoping somehow it might go away, but the evening had arrived.

He has booked his usual babysitter. Paula is a disabled navy widow from the council house next door who enjoys leading a proxy life through the Dyers. One of his favourite people in Oxford, Paula does not yell at the Jamaican family whose children everyone assumes are drug dealers. She does not shoo away those distributing flyers for Art Week, or the Labour councillor who comes knocking for her vote. She does not put up Brexit stickers in her window, run after rubbish men to persuade them to take her recyclables in the week when they collect household rubbish. Neighbours give her their keys. Delivery men give her Amazon parcels. Dyer would be happy to leave her with his secrets.

Before going out tonight, he asks Paula to superintend his son's homework on Trafalgar, only after which is Leandro granted leave to watch television or go on his Xbox.

'Yes, yes, now you go and have a lovely time,' she commands Dyer, sounding like his aunt. 'You never know who you're going to meet.' Although by now he does have an idea.

*

In the beginning, in Leandro's first term, Dyer had clamped everyone by the shoulders, hugged them, and for a while was centre of the party. And then the vitality ebbed away. He stood there, but unless there was a glass of wine in his hand, he had nothing to say.

As the weeks in Oxford passed into months, he had drifted back out to the margin, feeling like the spy that at university he once was approached to become. He watched parents salute each other at the school gates. The minute gestures of recognition, like secret handshakes; the alteration in the voices. He saw how they worked hard, focused, entertained well; Davos at Easter, summer in the Muskokas, with seats at the opera, Ascot, Wimbledon, Wembley. But kindred spirits were punishingly few. He did not share the aspirations which bound most of these people, their masonic sense of kinship. He had not yielded to their world; it was outside anything that mattered to him. He was poorer, older; his experience was in subjects and countries that held neither curiosity for them, nor profit. They made him feel like the survivor of a tribe that was dying out.

If Dyer's impression of other Phoenix parents was delible, the same could not be said of the opinions of a dominant section of English parents about Dyer. Their initial rush to embrace him had been coloured by an expectation that he was bound to share the opinions of his former newspaper. This, they discovered, was not so.

It wasn't merely Dyer's different attitudes towards Europe, America and the dispossessed which destabilised them.

Written on his face was the drear history of a messy private life and imprecise employment in a far-flung backwater. When they bloviated about their careers in the planet's commercial hotspots, he sensed their insecurity, a concern that in his response Dyer was likely to cross the boundary between wit and rudeness. What they ended up seeing was an abrasive, arrogant character who was the complete opposite of the person he concealed.

For the most part, his compatriots in Oxford were the archivists and cataloguers, the Portuguese medievalist in the house opposite, the young Polish woman in the porter's lodge who had been spat at in the bus on the day after the Brexit referendum.

Plus there were ridiculously wealthy exceptions like Gilles and Silvi Asselin.

A bayoneting wind had set in as he walked up Ward Road clutching a copy of his book. He thought of February in Rio, the yellow sand, the warm tessellated pavements beneath his bare feet, a bar–café in the eighties just along from where Joaquim Nabuco met Ipanema, Astrud's converted maid's room with a ceiling fan.

The grey light fell on a detached modern house the size of a large rectory. A man in a tight dark suit opened the security gate and pointed the way across the pale gravel. The lights are on in the tall rooms where people move between gilt-framed portraits.

Silvi greeted him in the hallway. Her figure compressed into a shiny jacket, liquorice black. She was wearing her latest lipstick ('burnt rhubarb') and, around her graceful neck, a string of green jade beads.

'This is for you,' said Dyer.

'Did you write this?' a beringed hand flying to her face, as if he had handed her a menu.

A pot plant looked monstrously at him out of the jardinière.

'Oh, darling,' said Gilles, appearing suddenly with an open magnum of Jacquesson, and peering at the cover, 'that's the kind of book you *love*. You should do it for your reading group.' And to Dyer, 'You know Silvi went out with a writer.'

'Gilles.'

'Who was the writer?' asked Dyer.

'He wasn't a proper writer, Gilles. That was just a silly thing about scarves.'

'She likes to argue,' he said.

'I love to argue,' she smiled.

'He wrote that history of Hermès,' said Gilles, filling a crystal flute which he handed to Dyer. 'Here. Try this. If you don't like it, fuck off.'

There is a price for arrogance, but Gilles Asselin could afford to pay it. In his alpaca evening jacket with a blue velvet lapel, he exuded the burnt-rubber smell of deals that had left nations scorched. In colonial Brazil he would have been a *bandeirante*, hunting for gold and precious stones, rounding up Indians and crushing the uprisings of black slaves, bringing them back in chains. In the twenty-first century, he ruled as a *banqueiro,* on the hunt for insider knowledge that would leapfrog him ahead of the game. He had lived his life in accordance with a complete lack of conviction and no ideology other than to make money. His mantra, he told Dyer during one of their touchline chats, 'How do I shove my way into immediate profit?'

Dyer never concealed from Gilles that he considered him to be a moral hunchback, yet his voice with its undertones of French was listened to with respect in boardrooms from the City to Seattle. Wherever in the financial world you looked, Gilles dominated, he dazzled and bewildered. One of his specialities was debt: 'No assets or personnel to worry about.' He was rumoured to have brokered the deal which had caused Greece to default, then the deal that secured Greece's bail-out. He had bought Argentina's debt and taken her Tall Ships as collateral. The Ukrainian debt, so that he could advise the finance minister in Kiev on how to restructure his economy in a way calculated to benefit Gilles's investors. Governments were among his clients.

At the heart of his operations, nourishing them, lay a colossal vacuum. 'There's three times more debt than equity out there. If you set up all the financial assets in the world, there is $120 trillion GDP and $400 trillion debt.' In this black hole Gilles flourished. He derived a sizeable portion of his company's profits from betting on the volatility indices.

With noteworthy patience, Gilles had tried to explain his method to Dyer. 'Let's say I think the BP share price, currently at £6, is going to collapse on some news. I call my prime broker in New York, borrow BP shares and place an order to sell them forward at £6. All I care about is that I have enough margin collateral to cover my bet that BP is heading south fast. If the shares go up, I have to buy the shares to cover the short. But if the share price goes below £6 on the news, I'm in the money … if they hit £3, I buy them back at that level and make multiples, because my only cost is what the broker charges me to borrow the shares.'

To Gilles, this was the way the world had always worked. To Dyer, it was gobbledygook.

On more than one occasion Gilles had told Dyer, or 'Jean', as he called him, 'You put too great a faith in Christ's promise that the meek shall inherit the earth.' Meekness was absent from Gilles's make-up. Control was what he sought. He had reached the stage where nobody questioned his financial clout, his blatant wealth, his global contacts. Yet were anyone to penetrate Gilles's urbane exterior they would soon learn that he sat on a volcanic temper, his natural irritability constantly darting to the surface to inspect a lure. That was how he first had appeared to Dyer at the Headmaster's Breakfast.

At this 'Fathers Only' gathering beside the Cherwell, it was not Mr Crotty who kept the fathers' spellbound eyes on him, laughing when he laughed, frowning when he frowned, even coughing when he coughed, as if he controlled the river and the trees, but Gilles. When he raised his breakfast bap to speak, no one could move; his eyes were fixed on them the whole time, holding their attention – all, that is, save for Leandro's father. Perhaps Dyer had interviewed too many presidential candidates. At any rate, something in his expression piqued Gilles enough to seek him out, win him over. But whatever Gilles hoped to achieve that morning, he failed. His brain whirred on, not dwelling on what he was saying, flicking his fingers, impatient, dissatisfied. He knew that he was boring Dyer.

So it came as a surprise when Silvi announced how much her husband had enjoyed talking to him. Gilles Asselin, it seemed, had taken a shine to Dyer in the knowledge that he could not afford him. Dyer's poverty was a condition as unassailable as the bells of St Barnabas. He was poor, but free in a way that meant he paid not a penny of attention to Gilles's luxuries or dominance, and in that unaccustomed freedom Gilles appeared to find a vicarious ease.

'I don't read books,' Gilles said to Dyer, adjusting the napkin around the magnum. 'My life is a book.'

'I never loved your looks. What I loved was your mind,' said Silvi. Her thoughts were always two notes away from a pop song.

'Darling, he said *books* not *looks*,' came a tart voice. It belonged to a chestnut-haired woman in odd-shaped glasses who had entered after Dyer.

'I don't read anything any more,' Gilles harped on, 'except Silvi's bank statements.'

Blurry pastels of snowscapes with chevrons of birds. A decanter on the sideboard like the glass chamberpot under his mother's bed. Silvi has arranged the flowers. She's left Gilles in charge of the wine.

The Jacquesson has yielded to a Sauternes. Even as Dyer sips it, he loathes himself. He knows that as soon as he's had a couple of glasses, he will go along with the party. Yet he also has to drink to get through it. An evening like this is a long-haul flight. After half an hour he's demented, with all his faculties poised to bolt, but by the end he'll be exchanging addresses and telephone numbers, he will see they're actually not so bad, his fellow passengers, they're all pilgrims on the same journey, part of the same humanity. He'll be one of them, even if he wakes up next morning with a rapidly beating heart, back to his old self, instantly feeling dread as he surfaces through the scum of his remorse: *Was I rude, did I show how bored I was, did I bore on too much?* But he won't be able to hide. He has to face them at the school gates. He has to talk to them under the harsh light of sobriety, when he can't remember how to live up to who he was the night before.

Aside from his hosts, who sat at each end of the gigantic mahogany table, Dyer knew none of the thirteen others present, some of whom appeared to be clients of Gilles. The only couple he thought he recognised – from a school

concert in January – were the Cubbages. Ralph, from California, and his intense-looking wife Bonnie, lived down the
street. It suddenly registered that Ralph was the person in
the 'Cal' baseball cap who Dyer had seen that afternoon
talking to Gilles on the touchline.

In obedience to Paula's command, Dyer glanced around,
ready to surrender himself to the evening. Silvi, whose pride
in her talent for bringing people together was reflected in the
trouble that she took over her placements, had whispered on
their way downstairs: 'I've put you between two single
ladies.' Dyer intended to start with the dark-haired woman
on his right; he had followed her to the table slightly
mesmerised by her two-inch yellow heels.

He has had love affairs since Nissa. Women like him. He
listens to them and makes them laugh. They know he has a
sense of humour about himself and pokes fun at his own
puritanism. They are touched by the stripe of sadness in him
which it's easy to mistake for something smooth, round,
solid and, if not necessarily complete, then centred – without recognising that it's his ledge out onto the void.

But nothing since coming to Oxford.

'Jocasta,' dropping her iPhone into her lap and holding
out a hand.

'John.'

She was slender, in her dissatisfied forties, in a translucent
flesh-coloured blouse. Her short dark hair stronger and
healthier than her face, which was rather plain. *One of those*

faces, his aunt would have said, *that looks as though it's been spat on and polished.*

'Haven't we met before?' she asked, giving him a sociable look.

'I don't think so.'

'Funny, I was sure I recognised you. You're a writer, Silvi was saying.'

'She's being generous. I have written one book.'

'I'm all athrob. Has it been bought for the movies? What's it about?'

'The indigenous tribes of the lower Amazon basin.'

She gazed at him as if at an empty fuel gauge.

'Now it's coming back to me ... ' Her eyes flicked down to her lap. 'You're the one who's lived in South America.'

'Do you like South American writers?' to help her out.

She lifted her head. She pretended she was studying the paintings. She looked at the wall and its dreadful potential.

'I've not really read them.'

She was more a people person. She had met everyone. David Beckham. David Cameron. Charles Worthington. 'Sorry, I have to get this. It might be my bed for the night.'

Her face went dead as she read her texts.

Raising her eyes back above the table, it took Jocasta a second or two to remember where she had mislaid their conversation.

'What's South America like? I've always sort of wanted to go there.'

Dyer opened his mouth and then closed it.

She looked at him encouragingly. Her charms were trying to come out, her coral lips, her glinting eyes.

But he could no longer do this. After seventeen months in Oxford, he could no longer describe the continent to her, the rivers, mountains, deserts. He couldn't tell her how it was his aunt who had been responsible for introducing Dyer to South America – after his mother died, Vivien had sent a plane ticket, pressing him to come and stay. How he saw the shadow of palms on the tiled wall, the yellow bunches of small plantains, and a spell was cast. He couldn't tell her about the limitless horizons and the lapwings' shrieks. Or the cities, Buenos Aires, Iquitos, Belém, the *favelas* in Rio, the *pueblos jóvenes* outside Lima. He couldn't tell her of obscure places like Rio Pico, Hortensia, Tres Cruces, Corbett, Satipo, or the village in the Peruvian jungle where he had passed five days in a sweat-drenched delirium. He couldn't tell her about the excitable fellow journalist he had known who went to interview Sendero prisoners in Lurigancho gaol – a scoop, Jaime kept saying, a real scoop – and was released with his tongue cut out. He couldn't tell her of the tropical night when he lay in a make-shift gondola beside a *canoeira*, a girl plying her trade in Iquitos's Venezia district, a pink birthday candle in the milk-tin, and the wizened paddler, his back to Dyer, rowing in steady, heart-shaped strokes out into the Amazon, unswerving as Charon. The fresh body in the grass under

80

the flyover. The name on the church door scrawled in the blood of the priest. The bar–café in Joaquim Nabuco where he liked to go to read. He couldn't tell her of the samba that pulsed through the river mist, the buzzards that drifted down from the mountains like open bibles, the jolt of freedom as he cantered along an avenue of eucalypts, out onto the straight dirt road, the smoke of burnt hay, the horse-radishy smell of the wild grass, the pricked back ears of the horse.

'South America,' he said carefully, 'is great if you like butterflies.'

'I *adore* butterflies.'

A waitress in a short black skirt with black stockings served them. The plates were blue Limoges and warm.

'Silvi, this is really good,' Jocasta called out.

'Gilles brought it back from Brussels.' Her pale, boss-eyed face drifted over them.

Soon they had finished their foie gras.

'*Amigo*, mind if I smoke?' she said to him.

'No.'

'It's all right, you won't get cancer. It's an e-cig. Not as good as tobacco, but better than nothing.'

'I don't mind. Really.' He sat with his arms to his side, like a man dining at High Table.

'You're a good *amigo*. That's the only Spanish I know.'

'They don't speak Spanish in Brazil.'

Jocasta inhaled, absorbing this. 'Yes, of course, I knew that. Portuguese. But do they have fortune tellers there?'

'They're called *pais de santo*.'

She exhaled. '*Pais de santo*,' she repeated, rolling the words around. 'I'll tell you something, when you hear it you're going to laugh. I was once told by a fortune teller –' and she pushed back her chair – 'that my sense of humour is really very, very amusing.'

He drank his wine. The claret, at least, was good. 'This,' Gilles had promised when pouring it, 'would loosen the morals of ancient Greece.'

Over her voice, fragments of male conversation.

'It's his vulgarity that is so goose-pimpling, the little vagina shapes he makes with his hands, the phallic ignorance.'

'Don't worry, I've still got *my* marbles. Despite what Athens would like!'

'The region was sliding into war until that deal was signed.'

Jocasta was telling a story that involved a man in Hong Kong who had treated her badly, and a speedboat. He gave up the attempt to listen.

He heard Gilles saying, 'Only two people have had their name linked to a month: Augustus and Julius Caesar.'

Beside him, Jocasta played with the napkin ring as if it were a precious amulet.

'Does this story amuse you?' Her dull pale cheeks. The outrage of a star whose whims were suddenly denied. He could see her going for someone with her Vampire Vape fla-voured e-cig.

Dyer, ignoring the sinister possibilities of tone, 'Infinitely.'

The arrival of the main course interrupted them.

The person on his other side, in a short-sleeved aubergine dress, was saying something to the man on her left. She turned to Dyer.

'Do you ever do that?'

It was the chestnut-haired woman.

'Do what?'

'Hide something in order that you know where it is only to forget where you've hidden it.' Just before coming here tonight, she said, she had sat on her glasses – tucked for safe-keeping behind a cushion. She looked at him dourly out of a warped bronze frame.

'All the time,' said Dyer. It was what his mother had done.

She had a slight lisp, like a dimple in her voice, and the irregular teeth of the English middle class. Straight shoulder-length hair, intelligent pale oval face. If Dyer had to describe his type, it wouldn't be her.

Her name was Miranda. She lived in a house at the end of the road with her mother, who had dementia. 'She'll step out in the evening and hail a cab and tell it to take her anywhere.' Once it took her to Malvern. 'I had to write a cheque for two hundred and fifty pounds.'

An educated woman in her fifties, she was divorced, like so many of her friends. She was still unresolved about the precise sequence. 'A lot of women marry what they can handle, not what they want.'

'Who did you marry?'

'Someone I couldn't handle – who do you think?'

He was a psychologist who had gone off with an Indian nurse he'd been leading a double life with in Battersea. A separate family, a birth certificate found in the glove compartment. That was three years ago. She quoted, in an injured voice, '"Trust not the light that men call love; 'tis but a phantom gleam."'

She confessed to feeling more exasperation than bitterness, furious at the careless waste, the cowardly act with which he had flicked aside her loyalty and love, and the streak of it salted her humour. 'Imagine the mental effort to keep both lives in the air. Still, it kept him fit and alert – most of the time. He once bought me a bunch of flowers for my birthday, but it was her birthday.'

She paused to take in a mouthful of guinea fowl. 'Have you come from London?'

He lived in Oxford, he had a boy at school here, he said.

'The Phoenix, I suppose?'

'Guilty.'

'What do you do? You don't look like a banker.'

'I'm writing about a tribe in Brazil called the Tupi.'

'Why, do you speak their language?'

'A few words. But it's virtually extinct now.'

'I remember being taught that with eighty words you can say just about everything. You can practically discuss Wittgenstein.'

'That may be true.'

'I think I'd like to learn Tupi,' smiling slightly and gazing into her glass. 'I've always been interested in linguistics.'

He looked sideways at her. While she was not what Dyer would call beautiful – she resembled Cézanne's wife in her short-sleeved dress – she had a marvellous smile.

'I could recommend some books.'

'Would you? I'd appreciate that.' Then, as if she thought he was saying this to be polite: 'I mean it. I would.'

The male voices were getting louder. Across the table, an American accent cut in. Ralph Cubbage in his tailored red jeans held up by an Argentine belt. Still gibbering about the Iran deal.

'… ballistic missile tests … weapons factories in Lebanon … harassment of our navy in the Gulf …'

'The US has been in violation of the deal from day one,' protested a burly man in a suit who sat across the table – a Hamburg banker who had inherited the family firm. 'Yet you can't tell me a single one of the agreements Iran is supposed to have broken.' He wore an Hermès tie, green, patterned with two yellow parrots facing each other on a branch.

'Of course I can,' said Cubbage, tearing at a roll. 'But I didn't come here prepared.'

'Give that man a nice tall glass of shut-the-fuck-up,' whispered Miranda.

'Do you know him?'

'Yes, I know Ralph Cubbage. He recently moved in opposite.'

He was mouthing 'More bread' to the waitress.

Dyer looked around to see that no one was listening.

'All right, eighty words on him,' he said.

Her glance skimmed back over the table, rising to the challenge. 'Nuclear physicist. Berkeley – i.e. Livermore, the US weapons laboratory in California. Arrived here at Christmas to take up a post at the Clarendon. Married to the oh-so-pious woman sitting on Gilles's left. Bonnie is a prominent member of the Church of the Open Door. They have a daughter at the Phoenix who plays the cello and whom they treat as the next Jaqueline du Pré.'

'A nuclear physicist,' said Dyer slowly, to let the reality of this take shape. 'You have fifteen words left. Go for it.'

She re-examined Cubbage through her squashed glasses.

'I don't know you well enough for another fifteen. How about always disagrees with the last person he has spoken to. And an artesian bore. I will throw in for free that *cubbitch* means "greedy" in Jamaican.'

'Well, that's him in his nutshell, almost,' said Dyer.

Her forthright nature was a blood transfusion. He recognised the lack of filter that others flinched from in him.

'Gilles?'

'Our resident predator? Easy peasy,' said Miranda, and swivelled her gaze to the end of the table.

He waited while she refocused. He was beginning to enjoy himself.

Their host was talking to a thin little man with gloomy eyes who was in the middle of a divorce.

'They're looking at one third for you, one third for your wife and one third for them. The worst word in their diction-ary is "agreement".'

Her index finger pressed her misshapen glasses further up her nose. 'Gilles is a parasite ant. He bites the legs off other members of his species and turns them into living silos. His victims grow exceedingly fat and blubbery, and in winter he eats them. He may be Canadian, but don't let that mislead you. He may be tall. Don't let that mislead you either. He has the faults of all men under five feet three. And also, let me tell you, he takes pleasure in pain.'

'How do you know?'

'I tell you, I know these things.'

'Anything else?'

'Haven't I used up my allocation?'

'But I'm getting to know you better. Go on. Take another eighty.'

With an air of collusion, she said: 'He doesn't have a per-sonality, but that's him. He's not a people person, he never will be. He sees the world as a system geared to optimise revenue for his company. He's constantly tipping me "the next big thing" to invest in, although I have no savings to speak of. I do honestly like to think it's because a tiny bit of him wants to help me out. One day it's genetic and data science, the next day it's bio-synthesis and the creation of proteins. If you want my opinion, he's right now on the prowl for a new mission.'

'A mission to do what?'

'Oh, run the universe, I expect, as everyone tries to do who makes a lot of money and then uses philanthropy to cover up the original sin.'

'Will he succeed?'

'I vastly doubt it.'

'Why not?'

'Because whatever was once good in his character has been gangrenated – if that's a word – by prosperity. He has paid for everything and he wants a free pass. He wants us to cut corners with the truth. But there are people who won't let him do that.'

'People like you?'

'And you perhaps?'

'Don't you like him?'

'I like Gilles about as much as a cat loves a crow.'

'Then you hate him?'

'No, no, not hate. But something close to it, yes.'

'So why are you here?'

'Someone dropped out at the very last moment, didn't you hear? Someone called Updark. Subject to Better Offer, I have a feeling. He's having dinner tonight with the Foreign Secretary, apparently. Silvi rang me, furious. I'm the spare gooseberry who is always on tap. Otherwise there would have been thirteen round this table, and you may be surprised how superstitious Silvi is. I don't mind, I have no pride. Very occasionally, you do meet somebody interesting. And it makes a change from scrambled eggs with Mum.'

'Who keeps Mum from haring off tonight to Malvern?'

'A nice maths student at Magdalen to whom I pay ten pounds an hour.'

Gilles, with a full decanter, suddenly loomed over them like a fighter pilot. 'To hell with the expense, give the canaries another seed,' replenishing their glasses. He bent closer. 'Just don't believe a word she tells you,' his voice lazy and larval and powered by riches acquired too easily. 'Do not believe a word.'

After the port had circulated a second time, they went upstairs.

The waitress pointed the way to the loo. On the walls were photographs of Gilles in his speed-skating days. An Olympic silver medal at Nagano. Taking the corner at a world championship in Montreal, leaning sideways with his gloved hand touching the ice.

The man who came and sat on the cherry-red chesterfield beside Dyer still had the huge square knees of a skater. His trousers strained at the seams.

'Tell me, Jean,' Gilles said genially, slowly swirling a honey-coloured liquid around a large glass. 'Rustum Marvar.'

'What about him?'

'I saw you talking to him this afternoon. He was behaving in an unusually ecstatic way. What was that about?'

'His son scored an amazing goal. Didn't you see?'

'Is that all?' still swirling. 'It seemed rather more than that.'

'I don't know him well,' said Dyer guardedly, judging the direction of the question. 'I've only met him once before.'

'Just wondered what you make of him, that's all.'

'I like him. Why?'

Gilles laughed, disappointed. 'I don't know, he strikes me as a little ... well, incoherent. A few days ago, he was in a flap about letting his son come here for a sleepover. Now all of a sudden he couldn't be more relaxed.'

'He's a scientist, Gilles. Up and down.'

'I suppose so,' said Gilles, staring into his glass. 'I suppose so.'

Everyone got to their feet. Only Cubbage lingered for the rum which Gilles had purchased from Hemingway's cellar in Cuba.

Headlights in the rain. Sable coat. An overly wrapped figure with a night-case – Jocasta – stood in the open doorway thanking Silvi for a wonderful evening. Out in the street, engine running, a taxi was waiting. She tripped towards it on her high yellow heels like a seagull that has gorged so much it can hardly fly.

'It's been fun, I must say,' said Dyer, kissing Silvi on the cheek.

Over her shoulder, the gravel glinted in the security light.

'I'll ring you about Saturday,' she promised, already looking ahead to Pierre's birthday party. 'You must tell me if there's anything Leandro doesn't eat. Oh, and thanks for the book.'

Chapter Nine

THE FOOTBALL MATCH ON THE following Saturday was against Winchester House, in Brackley, twenty-two miles away. To celebrate his birthday, which fell next day, Pierre Asselin had invited the Phoenix team home for a sleepover after the game. Leandro never wanted to go to the house of anyone who didn't have a father, preferring to be with friends whose dads were very visible, but he liked Gilles, and was somewhat in awe of his speed-skating past, having seen a photograph of him crossing the line in Japan that Gilles carried on his phone and had shown to Leandro after a practice.

Dyer would have the house to himself for the weekend to work on his book.

Late on Saturday morning, Dyer tore himself from the Taylorian. His research had suddenly become a lot more interesting, sparked by the monograph that he had ordered up the week before.

Dyer was investigating the first European settlers in Brazil: among them, three weeping convicts left behind in May 1500 on a beach south of the future city of Bahia. The Portuguese chronicler, Pêro Vaz de Caminha, who witnessed their distress from the deck of his admiral's flagship, reported that the men's death sentences had been commuted in exchange for their learning about the customs and language of the naked Tupi.

Not much was known concerning two of the convicts, but an historian at Coimbra University had traced descendants of the third – 'a banished youth' called Afonso Ribeiro – to Belém on the mouth of the Amazon, a thousand miles north; new documents had led to the discovery of a family of Ribeiros living in the port area.

Belém was a city which resonated for Dyer. It was where one humid evening in an otherwise deserted riverfront restaurant he had stumbled across the police colonel who had arrested Ezequiel. The only other person in the Cantina da Lua was the waiter, Emilio Ribeiro, a lugubrious fellow who hurried for no one. A connection with Afonso Ribeiro, the first European to speak a native Latin American language, seemed highly improbable. Almost everyone in Bahia was called da Silva; most likely, the same held true for the Ribeiros of Belém. Yet it was a sign which the superstitious ex-journalist was reluctant to ignore. For Dyer, as for another ex-journo he admired, Graham Greene, coincidences were not merely spiritual puns, they 'beset our past like the traps set for leopards in the jungle'. For most of his life, Dyer had considered extraordinary coincidences to be the lazy novelist's gambit. Only since returning to Oxford had he started to recognise that it took an historian to set leopard's traps.

Dyer perceived the waiter's surname as an omen. For the first time in months, his life had taken on a new rhythm. He felt like the Portuguese admiral Pedro Cabral on the deck of his four-master, tossed upon boiling seas, his spanker sails buxom with a sudden wind from the south.

Shortly before 1 p.m. Dyer returned Professor Madrugada's book to the stacks. Before unplugging his laptop, he checked the headlines. A mass extinction of antelope herds in the Russian steppes, allegedly linked to climate change ... an Australian mathematician missing on a bush walk ...

Dyer's attention glided to the Middle East. The Iranians were protesting about the US president's visit to Saudi Arabia and the Saudis' purchase of $100 billion of US arms. Meanwhile, the latest US Defence Secretary was defining the three gravest threats facing America as Iran, Iran, Iran. Dyer wondered how Marvar would receive this news.

Outside struck the full winter chill of Oxford. There had been a frost in the night. The windscreens of the cars parked beside St Barnabas school stared blindly at him, opaque beneath membranes of ice. Dyer meandered back to Jericho through patches of mist, trying to recollect where he had parked his frog-green Beetle.

In the mist with his coat he was a bluster of dust. Dyer was halfway down Great Clarendon Street when he recognised Marvar leaning against the wall inside the entrance to the Oxford University Press. During the week, this was where smokers congregated – editors and managers discussing redundancies and bonuses, and – who knew? – Dyer's book. This morning only three people stood sucking on their cigarettes, printers and shift-workers most likely, plus one solitary large flabby figure.

'Rustum?'

You are what you are when no one is looking. He turned and blinked at Dyer as if he hardly recognised him. His hair seemed more matted, his eyes duller. He had the face of a derelict, one of the homeless men on the pavement outside Blackfriars whom Dyer passed every morning, invariably staring at a book upside down in the hope that Dyer would mistake them for a former student whom life had unfairly elbowed into the gutter.

'It's me,' Dyer had to remind him. 'Leandro's father.'

Marvar scratched his arm. His coat was on tight, he had done up every button.

'John Dyer...'

His breath, visible, mingled with the smoke leaving his nose. He was not himself. It was as if something dreadful had happened to him.

'Are you coming to the football match?' said Dyer. 'I can give you a lift.'

Marvar threw away his cigarette and clutched Dyer's arm.

'No, no, I can't.' He looked directly at him. Behind his glasses, there was a dancing flicker in his eyes. 'Dyer ... have you a second?'

It occurred to Dyer that Marvar's behaviour might be connected with the news about Iran. He checked his watch. The match began in forty minutes.

'Listen ...' he decided. 'My place is around that corner, literally. We can go there.'

He would hear what Marvar had to say. If he drove fast, he could still arrive in time.

With an odd sudden tilt of his face, Marvar glanced both ways up Great Clarendon Street. There was a silver Golf parked on the other side, its windows fogged up. He gave it a nervy look.

'Yes, yes. All right.'

He walked in quick strides beside Dyer, breathing in gulps.

Dyer showed him in. It was the house where he had lived for a year and a half: tiled floors, the pâté-coloured staircarpet. From the window in the small sitting room, you could see the canal. The landlord lived in Wolvercote, and favoured round white doorknobs from Homebase and white crockery.

Converted from a garage, the place was not to everyone's taste, with its creaking furniture and single-glazed windows that rattled in a hard wind, letting in the sound of trains. The upstairs smelled of new carpet, and the radiators emitted a sharp gurgling noise when the heating came on. At the rear, French windows opened onto a courtyard with a wooden tub containing a magnolia.

Marvar tripped over the two bicycles in the hallway, and sent Dyer's fishing rod clattering. Balance regained, he stumbled into the kitchen area.

Dyer propped the rod back up and waited for him to finish unbuttoning.

'Have a seat.' He took Marvar's coat and went to hang it up in the cupboard under the stairs, next to his tackle.

Re-entering the room, 'Tea? Coffee? Something stronger?' On the draining board was a glass with a red halo at the bottom.

Sprawled awkwardly on a hard chair, Marvar looked slowly about, like a passenger who lingers after the plane has landed. He was wearing a suit tailored for someone, if not for him then his father or grandfather; midnight blue, old-fashioned, turn-ups. The jacket strained over his stomach.

'Sure,' Marvar said vaguely, listening to the clangs. There were workmen in the next house. They had been putting up scaffolding.

He sat there while Dyer filled the kettle. His eyes moved over a photograph on the wall of Dyer in the *favela* with his class, to a drawing by one of the orphans, before landing on the notes scattered over the kitchen table.

'What are you working on?' after a pause. Without his coat, he breathed more evenly.

Dyer told him.

'Are you a good writer?'

'My English teacher at the Phoenix said if you want to be a good writer, you have to be a horrible person.'

At this, Marvar laughed. He was ready to laugh. He leaned forward, twisting his neck to decipher Dyer's notes. 'I'd like to read something you've written.'

Dyer knelt before the Ikea bookcase and picked out a book, sandwiched between a copy of Basil Bunting's collected poems and an early novel by Mario Vargas Llosa, and handed it to him.

He inspected the spine. 'J. W. Dyer. This is you?'

'Not as often as I'd like it to be.'

Marvar fingered the book listlessly, not seeing. He was too fat and the walls were too thin. He might have been thinking of another book.

'Have it,' said Dyer. 'It's for you.'

It was his last copy. He could order another. The half-dozen that his publishers had sent him, he had wasted as dinner-party gifts.

Marvar flicked to the title page. 'Then you must sign it,' and stood respectfully up. The book lay open in his palms, drifting in the thermals.

Dyer patted his chest, pockets. From a broken-handled mug with a phoenix on it, he plucked a biro that didn't work.

'Why,' he muttered, 'do writers never ever have anything to write with?'

He unzipped the leather shoulder bag containing his laptop, and dug out a propelling pencil.

Marvar remained standing while Dyer took the book from him and sat down at the table and pondered an inscription. The sound of hammer against scaffolding came through the wall like a gong. The renovator's wand hadn't yet touched Paula's house on the other side.

'Your ex?'

Dyer looked up.

On top of the bookcase, the black-and-white photograph of Astrud loose in a maple frame.

'One of them,' he said.

Nissa was upstairs, in colour, on a wall in Leandro's bedroom – with a smile on her face that Dyer could imagine darting between their son's ribs every time Leandro looked at it. Her beauty was not in doubt, only what it let her get away with. That she might be a stove that smoked whenever it blew, as his aunt tartly put it, Dyer had been slower to recognise than Vivien who, after at last meeting Nissa, observed to him while she thoughtfully adjusted the knitted cosy on her teapot, 'I like her, John, I do. I just can't help feeling that with Nissa the half seems always more interesting than the whole. It's something Hugo's noticed, too. Did I ever tell you what he said after our first meeting? "A great face always comes with a price tag," and it's perfectly true, my dear.'

Had Nissa ignored Leandro altogether, it might have hurt less. For the first year, she was content with the progress reports that Dyer made a point of writing to her at the end of each term. Yet now that her twins were down for an English prep school, she had started to show more interest. A fresh demand plopped through the letter box every few weeks, along with the gas and electricity reminders. For Leandro's school report, his team photograph, his waist and neck measurements, as if she was trying to reclaim him by reaching out through the arms and legs of the shirts and trousers that she wanted to send. The clothes arrived, but Leandro wouldn't touch them. She would have made a perfect Phoenix mother, thought Dyer, who had not seen it coming. What he saw, he did not tell Leandro – who had never asked – was that the woman he believed he loved had escaped him for someone wealthier. Which wasn't how Nissa saw things. 'It's not me you're fucking.' She wiped the tears from her eyes. 'It's Astrud.'

Marvar was still looking at Astrud's photo. It was taken on her parents' terrace in Petrópolis, at dusk. She was leaning against the barley-sugar irons of the balustrade, staring at him. Not beautiful, not ugly. Her candour had nothing artificial about it. She was telling him to get a move on, she needed to turn down the gas on the *moqueca*. She was three months pregnant.

'What's her name?' Marvar asked.

Dyer's mouth formed the word. He felt a phantom heart-beat just saying it. He remembered saying her name for so long. It wasn't something you could talk away or find words to soothe; it was a part of himself which was empty and would never be filled. The same with their baby daughter. He could see her growing up, but she would never grow up.

That hammering again. A barrister from Putney had bought the house. He had a boy and a girl going to the Phoenix in September.

After Dyer told him how Astrud had died in childbirth, Marvar fished out a wallet and produced a photo. 'My wife.'

Dyer saw a face like Samir's: large eyes, very dark brows, long thick black hair, a small straight nose, and slightly uneven front teeth that lent an elfin element to her smile.

'And here – with my daughter.'

The baby girl in her arms, she could have been only a few months old.

'What's your daughter called?'

'Jamileh,' in a small voice.

'And your wife?'

'Shula.'

'She looks lovely.'

'Oh, she is, she is a very brave, clever woman. My half-ness.' It was almost a whisper

'You told me you were divorced.'

Marvar inclined his head. 'I lied.'

Dyer looked up. 'Any reason?'

Marvar's faint brown skin stretched over his skull exposed a small pulse that Dyer had not noticed before, showing the race of his thoughts.

He pulled up a chair and sat down, making it creak. People always look around before they lie. He met Dyer's gaze directly.

'May I have a coffee?' as if this was not the only decision he had reached. Lies weren't going to get him anywhere.

Chapter Ten

EVERYTHING STARTS OVER A COFFEE, he remembered her laughing. Not that Marvar drank much of his. He kept getting up and wandering over to the window, speaking to the window as if to the sky. He belonged not in that room, but in a desert landscape the colour of his coat, rimmed by volcanic peaks, the dogs panting, the groan of the water-wheel, shutters closing, opening. Outside, coming off the canal, the Oxford mist suspended Marvar from normal times, from this red-brick house in Jericho where he stood, or sat noisily down, his lungs wheezing, trying to work out how to explain to Dyer what motivated him to behave in this strange jittery way. And all the while from next door that bang bang bang.

It emerged in fragments between sips. He was afraid of saying too much. He hardly knew Dyer. They'd had – what? – two conversations. Even so, his instincts told him that

Dyer was a person to trust, who might understand. Anyway, who else could he talk to? There wasn't anyone.

He spoke as if his mouth was dry. Yes, he was still married, and happily. But his wife Shula was a hostage in Tehran. They had not let her travel to Oxford. They would let him bring Samir, but not his wife.

Marvar couldn't deny that it had come as a surprise when the Clarendon laboratory invited him 'in a spirit of reconciliation' to spend three years at the Department of Physics in Oxford. He was a junior spectrometrist. Iran had plenty more experienced physicists – plus his mother had been a Christian.

Subsequently, he learned that his name had been put forward by a Dutch scientist, a visiting fellow at Tehran University, who sometimes sat and talked to Marvar in the canteen.

'You may accept.' It was clear that many consultations had taken place before his head of department summoned Marvar and gave him this news in a calm, dispassionate voice, and then the conditions. His wife had to stay behind, he had to report back on his own research every month, he was to avoid making contacts outside his team at the Clarendon. If anyone questioned him, he was to represent himself as a single father. The West was full of them.

It was Shula who had decided. An opportunity to work in Oxford – it was not likely to come again, and Samir would benefit; the government had consented to pay for his schooling.

'She said to me: "No question, Rustum, you have to go."'

Father and son had arrived in England soon after the signing of the international treaty that suspended Iran's nuclear programme in exchange for sanctions relief. A thirty-year stand-off – three decades of 'mutual demonisation' – had come to an end. Tensions relaxed further as Iran began again to export oil. Marvar received no more instructions. He lived with Samir in digs in Merton Street. He got on with his work. He ate takeaways; he never went to parties. Last summer, he'd flown with Samir to Tehran to visit Shula, by then six months pregnant. Marvar was back in Oxford when Jamileh was born three months later. He had been looking forward to seeing his baby daughter for the first time in March, at the annual meeting of the Iranian Atomic Energy Organisation.

'But these last weeks – the atmosphere has changed utterly.' America's threat of sanctions had sent the Iranian authorities berserk, he said. 'Every day, they issue new orders to those who have dealings with the West. At the same time, they are arresting people.'

Marvar's research at the Clarendon now obsessed them. They insisted that he report back not every month, but every week, in detail. That was not all.

'I'm not a spy – no, no, you mustn't think that. But my people are very suspicious, you cannot believe how suspicious. They have made other conditions. They want to *make* me into a spy.'

He spoke in a low voice as if petrified of being overheard. 'I have to report on the rest of the team. If they are not satisfied with ... I can't think straight.'

His pace had faltered. He needed to swallow before he could go on. With an unexpected sob, he said: 'I have heard from my cousin that Shula has been taken away.'

In his large brown abstracted eyes was the horror of a man who might never see his wife again. Rejas had shown the same anguish when talking about Yolanda.

Dyer would not have become a journalist if he had trusted people. He had been trained not to believe, it was a requirement. People lie the whole time, most of all to themselves. Thirty years in Brazil had taught him to approach Marvar's story with caution.

Obscure to Dyer was who 'they' were. His knowledge of Iranian politics came from what he read in the news. Was Marvar referring to the Iranian Atomic Energy Organisation? To his university faculty in Tehran? To the Revolutionary Guards? Or to a secret faction closer to the Ayatollah?

He lifted the cup to his lips, waiting for Marvar to go on. When he sipped his coffee he felt clear, calm. In Rio that day. He had met her one dry lonely afternoon. She was like the first coffee of the morning. She made things come alive, which is also to make them come true.

It was one of Marvar's tics, when agitated, to raise his right hand from his sparse beard to the top of his head and pat down his hair until it fell over his eyes.

'I don't know what to do ... I was going to church to ... I feel everywhere I go ...' The rest of the sentence stayed in his mouth.

'You feel you're being watched?' supplied Dyer.

Marvar nodded. He had to clear his throat again.

'By who?'

'Cubbage, for one!' exploding with resentment.

Dyer put down his mug. 'What, Amy's father?'

The very same. Ralph Cubbage, of the carroty hair and tailored red jeans, the large black Lexus and Berkeley baseball cap, who in January had been appointed deputy head of Marvar's department. An Australian professor was nominally in charge, but Cubbage acted as the day-to-day supervisor. From the first morning when he bristled through the Clarendon's pompous orange-brick entrance, up its wooden staircase and along the corridor to Professor Whitton's room overlooking the Parks cricket pitch – two long white communal desktops surmounted by eight large screens – Dr Ralph Louis Cubbage Jr. had behaved as though he had an unwarranted claim on Marvar's work.

'If he's not working for the CIA, then – what is your saying? – I'm a Dutch person.'

Cubbage was not alone in his interest. Everywhere Marvar now glanced he saw a wolf-eared shadow. Aside from the Americans and the authorities in Tehran, Marvar seemed particularly fearful of the Israelis, who, between 2009 and 2012, he said, had assassinated seventeen Iranian nuclear scientists. Recently, Marvar's professor at the Clarendon had received two visitors who purported to be plasma scientists from a lab in Tel Aviv. They gave him a severe inquisition about his work, but were noticeably evasive about their own establishment.

Then, in no particular order, came the Saudis, the Russians, the Chinese, the British, the City, Wall Street, weapons manufacturers, Iranian dissidents – even the oil industry. Marvar muttered, 'The thing is so big, they would have to be on top of any renewable revolution.'

Dyer heard this without commenting, as a doctor listens to a hypochondriac rehearse their symptoms. Little mental effort was required to see that Marvar could be an eruptive, discomposed personality, with extreme reactions to people and situations.

'The truth is, I never expected it …'

His voice was disincarnate. His heart was in a state of considerable nervous excitement over the fate of his wife and daughter, but Dyer had the impression – once again – that it overspilled with other passions.

'… I never expected to have results …'

'I'm sorry,' Dyer said finally, after Marvar had jumped to his feet. 'What are these results you're talking about?'

Marvar stood stooped by the window, white mug in hand, a faraway glaze in his eye. The dense mist, evocative and deceiving, drifted over the empty boatyard, now and then thinning to reveal the canal. The tinder path opposite, with barges tied up; along the near bank the backs of narrow lawns sloping up to Edwardian houses, and modern developments, gardenless, with balconies and sheer facades like Venetian palazzos.

'Look, how lovely it is over there.' He turned his lost face to Dyer, as if chasing his last chance for joy. 'Let's go out.'

In between clangs from next door, the bells of St Barnabas chimed twice. On a frost-hardened field in Brackley, the whistle had gone and Leandro and Samir would have started playing – with neither of their fathers watching, it depressed Dyer to think, as he went to retrieve Marvar's overcoat.

Marvar stood abstractedly putting his coat back on while Dyer telephoned Silvi Asselin to tell her that he couldn't, after all, make it to the match this afternoon, nor could Samir's dad, and might she be able to give their two boys a lift home for tonight's sleepover?

Silvi was determinedly good-natured; Gilles was always cancelling at the last moment. 'You'll miss the tea,' was all she said. The match teas at Winchester House were the best.

They crossed the bridge and walked along the towpath, Marvar every now and then glancing back. The canal flowed slowly, darkly; twigs and bottles were trapped on the surface like tar. Nothing seemed reflected in it, no birds, no clouds, no streak of sunlight. Ducks submerged and rose, shaking their heads near the far bank. Smudged by the thinning mist, solitary men crouched beside black nets fishing for tench.

As they walked, Marvar started to tell Dyer a curious – no, a fantastic – story. He would not have spoken so freely before coming to England. But in the more libertine atmosphere of Oxford, he had discovered that you can say what you like and the sky doesn't fall in.

They were passing a moored-up barge when Marvar turned to him. 'What do you know about nuclear fusion?'

Physics had eluded Dyer; after maths it was his weakest subject. Not even Rougetel, fluent in the sciences as he was in the arts, could help him make better sense of it. In fission, Dyer scrambled to recall, atoms were made to split; in fusion, they were forced to merge – producing potentially immeasurably greater power. He had learned all this at the Phoenix, from a young master who couldn't have been more than a few months out of university.

'Everything I know about fusion,' he told Marvar apologetically, 'could be written on a post-it note.'

'A post-it note?' said Marvar, smiling almost for the first time, and then throwing back his head and bursting into laughter, after Dyer had explained what, exactly, a 'post-it note' was. 'Everything I know, too!'

Marvar gestured at the grey afternoon sky. 'To put it in one line, fusion is what is happening in the sun – if we could get to see it in Oxford – every second, every minute, every day. It's why the stars sparkle. So why not here?'

This had been the challenge facing scientists for eighty years, the holiest of grails. If we could replicate on earth the processes of the sun and the stars, then in a flash our energy problems, global warming, would be sorted. For ever!

But how?

He was looking at Dyer with incredibly tense eyes. 'Well, it can be done,' and gave a distressingly pinched laugh. 'I have found a way.'

It was Dyer's turn to burst out laughing. But he corrected himself when he saw Marvar's face, and he did not question a word of it by the time that Marvar had finished talking.

Marvar's mood had shifted, his tempo had quickened. Once he began, he did not stop. Every sentence he spoke made him need to speak another. Before, he had sounded furred, tense, but now, with no one to overhear him save for Dyer, he spoke clearly, coherently, as if in a confessional.

Marvar unlatched the gate into Port Meadow and for the next ninety minutes gave an impassioned account of his recent research at the Clarendon. The large meadow stretched flat to the river, unploughed for millennia, a grazing pampa for cattle and horses. From across it, they would have seemed like two academics deep in talk, one of them engrossing the other in his subject – the history of our future energy.

Chapter Eleven

'IF YOU HEAT SOMETHING REALLY hot,' said Marvar as they walked towards the weir, 'it goes ballistic. It's like shutting a kid with tantrums in a cage – like shutting Vasily in a cage.' Dyer had to think of Vasily as a plasma. 'When you heat plasma, it doesn't like it. It goes whistling around, creating instabilities, and takes on a mean-minded identity of its own.'

Until now, there had been no breakthrough in heating plasma to a 'self-sustained burn' – that is to say, to the point where the plasma generated more heat than was put into it, although there had been many experiments using exotic metals, super-conducting magnets, giant lasers and so forth.

Always, the instabilities got in the way.

In the south of France, the world's most advanced nations had chosen to build a big expensive reactor costing $25 billion. But this wouldn't be tested for another eight years. Even then, ITER could very well fail like the Zeppelin, or like the fission breeder reactor in America, fifteen years in the making, and closed down before it had conducted a single experiment.

Other than in a hydrogen bomb, which needed to be triggered by a fissile atomic explosion, the most successful attempt to replicate fusion peacefully on earth had been at the Culham laboratory outside Oxford: here, in 1997, in a gigantic machine the size of the Pompidou Centre, fusion had been achieved – if for less than a second. The trick was to keep fusion going for much longer, and on a vastly smaller scale, but this had eluded the world's scientific community. Cold fusion, tokamaks, stellarators, magnetic confinement – each had held up a flickering promise. Not one device had proved to work. A self-sustained burn continued to stay out of reach, a chimera.

'That is, until 7.32 p.m. last Friday.'

But Marvar was rushing ahead of himself. None of this would make sense unless Dyer understood the nature of his research.

'Pauli? You have heard of him?'

Dyer admitted that he hadn't.

'Pauli was a pioneer of quantum physics,' Marvar went on, with an erudite smile. 'He was watching a revue at a theatre in Copenhagen when the exclusion principle came to him.'

Marvar had his brainwave after going to see Samir play at Summer Fields.

'Do you know what gave me the idea?' Marvar said, gathering momentum. 'The football!'

In order to make the 'burn', you needed to squash atoms into incredibly high densities. 'The problem is, it's like wrapping your fingers around a party balloon and then trying to squeeze. The balloon squishes out between your fingers and you can't do it.' The only way of attaining fusion was to create an absolutely symmetrical profile. 'We have never achieved coherence all the way round, that is to say a perfect spherical wavefront – like a wave arriving along the beach at the same time.' At Livermore, where billions of dollars had been spent on this, an array of long multiple lasers each one the size of two football pitches were beamed onto a target pellet so minuscule that you almost couldn't see it, and every single time there had been spots.

'Spots means squishing. It means it is not symmetrical.'

Marvar was watching Samir in the act of taking a corner kick when his mind made an acrobatic skip: what if you could find a way of producing an utterly symmetrical implosion *from a spherical laser*?

It blasted him in the face. The match was still going on when he hurried from the pitch and tore back to the Clarendon.

Over the next days, he didn't stop making calculations, on paper napkins, the backs of menus, yellow post-it notes ('now I know what they're called') – 'in sandpits even!'

What he had realised: size didn't matter. The machine didn't need an elaborate magnetic cage, it didn't need to be enormous, it didn't have to be like Wembley. 'It could be no bigger than a football.'

The audacity of it. His idea went against the received wisdom of every internationally known scientist. But he couldn't breathe a word to Samir, whose kick had inspired it. He couldn't log on to his computer, it was likely to be monitored, and so he entered his calculations into a notebook that he kept in his coat. It was vital that nobody suspected what he was working on. Marvar's team believed him still to be plugging away at plasma focus, and so he continued to conduct experiments with a tungsten-tipped electrode, making careful records, but these experiments were a decoy. He devoted the rest of his time to creating his 'football'.

'For three weeks, I hardly left the lab. The materials were all there, I didn't need much.'

He slaved through the night; there was less risk of being interrupted or observed. He tested a number of lasing mediums before fixing on the one which worked: 'It was silly of me not to have thought of it sooner, a nonlinear optical crystal that I'd experimented with in Tehran.'

Marvar had constructed a blanket out of this to wrap around the hot plasma, using the blanket as a laser. 'I'm making it sound simple. It wasn't simple.' The uniform thickness of the blanket was critical. 'To achieve the smooth wavefront, I had to mix in other lasing materials as well.'

'Go slow, please,' said Dyer. 'What other materials?'

Marvar reeled them off. (On struggling next morning to remember the details of their conversation, Dyer had a burn of regret that he hadn't reached into Marvar's pocket and borrowed his notebook. In his hangover, he was unable to recall if Marvar had said neodymium or monazite or bastnasite, or any of the candidates that Dyer googled. What he did grasp: Marvar had found a way of doping sand from rare earths to make crystals which, when added to the principal lasing medium, smoothed out all instabilities and dramatically increased the neutron production.)

Then, last Friday evening, behind a shiny red door in the Clarendon, after everyone had left for the Magdalen Arms to toast Professor Whitton's Fellowship to the Australian Academy of Science, Marvar took a pellet of frozen deuterium contained in a thin shell of plastic, and placed it inside his laser. The icy outer surface of this central pellet was one spherical mirror; the outer edge of the blanket was the other mirror, forming the laser cavity.

'Not crazy, it just required exquisite alignment between the two.'

'How did you support the pellet – if it needed to be dead in the centre?'

'Excellent question!'

Whitton and Cubbage in their experiments used a tube five microns in diameter – 'but that still causes very noticeable perturbations to the symmetry.' Marvar's solution: magnetic levitation.

He looked up. Dyer was flailing again.

'Let's not go into that now. Let me tell you what happened.'

Shortly after 7.30 p.m. Marvar stepped back from the target chamber behind a lead-lined concrete wall, slipped a pair of safety goggles over his eyes, and switched on the power supply. Through the bright green lenses, he watched multiple laser pulses launch shock waves into the pellet, sending waves that rocked back and forth, back and forth, getting stronger and stronger, like the waves that Samir used to slosh in his bath – 'his mother hated it!' – until all at once the lasing atoms broke through, 'creating a pulse of beautiful, spherical light'.

It was not a sustained reaction; it lasted until the fuel was burned up – this carefully calculated by Marvar in order for him to survive the high-density implosion. In a molten hurry before any of the team returned, Marvar then measured the size of the reaction with the Clarendon's time-gated X-ray camera, the burn duration with the X-ray streak camera, and the neutron yield with the lab's new neutron activation detector. He scarcely dared breathe the result.

He drew himself up and looked fully at Dyer.

'I had not just good compression, it was better than that. I had perfect compression. When I checked the data, I had created more energy than I had used.'

Marvar said, blazing: 'I had got the conditions for fusion using a machine no bigger than Samir's football on the space of your kitchen table.'

Chapter Twelve

MARVAR TURNED AWAY. IN HIS coat, he stood on the bank and stared at the trees. An excursion boat was roped to the far side, chairs stacked up on deck. A young woman's muted laughter came from the bridge.

Dyer opened his mouth and he forgot what he was going to say. It was incredible what Marvar had told him. If true, the implications were immense for everyone, for all time.

But was it true?

When they'd set out from Jericho less than two hours earlier, Dyer couldn't help feeling that Marvar was treading the line between deception and self-deception. His scepticism had not dissolved as Marvar described his football-shaped laser. It was hard for Dyer to suspend disbelief about a junior researcher from Tehran – who must have been under surveillance already, given the history of the Iranian nuclear programme – being able to make such a significant discovery, on a Friday evening on his own, without leaving any trace.

Dyer now made an about-turn.

Unlikely as it seemed, here was this solitary Iranian in his late thirties, in exile in this city of striped ties and black gowns and rain, naive, passionate, who never expected to crack nuclear fusion, but who might have succeeded where teams of scientists and government-funded organisations had failed.

It never ceased to amaze Dyer, the stuff we didn't know, which it took the ingenuity or the sheer good luck of one individual to come along and clarify. Marvar's fortuitous discovery – a new continent of knowledge entirely – was it so different from Cabral's random discovery of Brazil after a storm at sea forced the admiral to turn westward?

Just for one instant, Dyer wanted to relish the outrageous outside chance that Rustum Marvar was more than a fugitive physicist in a dun-coloured greatcoat. He was a symbol, exquisite and indelible, like a figure on the stamps that Dyer collected as a boy to commemorate the moment when Alexander Fleming discovered penicillin, or the Wright brothers took off from the ground, or Marconi heard an impossibly far-away voice in the crackle.

A dense layer of cumulus lay overhead, an ice-floe of it. If you concentrated, you could see that it was moving. A fitful wind carried the smell of fresh cow pats and horse dung.

Dyer was uncertain how long passed before he heard himself say, 'What do you plan to do?'

'I don't know,' Marvar replied in a lifeless voice, speaking with his back to Dyer. There was something sad about him, like a man who had worked hard and still failed an exam. He took off his glasses and rubbed one eye and then another with the sleeve of his coat, and put his glasses back on. His movement had an excruciating slowness to it as he turned. 'I really don't know ...'

Dyer knew that he would remember Marvar's expression for a long time, the hollowness in his brown eyes. If Dyer expected them to reflect what Marvar's eyes alone had seen, he was shocked. There was no pulse of light in them. Where elation should have been was a nameless, infinite dread.

'... You see, in my country, everything evil is having the time of its life.'

The change was astonishing. A new person was speaking, in an indescribably sad voice, who didn't need to remind Dyer how, in the cause of religion, the Ayatollahs had created a fascist state that rivalled the fascist states of 1930s Europe.

'You wouldn't believe the wickedness that is being done in the name of good – it's big.'

Iran was supposed to be a country dedicated to God. It was not. Religious diversity was despised, said Marvar, his voice tightening. 'I'm not a religious person, but my mother – she was a believer, and how she suffered because of it. How she suffered!'

Soon after his father's death, when Marvar was seven, his mother had converted to Christianity. She experienced no repercussions at first. Then, five years ago, she was detained as she left the Janat-Abad church in Tehran, and her Christian books confiscated. Eventually released, she was reminded that apostasy was punishable by death. She died of pancreatic cancer eleven months later, still unable to worship freely.

What Marvar believed in was science. He seemed not to have considered his position when he began his research, the implications of success: he had been pursuing his goal purely for science's sake. Now he had to confront the political realities of his discovery.

The intolerance shown to his mother had germinated an already rebellious seed. Marvar was a student at the University of Tehran when he came across Werner Heisenberg's line that 'effective resistance can only come from those who pretend to collaborate'. This impressed him, but less than the injunction of another atomic physicist, Fritz Houtermans: 'Every decent man confronted by a totalitarian regime ought to have the pluck to commit high treason.' In the liberating world of Oxford, exposed to scientists from every part of the globe, he had mustered the courage. He had resisted passing on his latest research to Tehran, despite the sharpening pressure on him from the Revolutionary Guard.

'I have still not alerted them.'

Inevitably, the Guards and their Mullah bosses would view his behaviour as treasonous, but Marvar had worked tirelessly to brush over his tracks. He had locked his notes in a safe in Oxford, while, to the Iranian Embassy in London every Saturday, he continued to send routine reports and theoretical studies – 'bromides, essentially'. He copied these in to his team at the Clarendon. Until the arrival of Ralph Cubbage, Marvar had managed to keep his Australian professor in the dark. In Professor Whitton's eyes, Marvar was a diligent if unsociable junior spectrometrist who dabbled not terribly successfully with magnetic levitation. It would never have crossed Whitton's distracted mind that this plodding thirty-nine-year-old Iranian researcher had made imminent the feasibility of cheap fusion, any more than it would have entered the thinking of Marvar's masters in Tehran when they permitted him to go to Oxford.

But someone must have suspected. The idea that came to Marvar on the Summer Fields' touchline excited him so much that it booted all else from his thoughts. When he made the obvious mistake of sending a happy text message to Shula, his fate was sealed.

Word raced back to Tehran, either from the Embassy or else from another source, that Marvar was not being transparent, that he was hiding something. It was too soon to say what they knew, whether they had any inkling of what

Marvar had done, but they must have suspected, given their reaction.

Two figures featured prominently in Marvar's nightmares. A General Damghani in the Revolutionary Guard who had lost his son in a gas attack against Saddam; and above him, an elderly Ayatollah from Qom, cultured, an expert in medieval poetry, who had been tortured by the Savak. This powerful duo were in charge of all Iranian physicists working abroad. They regarded America and Britain – after Israel – in the same light as had Saddam, and they lived by Saddam's mantra: 'He who arises to kill you, arise earlier and kill him first.' Swift to suspect Marvar of betrayal, they called for an urgent new check on his background, and then made a decision. He must be brought into line – before the temptation seized him to share his research with another party.

Marvar's warning was delivered last Thursday morning to his pigeonhole at the Clarendon. He had inserted the memory stick in his laptop, and found himself listening to a sound recording, no words, merely muffled noises. Less than thirty seconds later, he yanked it out, ran from the room, down the corridor, into the toilet, and vomited.

He said in a flat, used-up voice: 'You must understand, it's not hatred they feel. It's something deeper.'

For the next twenty-four hours, he revolted against his imagination. What he had heard was not true, there was no proof, the recording was a set-up, these were actors, it was too soon for the authorities to have reacted.

Then on Friday he received his cousin's anguished message. A group of men had turned up early one morning at Marvar's home off Hessabi Street where Shula was kept under house arrest, and taken her and Jamileh away.

Marvar knew from friends what was likely. He read books, newspapers. It was impossible for him not to reconstruct the scene. To supply, unedited, the images and sounds of that day.

The beating on all the doors, the footsteps on the roof.

Chapter Thirteen

SHULA WAS HOLDING JAMILEH WHEN they barged in. A group quite different from those in the parked car, whom Marvar had come to recognise over the summer. Men with beards and tight collars buttoned to the throat and wearing black baggy sirwal trousers a size too large. They would have shown Shula a photograph of herself and asked if it was her. Once she had confirmed that it was, they would have searched the house, even looking inside her slip-ons that he had bought in the Ducker's closing-down sale. They would have discovered Shula's radio tuned to the BBC Persian service. Tucked under the baby's mattress they would have found the English novel that Marvar had purchased in haste from Blackwell's before catching the bus to Heathrow. They would have blindfolded Shula, not allowing her to wear her shoes, and forced her outside to sit in the unmarked Paykan. They would have driven her, still clutching Jamileh, to the detention centre in

Kahrizak and pushed her down a narrow corridor to a cell. Tiled floor, no windows, dark, the stench of faeces. Deaf to the baby's screams, they would have grabbed Jamileh. Having covered her lustrous long black hair with a plain scarf, they would have slapped Shula, thrust her against the wall, stamped on her feet with their army boots, and then knotted her wrists and ankles to an iron bed. They would have hit the soles of her feet with a cable, all the while saying nothing, not asking questions. Before leaving, one of them would have tossed a blanket at her. Moments or hours later, Shula would have woken, feeling something move on her lips – until she realised that ants were crawling into her mouth and up into her nostrils. At some point, the men would have returned to untie her so that she could defecate in the corner. They would have gripped her by the shoulders, and half-carried her to another room, and only then would the blindfold have come off. As her eyes adjusted to the light, a black-bearded cleric in a black turban would have entered, sitting down at the bare wooden table between them. He would place a book on the table, and she would see that it was the English novel that Rustum had given her. She was an infidel, the turbaned man would begin. When he touched her, when he touched this filthy book, he became dirty, just as Jamileh became dirty when Shula fed her, and he would tell Shula that her milk was religiously prohibited because she was a non-believer, and she would not be allowed to bring up her daughter as a non-believer in an Islamic country, unless she cooperated. Then a guard, his face covered with a woollen mask showing only his mouth and eyes, would place a metal bowl on the table and Shula would see that it was filled with dried fruit. The cleric, after inspecting and selecting a date, would explain what other troubles she was in. She would be contaminated and tainted for ever unless she confessed and disclosed what her husband was hiding, which foreign agents he was seeing, what exactly he had revealed to them. The cleric would have listened, eating his date, and then another, while she insisted that she had no knowledge of her husband's work in Oxford; Marvar never talked about it, she wouldn't have understood even if he had, she was a student of literature, not a nuclear scientist. 'Then what about this?' the cleric would respond, and slide a note across the table that Shula would unfold with trembling fingers, on which were typed the words: *Halfness, you changed the world for me – & again with our son & daughter. Now I may have done something!* 'What do you suppose he is talking about?' And Shula would shake her head, 'I don't know, I don't know,' and after a long pause the cleric would say, 'What about his Christianity?' Did her husband never talk about going to house churches and attending services that were against national security? Again, Shula would have shaken her head, this time more vehemently, and exclaimed in her most exasperated voice, 'That was not Rustum, that was his mother!' At this, the cleric would look at her, and it would need no words to say what he was thinking: *Like mother, like child.* Then he would give a nod for the masked guard to place on the table another bowl which was filled, so the cleric would explain before she retched, with her own filth. She had to cooperate or eat it. And she would have looked at him as if he really was insane, or she was. When she had stopped wiping her nose and was in a state to continue listening, he would say, 'Do you want to see Jamileh again?' Unless she ate it, she would never hold Jamileh in her arms. Her choice. He would have talked to her, chewing his dried-up fruit, while he wrote down her charges one by one on a sheet of paper, glancing up now and then to observe her progress, or making his way into a corner of the room to pray. Only after she had forced the last of the bowl's contents into her mouth and swallowed it between sobs, gagging, blocking her mind, thinking only of Jamileh, would he read out what he had written. He would be charging her with the crime of national security and 'collaborating with enemy states', to be tried by Branch 13 of the Revolutionary Court; the crime of disrupting public opinion – indicating the novel – by spreading false information and immorality, to be tried by a special Court in Region 21 of Tehran; and – most serious – the crime of insulting the prophets and the Supreme Leader Ayatollah Khamenei, to be tried in Branch 16 of the Criminal Court. He would ask her to sign the piece of paper, and when – instead of picking up the pen and writing her name with the hysterical relief of nine out of every ten who sat there – she dragged her gaze up through his thick beard, over his plump lips, his pitted nose, into his eyes, thinking how much enmity comes out of two small pools which a thumbnail could extinguish, and said in a low searing voice that she would not commit this shitty perjury, even if that meant not seeing her daughter, because what good to a child on Allah's earth was a mother who consented to lie in this sordid way, so that from now on whenever she looked into herself she would be afraid of seeing someone else, because she was innocent of these charges, as he well knew, he would meet her flaming gaze with no expression, and when she had finished speaking he would fold the sheet of paper and slip it into the novel, stand up, and before turning to leave, give another nod to the guard. After the cleric had closed the door behind him, the guard would tell her that she would be raped so that she could not go to heaven. He would take her to the prison library that was used for praying. They would rape her from behind and in front, both sides. Three men. In the library. All the time a hand, with dark hair on the knuckles, over her mouth. After half an hour, she would hardly be able to stand. She would be led back to her cell holding her stomach, walking in small steps, leaning forward. The guard would put her blindfold back on. He would retie her by the feet and hands to the bed. As an afterthought, he would cover her shoulders with the blanket. The last sounds that she would hear before she fell unconscious would be the grating of the guard's heavy key and the hoarser cries of Jamileh along the corridor.

Chapter Fourteen

DYER COULD TELL – YOU ONLY had to look at him – that Marvar had exhausted himself swatting away the images. There were nights in Belém when the bats zinged back and forth in front of your face, as if someone was shooting them. That was how Marvar held up his hands. It was going round and round in his head, what might have happened, what he could do.

'Have you spoken to anyone?' Dyer said finally. Here, on Port Meadow, beside the Thames, the whole thing seemed melodramatic, extreme. So implausible.

'No … I can't tell Samir.' He had had to keep his excitement and then his dread from his son.

'A doctor, perhaps,' although Dyer did not mean this in the way that it sounded to Marvar, who looked bewildered and exposed.

'You don't believe me …'

'I didn't say that –'

'I'm not delusional,' his face haggard.

Dyer replied in the controlled, neutral tone of the seasoned reporter. Behind him, the years of patient questioning. Telephone calls, long bus journeys, the sun on his unshaven face. The words of his first editor in his ear. Doubt and you'll not be deceived.

'Please. I'm trying to get this straight. You're worried that your wife might have been tortured and raped because you sent her a joyful text?'

'You don't understand these people, John Dyer,' he said from within his invisible hole. 'I thought that you at least … with your experience of the Shining Path … would know what human beings are capable of … would see that I'm saying the truth.'

He had to pause to catch his breath. But he had not finished. 'I always hoped, because she had a marvellous thing for life, that she would escape … She had always managed to … She had an animal's instinct for survival. When I heard her as a petrified animal, it went quickly through my head, "God, she's lost." Now I've stopped hoping.'

The helplessness in his voice was enough to tell Dyer it was true.

'Is there no way to secure Shula's release?'

Oh, nothing could be simpler, said Marvar with an unconvincingly pleasant smile. One call from his mobile would do it – to General Damghani, revealing what Marvar had achieved nine days earlier in a room on the second floor of the Clarendon, and how to repeat the experiment.

Marvar had wanted to shout it to everyone! He agreed with Robert Oppenheimer: 'A scientist cannot hold back progress because of fears of what the world will do with his discovery.' Even to Dyer's imperfect understanding, the implications of Marvar's breakthrough were groundbreaking, although the word did not seem strong enough. Chances were that Marvar, if he was telling the truth, had broken more new ground than Oppenheimer. Not only did fusion matter, it was probably, given the way we were heading, the single thing that mattered. His spherical laser. The sun on earth. What tremendous consequences, in the right humanitarian hands, for our planet. No mining for coal. No fracking for gas. No oil spills. No more pollution. *No more global warming*... An inexhaustible supply of energy at little cost; all it needed was water. The fabric of world energy would change overnight. Deserts would be irrigated. Places bypassed because previously so dry would become the most fertile. With the assistance of reverse-osmosis water purifiers, the Tigris, the Euphrates, the Sinai would be gardens of Eden, creating food for the world. There was nothing that Marvar's nuclear 'football' might not improve. In the right hands.

But an equal force held Marvar back. What if his discovery got into the *wrong* hands? This was the prospect that paralysed him.

'Don't you want the Clarendon to know what you've done?' said Dyer, not certain how to continue.

'And have Cubbage pass it to America!'

Marvar didn't trust the Americans to use the technology peacefully. Dyer mustn't be lulled by the siren voices of men like Professor Whitton who insisted that fusion was safe. 'Don't believe anyone who tells you it's clean.' Oppenheimer's appalled reaction to the H-bomb was the correct one: it was like the plague of Thebes.

Yes, cheap and easy fusion held out the prospect of salvation, but in the same fiery breath it threatened a destruction that had no parallel in history, save for the kind of meteoric explosion that had once gouged out the Mexican Gulf and destroyed the dinosaurs.

Today's dinosaurs were the American president on one side, and on the other the fanatical Revolutionary Guards who had arrested Shula and Jamileh, and pledged to incinerate Israel from the face of the earth. Whatever promises they had signed in order to secure the nuclear agreement, Dyer needed to know that for the past forty years these men had sought nuclear weapons. The US president's belligerent behaviour had prompted the Guards to renew their search. Fusion would give access to a new type of weapon whose limits could not yet be imagined. Marvar's device – with no great alteration – would grant the Guards an obscene dominion, not merely over Israel, but over the Middle East and beyond. North Korea could supply the rocket. But you wouldn't need a rocket. You wouldn't even need high planes bombing. A single bullet would do. A bullet with a capsule in it, containing deuterium-tritium fuel, fired at extremely high velocity. The Empire State Building. The Taj Mahal. Big Ben. The Bodleian. Marvar held up two fingers and pointed at a family of ducks drifting beside the riverbank. Boom boom boom.

Marvar had gone through it all, over and over. He was aware – his last twenty years had trained him – that people would welcome his invention for good reasons and for bad reasons. Then there were those who would not welcome it at all – for the reason that Marvar was Iranian. Two obdurate enemies of fusion were Russia and Saudi Arabia, among the most unstable countries in the world. 'If someone said: "We now have the technology to change the planet: no more petrol, no more coal, no more gas," how would Putin treat that? How would the Saudis? The oil cartels would be demented.'

Financiers, investors, hedge-fund managers – they'd all want a share of the knowledge, Marvar said. 'The cost of world energy is seven trillion dollars per annum. One per cent is seventy billion. If you were to license the process, you'd get more than one per cent. It would dwarf the riches of the richest ...'

It was against Marvar's every dictate to hand over his knowledge to those who would abuse it as they'd abused Shula. At the same time, his heart was full of his wife.

Raped, with a mouthful of ants, not knowing what he had done.

Dyer saw it with terrifying clarity. Marvar might get his wife back by telling … But if he told … His dilemma was inflexible. That was why he stood there like a salmon flapping on the bank. Everything in his face, the way he moved his shoulders and ran dismayed hands over his coat, feeling for the answer in the cloth between the buttons, showed his desolation. He was not here. He was somewhere else, in his own cell, alone.

They had walked beyond the weir to the stretch of river where the college eights practised. The clouds had dispersed and there was a band of clear sky, page white, above the trees. A light wind was swaying the branches. The Thames murmured, horses, cows, ducks. On sunny mornings, Dyer would run here. Had anyone the right to annihilate this? From somewhere, he heard the metallic notes of a marsh tit.

Marvar heard it too. In his coat, he stood and stared at the bare trees, searching for the source of the sound. He seemed infinitely sadder, now that he had unburdened himself. He had talked to Dyer as if he wanted to prolong the world for as long as possible without this knowledge. ('How long would it take otherwise?' 'Years!') He had no words left to say. Birds wheeled overhead, disappearing. The wind blew ripples on the water. He was one of the barges on the canal, rudderless, pot-plants in the little curtained windows, beer cans, the refuge for vagrants. He was back where he started when he stood blinking at Dyer outside the Oxford University Press, not knowing what to do.

Dyer pointed.

'Look. He's over there.'

Marvar followed the direction of Dyer's finger to a dark tiny speck, balanced on the middle of three telephone wires like a solitary musical note.

'He? How can you be so certain?'

It was Dyer's turn to tell Marvar something he didn't know: it had been an amateur who discovered that male cuckoos do the singing, as was the case for all songbirds.

Marvar shook his head; he had no idea. 'You mean,' in a slow, fascinated tone, 'that if you hear a bird singing, it's a male ... Now that *is* incredible.'

For perhaps ten seconds more they stood in silence and listened, until the bird flew off.

Marvar gave a little sigh. He gently rubbed the back of his knuckles. 'The atomic bombs – they had male names too, you know.'

Just then, as if a door had opened, a cold gust sprang up. Dyer looked at his watch. The football match would be over. Their two sons would be tucking into their prawn sandwiches and banana cake, supplied by a caterer in Summertown.

'Why not come home for a drink – unless you've got other plans?'

'Plans?' It was an empty laugh, but a laugh nonetheless. 'I have no plans.'

As they turned to go, the geese came over low up the river, a wedge of large brown Vs, sharp against the darkening sky, babbling, surging on.

Chapter Fifteen

FOR THE SECOND TIME THAT afternoon, Dyer relieved Marvar of his coat.

'I could do with an overcoat like this. Where did you get it?'

They were standing in the hallway, next to the fishing rod.

'Shula had it made for me before I came here,' said Marvar.

Stitched into the collar was a label that Dyer hadn't noticed before. It showed a red egret and a word in Farsi – the name of a master tailor off Laleh-zar Street, Marvar explained. 'He warned her that Oxford is exceedingly damp.'

Smiling, Dyer went to hang it up again.

Leandro was at a sleepover with Samir. They could drink. They could talk. Marvar could decide what he was going to do.

He heard a chair groan as Marvar sat down.

Coming back into the kitchen, Dyer flapped open a cardboard box and pulled out a bottle, showing it. 'I've only got white.'

'I'll drink white wine.'

'I'll put it in the freezer.'

'Don't worry, I'll have it warm.' He looked at the label. He was not reading it.

Dyer poured the glasses.

Marvar picked up his. He drank as if warm white wine and he were made for each other.

'Who else knows about your discovery?' asked Dyer, sitting down.

'Just you. You're the only one.'

Marvar had dismantled his spherical laser. But it was easy to make another – if you knew how, if you had the formula. You only needed the formula.

'Where's that? On your laptop?'

'Don't worry, it's safe. I'm not so foolish.' He would never risk putting anything on a computer. Every Tom, Dick, and Ralph could hack into it. Every Ayatollah too, mirthlessly.

His aversion was understandable. It made Dyer suddenly think of Rejas, who had told him how Ezequiel never wrote anything down, and neither did Socrates or Jesus. '*The problem with text is that it assumes its own reality. It cannot answer, and it cannot explain.*'

But Marvar hadn't gone quite to that extreme. He ran a finger around the rim of his glass. 'Know the best way to keep a secret? With a pen and paper – like in the old days. But you're a writer,' gesturing at Dyer's notes and his book, still open, on the table, awaiting an inscription, 'you know that.'

Marvar had condensed his planet-shifting invention to an algorithm on a single piece of paper. Handwritten. One copy. 'You don't need any other.'

That was the beauty of science, he said. It wasn't so hard to understand as love or war. Everything could be lasered down into a few letters and numbers which you could hold in your palm.

Yet the problem remained. Who to give it to? Marvar widened his eyes, staring fiercely through his glasses at his open palm as if he would read the answer there.

Give it to the Mullahs and perhaps get Shula back, but risk them weaponising his discovery? Give it to his Australian professor at the Clarendon, but risk it passing into the hands of Iran's enemies? Did he entrust it to the most respectable body within his field – the European Atomic Energy Community, say? Or did he broadcast it to the world, through Wikileaks or a newspaper? Was the answer 'everyone' – or 'no one'? What if Marvar couldn't find anybody who was deserving of this information: 'What if there is no right person?'

Plainly, it was tormenting him, the lack of a solution.

They soon finished the bottle. Dyer opened another. It was a New Zealand sauvignon from the Co-op.

'Do you want a pizza?'

'A pizza?' said Marvar.

'I can ring for one.'

'Why not? The last pizza,' he waved his hand merrily, like a conductor.

'I hope not,' said Dyer. He got up and dialled the number from the post-it note on the fridge, ordering a quattro staggione for himself, a margarita for Marvar.

'Twenty minutes,' said a foreign-sounding male voice.

He refilled their glasses.

Marvar took another large swallow and stared across the room.

'Yes, maybe *you*, J. W. Dyer, *can* imagine it,' he said, and swivelled his eyes from the bookshelf back to Dyer, and then to Dyer's open book on the table. 'You write a book, you put years into it, your life ... and *no one publishes it*. All that hard work, you don't have *one single reader*.' He drained his glass and took the bottle and poured more wine into it. 'I had a teacher too. Lovely old woman. Piano. "Music unheard has no value," she used to say. And it's true, it's true.'

Dyer looked at him. 'Oughtn't we to see how our sons are getting on?'

'Yes,' said Marvar, suppressing a burp, 'let's do that.'

Dyer found Silvi's number and dialled it. 'Hi, Silvi, John here. I've got Rustum with me. That's right, Samir's dad. We were wondering how the boys are doing?'

Following a brief conversation with Silvi – they were fine, Gilles had made cheeseburgers, everyone now was in the games room playing Fifa – Dyer was passed on to his son.

Leandro didn't seem to hear him, gaming no doubt. After extracting from his son the earlier score – 3–1, to Winchester House – Dyer asked: 'Is Samir there? His dad wants a word.'

He handed his mobile to Marvar.

Dyer started to tidy away his notes on the Tupi while father and son spoke. Even so, it was hard not to overhear when Marvar's voice became concerned. 'But Samir...' he said, holding on to the table. He scraped back his chair and rose unsteadily to his feet. 'It didn't stop you playing?' He was frowning. 'Huh, don't I know the type...' patting the top of his head. 'No, I'm with Leandro's dad,' and then a few words in Farsi, rather as Dyer spoke to Leandro in Portuguese when they talked about people in front of them. At last, Marvar said: 'What time am I collecting you? Six? That late? Oh, there's a party... Yes, yes, Ward Road, I have the address. Bye, darling... Love you too.' He kissed into the phone and put it to his ear to listen, but Samir had rung off.

'Anything wrong?' Dyer asked.

'Samir's hurt himself,' grimaced Marvar, returning the phone. 'There's some big boy at Winchester House. He called him The Pubic. Does he mean precocious puberty?'

Dyer laughed. 'They usually have one boy who's six foot two and clearly shaves. But he's OK?'

'He is good. It's only his shin. It is nothing to worry about. We will still be able to go walking,' he said with forced

143

cheerfulness. Then in the way that people redundantly repeat what has been overheard, 'I said I'll collect him at six tomorrow afternoon.'

The buzzer went. And again. Longer this time.

Marvar shot a look at Dyer. The muscles tightened around his eyes.

'The pizzas,' clarified Dyer.

An Albanian boy on a motorbike handed them over. Dyer unpacked the pizzas from their boxes onto plates. Marvar nibbled dejectedly at his margarita.

It was no longer light outside. The darkness was crushing him.

'Where's the loo?'

'Down there, on the right.'

His shadow, magnified, cartwheeled across the wall.

'I know she's dead,' he hiccupped, when he returned.

He lay back in the chair. The pulse was racing in his temple.

'You have no proof,' said Dyer.

Marvar was leaping ahead, chasing the worst again. His conversation with Samir had startled something. He was like a sheep who had scented the slaughterhouse.

He hiccupped again. His wife was in Tehran, in a tiled room, behind a locked door. She had cramp in her legs, her lips were swollen.

'No, no, she's dead, or she might as well be. What she loved in me is gone – because she will take it with her. I feel

a large piece of me is no longer there. But as long as I live –
and Samir lives – then she is not gone. While we live, she will
not be completely dead.'

It sounded like a speech that he'd rehearsed in the loo.

'You don't know,' Dyer insisted. Marvar was saying this
just to see how it would feel. He wanted to test his capacity
to survive his wife's death. But they wouldn't kill her till
they'd got hold of Marvar.

Across the table, his hard corroding smile. 'I do. I do
know.'

He stopped speaking. The room was without a sound in
it, quieter than the Taylorian. When the church bell struck,
the chime was unnaturally loud.

Then he burst into tears. He had lost his footing. Up
until now, God himself couldn't have made a coward out of
him. But he was cracking, there was no doubt. His confession hadn't given him succour. He had been looking to
Dyer for absolution. Or for Dyer to tell him what to do,
maybe.

Dyer went to the loo.

When he came back, he was surprised to see Marvar's
chair empty.

Marvar stood by the fridge. Strangely calm, he seemed to
be peering at the Pelé fridge-magnet which Vivien had given
Leandro, and – clipped to it – a yellow post-it note scribbled
with telephone numbers for pizzerias, cleaners, doctors,
plumbers ... the kitchen of Dyer's life.

At the sight of Dyer, Marvar stepped away. He resumed his seat and pushed Dyer's book across the table. It was as if all his nervousness had been replaced by resolution.

'You never wrote a dedication,' and handed to Dyer the propelling pencil that he was holding. 'Go on. Write something. For me.'

Dyer accepted the pencil and looked at the title page. He still hadn't worked out what to write. He was aware of Marvar sizing him up through his round wire spectacles. It was always like this, he thought, sitting down.

The last words Dyer remembered him saying: 'Ah, yes. You had a wife and daughter,' as he picked up the photograph of Astrud, stared at it, and put it tipsily back.

That night, Marvar slept in Leandro's bed. He was in no state to walk home to Merton Street. And although he didn't say so, obviously worried about who might be waiting for him there.

He had gone when Dyer woke in the morning. He had taken the book, but not his overcoat. It was hanging with its collar up next to Dyer's tackle in the cupboard under the stairs. Marvar must have searched for it and not finding it he must have left.

Chapter Sixteen

IN THE NIGHT, DYER DREAMED a line of poetry which seemed so true, so wonderful that he had to bring it to the surface to be preserved when he woke. He dragged the line through the vertical meadow of his sleep and having kept it warm and tender in his mouth like a gun-dog with a bird, he dropped it before his waking self.

After writing it down, he went back to sleep. In the morning, he picked up the sheet of paper that he had put on his bedside table between the photos, books and possessions, and read: 'Ordinarily he took the train.'

Groggily, he belted on his dressing gown.

In the meagre light, the chill vacancy of Leandro's room. On the draining board downstairs: two empty wine glasses, a white mug three-quarters full with cold coffee, Marvar's barely touched pizza.

In Brazil, 'pizza' was slang for a crime which suffered no legal consequences. Marvar had committed no crime – so far as Dyer could tell. He must have shambled back to his digs in Merton Street.

Dyer drew the curtains, peered through the French window. The mist reeked out of the canal and shrouded the buildings. Over the neighbour's fence and the grey tiled rooftops, the clang of bells. It could have been Belém – the narrow roads off the square and little two-storey houses painted in pastel colours, with front doors onto the pavement. But it was the energetic vicar of St Barnabas tolling him to morning service. Marvar yesterday had been on his way there, Dyer now recalled. He was dressed up for church, dressed to pray, and had paused with the smokers outside the OUP for a cigarette when Dyer strolled out of the fog.

The bells stopped, tossing Dyer back ashore in Jericho. Should he call someone? But who? He'd cross that bridge after breakfast. Once he had set down all that he could remember of his conversation with Marvar.

Despite his aching hangover, Dyer forced himself to the kitchen table, and, with a full pot of coffee beside him, started to write out the story before the details vanished into the mist. His return to England had coincided with the revelation that Microsoft, thirty years before, had inserted into every programme a device which allowed the US intelligence services access to your computer. It hadn't required

Marvar to remind him that the best way of safeguarding a secret was with pencil and paper.

Much of what Marvar had told him was too technical, and Dyer left out a lot; as well, he may have misremembered certain things. Still, it was a relief to be exercising his reporter's muscles, to be writing, back in the flow. Over the past months, his mind had lost itself in the Cherwell's weeds, but now it was on fire with what Marvar had said. By transcribing this onto sheets of A4 in shorthand, Dyer was making it real. Exactly what he would do with it, he had no idea. All he knew: Marvar's story was unlike any he had heard.

Flooded with coffee, Dyer raked back through their few encounters. Marvar's abrupt disappearance during the Summer Fields game – that must have happened after Samir's corner kick set the ball rolling, as it were. When Dyer first met him beside the sandpit, Marvar was scribbling mathematical formulas in the sand, tantalisingly close to a solution. Their excited embrace on the touchline following Samir's goal against Horris Hill would have occurred within hours of Marvar's successful experiment. Small wonder his ecstatic reaction.

Yet Marvar's face last night was drained. He had talked like a man under attack from every direction, who didn't know which way to turn. In the lucidity of his despair he chose to confide in Dyer.

Both their sons had been bullied by the same boy. Was that the reason, though?

Something about Marvar's behaviour at the Horris Hill match had stayed, unexamined, in Dyer's mind. How he raised the subject of Rejas and kept returning to him. The policeman's story fascinated Marvar. But not so pressingly as Dyer's reasons for keeping the story to himself, refusing to publish.

Dyer could only guess that Marvar had longed for an honourable way to be relieved of his responsibility. His options were narrowing with each moment, he didn't have much time. He was passionate in wanting to save Shula, but the one means that he could think of to achieve this was out of the question. He had to look for his answer elsewhere.

In his paralysed state, it was easy then to understand why Marvar should have sought the help of his mother's God, a god he had hitherto not believed in. What he had been on his way to pray for in St Barnabas, when forestalled by Dyer, was to have the decision wrested from him.

In those circumstances, who do you trust to give you release? You can't trust your government – or any government. You can't trust your professor at the Clarendon, who has but the haziest notion of who you are. You can't trust your wife, because she's lying semi-conscious in a prison cell in Tehran. All you're left with is a superannuated ex-journo you met at a school sandpit and once stood beside on a touchline. You have to trust someone like John William Dyer, author of *A Social and Cultural History of the Lower Amazon Basin* (OUP, 2001), a man who had nailed himself so stubbornly to the mast of his high principles that he sank a reasonably promising career by keeping mum.

Shortly after 6 p.m. Dyer drove to the Asselins' to pick up Leandro.

Over the car radio, he caught the last item of news: about the Australian mathematician Todd Angle who'd gone missing on a bush walk in Tasmania's south-west. Dyer was about to turn it off, but the phrase 'So the whole world can know' stopped him. A friend had received a letter from Angle two days after he disappeared, beginning with these words written boldly across the top, and containing Angle's philosophy on reality and a mathematical theory explaining the ideal tax system. 'I wondered if Todd had committed suicide, but came to the conclusion he had changed a lot since I last saw him.'

Meanwhile, the main news concerned the worsening situation in the Middle East. The American president was promising to 'dismantle the disastrous deal with Iran'. In response, Iran was ratcheting up the rhetoric. 'Israel is no longer needed to exist near us.' Any further provocation, said a spokesman in Tehran, and Iran was prepared to restart its nuclear programme 'within hours'.

Chapter Seventeen

THIRTY HOURS ON, DYER'S MIND remained congested with everything Marvar had told him. Dyer had lived more on that day than in the last seventeen months; who would have predicted that it would have been so after they ran into each other outside the Oxford University Press?

Yet when Dyer went over it again, he wondered whether Marvar was not being violently overdramatic. Was it possible that no one had laid a finger on Shula, and Marvar's fears were the product of his disturbed imagination?

The truth has its own smell. There was nothing feigned about Marvar. Even so, Dyer worried that a long period of inactivity had made his own judgement defective. 'Never put a wet car in a garage,' his father used to say. 'It goes rusty.' Had this happened to Dyer?

He looked forward to a few hours of not having to think about nuclear fusion, for which he had anyway no spontaneous talent; to losing himself, instead, on the coast of sixteenth-century Brazil. The bay below Monte Pascoal. The crump of waves on a high-banked shore. The Portuguese fleet is at anchor.

A cold breeze had blown up, an Oxford breeze, knife sharp, with dead leaves in it, and empty paper cups. Dyer wrapped his scarf tighter. Emerging from Little Clarendon Street, he walked past St Bennett's, past the Eagle and Child where Tolkien used to meet C. S. Lewis for a beer, past the newly refurbished St Giles's Café, once upon a time a greasy-spoon where he and his best friend Rougetel escaped from school on Saturday afternoons to eat an illicit egg on toast.

The breeze heightened his senses. Passing the Oxfam bookshop, Dyer caught a smell of body odour and urine. Ahead, he recognised a Phoenix parent. A donnish-looking man in a black beret, unbrushed grey hair growing in every direction: the father of the second boy demoted from the football team, whose name had slipped Dyer's mind. He was giving wide berth to a dishevelled accordionist seated cross-legged on the pavement.

Blue tracksuit with pale stains on it, scabs on the backs of his hands, sharp teeth blackened around the stumps, and his eyes wincing as if it wasn't music he was squeezing out of his box, but smoke. The tune was always the same one.

The face staring up had the bitter, porcine features of someone who had never been taken seriously, who had had to fight for every scrap. A thick paperback was open, upside down, pages stained, on a sleeping bag beside him, together with a half-bottle of rum.

He stopped playing. His left hand stretched out, clutching a McDonald's coffee cup filled with coins, and jingled it.

Dyer was about to enter the Taylorian when he heard a muffled voice call his name. He looked around. A sleek black Audi was parked in the bus lane parallel to the entrance. Knuckles rapped at the tinted rear window, which lowered further to reveal the blotched features of Lionel Updark, who fastidiously dislodged his Apple headphones.

'John, do you have a mo'?'

Dyer wanted to turn away. He gestured at the Ionic facade behind him. 'I was about to go in there.'

The driver sprang out and seamlessly opened the far-side door.

'I'm the last person you want to see, I know,' said Updark, with a crimped smile, making a little Boy Scout salute with three fingers, and then wrapping the white cable around them and putting it into his pocket. 'But this shouldn't take long.'

Dyer climbed into the back, in his mind cursing the red light that he had dutifully obeyed at the pedestrian crossing. The car glided off down the Woodstock Road.

'Where are we going?'

'Patience, John, patience.'

Beside him, Updark, in a black coat, sat with his hands in his lap, looking out of the window. The sun lay hidden, smothered by fast-moving banks of cloud, intense white, like the glaze on an iced bun. Lights were still on in some of the houses they passed.

The car slowed down by the speed camera opposite Lynam's primary school, and after an interval it accelerated on. Over the roundabout. Onto the A40.

It was falling into place.

'Anything to do with your new posting?' asked Dyer in a dry, flippant tone. Instead of heading to the Faubourg St Honoré and the former palace of Napoleon's sister, Updark was whispered to be on temporary secondment to an outreach of GCHQ.

'All will become clear when we get there,' Updark said. He brushed some hairs from his trouser leg. 'What do you reckon, Peter?'

The driver answered twenty minutes. Dyer knows suddenly where they are going. Not to the Updark pile in Woodeaton, where he had tipsily complimented curly-headed Audrey – that was her name! – on her clinging scent. ('That smells exotic, what is it?' 'Oh, something I got in the souk in Rabat.') But to an anonymous corrugated-iron warehouse in a business park outside Eynsham where he will be obliged to leave his shoulder bag in reception and submit to a close body search and, after a security wand waves him through, follow Updark up a perforated-metal staircase, through a steel-lined corridor and screened co-axial cables, into a large open-plan room with floor-to-ceiling windows.

The tune of the wheels on the straight flat road removed them from the present.

'Sorry not to see you at the Asselins' the other evening,' said Dyer.

'Something came up,' Updark replied in a grave voice.

'You'd have liked the person who took your place.'

Updark made no response. Dyer thought of Miranda assessing Updark through squashed glasses to encapsulate him in eighty words.

'How's Beatrice?' asked Dyer after a while, and receiving no reply, 'Spassky?'

Ignoring him, Updark said in a retrospective tone, 'Did you see that Slimy has died?'

Only to Dyer out of all the parents at the Phoenix would this name have resounded. It was as if, in an obituary in the *Phoenician*, Updark sought a trench in which the pair of them could shelter, before hostilities resumed.

'I did read that. A miracle he evaded Yewtree.'

'Remember Parkhouse?' said Updark, investing the name with respect and authority. Hair was springing out of his nostrils. He was touching a plaster on his wrist.

Dyer thought back. He would play the game. 'Robin Parkhouse?' There came to him a round face in a blue-and-yellow striped blazer. 'Captain of cricket?'

'I saw him not long ago,' Updark went on. 'He told me how he took his son round a prep school in Dorset, all set to enrol him, when, just as they were leaving the headmaster's study, a door opened along the corridor – and out stepped Slimy!'

Dyer couldn't hold back his smile. 'That would have been a shock. Although, I have to say, he never beat me.' Slimy Prentice had merely hurled Dyer's math's prep into the bin, saying: '*This, Basil, is damned unamusing.*'

'Nor me,' reflected Updark, rubbing a distracted finger up and down his wrist. 'He wasn't such a bad teacher, actually. Remember him telling us, "Knowledge is power"? Of course, Slimy didn't let on he was quoting Bacon. Still, it's quite true.' Then: 'Seen any of the others recently?' He meant from Upper One.

'I've been living abroad – like you,' Dyer pointed out. It was a bit too early for such cocktail-party banter. He had gone out of his way to avoid Updark at the gathering in January, because this was just the kind of conversation they might have had.

'I did go to the last reunion,' Updark said. It was where he'd met Parkhouse. His face had a scorer's concentration as he recollected the gathering at the In and Out Club. 'Funny how we all recognised the strong impact the school made on us, how vividly we recall it even now, and how difficult it is to communicate much of what we experienced then to our wives.'

Dyer had declined the invitation; this club was where his newspaper editor had taken him for lunch when recruiting

him. But he could picture the get-together. The long polished table like the deck of his uncle Hugo's yacht, the
partridge with bread sauce, the club claret, the white heads
in black tie, the souffléd features of accountants, lawyers,
civil servants, bankers, teachers, all scrambling to recall each
other's nicknames for the chance to voice them once again.
What fates had they found, Splash and Boggy and Wiggy?
Leaving the gate, up Bardwell Road, with their Latin and
Greek, their not-bad maths and indeterminate ambitions.
Did they unify themselves, or fall on the trail? Did they find
their Guineveres?

'Who else was there?' Dyer asked dutifully. 'Finnock, I
suppose.' The former head boy who was eternally coming
back.

'Finnock died. Poor Finnock. Forty-six. Cancer.'

Dyer thought of the others in his dorm. 'Garridge?'

'Garridge is in Perth.'

'Doing?'

'I think he makes outdoor garden furniture.'

'Rougetel?' said Dyer impulsively. Once you started, how
hard to stop.

'No idea. Though I can't say I knew him well, being as he
was in the year below.' His eyes narrowed at a recollection.
'Friend of yours, wasn't he?'

'He was a friend.' One who possessed what Dyer, aged
twelve, had only read about in *Jane Eyre*: the attribute of
stainless truth.

'Didn't he live in South America?'

'That's right. Bolivia.'

'I remember him running away ...'

Where was he now? All of a sudden, Dyer wanted to rescue Rougetel from time, before Updark got to him first. His pale freckled face swam back. Halfway through his first term, Rougetel had asked his grandparents to collect him at a given hour from the postbox outside the boarding house, and when they didn't, he caught a train to London where he was picked up by the police, who were waiting on the platform.

'... It caused a great impression. A rebellion!' Updark laughed uncomfortably, shaking his head. He himself had never rebelled. He had followed the path laid by his parents and grandparents. 'Ever see him, do you, Rougetel?'

'Not since I was twenty,' Dyer calculated. On a rainy summer afternoon beside the Thames near Hampton Court. A slim figure stood on the riverbank, watching Dyer and his crew lift their boat out of the water. '*Hello, Basil.*' Dyer, glancing up, recognised the person in black jeans with a backpack. The two of them had talked in an awkward way over the upturned shell, but by the time Dyer had finished loading the boat on the rack and returned to the river, the towpath stretched up and down, blank, like an old telephone number. 'I've no idea what became of him.'

Not quite true. There'd been one other sighting, bizarre and unsatisfactory, in a letter from Trundle who had started a business selling outboard motors in Benin. *'You won't believe this, but guess who I spied in a voodoo procession in the centre of Ouidah?'* Trundle had shouted his name and the man had looked up and hurried on. *'I'm positive it was Rougetel.'* That was eighteen years ago.

Updark was still at the reunion dinner. 'Funny how someone you thought was a complete dunce becomes head of Unilever, yet the one you'd put your money on to do well...' He examined Dyer. 'But you've done well. In your field.'

'Quite a small field it was.'

'Yes,' nodded Updark with that indulgent tone he had, 'but a field is a field is a field. Now who was I talking to about you ...?' He picked another hair off his trouser leg. 'Whoever it was reminded me of something I've been meaning to ask. Why were you called Basil? You're so not a Basil.'

The driver's eyes were listening in the mirror. Dyer gave a defeated smile. How many years since he had heard that name? Not, probably, since his encounter with Rougetel outside the Molesey Boat Club. He could still see his black jeans and the side of his head.

Dyer began to tell the story. 'It was that physics master.'

'...Jumbo?'

Dyer nodded. 'He asked us a question in class. I stuck up my hand. "Yes, you, Basil." "Sir, my name's not Basil." "Well, it is now!"'

'For a long while I used to wonder why he chose to call me that. I didn't know then, and I don't know now.' By the end of that term everyone was addressing him as Basil – even the headmaster. Dyer mused: 'It was probably Jumbo's way of striking back – for the nickname we'd given him.'

'I don't believe I ever had a nickname,' Updark said after a pause. He looked out of the tinted rear window. The light falling on his cheeks emphasised the shiny nodules on his skin, the red welts, swollen and scaly with damp patches, like Ezequiel's psoriasis. 'But it's funny how things stick. I still think of you as Basil.'

They were turning into Eynsham.

'There's something I'd like to ask you,' said Dyer.

Updark rotated his head in a slow arc, and looked at Dyer with a groundless grin. 'I'm all ears.'

'Whatever happened to your face?'

Chapter Eighteen

UPSTAIRS, THEY SAT ON WHITE plastic cubes at the side of a neon-lit open room. In the space around them, a dozen or so figures, some casually dressed, some in ties, were hunched over computer screens or talking by the large window which overlooked the car park. The screens were mounted on long narrow tables. From time to time someone wheeled out from under one of these tables a box-shaped white cabinet with drawers, and pushed it towards a colleague.

Dyer's quick eyes took in: potted plants by the window, a message pinned into a sound baffle, 'Remember your neighbours, please no curry', no clutter, hardly any paper, and despite all the knots of conversation, an overall feeling of soundlessness.

Updark waved at a woman working at a desk in the area they were sitting in to bring two coffees.

'Milk?' raising her eyebrow at Dyer. She could have stepped from one of Vivien's fashion magazines, in a short navy skirt with scarlet dots on it, and dark stockings. Her auburn hair was piled up in a dated bun, and two loose strands trailed over her ears.

'None for me,' said Dyer.

'The usual splash, thanks, Lorna.'

They were waiting for someone to join them. He arrived at the same moment as their coffees. A younger man, lean, unshaven, open-shirted, in a green tweed jacket. His short brown hair looked recently cut. He had a small mouth.

Updark introduced him. 'Roland Hissop. Iran desk.'

'Hi,' with a firm grip. His other hand held a clipboard.

'Hi.'

'John and I were at school together,' Updark explained. 'We've been catching up.'

Hissop, too, it appeared. He knew of Dyer's work in Rio, he said. His first posting had been Venezuela.

'I was sorry to hear about your wife,' settling onto a cube.

'Which one?' asked Dyer, more sharply than he intended.

'Oh, I thought there was only the one.'

'Not really. But you haven't brought me here to discuss my marriages.'

'Quite right,' Updark said. He had hardened back into a stern and watchful administrator, as self-contained as the biscuit tin which he now scraped open and offered round. 'Flapjacks, anyone? Lorna made them.'

Dyer shook his head.

'Thanks,' said Hissop, taking two.

Updark started to reach for one, but decided against. 'We have brought you here,' returning the tin to the top of the white cabinet between them, 'to talk about Rustum Marvar.'

Of course. This kidnap. It could only be about him.

Dyer took a procrastinating sip of lukewarm black coffee. 'What about Marvar?'

'Interrogation session,' said Updark, 'coming up.' He produced a notebook and pen from his jacket. 'You and Marvar are friends, I understand?' He looked at Dyer enquiringly.

'Friends is too strong. We each have a son who was bullied.'

'Ah, yes, by that Russian boy. A malevolent lump of lard, Beatrice informs me.'

'Anyway, it's been sorted.'

'*Agam quam brevissime potero* – I wish to be as brief as possible.' He drew out his cuffs. 'Do you know where Marvar might be at this moment?'

'No. Why?'

'He's gone missing. So has his son.'

'Since when?'

'They left an address in Ward Road shortly after midday yesterday. Neither has been seen since.'

'That's the Asselins' house ...'

Dyer felt sick in his vitals. He could hear the creaking of plastic. Updark's face was furrowed as he lowered his head.

'Your son was there, too, I believe.'

'Yes. It was Pierre's birthday. He'd invited Leandro and the rest of the team for a sleepover.'

'Mrs Asselin says that Marvar turned up before lunch and whisked Samir away without so much as a hi or a thank-you. She was downstairs at the time. Didn't even see him.'

'That's odd,' said Dyer, who distinctly now recalled Marvar arranging to collect Samir at six. Leandro hadn't mentioned that Samir had left the party early. Then again, if Leandro was submerged in a computer game, he wouldn't have noticed anything. 'Could it have been someone else who picked him up?'

'The butler described a man who did resemble Marvar, and we've asked to see the security tapes.'

They were taking a lot of trouble for someone who had only been missing for half a day.

'Why do you think Marvar arrived so early?' asked Hissop.

'I've no idea. I know he was worried about an injury to Samir's leg. But it didn't sound serious.'

'We need to speak to the last person who saw him,' Hissop said.

Updark pressed the tips of his fingers together. 'Silvi Asselin said he'd been with you.'

'That was on Saturday.'

'Talk us through that, would you?' said Hissop.

'I bumped into him outside the OUP.'

'When exactly?' asked Updark, notebook open, pen poised.

'It would have been shortly after one p.m.,' said Dyer. 'He came home for a coffee. We went for a walk on Port Meadow.'

'How long a walk?'

'Oh, a couple of hours.'

Hissop looked at Updark.

'And then?'

'He came back to St Barnabas Street. We had a pizza, two bottles of wine, and he stayed the night. He was worried he had drunk too much, so I offered him a bed. He was gone by the time I got up.'

'Weren't your sons playing football on Saturday afternoon?'

'They were.'

'Am I correct, John, in thinking you would normally go and watch Leandro?' Updark's politeness was self-willed. Until two months ago, he and Dyer had known each other only by their surnames. His use of Dyer's Christian name took Dyer back to the emotion he felt when in a novel the author addressed him as 'Dear Reader'; it was disconcerting, unearned.

Stick to the truth as close as you can had been Dyer's rule whenever detained by the Policia Militar. He replied: 'We got talking, and suddenly it was too late to drive to Winchester House.'

'Talking about what?'

166

'His wife and baby daughter, mainly.'

'What about them?'

'He said they'd been arrested in Tehran. And worse.'

'Talk about his work, did he?'

Dyer looked at Updark. 'He's a physicist. It's not my subject. I'm a South American hand, remember.'

'But you ask questions, you're curious.'

'Exactly, you're a journo,' said Hissop.

'Was.'

'You're always an ex-journo,' in a knowing voice.

'Did he talk about his work, John?' said Updark. He was fretful, like a desk-bound colonel.

'A little.'

'How much is a little?'

'Not much.'

'Seem excited, did he?' said Hissop.

'A little.'

'I wish you wouldn't say that,' said Updark. '"Little" pulls no man off his horse. Did he talk of magnetic confinement or plasma focus? Did he tell you about that? You spent a couple of hours chatting, remember. You're the one person who seems to have had anything resembling a conversation with him.'

'Like I said, he was worried about his wife and daughter.'

'So how could you tell he was excited?'

'I can see you're excited by your work, but I don't expect you to talk to me about it.'

Updark exchanged an impatient glance with Hissop. He had gone beyond Dyer and it was irksome to be treated as still in the same class. The muscles in his jaw tensed, as if he had clamped his teeth on a nut.

'Look, I can't force you to tell us. Only you know what Marvar said to you. But if you are willing to tell us, then we'd very much like to hear.'

'I really don't have anything to add.' *'I know I can trust you not to say anything.'* It wasn't only what he'd promised Marvar. He was unsure, suddenly, of their motives.

Already, this was too much for Updark. 'You were always a quick boy, John,' in a tone suggesting that Dyer was no less rebellious than his best friend Rougetel. 'But you're not doing yourself any good. You may end up wishing your ears were a little deafer.'

Dyer gave him a sturdy smile. 'Now why, Lionel, should I wish that?'

'Let's put a few cards on the table, shall we? Long story short, it is conceivable that your friend Rustum has made a scientific breakthrough.'

'A revolutionary breakthrough,' echoed Hissop, taking another bite.

Dyer looked from Hissop to Updark, who would have to be calmed down and outwitted. 'I'm sorry, but what are you talking about?'

'You know, John, I have a little problem with stupidity above a certain temperature.'

'You've just praised my intelligence.'

Updark looked at him severely. 'I don't think we're hearing each other.'

Dyer only smiled. 'I'm all ears, Lionel.'

'Let's start with: I am going to take everything you've told me so far *cum grano salis.*'

'But I haven't told you anything. Plus, I'm not sure what I've got to say. And if I did have something to say, you have reminded me I am under no obligation to say it. Actually, I will have a flapjack.'

The mask of affability had definitely slipped by the time Updark resumed.

He said to Dyer – it was important this was made clear, 'This is D-notice, right? Right, John? National security. You tell no one. But no one.'

'Right.'

'There is a possibility – I stress possibility – that Marvar has bypassed the whole bunny game and found a new way to solve our energy problems.'

Dyer tried to consider this calmly. 'What makes you think that?'

'You'd hardly expect me to reveal sensitive information. Let's say that data has been discovered on one of the machines at the lab, and our cuckoos in the Clarendon seem to think it points to a result. Just how Marvar achieved this result is the mystery that is confronting us.'

'It sounds,' Dyer said, 'as though you were already monitoring him.'

'We've found his computer,' said Hissop, sidestepping. 'We've found a safe he used. We've searched his rooms. He's been crafty. He's left no trace.'

'Apart from this,' said Updark, and flicked his fingers. 'Give us that napkin, Lorna, will you?'

She opened a drawer in the cabinet and brought something out and put it down next to the biscuit tin.

Updark said: 'We picked this up in the café where he liked to take breakfast. The waiter overheard Marvar talking to himself before he leaped up and rushed off. He sounded pretty excited about something – so excited that he forgot to ask for the bill. This was last Friday morning. One week and three days ago.'

He unfolded the white paper napkin with tremendous care, as if it might detonate. Scribbled on it in black ink, among the coffee stains and dried egg yolk, was the beginning of what looked like a mathematical formula.

'Mean anything to you?' asked Hissop.

'It may be nothing,' Updark broke in, 'but we can't afford the risk of it being something.'

Dyer stared at the scribble. All at once, the sandpit reeled back. In among the small, imperfectly obliterated mounds, the same figure 7 and letter M.

They were watching him closely.

'It looks like fried egg.'

Updark stood up and rammed his fist into his palm. His cheekbones were livid, as if they had been slapped and weren't suffering from the mysterious allergy that he had contracted immediately on his return to England, as he explained to Dyer in the car, and for which he was having to undergo patch-testing. Three days, Monday, Wednesday, Friday. A plastic sheet on his wrist, with aluminium chambers containing allergens for 'suspect agents'. Updark was relieved to speak about it, sharing the details as they came up the stairs, once Dyer's person had been thoroughly searched – Updark's interrogation by two top dermatologists in Milton Keynes, their prognosis. Had he been bitten? Had he used another shampoo, soap, shaving cream? What had he done differently, where had he been? They were speculating, really. There was no diagnosis for it – *Granuloma faciale* was the best they could do. 'They don't know, that's the point. Sometimes it just disappears.' They weren't ruling out stress, he had told Dyer optimistically.

Not much optimism in his face now.

'You're pulling my pisser, Basil.'

Reverted to a nickname, Dyer could have been back in Upper One.

Updark reached up and smoothed his hair. He liked people who had been at the Phoenix to remind him of himself when he was at the Phoenix, with the world laid out before him. Dyer did not. 'I don't think you appreciate how high the stakes are. The numbers, damn you. Look at them.'

Dyer pushed away the napkin. 'If you recall, I was never good at numbers.'

'He didn't give anything to you?' Updark persisted. He was still standing. With his blotched red face. Yanking a disobedient creature by the leash.

'Why would he? As I told you, I hardly know him.'

But Dyer's mind was racing. His account of their conversation, which he had devoted much of Sunday to writing out – was it downstairs in his shoulder bag? On the kitchen table? He had a memory of moving the pages to one side on Sunday evening as he helped Leandro plot the disposition of the British and French fleets at Trafalgar.

Updark was rapping his notebook against his leg.

Just then, Lorna interrupted to say that Updark was wanted upstairs.

'I'll be back pronto,' he promised in a detached voice. His glance flickered again to the paper napkin on the tray. Then he closed his notebook and slipped it into his jacket pocket and left.

Hissop said: 'I think we need another coffee. Lorna!' and to Dyer: 'She's my secretary.'

'I'm not really his secretary.'

'Well, whatever you are, please get us some more coffee.'

To Dyer, taking his white mug from him: 'Black still OK for you?'

He nodded, and suddenly recognised what was familiar in her voice – as unmistakeable as the sound of the curlew

– and in the gingery taste of her flapjacks. 'Where up north are you from?'

'Near Sedburgh.' She looked at Dyer. 'With that accent thy's not a southern soft either.'

'Too right I'm not.' His mother's family were from Clitheroe. They hardly ever crossed the Shap Divide to go up to Penrith, he told her. His grandmother viewed everyone not from their region as an 'off-comer', could barely bring herself to speak to them.

Her turn to smile. 'You don't seem very keen, either, to share what you know. Maybe once you have the full picture, you'll see why it's so important that you help us as much as you can.'

Left alone with Dyer, Hissop said to him: 'Iran. Ever been there?'

No, said Dyer, but there was a time when his newspaper had wanted to send him, and he was tempted. In the 1950s, an English poet he admired had served in Tehran as the *Times*'s special correspondent, until his expulsion.

Hissop had not heard of Basil Bunting. He brushed the crumbs off his shirt. 'Time I was there, it wasn't very funny either. I tell our chaps: Don't lose your temper. Count to ten on lots of occasions. If you say: "Listen I'm not going to pay you, you arrogant bastard, because you're lazy and corrupt," you're not going to get over the border in a hurry, but this is what our American friends tend to do and wonder why they're not home in time for dinner.'

'What were you doing there?'

'Long story, don't worry about it. But you've worked in South America. You know the smell of the lonely roads at night.'

Presently, Updark returned. He retrieved from his jacket the small spiral-bound notebook in which earlier he had entered Dyer's answers, and glanced at it. 'Where were we? Oh, yes, you were saying Marvar didn't give you anything.'

'That's not quite true,' said Dyer. 'He did leave his overcoat behind. I've been wondering how to return it. If he's gone missing, that explains why I haven't heard from him.'

The unstiffening was minuscule, but Dyer detected a relaxation in Updark's response, as if he was quite pleased that Dyer had mentioned the overcoat. 'You have no inkling where he might be?'

'None at all.'

'These physicists love to go hiking,' said Hissop, somewhat joylessly. 'They say it's good for clearing their minds,' and he read out the names of four scientists and their favourite mountain ranges. 'Did Marvar mention any hiking?'

'What, in February? Without his coat?' Dyer laughed. He wasn't going to tell them about Ullswater, and he could be reasonably certain that Marvar hadn't told anyone else. 'You've seen him,' appealing to Updark. 'He's an alien to all forms of physical exercise, I'd have thought.'

'If he is on the run, then he'd better clean his rear mirror,' said Hissop in the same bleak tone. 'There are a lot of people who won't rest till he's told them what he knows – or else he's chopped up in bags in their freezer, to borrow a phrase. And I mean a lot.'

'Before we get into that,' said Updark, 'I still haven't formed a clear picture of the man. Roly?'

'"Rude, sarcastic, touchy, withdrawn, monosyllabic,"' Hissop read from a page clipped to his board. 'But also: "Smart, loyal, witty, patriotic, creative, deft."'

Updark turned to Dyer. 'How did he impress you?'

'I barely knew him, as I keep saying. But if you want me to add to your list, I'd say honest, sensitive, confused, frightened, and, as I told you, physically out of shape.'

'Not a rabble-rouser then?'

'I wouldn't have thought so, no.'

Updark sighed. 'Show him, Roly.'

Hissop unclipped a photograph and handed it to Dyer.

The colours had faded, but Marvar could be seen clearly. Much younger, leaner, his features sharpened by a moustache, like a leftist student. He was marching in a crowd down a foreign street under a blue sky. He held up a placard and his mouth was open as if he were shouting something.

Dyer smiled.

Updark studied him. 'Did he tell you he was an activist? No, I don't suppose he did.'

'If he was an activist,' said Dyer, who all at once could picture Marvar fired up – by Heisenberg, by Houtermans, by the regime's treatment of his mother – 'then I'm sure it was for democracy.'

'Did he tell you that he studied engineering before he switched to physics?'

'He did not.'

'Well, let's put aside for the moment that most jihadis have engineering backgrounds. Let's also agree that he was demonstrating for democracy, and that he is every one of those things you say he is, and he was not sent as a spy by the regime to continue research that would benefit them. Let's further assume that since leaving Iran he has become a really good mechanical engineer as well as a plasma physicist, and that he has by some extraordinary and unanticipated miracle done what we think. But here I come to something that puzzles me. No one else rates him so highly. Not here, not in Tehran, not anywhere. The man who wants to crack fusion has to take a pretty big size in hats. From whichever angle you view it, Rustum Marvar's head doesn't fit.'

Hissop nodded. 'Frankly, he was below our radar.'

'Not only *our* radar.' Updark glanced at Dyer. 'I'm only telling you what my people tell me. Your friend Rustum is not exactly high up in the pecking order of brilliant Iranian scientists. The chief nuclear negotiator has never heard of him. Same in Oxford.'

Hissop said: 'He has no affiliation with any college. He doesn't have students. He's basically just a junior researcher, part of a group of eight PHD students with a professor in charge.'

'What does his professor say?' asked Dyer.

Hissop coughed. 'Marvar wasn't terribly well connected to the head of the group.'

'Professor Bruce Whitton,' Updark expanded acidly, stretching out his leg, 'is a great believer in the doctrine of economy of effort. He is more interested in another branch of plasma research, and is far too busy raising money for that, plus going to All Souls for dinner. He professes incomprehension at the idea of Marvar's so-called breakthrough. Roly?' He picked up his mug, waiting for Hissop to locate the note.

Hissop read out: '"Plodding, erratic, paddling his own canoe up a dead-end tributary of plasma focus." Whitton finds it beyond inconceivable that this man should have stumbled on the answer to nuclear fusion. "What did he use as fuel? He didn't have access to tritium." Also, Whitton is in a rush to remind us that a lot of the claims in the past have turned out to be bogus. They appear viable at first, but scratch – and the evidence doesn't exist. There was that German scientist in Argentina in the 1950s. All that palaver about cold fusion in the 1980s. Then the false dawns with ZETA and TFTR and JET. One after another, each of these so-called discoveries has been dissed.'

'Then why not listen to Whitton?' said Dyer, marvelling at how easy it had been to lead them into full disclosure.

'As a matter of fact, Whitton's not our main source on this,' said Hissop, flushing.

'The thing that's changed,' said Updark, as if Dyer's question had been answered, 'is that a single entrepreneur sitting in a room now has the tools and the lack of bureaucratic encumbrance to outdevelop and outsmart governments. You don't need big labs. All you need is a very small team on a very small budget.'

'What about others in the group?' persisted Dyer. 'Wouldn't they have an idea?'

'Roly, you've spoken to them,' said Updark. 'They had little or no contact with him, am I correct?'

'He seems not to have collaborated with anyone else on the team,' Hissop confirmed. 'Whitton ran a pretty open lab. Not much security. Marvar was free to come and go.'

'What we are saying,' said Updark, 'is that he's not a high-value asset. He doesn't count, he doesn't move the needle, he's small fry. But then again – and it doesn't really sound logical – if anyone is going to break through the fusion barrier, it's likely to be someone who has been ignored. Discoverers are dull. Look at Fritz Zwicky.'

'Who's Fritz Zwicky?' asked Dyer.

'Responsible for arguably the most spectacular discovery of the twentieth century. *Dunkle Materie*, or in plain English, dark matter. But for forty years no one took him seriously

– just like our guy. No, the part that is hard for me to believe is that Marvar did this in a university lab over what sounds like a weekend.'

'There are surprises. Surprises happen.' Hissop was leafing through his notes. 'There was widespread under-estimation in the West after the Second World War of Russia's capability to make bombs. Then in the 1960s the Russians achieved great advances in fusion with the tokamak. We've probably committed the same miscalcula-tion with North Korea. But up until this moment,' referring to his digital watch, 'ten-thirty-seven a.m., Monday, twenty-eighth of February, two thousand and blah blah, no one has found a simple way to achieve fusion – and definitely not without massive government backing.'

'So if it isn't bullshit,' said Updark, 'the next question we have to ask is this. If he has indeed found a way, then has he done so on his own, or is another government now involved? And if our errant asteroid hasn't done it on his own, has he done a bunk? And if he hasn't done a bunk, has he been taken, and if so by who?'

He folded his arms and sat back. 'Roly, could you ask Lorna if we might trouble her for a moment?'

Chapter Nineteen

WHILE HISSOP WENT OFF TO fetch Lorna, Updark unfolded his arms and helped himself to one of her flapjacks. His attitude was less peevish, more reconciliatory, as if he was thinking that Dyer might be softening up a bit, but had first needed to be told things in order to play the game.

'Fusion research has been declassified since 1958. Inter-cooperation is the name of the game. Want to know the cynical reason? Because no one has the knowledge, it's so bloody difficult. But the moment it looks like someone is going to make a dollar out of it, then cooperation will be flat on its face. Right now, there's a race on in Livermore, in Cadarache, in Moscow, in Beijing – in various places around Oxford, too.' He spoke in the confident voice of this city, the baritone that commanded ships and government ministries and embassies.

'These things always come much quicker than you think. That's why everyone lives in terror of the other side's advantage. There's not a scientist on earth who wouldn't stamp on his grandmother's neck to be first with the discovery.'

His teeth clamped down, scattering flakes of oatmeal. He pondered as he slowly ate, a ruminative expression settling on his face.

'Has Marvar beaten them to it? If so, does that mean Iran has the knowledge? Because this would change the whole game of marbles.

'We know the Mullahs are desperate for any edge in the nuclear stake. The rhetoric coming out of Tehran suggests they might have got hold of something. That's what the Americans feel.'

'You mean Cubbage?' It came out uncalculated and Dyer instantly regretted it.

Updark stopped chewing. He lifted his chin. 'Now why would you say that?'

'I can put two and two together as well as anybody.'

'Did Marvar talk to you about Ralph Cubbage?'

'He had his suspicions about him.'

'So he did talk about Cubbage,' Updark insisted in a berating tone.

'Only that he suspected Cubbage of working for the CIA.'

'A moment ago, you said Marvar hadn't told you about his work.'

'I said he told me a little.'

'Partial to a bit of flower-arranging with the truth when it's inconvenient, are we, John?'

'Look, what's the point of asking questions if you've made up your mind?'

'You're still fobbing us off,' said Updark, anger further colouring his face, 'is what's poking out at me like a dog's balls.'

'Well, you'd know more about dogs' balls than I would,' said Dyer in a defiant voice.

Silence.

'How are the flapjacks?' came Lorna's cheerful voice.

Hissop stood behind her.

She handed Dyer his mug, full to the brim with more warm black coffee.

Dyer smiled at her. 'Exceptional.'

Updark groaned: 'Marvar knew about Cubbage.'

Hissop let out with irritation: 'Cubbage is a real pain in the orchestra stalls.'

Unbothered, Updark looked over at Dyer. He conceded sulkily: 'We're not happy with the Americans.'

Dyer was conscious of Lorna bringing over a cube to sit on. 'Why is that?'

'Why. Is. That,' Updark repeated very slowly. 'Let's ask Lorna,' and to Dyer: 'Lorna's our Chief Analyst. She knows all about Americans. Please tell John what you know, Lorna.'

Lorna impressed from the moment she opened her mouth. She was like his straight-talking aunt when Vivien showed her training and danced. Under that skirt, that smile, all sinew and steel.

She looked directly into Dyer's eyes. She didn't need notes. She was in command of her material.

'Where do I begin?' in her North Country voice that summoned up for Dyer a small front drawing room in which his grandmother only ever used to serve tea on a silver tray with home-made Eccles cakes, exactly as she had taught both her daughters to bake.

'Do I start in the 1950s, when the Americans refused to share their nuclear secrets? Which didn't stop us going from zero to having the H-bomb within three years.

'Or do I jump to 1975, when Henry Kissinger agreed to sell nuclear energy equipment to Iran for six billion dollars' worth of business, with his besties Cheney and Wolfowitz and Rumsfeld?

'Or to the year of our Lord 2000, when those selfsame individuals stopped at nothing to deny Iran access to identical technology?

'Or do I fast-forward to the decade between 2005 and 2015, and to America's claims that it was the US who paid the economic price once sanctions were imposed on Iran, when in fact it was the EU who suffered most economically?

'Or should I kick off in 2015 when, behind our backs, the Americans used the EU's oil sanctions as their biggest card in the secret negotiations that they had with Iran, in fundamental violation of EU sovereignty?

'That's not such a bad moment to start, since it's also the year Republican senators with outstretched arms welcomed Israeli lobbying against the deal – when Israel was not even a party to the agreement. And yet the Republicans didn't allow us – America's closest ally – to have any say in the debate. As of this moment, it's the old guard in the Republican Party who pose a greater threat to world peace than the Revolutionary Guard in Tehran. After my experience with both sides – and I was at Livermore during the failure of three weapons tests – I am coming to the conclusion that it may be easier to negotiate with Iran than with Congress.'

Dyer listened to this in silent admiration. 'Then why don't you?' he heard come out of his mouth.

'We,' Updark corrected Dyer. 'We.'

'Two good reasons,' said Lorna, still looking at him. 'Firstly, negotiating with Satan is against the Koran. Secondly, it's becoming harder to persuade the Iranians that even Satan has prospects. Each utterance from the White House feeds into their paranoid picture that the US and the UK are still out to get them. Even at the top, their thinking is clouded by conspiracy theories. If they don't see one, they'll create it. Seizing a tanker or two is just the start.'

'I think Lorna's saying that we continue to be viewed as Satan in Iranian eyes.'

'Of all the world's arrogant powers, we are viewed as the most evil. But I am also talking about a political system that is capable of taking on a life of its own, as Roly here can testify.'

'Hear hear,' said Hissop.

'History lesson,' said Updark, nodding, 'coming up.'

Lorna kept her eyes on Dyer. 'Iran is a country with a proud seven-thousand-year-old civilisation that is only now starting to recover from a religious over-reaction to two Western governments – the US and the UK – which overthrew its democratically elected leader in 1953. And why? For the apparently treacherous reason that Mossadeq wanted the oil wealth of his country to be shared by its people. Iran could have built a bomb like North Korea ages ago had it wanted. But why bother? There was no need, not when the US was making such a comprehensive mess of its foreign policy. Leaving aside the unhelpful fact that the US has not been able to defeat goat-herders in flip-flops in Afghanistan, there is the troubling example of the present incumbent in the White House.'

'Who may have earned the right to be considered, forgive my Farsi, the biggest spurt of piss ever let out of an American prick,' said Updark, licking his fingers.

'And why is the US president behaving like this?' continued Lorna. 'Baldly put, he cannot accept how far the balance of power has shifted since America's disastrous 2003 invasion of Iraq and the defeat recently of Isis in Syria, for which, I might add, he needed the tacit consent of Iran.

'In short, who are the two chief beneficiaries of America's strategic mismanagement of the Middle East? Number One, Russia. Number Two, and catching up fast, Iran. The losers are America, the Saudis and Israel – who are each busy pinning responsibility for the region's ills on Tehran. The main reason why they want to ditch the nuclear deal is that it would knock out Iran as a regional player.

'Don't get me wrong. No one pretends Iran is the benignest power on earth. What I am saying is that all international assessment so far points to the fact that Iran is complying with its obligations. Iran may have had a nuclear programme before 2015, but there is not one scrap of evidence to say that it has had one since. That is why Ralph Cubbage would so dearly love to find any proof that Iran might be reneging on the deal. Marvar's discovery may not at this moment be weapons-focused, but it would be, as Lionel likes to say, the dripping sirloin that Cubbage's president is slavering for.'

'Thanks, Lorna,' said Updark. 'Sharp to the point as ever. And before I forget,' tapping the tin, 'remind me to give Audrey your recipe.'

She took it as her cue to stand up, adjust her skirt, and return to her desk.

He turned to Dyer: 'Questions?'

Dyer's regret to see Lorna go was mingled with relief that she had not questioned him directly about his conversation with Marvar. He looked at the two men. 'Where do you reckon Marvar is?'

'We've checked all flights to Iran,' said Hissop. 'He doesn't seem to have left the country.'

'But why return to that regime?' said Dyer. 'They've imprisoned his baby daughter. And possibly tortured his wife.'

'Which might indicate that he has made a significant breakthrough ...'

'To bargain for their release?' Updark slid in.

'If he's missing, isn't it more likely the Iranians have got to him already?'

'That is what we're looking into. If the Mullahs did believe that one of their own scientists had landed this whale of a fish in Oxford which would give them hegemony over all other nations, and yet hadn't whispered a word of it to his superiors, then the suspicion of extreme conservative hardliners would be boundless. Not much space for dissent in that lot.'

'He might have been abducted by the Al-Quds Force is what we're thinking,' said Hissop.

'They're like Augustus's Praetorian Guard,' explained Updark. 'I'm sure you remember your Classics – the best, most loyal legionnaires chosen to protect the Emperor, only in this case the Ayatollah. One of their jobs is to liquidate his opponents abroad. Before the treaty, they were responsible for a spate of assassinations.'

'So what are you saying? Rustum could be dead?'

'Could be,' said Updark. 'Abduction is more likely, though – so that he can reveal to the Mullahs every last iota of his secret.'

Hissop was studying his clipboard. 'Since early this morning we've been hunting a white delivery van registered in Cowley. A CCTV camera in Norham Gardens caught three bearded Asian-looking men bundling into the back a sofa-sized object which seemed to be missing its cushions.'

'In other words, it might not have been a sofa,' said Updark.

'But what if it was a sofa?' objected Dyer. 'And what if it's not the Iranians who've snatched him? What if someone else got there first?'

'Anyone in mind?' asked Updark.

'You said yourself there might be a lot of people after him.'

'What they're all after,' said Updark, pronouncing each word meticulously as if he were unpacking his sponge bag and arranging hairbrushes on a dresser, 'is his knowledge of how he might have done whatever it is he might have done. As, I should add, John, are we. I can't tell you what his contraption looks like, whether it resembles an omnibus or a blunderbuss, but already I've got the cuckoos in London saying: "*We've got to have one of these. British flag on top.*" This is the position likely to be adopted as well in Tel Aviv and Riyadh and Beijing. And indeed also by Mr Putin.'

Hissop said: 'Moscow has its own secret programme of scientists working on fusion, but if something interesting *is* happening in Russia we won't know until it's very late.'

Dyer thought of the nervous way that Marvar had eyed the cars parked in Great Clarendon Road. 'He was terrified that he was being watched ...'

Updark's smile was harsh. 'And not merely by the mad Mullahs. His fear of Israel, too, would be justified. Even before the treaty was signed, there were a number of reasons why you wouldn't want to be a scientist in Iran, among the most persuasive being that the Israelis bump you off.'

Hissop consulted his clipboard again. 'When the Israeli general in charge was asked how far he would go to stop the Iranian nuclear programme, he replied: "Two thousand kilometres." Even so, if Mossad *is* buzzing around Marvar's lab, then, as Lionel said, it's likely so too are the Russians, Saudis and Chinese.'

'And I tell you this,' said Updark testily, 'they're not all descending on our dreaming spires because they sniff the sweet scent of cheap energy. The popular idea peddled by Professor Whitton *et alii* that fusion can have no military implication is balderdash. This, in case you're still curious, is why we have brought you here today. This is why we have invested so much energy in questioning you and requesting your help. The ramifications, John, are extremely serious. And I do mean extremely. If Marvar has found a simple way to make a fusion explosion, it would make a lot of important people around the world very depressed. You then have the possibility of giving all other "bad guys" – I'm sounding like the American president – the chance to control the most lethal weapon ever invented, and to do it clandestinely, at little cost. I'm sure you recall that incident on the tube train in Parsons Green. One delinquent teenager with a grudge and a shopping bag of nails was enough to paralyse the nation for two days. Imagine what a dedicated group of disaffected teenagers each with a carrier bag containing a fusion device could do. If you're prepared to blow yourself up to kill one person, why stop there? Why not kill half a million? Coming to a theatre of death near you ... No. We've been to that movie, don't like how it ended.'

Dyer said nothing. He drank his coffee. The mug was institutional white, like his landlord's mugs in Jericho. He thought of Marvar holding his by the window, not drinking. Could he have taken Samir to the Lake District, in the footsteps of Wordsworth and Coleridge, to mull over in peace what to do? Is that why he had asked Dyer not to speak of his plans?

Finally, Dyer said, partly to deflect Updark: 'What if no one has kidnapped him? What if he's gone to ground for some other reason?'

'Such as?'

Dyer shrugged. 'Say to put his ducks in order before making a public announcement? There'd be a Nobel in this, wouldn't there?'

'And how!' said Hissop. 'Although, if it was developed at the Clarendon, Whitton would want to take his portion of credit.'

Updark scratched his cheek. 'I don't know, Roly,' he said. 'But then again, you've talked to these people. Do you honestly think it likely?'

'It has to be a possibility. To most scientists, ten million dollars is less important than the Nobel. But if I look at this from over an Iranian desk, there's one other factor we oughtn't to rule out. We haven't mentioned martyrdom.'

'Ah, yes, martyrdom,' said Updark, without obvious energy. 'Explain to Mr Dyer.'

Hissop turned to him. 'Some of us are prepared to die for things we want to go on being alive for. Marvar might be such a one. Nuclear fusion could be a sacred idea in which he believes, but also for which he is willing to negate his whole existence if the core idea becomes polluted. Maybe he consciously welcomes death, and, rather than entrust his discovery to the wrong hands, he has decided to take his secret with him into the next world, like the famous Shia martyr Imam Hussein in the seventh century.'

'Did he strike you as devout, John?'

Dyer thought of Marvar in his old-fashioned suit, pausing to draw on a last cigarette, before he pressed on to St Barnabas to pray to his dead mother's God for guidance.

'Possibly.'

'Then what about his son?' said Updark. 'Where does he fit into this posthumous scenario?' He looked at Dyer. 'John, I'm asking you. Do you think he could do that to Samir?'

Dyer thought of Marvar speaking on the telephone to Samir after learning of his injured shin. He thought of what Marvar had said to Dyer. *'We will still be able to go walking ... as long as I live – and Samir lives – then she is not gone ...'*

'No, to be honest, I don't.'

'So let's rule out martyrdom, Roly, shall we, for the moment? Right now, the facts – what few we have – are pointing in one direction.' Updark picked up the napkin. 'Aside from finding Marvar, our immediate priority, it strikes me, is to find out where he might have put the rest of his magic formula.'

The meeting was over. A car was arranged to drive Dyer back to Oxford. Updark escorted Dyer downstairs and waited for him to retrieve his shoulder bag.

'And John?'

'Yes?'

'No need to tell anyone about this. That, I think, would be a great mistake. Name of the game is discretion and secrecy. Oh, and nanny rules.'

'Nanny rules?'

'Tennis. Keep the score, and supply your serving partner with balls. If Marvar does get in touch, please fucking tell us.'

Chapter Twenty

DYER ASKS THE DRIVER TO take him back to Jericho. He knows that he needs to go home before collecting Leandro from the Phoenix. Why, he can't recall. He is recovering from being interrogated by Updark.

The driver's eyes in the mirror watch Dyer check his shoulder bag. It would be sensible to assume that they've downloaded his laptop. Fortunately, he didn't write up Marvar's conversation on it. But his shorthand notes – where are they?

The car drops him off outside his door. Dyer waits until it has driven away before entering.

At a quick glance, the house appears as he left it three hours earlier: the beds unmade, the washing-up not done. Magda hasn't been in to clean; anyway, she knows what not to touch.

But when Dyer looks closer, his anxiety mounts.

Nissa was on the wall at a different angle in Leandro's bedroom. That was not all. From the top of the downstairs bookcase, Astrud gazed at Dyer a fraction too squarely. Reflected in her mute expression, he saw masked figures searching the rooms. He could feel their fingers running through his clothes, his pockets.

His notes on Marvar were not on the kitchen table, nor on the shelf where he usually stacked away his papers. He ran upstairs again. The only note he could find, on his bedside table, was that line of nonsense he had dreamed.

Updark had been summoned away at one point during their interview. Were his men reporting back what they'd found?

In a state of absolute alertness, Dyer opened the cupboard under the stairs and checked his tackle bag. His superstitions began in fishing. He knew that he had arranged the lures in his fly book in a certain order.

It jarred him to see the fly book the other way up.

He felt suddenly weak. He couldn't control his thoughts. They blundered around in his head, glimmering up ghostly images of Updark's men poring over his interview with Marvar...

Next to his tackle bag, Marvar's overcoat remained on its wooden hanger. Collar turned down. They would have searched it as a priority, checking that nothing was sewn into the green lining.

That was the reason, it came back to him: Dyer had been going to take the coat to the Phoenix to give to Samir.

But Marvar? What about him? Along with his dust-coloured coat, he had left behind a heap of questions. Where was he? Alive, dead, captive?

And his revolutionary, world-altering formula – where was that?

Marvar – at this selfsame table – had left Dyer in no doubt that it was possible to consign his breakthrough to a single sheet of paper, and he had. But put it where?

Unable to concentrate, in no mood to return to the Taylorian, and needing to halt this torrent of questions, Dyer knelt by his bookcase and hunted through the spines for a volume to distract him.

He had sandwiched his favourite texts – poems and novels he wished that he could read for the first time – between bookends decorated with the cut-outs of a phoenix that Mr Barson, his carpentry teacher, had taught him to saw from a sheet of plywood. After selecting and rejecting Borges's *Labyrinths*, Dyer took out Basil Bunting's *Collected Poems* and sat by the French window and started to read. He had to remind himself: *You haven't betrayed Marvar. If Updark hauls you in again and wants you to explain your notes, simply refuse to answer. Point out that they were acquired illegally, and journalists never reveal their sources – a cardinal rule which applies to ex-journalists too.*

A fly was on his arm. He flicked it off and it settled on his right ear. He brushed it away again. After a while, his breathing returned to normal.

*

At 3.30 p.m. Dyer got into his car and drove to the Phoenix.

He felt a jolt of relief to see his son beneath the school clock.

Leandro crouched over his bicycle, helmet on, fiddling with the lock.

'Hi, Dad. What are you doing here?' in a puzzled voice, standing up.

'I have decided,' said Dyer, 'to give you a lift home.'

'What about my bike?'

'You can ride it back tomorrow.'

'All right,' said Leandro, and he removed his satchel from the basket, and started unbuckling his helmet. 'Just let me lock it up.'

Dyer made pasta for dinner.

Five minutes into the meal, Leandro raised his head. 'Dad, what are we doing for exeat?'

A quarter of his class had joined the Phoenix skiing trip to Davos at half-term. While Leandro had stayed in Jericho and played Fifa 18, one boy flew to Perth – and two girls to Hong Kong. Leandro was still trying to unscramble the mixed messages of being at a school with friends whose parents could afford to send them at regular intervals to distant locations, and having a father who was so constrained financially that not once since their arrival in Oxford had Dyer taken Leandro back to Rio.

Dyer mumbled something foolish, to the effect that he hadn't yet made a plan.

The truth was, Dyer was going fast through Vivien's legacy. The school fees went up every term. The latest bill had forced Dyer to ask himself if the upheaval from Joaquim Nabuco to St Barnabas Street had been worth it. Much of what Leandro was being taught seemed to be beside the point. What was he gaining at the Phoenix that he couldn't have acquired in Rio? A confidence, a background history, a knowledge of half a dozen poems and hymns, a group of friends who might help each other later on (or not)?

Or had Dyer uprooted his son to Oxford to repair a rip in his own fabric?

Leandro forked more spaghetti into his mouth, and went on slowly eating. He had worn the same expression in his first term, when other boys teased him for not having seen any of the children's programmes on television.

'Even Samir is going away somewhere,' he said moodily.

A little while later, Dyer not having responded, he lifted his eyes and asked, as if braced for a negative answer, but with feeling: 'Dad, when are we going to get a dog?'

'Have you decided what kind of dog you want?' hedged Dyer. He should have known that children hold adults to their promises.

'Yes.'

Dyer glanced at him. The pasta, his concentrated face. His blond hair had grown over his eye.

'One like Beatrice Updark has.'

Under Beatrice's supervision, Leandro had walked Spassky on his bright-coloured lead around the Hard Court. Not once, Dyer now discovered, but several times.

'I thought you didn't like Beatrice.'

'I like her dog,' said Leandro defiantly.

Dyer suppressed a smile. He remembered what Vivien had said about the Phoenix when encouraging him to send Leandro to the school. *'Your mother and I were treated as equals. We were taught we were every bit as good as the boys when we were as good as them. We learned to be competitive and ambitious and also adventurous – it was the girls who dared each other to go into the boys' dorms, not the other way round.'*

'I'm not sure about his eyebrows,' Dyer frowned.

'They're called furnishings,' Leandro corrected him with unusual authority.

Dyer wasn't going to rehearse all the arguments, but it prompted him to revive another of the offers that he had made to Leandro in Rio. 'Why don't I take you fly fishing, and we can discuss it?'

The upcoming three-day exeat coincided this year with the start of the fishing season. Dyer's proposal to look for a country inn, on a stretch of river where he might teach Leandro how to catch a trout, had a pacifying effect on his son. A little less downcast, Leandro cleaned out his fingernails with the tip of a pencil.

Dinner over, Leandro had homework to do. When Dyer offered to look over this once he had finished it, Leandro declined. He didn't need help, someone was already helping him.

Leandro opened his satchel as Dyer cleared the plates and briefly speculated in a back room of his mind who this person might be – Beatrice? Leandro's history teacher, Ma Burgeon? – before other thoughts – about his missing notes, Marvar, Updark – crowded in.

'Oh, Dad, I'm sorry,' pulling a face. 'This morning … I packed these by mistake.' With a penitent expression now, Leandro produced a sheaf of pages covered with Dyer's shorthand.

Dyer's chest went cold. His hands shook as he grabbed them.

'Thank God …' and collapsed noisily into a chair. 'Thank God.'

Updark had nothing on him! There was no evidence to link Dyer with Marvar's discovery – only these eleven sheets of A4.

Leandro looked up, startled. 'Dad, are you all right?'

'Yes, yes …' He was rereading the first page of his interview. He did not need Astrud's photograph to warn him. He had to hide this – or destroy it. The information must not be found in the house.

Dyer looked up from the page, white against the table, to his son. He didn't want to infect Leandro with his relief, his fear.

Leandro inspected him with touching tenderness. 'I hope you haven't caught my cold.' He bit his lip. 'I may have given it to Samir.'

Dyer leaned forward. 'You've seen Samir?'

'No, no, not today, he didn't come to school. Mr Tanner thought it was his injury, but Dad, it wasn't, he was walking fine. I bet you anything it was that flu I had. He wasn't feeling well at the sleepover, I could see.'

After Leandro went to bed, Dyer made himself a cup of tea. He added milk, and as he closed the fridge he was arrested by a memory of Rustum Marvar standing in the exact spot where he himself now stood.

Marvar had been staring at Leandro's Pelé magnet, his face, everything about him, altered from a moment before.

From two feet away, Dyer absorbed the image of the Brazilian footballer on the fridge door. Then the slow thought came to him. What if Marvar's eyes were fastened not on Pelé, but on the square of yellow paper protruding from beneath?

'*So that's what they're called!*'

Marvar had stopped on the towpath and thrown back his head in laughter when Dyer told him.

'*Post it. You mean, like a letter. Me to you?*'

But in the very next moment Marvar appeared conflicted, as though he had committed an error. Dyer's heart had reached out to him. He recognised the awkward emotion felt by someone who had suffered tragedy, when people caught them laughing.

Dyer stepped closer to the fridge. There seemed to be an unfamiliarity about his handwriting on the post-it note. His eyes scanned the names and the numbers that he had jotted down – for Paula next door; Domino's pizzeria; Magda, the Polish cleaner; the landlord's management company in Summertown...

Then he saw it.

Squeezed in between the letters and figures that Dyer had written, a single word stood out. It had been scrawled in a strange hand using his propelling pencil. Each capital letter as bold as an initial branded on a tennis ball.

'BOOMERANG'.

An apparently insignificant thing can be of huge importance, life had taught Dyer. He waited until the last chime of midnight faded into the Oxford darkness. He checked once again that Leandro was asleep, and then he put on an extra jersey and a black wool balaclava that he never wore, and stepped outside.

He had parked in St Barnabas Street next to the church tower. Before he climbed into his Beetle and started the ignition, he looked up and down the line of cars. No one followed him into Great Clarendon Street, or left along Walton Street, or right into St Margaret's Road.

It took Dyer five minutes to drive to the school. He drew up beside the pillar box and jumped out. Not waiting to lock the car, he walked fast along the pavement to the zebra crossing, and over the road. On the last occasion when he made this journey so late at night, after Rougetel had revealed the location to him in the bathroom mirror, bonding them for ever, Dyer had been wearing blue-and-white striped pyjamas and a paisley dressing gown.

He punched in the numbers and came through the gate. He ran as if towards a phone ringing. The street light shed the same dim orange glow. He knelt in the sandpit directly opposite where Rustum had sat, and started sifting with his fingers. He felt a drench of pure terror, but he was also distant, as though looking down on himself from the top of a bedside locker.

Almost immediately, his fingertips brushed against the outline of a solid object. This time, not the Airfix wing of an Australian fighter plane, but a Ziploc sandwich bag with a small hard-edged green folder inside, wrapped in wax-paper.

The shipping forecast was coming to an end, driving home. St Barnabas Street was as peaceful when Dyer got back as when he left. But something had shifted. He did not recognise the city, he could have been crossing Rio.

PART TWO

Chapter Twenty-one

Oxford waking in the dawn, the cold sunlight numbing and clear as morphine, the corn-coloured stone, the blazers in the windows, the cyclists. Tom Tower is visible above the roof tiles, like a Kaiser helmet. On a tented stall in the Broad, a man with Andean features lays out columns of panama hats to the sound of pipe music. He glances at Dyer, wondering if he ought to recognise him, drawn to how fearful he seems of being noticed, and decides that he doesn't.

Dyer sees the slimmer figure of his youth slip down the Turl. He follows him up Market Street, into the Covered Market. The Portuguese café more or less as he remembered. Same oatmeal lino floor, pale blue formica tabletops. He could be pushing open the glass-panelled door and walking in here fifty years before.

The Café Lisboa is where Dyer heads first thing, after dropping Leandro off at the Phoenix. More than anywhere else in Oxford, it reminds him of his childhood, but also of Brazil. For one thing, it's a place where you can speak Portuguese.

'*Puxa! É você, João?*' says Miguel, his habitual mask of melancholy creasing into a smile. '*Disculpe, não lhe reconheci com esse sobretudo.*'

Dyer looks down at the long overcoat he is wearing, and explains. '*Pertence a um amigo.*'

Miguel, who was born in Madeira, is a plump man with two strands of white hair across his skull. After the ritual exchanges about the uncle in Funchal, the granddaughter at Phil & Jim, Dyer orders a cup of tea and a rice cake.

A table is free by the pillar. Dyer takes off the heavy coat and hangs it over the back of the cane chair. A button is missing from the sleeve, and he thinks of Marvar's fingers on Port Meadow, fretting.

Settled in his chair, Dyer unzips his shoulder bag. First, he draws out the eleven pages of A4 which Leandro had returned to him, and sets these to one side. Then he pulls out the plastic Ziploc sandwich bag containing the corrugated green folder, lays it on the table and opens it.

From the folder he extracts a square of yellow paper, two inches by two – which Marvar must have ripped off a pad, since adhered to the back are two further post-it notes, both blank.

Dyer stares at this meteorite which has fallen into his scared hands. He holds it up, and struggles to make sense of what Marvar, in blue biro, has set down on both sides in meticulous, close-spaced, small writing.

Light from a plastic-shaded lamp falls on a jumble of figures and letters, some Greek, others Roman, some capitalised, others not, and on the reverse, beneath more calculations – qualities and names of the minerals to be used as lasing materials? – a sentence on its own: *Otto Hahn – 'contrary to God's will'*?

This terrible knowledge, which might set fire to the atmosphere, to water – or give us sun on earth. This is the original. There is no other copy. Buried in the sand for Dyer to find.

It was inescapable and inevitable as biography that Dyer should be the recipient. Any *pai de santo* peering into his shallow basket of cowrie shells could have told him: it was not by accident that Marvar had brushed up against Dyer's life. Marvar was like the surf which came in when he was running along the beach to Leblon, sometimes engulfing his legs, tugging him back, wet; a wave larger than all the others, unannounced, able to roll you over and over.

Dyer pictured Marvar writing it carefully down, his taut face. He must have buried it on Sunday morning before collecting Samir from the Asselins. Marvar had remembered Dyer's schoolboy story and had pinned his hopes on it.

He hears the sound of seashells being sifted. *'He has given you this knowledge for you to decide, because he was unable to decide himself.'*

The dread in Marvar's eyes. Dyer had seen it again this morning when he threw a careless glance at the mirror. It pained him to look at the face that stared back. Marvar's black spot had come into his hands, darker than anything that Blind Pew could have pressed into his palm, darker than anything he had a name for.

Except that it wasn't nameless, it wasn't torn from a bible or the Koran or from the book of any religion, and it wasn't black; it was banana yellow, composed of quite specific numbers and letters, and it came tagged with a quote from a German chemist.

Did that fear in Marvar's eyes explain his disappearance? Had the burden overwhelmed him?

Ludicrous as he had made Hissop's suggestion sound, Dyer wondered if it was conceivable that Marvar *had* stuck to his original plan and taken Samir hiking, and now was somewhere safe. Hissop had read out a list of physicists who at regular intervals escaped into the mountains to keep sane – Teller, Fermi, Bloch, Heisenberg. Marvar's abrupt departure caused Dyer to think of the still-missing Australian mathematician Todd Angle who had vanished while on a bush walk in Tasmania.

It made Dyer smile to imagine Marvar stumbling through rugged hill-country in mountain boots after he had buried his abstruse nuclear theory in the school sandpit. It was important to laugh. Otherwise it was all so damned unamusing.

Dyer climbed with Marvar a little way in his imagination. He wanted so much to believe that Marvar had arrived early at the Asselins' to take his son off walking. He wanted to picture him rising through the grassy fells above Howtown with Samir, looking down to Patterdale below. Then he broke off a piece of rice cake and put it in his mouth. No, it was too hard to conjure a coatless Marvar struggling up Fusedale with his son, stumbling and wheezing. As for the alternative scenarios which Hissop had posited, in their violence they too closely resembled the games on Leandro's Xbox. They lay beyond Dyer's willingness to believe. Easier to imagine that Marvar had melted into Oxford's thin air. He had disappeared in a storm, as Gustav Mahler was said to have done. He had burned himself out like a comet.

Yet if Marvar didn't come back ... if in some way he had been taken out of the equation ... then that left Dyer sole custodian of his knowledge.

About what to do with this knowledge, he has no script. He's not going to make a copy; Marvar wouldn't have wanted that. '*You don't need any other.*' And the algorithm is too long for Dyer to memorise.

If he can't copy or remember it, what other option does he have?

So quick, normally, to make up his mind, Dyer cannot decide. The friend of the missing Australian mathematician had given the letter that he had received posthumously from him to the police. Obviously, the thing for Dyer to do, sipping his tea, was to get this post-it note to Lionel Updark. That was the first path he should take.

But the prospect of handing over Marvar's information to Updark makes Dyer dizzy, disoriented. The fact that Updark socialised with Cubbage, and was supposed to be at the dinner party with him, puts Dyer off, given all that he has heard from Lorna about the Americans.

He stares again at what Marvar has written, and feels that he is being sucked backward in the current. These numbers and letters – like some abracadabra. $E = mc^2$ gave us the atom bomb. But Marvar's calculations? Is it possible to read too much into them? Could they be nothing more than clotted bilge, like Todd Angle's bushwhacked philosophy – or one of Dyer's maths preps for Slimy? 'This is fit only,' Slimy had said, 'for toilet paper.'

$7, M, Q_{fus}, nT\tau \ldots$ The muddle of figures, like the mistakes that the typesetters used to make. Dyer is tempted to view the whole thing as gobbledygook.

What he has been searching for is a simple algorithm for how to live. What did he want the world to think of him, who did he love best in it? His life was a coded set of letters and figures awaiting a solution.

Dyer thought back, as people in a crisis do, to where he had come from. A large part of him, too much, went back to Astrud.

He saw her sometimes in another, crossing a chequered floor to touch a shoulder, her eyes, the stubborn curl over her left ear that she was always brushing down. The bar is full, the book is open on the table with a fresh pencil mark in the margin. *'What are you reading?'*

And afterwards, the empty mornings and afternoons. In the evenings he sits at a table with a glass of cold beer and a book, watching the faces. A samba is playing. His face is wet. They were supposed to be his great days.

Vivien had tried to comfort him. Following the funeral at Nossa Senhora da Candelária in Petrópolis – Astrud in the coffin, the hands that had touched his shoulder – his aunt rang every week, compelling him to talk. *'It's bad to remember, but it's worse not to.'*

He had thrown his door keys at the doctor who brought him the news. In the sunlight of his first day of mourning, he was tearing at his own fur. He cut his hair. He couldn't listen to music, read a book, eat *moqueca*.

After she died, her dog didn't go into their room.

Even though a long while had passed since then, he could never stop it welling up. At what point had his mourning become pathological? When would he stop palming his hands against the memory, trying to warm himself? It seemed closer in time to him now than for many years. He was lashed to it like a convict. Healing from her loss would be the miracle.

'*Senhor João?*' It's Miguel, wondering what smiles followed by sudden sobs can have got into his normally taciturn customer. 'Another cup of tea?'

He tries not to look up. 'No, thanks, Miguel,' and reaches through the blur for a paper napkin.

Chapter Twenty-two

DYER TUCKED THE FOLDER BACK into his bag, shrugged his arms into Marvar's silk-lined sleeves, paid the bill and left. It was an odd sensation to walk through the Covered Market in another man's overcoat. Already, his fingertips had encountered a cough-sweet that smelled of Marvar's breath wrapped in tissue paper. He felt grains of sand in the pockets.

Marvar didn't have this coat when he revisited the sand-pit on Sunday; it was hanging up in Dyer's cupboard. Had Marvar left it deliberately as a parting gift, was he shedding his skin even then?

Compelled to walk at a different gait – the coat was warm, but too big, and it hung on him like one of Vivien's tea cosies – Dyer passed the fish counter, the shoe shop, the hair-dresser, Ben's Cookies, out into the High Street.

A bell struck nine. He yearned for the day before yesterday, and for the day before that. If he hadn't stopped to speak with Marvar outside the University Press. If he hadn't driven at midnight to the Phoenix. The bag on his shoulder weighed as if it had a body in it.

Dyer heard out the chimes and picked up his pace. He had walked slowly this morning to the Covered Market, as though Marvar would appear if he took his time. It was how he had walked before. He imagined that he would catch sight of her and then run and catch up, and they would walk on together.

His steps now were nervous, shorter. The people he passed knew nothing of the load he carried. A slip of paper could be so heavy.

Updark had given him his card – Dyer had left it on the bookcase beside the phone. He would overcome his reservations about the man and ring him when he got home. But the decision made, Dyer still felt uneasy. He stared down and jumped over a pavement crack.

Who else had spotted Dyer speaking to Marvar in Great Clarendon Street, or an hour later on Port Meadow, immersed in a conversation that nobody could have interrupted, or returning with Marvar to Jericho? What faces behind frosted windscreens had tracked them? Had those same eyes combed Dyer's house, or were they different ones? Even if Marvar hadn't been abducted, it was possible that whoever was in pursuit of him had extended their attention to Dyer.

It had happened in his life once or twice. There had come into his mind someone he had not thought about in years, and next moment this person had appeared. Never before, though, not even as he walked into the Cantina da Lua, up the stairs, through the bead curtain, holding a book – the same book Rejas was reading – had he experienced a premonition about an event, and it unfolded.

Dyer was making his way down Magdalen Street when a car swerved, skidded to a halt, doors flying open, and two men sprang out and ripped towards him. He had a staccato impression, rat-at-at-at, of black hoodies, gloved fingers clamping his arms, a silver Passat estate, exhaust fumes. A group of Chinese tourists looked on, gawping, as Dyer flailed out a hand, grabbing one of them, a young woman, by the wrist, and yelled at the top of his voice, at the same time clinging with every particle of his strength to his shoulder bag.

One of the hoodies fought to prise Dyer from the terrified woman, knocking him to the ground. The other hoodie knelt and trapped his head in an arm-lock, wrenching his neck and hoisting Dyer's gaze to the car.

He glimpsed a dark-skinned face peering out at him from the passenger seat, canal-black eyes without expression, until on studying Dyer closer, they registered a shock of surprise. Dyer heard a curt shout, an order barked in a foreign language – but what language? Arabic, Hebrew, Farsi? He couldn't be sure, either then or afterwards.

The two hoodies, nonplussed, suddenly released him, stood up and ran back to the car. There was a screech of wheels as they dived in, doors slamming, accelerated off.

Dyer lay not moving for a second. Then he picked himself up from the pavement, checked that he still had his bag, its contents were safe, and helped the Chinese woman to her feet.

She was shaken, but unhurt, she insisted.

He escorted her over to a bench to be comforted by her group.

The tour guide – black blazer with brass buttons; blue-red-and-brown striped tie – was an Englishman like Dyer, with a broad moley face. 'Who were they?' he asked Dyer in an educated, interested voice.

'I have no idea,' said Dyer.

'Might they have thought you were someone else?' with glances at the road.

'It's possible,' said Dyer, and after accepting the woman's assurance that she was fine, really, he went up the steps into the Taylorian.

Sitting down in the French and German reading room, after hanging up Marvar's coat, Dyer unzipped his bag and felt inside. His fingers had gripped Marvar's folder moments earlier, but he needed to touch it again, to be certain.

How fast the covering tide. From his leather-seated chair, Dyer looked down through the window, rubbing his jaw. Tilting his head, he could make out the pavement where he had been sent sprawling. A new group of Chinese tourists stood in line, waiting to cross.

The men in the car – where had they intended to take him? What did they want?

Then it hit him. The tour guide was right. They'd mistaken him for Marvar.

In yielding to his superstitious nature, Dyer had put on Marvar's overcoat as if it would help him decide what to do with the post-it note. Instead, the coat had made Dyer a mark.

Confused, intensely afraid – it had given him a real fright – he occupied himself in setting up his laptop. He plugged it in and stared hard for a moment at the screen. Then he reached out for Professor Madrugada's book, retrieved from where he had left it on Saturday: a stack in the main reading room, on a shelf reserved for surnames beginning with D. Opening it, he flicked forward to the page that he had marked with the white Taylorian slip, like a boarding pass. He took this out and resumed his journey into the Brazilian interior, but he was conscious of the man in the Passat, his dark blazing eyes, his foreign shout.

Dyer started when the door opened and a stocky young woman in jeans entered and tumbled her computer, charger, books, scarf, bobble hat, and a bottle of water onto the central table. Without glancing her pink round face in his direction, she unzipped her fur-lined parka and, after loudly taking it off, sighed, and walked out.

He felt the tension draining. *Is that how it's going to be?* He was alone in a hostile, unfamiliar world where everyone was a potential enemy. He was like Afonso Ribeiro, left to fend for himself among the Tupi. The serpent's hiss of the surf. The caravel in the distance a dot. He was going to have to learn a new language in order to survive.

He read some pages. The busiest hours of the morning passed. The library was his sanctuary. Here, he felt safe, unmonitored. The only thing looking down at him from the wall, above a bookcase of *Encylopédie Larousse* and a red metal rolling ladder, was an unexceptional painting in a tarnished gilt frame. It was of a bucolic classical scene, set high on a hill, with distant mountains below lapped in a blue haze, and showed a young shepherd, possibly Endymion, tending to the injured foot of a semi-naked woman, possibly Diana, who sat on a rock, with hunting dogs and putti hovering.

Dyer spent until the early part of the afternoon in the Taylorian, reading. His place by the window was good for that, even if he leafed through the pages not really taking them in, and several times had to go back over what he had read. Every so often, he stirred himself to make a note on his laptop or to look at the painting. He looked at the painting a lot. The woman in it reminded him of someone.

The Phoenix had no games or clubs on Tuesdays. School would be over by three-thirty, and he wanted to see Leandro; he was still shaken by the attack. At three o'clock, Dyer packed away his computer and walked back through the main reading room.

No one looked up as he passed. Here, at least, he was ignored.

The librarian behind the counter had purple-framed designer glasses and short peroxide hair.

'May I renew this?' Dyer asked.

If he had held a more senior library card, of the sort issued to professors, lecturers and PHD students, as Dyer briefly once was, he could perhaps have taken the book home, but something in his character suited Dyer to have it reserved for him, to read here, in the neutral limbo of the Taylorian, and then to renew the book should he require it for longer. This was the first time he had felt the incentive.

She accepted the book from him to enter the details.

'I don't expect there's a queue,' he murmured absently. 'I'm probably the only person to have requested it.'

She squinted at the screen. 'You *are* the first person. But that's not the point. It should be available for other readers. Meanwhile, your status as Mr ... Madrugada's sole reader to date is safe.'

'How so?'

'Data protection. I'm not allowed to reveal it – once I finish logging in these details,' speaking in slow motion, 'thanks to. the Bodleian's. new. Solo security system.'

She handed the book back. 'You can have it out for one more week. And just so you know, you can renew it yourself online.'

As he turned to go, she asked in a sharp, authoritative voice: 'Is that your coat?'

'No.'

She stared at him for a moment, the way his hands gripped his shoulder bag as if he had a newborn baby in it.

'Well, you can't leave it there.' That rack was for the staff.

He had been in such a state when he came up the stairs. 'It's not mine,' he insisted, feeling caught out. 'I was just borrowing it.'

She gave him a salty look and pointed to an umbrella stand in the passageway outside. 'You can leave it there.'

The black Audi had been parked outside the headmaster's house since lunchtime, apparently, and still Mr Crotty – or 'Crotch' as the boys and girls called him – had not emerged.

Mr Tanner wore a grim expression. He headed across the playground to his office in suppressed conversation with the pastoral care officer, a confident, clerkly, heavyset woman, unmarried, who was Crotch's sister.

Outside the Rink, standing in the cold, the mothers congregated. News that one of their number had gone missing had sent those who preferred to wag their tongues in the Bon Croissant drifting over to talk to one another. Nodding heads. Pursed lips. They stood absorbing the rumours, smiling gravely, trying to worm out what was going on. A face peeped around now and then at the gate, as if hoping to see Marvar come shambling through it, and not Dyer.

He had walked all the way from the Taylorian. He had walked as though freed, until he noticed the blonde head of Katya, her gloved hands rubbing each other, standing apart from the other parents. She had not spoken to him since the evening of Mr Tanner's investigation. Dyer had thought of her as little as possible, as if he was responsible. Seeing her there, he felt a slight tightening.

'Hi,' she said with an uncertain smile.

He looked at her – it was a lovely face. She might have forgiven him.

'Hi.'

She appraised him. His olive cotton shirt and his uncombed hair. The shoulder bag that he clutched with both hands.

'Aren't you cold?' she asked.

He drew himself up. 'Not really,' was all he said, ridiculous he thought, as if it had been the most natural thing to leave Marvar's overcoat behind, on this chill February day, on a brass hook in the Taylorian. The librarian was bound to identify the coat as Dyer's.

He would collect it next time, pack it into a bag, no one would notice.

Katya watched him with a strange look in her eyes.

There was the gargle of a Summertown voice a few feet away. 'He always avoided me.'

Without turning, Dyer recognised the speaker. Samantha Puckey. Part of a book group. He had helped her with her novel, it had not worked out. He was associated with the failure.

She was raising her voice to be heard. 'It's easy to be wise in retrospect, but I felt there was something not quite, I don't know, *echt* about him.'

'How are you?' he asked Katya.

The sun had broken through, weak, but flickering a silvery light over everything. The reflection in the noticeboard threw back her bright top.

She had seen Gennady off. He was not in a good mood, she said. She made a movement with her head.

He stood at an angle, keeping his back to the mothers. Her face was very white in the glass. He had the idea that she had been weeping. Just the cast of her jaw.

Her hand touched a mark on her neck. 'You've heard about Marvar?'

'Marvar?' To hear the name spoken was a shock. He wasn't prepared, he had been hoarding it to himself. It made real again everything that he feared.

Dyer didn't catch what he mumbled, but Katya construed it as encouragement to face and tell him.

No one had seen Samir or his father for two days, she said. The flu, is what everyone had thought. 'It's been going around.'

'I know.' But he couldn't pay attention. Behind her was the sandpit. There is sometimes one pose which endures. Marvar, sitting on the low wall, shoes in the sand. Looking at his fingertips as if the grains on them came from a desert.

She tossed a glance at the group behind him. 'They are telling me it wasn't flu.'

Katya was about to say something else, but then her son appeared and she thought better of it.

'Ah, Vasily.'

His hair was trimmed short as if his mother had cut it. He nodded at Dyer. 'Leandro is coming. I just saw him.'

He was less sullen than Dyer remembered.

Days earlier, Dyer had enquired about Vasily's behaviour towards him. Leandro, ever surprising, replied: 'Oh, Vasily's all right.' It reminded Dyer that Leandro didn't judge, kids protect each other. It still worried him, though, that Leandro might be identifying with the bully, and this was more about Leandro saying: 'Back off, Dad, let me deal with it.' Dyer knew that he would have to play out his concern. What he was observing was a process, a necessary step in Leandro re-establishing his footing with Vasily – although their friendliness hadn't yet extended to having Vasily over or going to his place.

On the other hand, his son's friendship with Samir had not advanced as Dyer would have predicted. Leandro's twinge yesterday that he might have passed his flu on to Samir had yielded to a more pragmatic view. Too bad. Tough luck. These things happen in sport. If you worry about the friend you gave flu to, you're sunk, you're never going to win, was Leandro's casual new attitude.

'I was off games for four days, remember. He'll be back soon.'

'What if he isn't?' Dyer had responded angrily, thinking of what might have happened to him instead.

Because what was becoming clear: a common cold was not the reason for Samir's absence.

'What are they saying?' Dyer asked Katya. It was one thing Marvar being abducted by hostile forces who would doubtless use horrible means to extract the information they wanted out of him, but for an eleven-year-old to be part of this was unthinkable.

Her face stiffened. She spun round and looked at him with the same expression that Vivien used to put on to say Not in Front of the Children.

'I will see you,' in a flat voice, and walked away with Vasily, leaving Dyer breathing in the air in which she had left her faint perfume.

Then it was Leandro standing before him. 'Dad! I didn't recognise you. Aren't you freezing in that shirt?'

Dyer was annoyed at being asked. The cold was the least of his worries.

Leandro went on looking at him, still mystified. 'Hey, I was going to bike home, remember?' He was finding it strange, this concern of his father's to ferry him about and turn up unannounced.

'I thought I'd walk back with you,' said Dyer feebly.

'Then can we go to Peppers Burgers?'

'Not today,' said Dyer. 'Tomorrow – after your history test.' There were lamb chops in the fridge. Unless eaten tonight, they'd have to be chucked away.

This reminder of his forthcoming test, on top of not being able to go to his favourite takeaway in Walton Street, plunged Leandro into a grumpy mood. He hitched his satchel further up his shoulder.

Overhead, the clouds were like foam behind a ship. The two of them walked down Phoenix Lane, through Park Town, and paused at the grassed-in oval, waiting to cross Banbury Road.

A public toilet had dominated this small lawn when Dyer was at the Phoenix. He remembered once waiting at the bus shelter opposite while Rougetel disappeared inside to have a pee. The boy who had re-emerged was unable to batten down his curiosity about the warning printed on a notice above the latrine. At the top of his voice, Rougetel shouted out to Dyer, standing in a line of serious-faced grey-haired women, 'Hey, Basil, what's a venner-real disease?'

Watching for a break in the rush-hour traffic, Dyer met his son's eye, igniting a crafty smile.

'Vasily's mother ...' said Leandro.

'What about her?'

'I saw you looking at her bosom.'

Chapter Twenty-three

'WHAT'S THIS?'

It was Leandro next morning who noticed the mark as he opened the passenger door. A neat purposeful scratch on the side, like a tag.

'Hooligans,' muttered Dyer. But he wasn't convinced. You don't leave an envy line on a seven-year-old left-hand-drive Beetle.

First, his attempted kidnap. Now this tridentine-shaped sinister scratch. In the way that after narrowly avoiding a serious accident you can become more reckless, Dyer decided to act.

Once he had dropped off Leandro at school, Dyer returned to Jericho, but instead of going to the Taylorian, he seized his shoulder bag from the passenger seat and walked back into the house.

He hung the bag on a hook in the hallway. Then, grabbing the cordless handset, he sat down on the sofa in the small drawing room. He had written out the number that Lionel Updark had asked him to call 'should you think of anything', but this was not the number he dialled. Something – a furry tongue at the thought of him, a sensation that his throat was closing up, like when he tasted walnuts, kiwi fruit or aubergines – still stopped Dyer from turning to Updark.

Silvi eventually answered.

When he heard her voice, Dyer obeyed an instinct not to wade straight in, as he might have done with Gilles. With Silvi, obliqueness worked better. He thanked her for the sleepover, Leandro would be writing. And he had a further reason for calling ...

At the other end, a suspicious 'Yes?'

How might he get hold of Miranda?

Silvi the matchmaker couldn't mask her delight. 'So you liked her?'

'That's not quite why I want to contact her. I promised her a booklist, but I forgot to take her number. I think she was serious.'

'Here, let me get her details. You know, I have a feeling she's away at the moment.'

He waited for Silvi to look up Miranda's address and telephone number ('I don't seem to have her email'), and wrote them down in his notebook, and her surname.

Silvi went on: 'I still haven't started your book – first, I have to finish *Some More Silky Ways*. Maybe after that, I will ask Miranda for your booklist! You must give her my special love when you see her.'

'I will.'

'You won't believe this. I said to Gilles, "I know she has a lady-from-Bucharest hairstyle, very not contemporary, but I can see John getting on with *that* one."'

'Actually, Silvi, is Gilles there?' If Dyer trusted anyone to come up with a plausible explanation for what had happened to Marvar and his son, it was Gilles Asselin.

Her husband was away, she told him in a different voice. In the Sinai.

'What's he doing there?'

'Buying up the desert, I don't know!' He had flown off on Monday from Kidlington.

'Back when?'

'He didn't say. You know Gilles. Independent as a hog on ice.'

'I wanted to ask about Rustum Marvar.'

'That's so awful. God.'

'Silvi, do *you* have any idea where Marvar might be?'

'He took Samir away before lunch, before the party. He didn't stay even to say hello, I never saw him.' Her tone was self-exculpatory. She had told the story before.

'You're positive it was Marvar who picked him up?' Or had Marvar already been taken at this point by the Iranians, the Israelis or someone else, and had they collected Samir as leverage over him?

'He did tell to Brian – our butler – that he was Samir's father. And the camera on the gate, Gilles has seen the pictures. He says for sure it's Marvar.'

'He was clearly in a hurry,' mused Dyer. 'Maybe they had to catch a train. Or a plane.'

'Maybe.' But her voice was not believing. Samir and Marvar had only been missing for a few days, yet she was imagining terrible things. 'Samir – I remember him waiting in the hall as if just now he is before my eyes.' It could have been her son. It could have been Pierre. 'Jean, if you learn anything, tell me. Please.'

They promise to pass on anything they hear.

Dyer had become more guarded on the telephone after his touchline conversation with Gilles about surveillance. He took the same precaution when surfing the internet, and had entered no further searches for nuclear fusion. It would have been suspiciously out of character, though, for him not to have shown an interest in Marvar.

Already that morning he'd googled Marvar's name. There was no report of a kidnapping. No suicide pact. No missing father and son jumping from Clifton Suspension Bridge.

He telephoned the *Oxford Mail*, the *Oxford Times,* BBC Oxford to ask if any bodies had been found.

Nothing.

In Dyer's heyday, the Updarks of this world counted on correspondents like him to tell them what was going on. Uncertain which way to turn now, Dyer behaved as any retired journalist might do when unable to verify a story, one furthermore that he still had to sort out where to place. He called his old newspaper and asked for Nat Royter.

Cub reporters, they had joined in the same year. Nat's ambition – which he achieved – was to be the political correspondent. He was one of very few survivors from the former regime, following the paper's sale to a thirty-year-old Qatari billionaire and champion of Brexit domiciled in Minorca.

They had met in the new Pimlico premises not long after Dyer's return from Rio. Through a blue flame, over a warm glass of calvados, was the last occasion they had seen each other, on the eve of Dyer's departure for Brazil. That was thirty-five years before. This time they had to settle for a snatched coffee in the lobby. Money was so tight in the newsroom, Nat said ruefully, that he couldn't leave his desk for long, and definitely not for a three-course lunch at Clarke's.

'They've given me the foreign desk too,' he said, 'bless 'em.'

'That would have pleased Frank,' said Dyer, recalling the bald, wry features of their first foreign editor.

'Frank Tullover,' murmured Nat. 'He who taught us: "Why is this person telling you this?"'

'That, and: "Always justify your expenses in the second para."'

Without a pause, they chanted in solemn unison as if it were a psalm: '"As I sat face to face across the table in Red Square with Kim Philby, the man who had brought Western intelligence to its knees, drinking, at his insistence, the most expensive vodka to be obtained in Moscow..."'

They looked at each other, then dissolved, shaking, into laughter, until rebuked by a glare from the receptionist.

Nat wiped the corner of his eye. His nose had broadened like his chest. He used to smoke thin cigars. He had the air of a man itching for a cheroot.

'You're looking young,' contemplating Dyer over a cup of machine latte. 'But you always did. Bastard.'

'The sun helped.'

'And no deadlines!'

'That too.'

Nat came from a wind-nipped landscape of salmon-fishers and poachers. In the year that Dyer left for Brazil, he had inherited a pear orchard near Hereford; it was his pipedream, then, one day to give up journalism and make perry. Yet the courage or the right moment had eluded him; he had become snared in the mantrap of London.

Seeing Dyer again made him reminiscent. 'When that job came up in Rio, not one of us understood why you took it.'

'There was no special reason,' Dyer reflected. 'My favourite aunt lived in Lima, and I had a friend at school who grew up in South America. It sounded different, interesting. Heath's government, rats in the rubbish, nurses on strike, power cuts – I didn't want to be around if that came back.' Plus, after his mother died, he had a craving to learn for himself, from experiences denied to his parents. They had come of age in post-war Britain, with rationing, whale meat, bedsits with gas meters; they could have brought nothing to the party that Dyer found going on in Brazil.

Nat had missed out on that party too. His carnival queen was Mrs Thatcher. The experience seemed to have soured him; he had not found the sun, the satisfactions of Corcovado, of tanned limbs. His face had browned like a pear.

'You got out at the right moment,' he told Dyer, his mouth turned down, 'even if none of us thought so at the time.'

Everything they had felt about journalism, the conviction, the adrenaline thrill, the confidence that what they wrote was read by a majority of the people they knew – this belonged to a pre-Columbian era. Today, Nat's op-ed pieces were dictated to him from Minorca. The paper carried the same masthead, but an incubus had sucked out its spirit as well as its circulation.

'They've sacked everyone, it's like a Potemkin village. Five underpaid students do everything, overseen by a few overpaid kapos – editors demeritus, essentially, not one of whom would have been given a sub's job on the old paper – who pander to the whims of the absentee playboy owner, and prowl about on seven-figure bonuses feverishly seeking ways to further slash costs. We don't print scoops, we print handouts.' It had become the kind of job that you turned your telephone off for.

'I'm sorry, Nat Royter left us over a year ago,' says a young woman's voice. She is unable to tell Dyer where he might be contacted.

He asks to speak to someone in the same department, but they're busy. He asks to leave a message. Could someone on the foreign desk call him?

'Can you say what it's about?' sounding no older than twenty.

'Iran.'

She has not heard of Dyer.

When no one calls, he rings again and is connected to a harassed male voice. This man also is young; he doesn't have a lot of time, he's putting three stories to bed.

Dyer feels sickened as he starts to explain himself. An image forms of the person at the other end, a face like Hissop's. Half-listening, half-prepared, hankering to be somewhere else.

'Nat Royter would vouch for me.'

'Ah, Nat,' with the edginess of a successor. 'Friend of his, were we?'

Quickly, Dyer explains his history with the newspaper, his two decades as its Latin American correspondent. He is ringing to ask about the situation in Tehran, one journo to another. 'Is it plausible that the Revolutionary Guard would imprison and rape the wife of an Iranian nuclear scientist based in the UK who may have defected?'

'Does a fish swim?' relenting a little. 'If she's a dual national, like that jailed mum, she might get away with not being raped. If she's Iranian, all bets are off. Why do you ask?' Dyer can hear him tapping away at the keyboard, mouth open, unshaven. 'Do you have someone in mind?' in the voice of someone who doesn't get out of Pimlico much, who hasn't yet visited Tehran, Rio. Possibly not even Malvern.

'Not really,' said Dyer.

'If your chap has defected, I hope for his sake it's not to us – unless he fancies spending the rest of his life in Langley. The UK is pretending to go along with the EU in helping out Iran to circumvent US sanctions. Don't believe it. I was at a briefing yesterday at the FO. This new extradition treaty the Foreign Secretary has signed – I'll be putting it online later. Basically, anyone the Americans slap in a request for, we fly them to Virginia.'

The whole exchange has been unsatisfactory, and recalls Nat's bitterest complaints. It spikes any lingering notion of Dyer's that the dark star of his nostalgia might have fertilised, about giving to the newspaper they both had worked for the first crack at Marvar's story.

Still, the young man's reaction confirms what Dyer in his old reporter's bones believes. If Marvar spoke the truth about his wife, then he was likely to be telling the truth about fusion. And if that were so, then the right recipient for Marvar's post-it note is not Lionel Updark.

'Wait, what's your number? If I hear anything ...'

Chapter Twenty-four

DYER RETURNED THE HANDSET TO its charger on the bookcase, beside Astrud's photograph, and then went over to where he had hung his shoulder bag, checking inside. The bag had not been in his line of vision. Although it was absurd to suppose that anyone had crept in and riffled through it while he was talking on the sofa, he felt the irrational need to make doubly sure.

He zipped it up and stood at the window, staring out. His conversations had depressed him, he was no further along. His mind kept returning to Marvar and his post-it note.

What do you do when something like this tumbles out of the sky into your life? Dyer yearned to hand it in, get rid of it. But if not to Updark, then who? He'd looked for signs and there were none. He had hoped the cracks in the pavement would tell him. If he had believed in a higher power, he would have implored it to point a way.

The post-it note was not his only concern. He couldn't stop thinking about the life-or-death implications of what he chose to do, for Samir, Rustum, Shula and Jamileh. He had already promised to withhold information. Yet further holding him back from reporting Marvar's findings to Updark or Euratom, or another neutral body, was Dyer's fear that the Revolutionary Guard would simply execute Shula, as they'd have no further need of her as a bargaining chip. Then again, if Marvar and Samir had been picked up, this would render Shula's life worthless to the unscrupulous entities who may have captured her.

Meanwhile, where to put this pestilential scrap of paper? Marvar's information was so radioactive that it ought to be kept locked in a vault with Madame Curie's cookbooks. It wasn't safe to carry about.

Dyer stands there with his thoughts.

On the far towpath, a shaven-headed man cast off a long barge. A woman walked by, pushing a pram that bounced up and down. Shula and her baby daughter. Too hard to think of them.

Easier to fret about Marvar's overcoat. Dyer couldn't leave that in the Taylorian – the librarian would inevitably associate it with him. Even though the coat had made him a target, he still felt responsible for it, a connection. 'Shula had it made for me before I came here.' The knowledge that Magda was about to arrive galvanised him to go and fetch it.

The overcoat would be too bulky to fit in his shoulder bag, but not into Leandro's canvas games bag. Quickly, Dyer emptied out the mud-encrusted socks, shirts, shorts into the washing machine.

As he pitched the soap pellet into the back of the drum, he remembered when a speculative North Oxford mother had congratulated him on being a modern father. He'd got that from his mother, he told her. 'She did the taxes, my father cooked.' When she died, he had needed to mother himself, and now he had to mother Leandro. He wasn't shy of doing this, it was just another role.

He turned on the washing machine and repacked into Leandro's canvas bag: Marvar's plastic sandwich bag containing the folder with the post-it note; his own eleven handwritten pages of their interview; his laptop; the collection of poems he'd been reading.

After writing out a list of tasks for Magda, and leaving three £10 notes on the table, he opened the door and walked out.

In the *favela*, to avoid muggers, Dyer took a different route every day. For the first time in Oxford, he changed his itinerary, not walking up Little Clarendon Street, but down Canal Street, over the pedestrian bridge, along the tinder path. Coming this way made it easier to observe if anyone was following.

He stares into the unflowing canal. It's like going back fifty years. He's twelve. He and Rougetel are walking into town along the towpath so that they won't be caught by Slimy or Jumbo. Rougetel's parents live abroad, in La Paz, where his father works for a telephone company. He's the younger brother Dyer never had, clever, unconventional, independent, who helps him with his prep, with whom he can play truant.

A quick twenty-minute walk had brought Dyer out into Hythe Bridge Street.

He checked over his shoulder as he turned into Worcester Street. How many times in the street or passing by in a car had he noticed someone he knew without them suspecting that he was watching; how many times had he been noticed by someone who chose not to make themself known, like a trout that had gone for his fly and he didn't see it?

Not recognising any of the faces, he continued up Beaumont Street, past the Ashmolean, into the Taylorian.

He breathed out to see no peroxided head behind the counter.

Still smothering the umbrella stand, Marvar's overcoat hung in the passage, its hem brushing the floor. Dyer stuffed it into Leandro's games bag. He was halfway down the stairs when he stopped.

It was here, on the grey anonymous staircase, that Dyer had the idea. He reached out to the wrought-iron handrail, turned, and began to retrace his steps. Gripping the bag, he pushed open the door at the top of the stairs and walked, heart tripping, across the soft coral carpet. Suddenly, he saw a way to throw his enemies off the track.

The walls of the big domed reading room were covered in books. Seven had been reserved by Dyer. These volumes were stored with many reserved by other members in a free-standing open case in the centre.

Dyer stooped to a pile on the second shelf. He ran the back of his index finger down the spines, until it brushed against the wine-red copy of *Uma Nova Luz Num Litoral Antigo,* by Sergio Madrugada (University of Coimbra Press, 2017). He tugged the book out and took it into the French and German reading room next door. As he'd anticipated, this was empty, the regular tiny band of Modern Languages undergraduates no doubt attending a lecture downstairs.

He sat at the end of a long table by the window and undid the blue canvas games bag, delving under Marvar's coat and pulling out Basil Bunting's *Collected Poems.* He opened this to a poem on page 72, and, drawing on knowledge acquired in this very room nearly three decades before, he started to create a code in his notebook, from time to time referring to the poem's last six lines, and altering certain letters into numbers.

His code established, Dyer dug out Marvar's folder and withdrew the yellow post-it note. He tore off one of the two blank post-it notes on the back and, using his calculations and comparing these with Marvar's – shielded in his left palm – he wrote out an altogether different algorithm on it, first one side, then the other, and finishing with the same words: '*contrary to God's will*'?

He checked it over one last time, this false formula with his Bunting code copied out in what he hoped resembled Marvar's handwriting. Then he tucked it back inside the green folder. As an afterthought, he slipped the third and last, blank, post-it note into his wallet.

Forty minutes had passed when Dyer folded Marvar's original yellow piece of paper into the penultimate chapter of Professor Madrugada's book, and returned to the stacks. He looked about. Three young women on the central round table, making notes. A chubby bald man in glasses, smiling to himself as he wrote a postcard. Reassured that no one was watching and there were no CCTV cameras to record his actions, Dyer reinserted *Uma Nova Luz Num Litoral Antigo* into the pile, and picked up his bag and left.

The blonde-dyed librarian had sparked the idea. The memory of her voice had trailed him as he was going down the stairs, the meaningful way she had raised her God-white head and said: '*You can have it out for one more week,*' after first revealing that no one would know that it was Dyer who had ordered Madrugada's monograph. Something in her manner had recalled his editor when he commissioned Dyer's valedictory piece on South America. It moved Dyer to treat the extension of a recondite library book with the respect that he once unfailingly approached every deadline. The date was arbitrary, of no significance at all, but it gave him another six days to work out what to do.

For now, until 8 p.m. the following Tuesday, Marvar's post-it note was safe between the pages of a book that no one was likely to want to read.

Dyer had needed something extraordinary to motivate him, to take hold of his spirit. Now he had it. Marvar's hard-edged folder had given Dyer a purpose and shamed him out of his morose mood.

He had not forgotten Gilles's touchline advice on how to avoid leaving a digital footprint. 'Stay away from cameras. Buy a pack of SIM cards, and rotate them so they can't get a pattern. And use a line of poetry for your password, no one will ever hack it.'

At the Vodafone store in Cornmarket, Dyer paid £5 for a pack of ten SIM cards. Before returning home, he stopped off at the post office in Walton Street and bought two padded brown envelopes.

Into the smaller one, he inserted his interview with Marvar, addressing it to himself. He sealed this up and folded it, along with a short letter, into the larger envelope, which he posted to a separate address copied from a page in his notebook that he then tore out and threw away, along with the notes for his code.

The letter read:

Dear Miranda,

Please forgive me for intruding on you out of the blue. I'm aware this request is unusual, but would you keep the enclosed package safe for me? I will explain when we next meet (better for tedious reasons face to face, and not by email/phone). Meanwhile, find below a list of books about the Tupi.

    With fond regards,
    abáûera,
    John Dyer

Moments later, Dyer was unlocking his front door when he heard the telephone whining in the kitchen. He raced inside, dropping the games bag onto the table, and ran to answer it.

'Hello?' came a voice from upstairs. 'Hello?'

Just the dialling tone. Marvar?

'It's all right, it's me, Magda,' he shouted.

She said something he couldn't make out over the noise of the hoover.

He called ring-back. The number was ex-directory. Updark? The journalist? Someone else?

Magda appeared, a tubby blonde whose hangdog expression reminded him of his college scout.

'It's been ringing and ringing,' she puffed. 'I didn't think you'd want me to answer.'

'No, you were right,' he said, and disconnected the handset. He felt some reason to do this that he could not define.

'I've made up your bed,' she went on. 'Oh, and a fresh duvet cover for Leandro,' tuning her voice to a more pleasant note. But she was very behindhand, she said, having taken her boyfriend to the bus station for a job interview in Bicester. She still had to empty the washing machine, hang out Leandro's damp football kit to dry, iron two of Dyer's white shirts, sew on a button, hoover downstairs. She might have been reciting a crime sheet.

A fly was buzzing against the windowpane. Dyer checked his watch. Twelve fifty. 'Then I'll get out of your way.' He was hungry all of a sudden.

Chapter Twenty-five

THE OLD BOOKBINDERS HAD BECOME more popular since Dyer's arrival in Oxford, and at lunchtimes it was packed. A French couple had bought the pub the previous spring. In lieu of pickled eggs and the local malt, plus, on certain days, a disreputable-looking unnamed battered fish, a blackboard advertised *moules marinières, croque-monsieurs, steak frites* and, all this week, a prizewinning wheat beer.

He glanced warily at the faces. The usual customers: French and Italian students in knee-length coats; middle-aged Brexit voters from the council houses and barges; on stools at the bar, a local divorcée and a retired professor of Spanish, one looking dreamily up in the air at the paper banknotes, denominations from foreign countries, that a previous landlord had pasted to the ceiling, the other at the *TLS* open on his brown corduroy lap.

Dyer pushed his way to the counter and ordered half a pint of bitter and a ham-and-cheese baguette from a narrow-faced woman drying glasses.

'I'll be through there,' he told her, accepting his change.

Taking his beer, Dyer ducked his head under the beam and passed into the lower-ceilinged room at the back. A rectangle of daylight slanted through the open door, pointing the way to an unoccupied table.

He put down his glass and, leaving his scarf to guard the seat, walked back through the pub, to the loo.

On his return five minutes later, he smelled something familiar.

Dyer had sat down before he noticed a figure in the corner. Her blonde hair bound up, she looked around like a girl in a foreign town, smiling.

'Hi.'

Bone-coloured jacket. Slim green jersey pulled tight. His face became different when he recognised her.

Now he was able to place it, that giddying odour.

His voice said the name whose lips, he realised, he had not stopped thinking of.

'Katya.'

She accepted his kiss, cheek forward, not moving.

'This is unexpected – what are you doing here?'

She seemed to be thinking.

'I wanted to see ...'

He waited. 'What?'

She shivered and shook her shoulders, like someone resisting a caress. 'Where we were going to have our "bitter" …'

He glanced down at her empty table. 'You're not drinking?'

She looked quickly at him. 'Whatever you are drinking,' she said.

Soon he was back.

'Long overdue,' clinking glasses.

She took a sip. It was a half-pint of Marston's Old Empire. 'Not bad,' in a neutral tone.

'You're being polite.'

'I am not so,' she said in her strange accent. 'But I like it. Quite,' scrunching up her small nose. 'I think.'

A smell of garlic came from the kitchen. Her green jersey was the colour of billiard cloth.

He dropped his eyes, and made circles on the beermat with his glass. 'How's Vasily?' he risked.

On a leather cord around her neck was a silver leaf. Katya touched it now and then, as, without going too deep into the subject, she told him about her son. He was studying for Common Entrance. He hoped to get into Harrow. The transition from Moscow to Oxford had not been smooth, but Vasily was happier now, she said: 'Although he is finding English history hard. The "Rocket" of Stephenson …'

Dyer laughed. 'Leandro has the same problem with Trafalgar.'

She searched his face. She had such a broad naked smile when he talked about his son.

Grateful to Katya for not alluding to the incident which had sabotaged their flirtation, he told her how it took Leandro three terms to find his footing, despite Dyer's connections with the school.

'I was rung up in the first week to say Leandro didn't have the correct black shoes – trainers wouldn't do.'

Not even in his trainers must Katya run away with the idea that Leandro always excelled on the sports field. In his inaugural rugby game, Dyer said, never having played rugby, Leandro failed to observe the boundary lines and was shouted at by the coach.

'He kept running right off the pitch and into the crowd. Mr Tanner yelled at him in such a mean way.' He picked up his glass. 'If I'd been Leandro's mother, I'd have given him a very expensive Lamy pen to make up for it.'

'Why didn't she?'

'His mother lives in Brazil,' said Dyer quickly. 'She doesn't communicate much. And to be fair to her, nor do I.' He hadn't told Nissa when Leandro had nits.

'Brazil is long way,' she reflected. 'Longer than Moscow.'

'It is far.'

'And Leandro – he misses her?'

'Of course,' said Dyer. 'Well, I say that, but I think he real-ises she's not there for him. She's remarried, has other children.'

'Do *you* miss her?'

'Leandro's mother? No. Yes. I don't know.'

'You feel about her what I feel about this?' She picked up her beer and shutting her eyes took another sip. Her eyes when they opened had a sterner expression. 'What happened?'

'To me and Nissa?' He reached for his glass as if it con-tained an explanation. Spelled out in the rising bubbles was an orgy of misconception. A couple who knew nothing of each other's past, who had foreseen a future together that neither of them could hope to possess. 'She fell out of love,' Dyer said at last, and took another sip. The beer had a differ-ent flavour, as if it was reacting to his memories.

Katya put her glass down. 'And you?'

He said thickly: 'Oh, she'd tell you I was never in love in the first place.'

She looked at him, all attention.

'Then why did you marry?'

'We didn't marry. We got engaged, but we never quite pulled the noose.'

'Noose?'

He made a motion around his neck. 'What the hangman does.' After a pause, he said: 'That was a joke.'

'You English,' she mused, shaking her head. 'I only believe when you are joking.'

'Really, only then?'

'Yes,' with a jolting smile. 'Only then.'

Before she could go on, he said in a parrying voice: 'What about you and Gennady? It's not easy, living in separate countries.'

He thought she was fastening an earring, but she was touching a mark on her neck.

'How did you both meet?' he pressed.

Her eyes gleaming, she stared at the glass, its brown unrefrigerated contents. They were at university together in Moscow. He had been an accountant, that was how he had begun, she said.

'But you're from Murmansk, I thought …'

'Murmansk?'

'You were a beauty queen in Murmansk, is what I heard.'

'Who told you?' frowning.

'Someone in Summertown, I forget.'

She lowered her face. 'I wasn't beauty queen.' She came from Muranovo, thirty miles north of Moscow. 'I was born on estate of great nineteenth-century Russian poet Fyodor Tyutchev.'

'Did you study accountancy, too?'

'No,' she said.

'Poetry?'

'Physics.'

He sat back in his chair.

She smiled, slightly sorrowful. 'I'm my father—'

She was interrupted by a young woman with short blue-streaked hair holding a plate, who he knew was slightly deaf, which was why it sounded almost like a shout: 'Who ordered the baguette?'

'Me,' raising his glass. And to Katya: 'Are you hungry? Why don't we share this?'

'I can—' reaching for her square red handbag.

'No, no, I've paid already. Let this be on me.'

He broke the baguette in two and gave her half. They ate in a silence that neither seemed willing to break. Voices could be heard in the other room. Someone was saying: 'He lives in a bungalow and has a beard and all the rest of it.'

Dyer waited for her to finish eating. 'Gennady works for GAZPROM, he told me.'

'If Gennady says so, it must be true,' with dulled eyes, pushing the plate away. She tried to smile.

He said carefully: 'Do you not believe your husband's every word?'

She raised her eyebrows as if complimented, and looked past him through the open door. She kept her gaze there, lifting and dropping her glass onto the beermat in between sips, and talked about her marriage.

It was no secret in Moscow, why should it be in Oxford? She and her husband were estranged. Gennady was a beneficiary of the asset grab that characterised Vladimir Putin's Russia. Her own words seemed to bore her as she explained how he was close to Putin's inner circle, but in the process of becoming connected and wealthy he and Katya had grown apart. They rubbed along, but it was clear, from her sad expression – and from her solemn admission in an embarrassed voice that they hadn't made 'any love' in six months – that the cartilage between the bones had worn away. The sole bond keeping them together was Vasily.

Her husband, an ardent Chelsea supporter ('he has many shares'), had not been happy with how Katya had handled Vasily's demotion from the first XI. She still had a mark on the side of her neck where Gennady had expressed his frustration.

She turned her face to the lozenge of daylight pouring into the room, and now Dyer saw it.

He had thought it was a small birthmark. He felt his tongue with no saliva press against his teeth.

She bent her head and sat there, waiting.

He stares at her and feels diminished. He is aware that he is blushing. Words rise to his mouth. 'Do you want to come back for coffee?'

On her face is the stern look which means she is mulling it over. Her breasts lifted under her jersey.

'Sure.'

Chapter Twenty-six

IN THE KITCHEN, HE SWITCHED on the grinder.

Magda had left. A note beside the sink in her large child-like hand asked him to buy more Ariel washing capsules. 'Not the liquid!'

Katya had walked out this morning not wearing a coat. She stood still in the middle of the kitchen with her arms crossed, her eyes darting from the bookshelves, the photographs and pictures on the walls, the landlord's impersonal, creaking furniture, out into the patio. The magnolia tree in its half-barrel tub. On the washing line were Leandro's football socks and shirts that Magda had pegged out to dry.

The kettle boiled. She uncrossed her arms and glanced at Marvar's overcoat, which Magda had taken it upon herself to liberate from Leandro's games bag and drape over a chair, and shuddered. 'It's cold,' she murmured in her low raspy voice.

She left him pouring out the mugs, and went upstairs.

'Katya?' he called after her. 'If you're looking for the bathroom, it's down here.'

Then: 'Your coffee's ready.'

No answer.

Heart drumming against his ribcage, he climbs the brown staircarpet.

She stood in his bedroom, her back to Dyer. She had removed her jacket and put it on the bed. Hearing him enter, she lifted her hand to behind her head, unbound her hair. Shook it loose.

Taut as a bough, he said: 'Katya?'

She turned to him without a word and stepped forward – he could smell her breath, the faint whiff of pale ale – looked at him, then opened her mouth and pressed it against his.

There were fresh sheets on the bed. There had been a report on the news. The Americans were suspending themselves from the nuclear treaty, the Iranians were going mad. A boy on the towpath was talking to a skinny man with a backpack. The mist, as if it had drifted in from the nearby cemetery, was disintegrating the branches of the trees. She bent over to take off her shoes. The jersey tightened on her shoulders, and then she was pulling it up over her head.

His heart stumbled. Stretched out on her back. The shape of her breasts. Long legs apart on the sheet, the small dark-blonde triangle of hair between them. All that she had on was the silver leaf on the cord around her neck. *The innocence of this people is such that that of Adam could not have been greater.* Her mouth is hypnotic. She knows she is attractive, her effect.

She was thirty-six. Her son was listening to his history teacher, brows knitted. When she reaches up to put her hands on his chest, her breasts throw a shadow on the pillow.

Feelings don't have manners. They roll over and over. Dazedly, he sees her spread out beneath him. Her splendid behind raised, her buttocks glossy and firm, like conkers. Her throat half-turned, exciting him on. As he enters her, he knows the code to the universe, he sees it flash before him, dazzling and shining, and then fade and disappear.

She held him from behind, her pubic hair soft against his buttocks. In spite of the beer, he could smell her perfume. He turned to ask what it was. She looked at him and smiled. 'Perfume? No, I'm not wearing perfume. You must mean me …' glancing down. 'Oh, I know, it's my BB cream.'

He kissed her neck, now covered with a shimmer of perspiration, and tasted a sudden oily residue in the back of his throat, the aggressive bleachy taste of a laundry tablet. Then he realises that it's the cream, and she has applied it to camouflage the dark bruise that lies beneath her skin in the shape of a fish under water.

She shifts underneath him and runs her fingers over his back, in between his buttocks, delving. His hardness returns. She licks the tips of two fingers and slides her hand down. Gravely, he opens her legs. He is hard inside her, back on the pitch, no longer watching but playing. Soon he is kicking the ball into the sky, into the sun, her mouth against his ear: 'Now.' He kisses her shoulder, her lips. He holds her in his arms and falls abruptly asleep to the sound of bells and trains. In his history lesson, Ma Burgeon has finished telling Vasily about the first victim of the railway, the MP William Huskisson, run over in 1830 by Stephenson's steam engine.

Dyer woke to see Katya getting up from the bed. She walked on tiptoe like a ballerina, straight-backed. He listened to the tread of her bare feet down the stairs, and raised himself on one elbow.

Her underwear on the floor. A thin white slip, the colour of mist. Swallowing every light in the room.

His head feels strange, as though he's slept for some time, even though his watch says it's only three o'clock. He falls back to sleep for a bit.

Downstairs, the sound of flushing. When she reappears, she is wearing Marvar's coat like a dressing gown, with her arms thrust into its pockets.

'You have taken off phone,' she observes.

'Someone kept ringing and hanging up,' he says.

'What if it is Marvar?' she asks.

He looks at her. Her white breasts, marked in red blushes where his tongue and teeth have travelled, stand out against the green silk lining.

'You know that's his coat?' he says after a while.

'I know, I recognise,' looking down. Framed by the camel-haired lapels, her collar bones are quotation marks.

'He left it behind.'

'Maybe he wants it back.' Her eyes are misleadingly calm and clear.

'I wish.'

'You were friend of his?'

'Not really.'

She removes her hands from the pockets and sits down at the end of the bed. 'I saw you speaking to him,' caressing his ankle through the sheet.

'When was that?' He was weighing her motive.

The grey in her eyes looked darker, the same shade as her bruise, full of hidden flashing thoughts.

'That night. By the sandpit. Remember?'

'Oh, yes. We were discussing Vasily.' He said it quite decisively.

A frown screwed up her face. She turned and looked at him sharply.

'Marvar was working on fusion, no?'

He felt himself tilting. 'So I gather. I don't know much about fusion. Do *you* know about fusion?'

She was silent, tense; it was as if they had stepped together into a cave.

'It was my father's subject.' She made a dispersing gesture with her hand. 'It is said he was doing good work,' something rounding the earlier hard edges of her voice.

'Your father?'

'Rustum Marvar,' slightly huffed.

'Who told you that?'

Her eyes met his and in the light of that room he could see the strain in them. 'His professor.'

He lay back on the pillow and crossed his hands behind his head. 'I really don't know. Right now my subject is sixteenth-century Brazil. The twenty-first century can go screw itself.'

She said nothing. On her face again, that stern expression – when a noise startled her. Her breasts quivered as she twisted around. 'What's that?'

Sitting up, he listened to the snarling radiator. 'Oh, that,' and lay back. 'The heating must have come on.'

She turned her head to the wall, and he was not prepared for what she said next. 'It must be expensive, the Phoenix. For a writer.'

'It is, it is,' puzzled by this twist in the conversation.

'Where will Leandro go next?'

'Probably not where his friends are going,' he told her curved back.

'Perhaps he could be helped?'

Lifting her shoulders, she patted the overcoat like someone still wanting to check the pockets even though she had been through them already. 'Gennady's people ... they would pay many dollars to discover what Marvar knew.'

His mood had changed, in blade-sharp contrast to the previous moment. He looked out at the Oxford afternoon, not moving his gaze from the window. 'Maybe they should ask Marvar's professor. It would be cheaper.'

She shifted her buttocks on the bed. 'He knows nothing.'

Through the small window, the unflowing canal. A dog was sniffing in the mist at a rubbish bag. The light was fading. It would be time to go soon.

He could taste her cream on his tongue. 'What about Marvar's people, what about the Iranians? They might have an idea.'

'Gennady says only Marvar has this information,' in her discoloured voice.

A bicyclist pedalled slowly by. Dyer brought his eyes back into the rented room.

'Why should he think that?'

Her hands were inside the coat, running over the pale lining which had the sheen of something freshly flayed.

'The Americans. It's what they believe.'

'And your husband believes the Americans?'

She made a movement with her head. It was hard to tell what she meant. 'He believes what he knows.'

'He knows an awful lot, it sounds.'

Katya shrugged.

He reached for his shirt on the floor. Next to it, her stockings lay crumpled up like a shed skin.

'The sooner Marvar is found, the better. If you ask me.'

'Unless,' she said meditatively, turning, 'he gave the information to someone else.'

'Like who?'

He caught the undertow in her eyes. For a second, he saw Vasily's face.

'I don't know. A friend. Perhaps he left it in his coat,' sliding her hands back into the pockets. She smiled oddly. 'Perhaps he gave it to you?'

The way she looked at him. With those eyes. It seemed to Dyer that she was concentrating closely on what his answer would be. In that instant, she was a very good imitation of a pit viper.

He felt, as if someone had taken him by the elbow and steered him round, that he saw her properly for the first time. A mighty current of sadness flows through him. He remembers Vivien's words when he told her about meeting Nissa at the photographic exhibition. '*Exhilaration, my dear, is the warning of disaster.*'

Right now, he doesn't want to know if Katya is working with Gennady, or if Gennady has made her do this, or how Katya knows Whitton's most intimate thoughts, or if she slipped something into his half-pint of Old Empire while he was in the gents at the Bookbinders so that she could later search the house. Something had switched off like the TV in his boarding house on Saturday nights. From the boundless distance of six feet, she shrank and shrank until she was a small flash on a dark screen.

'No,' he joked, retrieving his underpants, wanting to cover himself, his head still spinning and groggy, 'the only thing Marvar gave me was a hangover.'

Katya stared at him intently, absorbing what he had said, and then her eyes were swimming away and she was muttering in a language that he didn't understand. She looked as if she was rewriting something inside herself. Her hardened grey eyes were embers. Something enormous was reflected in them, like the glow of a distant city at night, but she was paying no more attention to Dyer than if he had been a games bag of wet muddy socks or the dead bluebottle on the carpet that had escaped Magda's hoover.

'We'd better go and fetch our boys,' he said.

She pulled off Marvar's coat and picked up her jersey and underwear and started putting them back on.

He dropped her at the school gates, waiting for her to get out before he drove on to find a parking space.

'Bye, then.'

'Bye.'

They didn't kiss.

It was one of Nissa's quarrels with him, how he said goodbye without operatics.

Chapter Twenty-seven

DYER DROVE TWICE DOWN CHADLINGTON Road before he found a parking spot. He sat in the car, wound down the window.

The shock. The first sensation is numbness. Then a sharp, burning sear.

It was biting his insides. Her pale nipples, that spectral coat, her eyes hating him. Lacerated, he no longer feels transparent; she had hurled a stone into him – everything was shattered. Beneath the fractured surface, shapes dart off.

'The brutal fact is, my dear, she's taken you for the most monumental ride,' is what his aunt would have said.

The rasp in her voice like virgin snow. He had thought that she liked him; she had never said that she didn't. Their interactions were friendly before he met Marvar, so that must have been genuine.

How badly he'd underestimated her. He had failed to recognise the warning in her eyes until she stood naked before him with her hands buried in the depths of Marvar's pockets. Never had he received such a look, it was a horse-kick. He realised, then, how utterly she'd bamboozled him.

Of more urgent importance: had Katya believed Dyer when he told her that all Marvar had given him was a hangover?

'You English. I only believe when you are joking.'

Suddenly, his fate, Leandro's too, seemed to hinge on a stupid quip.

Dyer couldn't see Leandro's bicycle propped against the wall.

He looked up at the clock. He was late, the playground deserted.

She must have collected Vasily and left.

'Have you seen Leandro?' he went over to ask Mr Tanner, who since Tuesday had planted himself in a visible position by the gate.

'Wasn't he on his bike?'

If so, Mr Tanner said, he was bound to have left by the exit on Phoenix Lane. He avoided any reference to Samir or to Samir's father.

Dyer drove quickly home, his mind making odd leaps. Under the lethal stimulation of Katya, he had taken his eye off Leandro. Brushing aside the legality of speaking on a mobile phone while driving, he called Leandro as he turned sharply into St Margaret's Road. His panic intensified to receive no answer.

He parked beneath the church tower, and jogged along the pavement.

At the far end of Canal Street, his next-door neighbour was stooped over a brown paper bag. Its bottom had ripped, spilling her shopping into the road. The spectacle of Paula scrambling after cans of Co-op beans and pineapple chunks pulled Dyer up short.

Against his every wish to press on and check if Leandro had arrived back safely, he stopped to assist Paula, gathering up the scattered cans, and then carrying them in his cradled arms round the corner, into her kitchen. It smelled of air-freshener and the skirting was painted in blue veins to look like marble. He was set to leave, anxious to be home, when he noticed, through the nylon lace curtains, an un-familiar car.

The curtains were translucent like the wings of a damsel; he didn't need to open them. There was a man seated in a parked brown Skoda. He leaned forward far enough for Dyer to see that he was watching his house, but not far enough to see Dyer.

Paula crumpled up the torn bag and dropped it into the bin.

'How did Leandro's history test go?'

'I haven't heard. Listen, Paula, can I climb over your fence? I've locked myself out.'

Seconds later, he was jumping down into the patio and pushing his way past the magnolia, under the washing line, his face slapping against damp socks and shirts, to the French window.

Inside, a light was on. Dyer tapped the glass.

Nothing stirred.

He tapped again.

Silence.

He tried the window. Unlocked.

'Leandro!' he yelled, even as he let himself in. 'Leandro!' His voice reverberated through the house.

There was no answer.

He ran across the room.

The kitchen seemed as it was when he bundled Katya out less than an hour before. Two mugs of coffee by the sink, undrunk. His shoulder bag on the hook in the hall, doubtless filleted by Katya when she came downstairs. She was unlikely to have had the chance to search Leandro's games bag, though. Magda had tucked this out of sight into a gap beside the washing machine.

Dyer pulled out the blue bag, unzipped it. His laptop was inside, along with Bunting's poems, and, right at the bottom, the transparent sandwich bag in which Marvar's little green folder bobbed rather like a tropical fish. Dyer looked for a moment at the folder as if he had been watching it since a little boy and it was a float that he was waiting to see disappear under the water.

With tender care, he brought out the folder, opened it. The false yellow post-it note was still there.

Packing everything back into the games bag, he hared up the stairs and raced down the corridor, opening doors.

Spread out like a skinned carcass on the permafrost, Marvar's overcoat was on his bed where Katya had discarded it.

Dyer stepped across the landing into Leandro's bedroom. He stood by the window and, keeping out of sight, glanced down.

A dog barked as darkness fell on the street. Over the canal came the sound of a train. The brown Skoda was parked opposite, the lean face inside outlined by the glow from a mobile phone.

Dyer thought: *That's what they do in Brazil if they want to roll you – they watch you till they know the pattern on your wallpaper, the colour of your shirts. And then, when you least expect it, they strike.*

Had someone kidnapped Leandro?

He sat on the bed, his hands fumbling as he redialled his son's number. In his impatience, he left out a digit, and had to start again.

Nissa smiled down at him while he waited for the purr of the ringing tone. He pressed the phone to his ear and listened. One, two, three, four times.

Again, no one picked up.

Mad thoughts of ringing the police, Updark even, were interrupted by the sound of the front door slamming.

Downstairs, Leandro was surprised to be enfolded by his father in a very tight hug.

'Hey, Dad! What are you doing?'

'When did you get back?'

'About twenty minutes ago.'

'Where have you been?'

'I popped out to the corner shop,' and held up the Match Attax cards to which he had decided to treat himself after all his hard work. 'Where've *you* been?'

'Helping Paula. I'm sorry I missed you. I was running late...'

'I called you,' said Leandro. 'Mrs Updark lent me her phone. I don't know what happened, but it was weird.'

'I've changed my number. Here, let me give you the new one.'

He wrote it down and handed it to Leandro, whose perplexed expression hadn't changed.

'Dad, the landline wasn't working either. Magda had unplugged it...'

'That was me.'

Leandro frowned. 'I thought it was Magda. Oh, and she didn't make your bed.'

'She made yours,' said Dyer, not wanting to open that can, and walked over to the fridge and looked inside.

Four bare shelves glared back. He hadn't bought dinner. He hadn't bought anything.

'Dad...'

He tensed. What was Leandro going to say? '*Are you having an affair?*'

'My history test—'

'And I want to hear how it went.'

Dyer closed the fridge and turned, he had remembered his promise. 'Why don't you tell me all about it at Peppers Burgers?'

Less than a quarter of an hour later, after Leandro had changed out of his school clothes, and both of them had taken a shower, Dyer called in a sharp voice as his son headed towards the front door: 'No, Leandro, wait! This way.' He opened the French window and stepped into the patio. 'Let's invite Paula. She'll want to hear, too.'

The brown Skoda was no longer there when the three of them returned, shortly before nine o'clock. Paula said good-bye with a little bow. Her husband had been a submariner; he had taught her not to waste words. 'Thank you, both. What a nice surprise. You're welcome to climb over my fence whenever.' She was glad the key had been found, though.

Dyer unlocked the front door. He had left the lights on downstairs. He came into the kitchen. Quick look round. All in order.

After Leandro disappeared to his bedroom 'to read', but most likely to play Fifa 18, Dyer took out his laptop and put it on the kitchen table. Ever since he'd dropped her off, he had been champing to look up Katya Petroshenko.

It was a risk, his searches could be traced. Yet as with Marvar, he might raise more suspicion if he showed no interest.

Not knowing how to say anything in Russian, not even hello, he typed Katya's name into his browser. A sweep of Russian websites yielded one hit: a reference to Gennady Petroshenko, associate director of GAZPROM (m. 2004 Katya 1 s).

Without her maiden name, Dyer was not going to discover more. Frustrated, he replayed their conversation in his head. She had been more miserly with her details than Marvar.

He went to the loo, then tried again.

In the forgotten footage, a phrase came back. *'I'm my father'* – whatever that meant – was virtually the only information she'd given away. That, and a town near Moscow which wasn't Murmansk.

She had mentioned a poet. Tyutchev. Dyer looked him up. Feodor Tyutchev. From Muranovo. That was it.

It was a swing in the dark. Dyer called up scientists born in Muranovo. And straight away there he is, Vasily Lavramarov, b. 1941. Looking just like his grandson, like Katya.

Until the moment he saw her father's face, Dyer refused to believe what he had already guessed. But his doubts evaporated when he read that the atomic physicist Vasily Lavramarov was a member of the 1969 nuclear fusion delegation which had been responsible for building the T-3 tokamak. His old newspaper might have demanded a second source; Dyer needed no further verification. Katya was a child of nuclear fusion. She must have been spying on Marvar since the day she arrived in Oxford, and reporting back to Mr Putin's chum, Gennady.

Dyer didn't know how to feel. In his pride, he hadn't wanted to believe it was all a ruse, her admiration for Leandro, her hurt over Vasily, her attraction to Dyer. The fact that she was sitting seductively in a pub by herself at lunchtime.

She had observed him talking with Marvar, and, after that, wearing Marvar's coat, and in concert with Gennady had taken the decision that Dyer was a stone that needed to be turned.

Once she had decided that Dyer knew nothing, he was what he said, a washed-up journo desperate to find relevance in a sixteenth-century Portuguese colony in Latin America, then he was history, as unnecessary and pathetic to her as his subject.

Dyer closed his laptop. Yet it didn't stop the roar in his head. The din was like the tune of that homeless accordionist, the same questions going round and round and round.

If he was to believe Katya, the Russians weren't holding Marvar. But neither were the Americans, because Updark wouldn't be looking for him if so. And nor were the Iranians – if indeed it was the Iranians who had tried to grab Dyer. Who, then? The Israelis? The Saudis? The Chinese?

Or was this a wild-goose chase, and Marvar remained at large?

Dyer didn't want to admit to himself that Marvar might be dead. His essential innocence could not be violated, somehow it would endure. Then he thought of the overcoat upstairs on his bed, like the hide of a hunted mammoth.

But whether Marvar had been captured or killed or was treading the moors around Fusedale was somehow irrelevant. The scrap of paper that he had buried for Dyer to find had made him more alive.

Marvar's worn face, the pain in his eyes, had affected him. Dyer might be impotent to protect Marvar, yet in respect of his post-it note he was not powerless. Marvar's strange conviction that Dyer would know what to do with this had motivated every stubborn and perverse atom in Dyer's nature to safeguard the information that Marvar had risked his life – and his family's – to put into Dyer's hand.

Dyer didn't for one moment believe that he himself wasn't in danger as well. From the instant that he lifted the Ziploc sandwich bag out of the sandpit, a persistent fear had stalked him that he never expected to feel in Oxford. The pull in his gut when walking at night, the only white face, through the *favela*, past the flickering gauntlet of milk-tin braziers, followed by eyes that tracked his smallest movement.

His fear was a hook that dragged him through the water. He couldn't shake it off. Even if Updark and Katya believed that he had no further light to shed on Marvar's breakthrough, behind them other silhouettes – malevolent, dark – flared up and vanished before he could identify them.

Who was telephoning the house? Who had left that neat scratch mark on his car like a hieroglyph? Who were the men in the Passat? Who was the man watching in the Skoda with the serrated intensity of a shoeshine boy, his lean face ghoulishy underlit from his phone?

Those who needed convincing that Marvar hadn't given his algorithm for whatever odd reason to Dyer ...

By appointing him custodian, Marvar had exposed Dyer to a hounding pack of invisible but ferocious savages who, were they ever to suspect Dyer of deceiving them, would stop at nothing to bathe their spears in his blood and in his son's blood too.

Leandro's lava lamp was off when Dyer went upstairs. In the dark, he peeped out between the curtains, and saw that the Skoda had not returned. He kissed his sleeping child goodnight, closed the door gently, then crossed the corridor into his bedroom and switched on the light. Marks on the furrowed sheets triggered a quick memory. But something was wrong.

Marvar's coat is not on the bed.

He runs downstairs, three steps at a time.

On the hook in the hallway, Dyer's leather shoulder bag. Beside the washing machine, Leandro's blue canvas games bag from which he had retrieved his laptop less than half an hour earlier. He opens it, rummages inside. His fingers pull out Bunting's *Collected Poems* and the Ziploc sandwich bag with the green folder.

The folder is empty. The float has gone under.

They were professionals who had known what to look for. While Dyer and Paula ate their chicken burgers and listened to Leandro enthuse about how Nelson's fleet, sailing perpendicularly, had carved a breach in Villeneuve's horizontal line of ships, someone had entered the house and gone over it with the finest toothpick.

Dyer totters, unbalanced, across the orange tiled floor and slumps onto the sofa, causing its cheap wood frame to squeal.

Not simultaneously, but almost, he experiences a pang for Marvar's missing overcoat, before relief floods through him. The horrible hook had been yanked out of his mouth. He wasn't free, yet, but the tension had slackened, he had secured a breathing space.

For the moment, he and Leandro were safe.

Because whoever had stolen the coat had also taken one of Marvar's two spare post-it notes.

A long time ago, Dyer had read that when being pursued by an elephant you must shed an article of clothing in the hope that the animal will stop in its tracks and attack it. You have then a chance of gaining ground. To throw his anonymous pursuers off the scent, this is what Dyer had done: he had left them another post-it note covered with abracadabra.

They would have their energies consumed in cracking Dyer's code. He had concocted his deliberately misleading algorithm out of a verse by Basil Bunting, substituting letters for numbers, and introducing a few capital letters from the two last stanzas of Bunting's 1932 poem 'Chomei at Toyama'. Whether or not Dyer believed in Rustum Marvar's claim for fusion – and the stubbornmost part of him resisted – his own formula, based on a Baconian code picked up during his stint as a postgraduate, was no more nonsensical in his eyes than Marvar's original. Plus it had the merit of being based on something that Dyer could understand.

> *I have renounced the world;*
> *have a saintly*
> *appearance.*
>
> *I do not enjoy being poor,*
> *I've a passionate nature.*
> *My tongue*
> *clacked a few prayers.*

It was the poem he had been reading in Rio when the hand of a young woman touched his shoulder.

Chapter Twenty-eight

THE FIRST WEEK OF MARCH. Walks to school. The streets are sniffing spring.

In the Bon Croissant, they are sharing scurrilities: 'Dyer's carrying on with Katya.'

'He can't be, her son bullied his son.'

'No kid gets dumped by his mother like that.'

'She's got twins with someone else who are going to Summer Fields.'

'*Did* he work for the *Daily News*?'

'I've never read anything he's written. He once gave me his book when he came for dinner. Forgot to sign it, though. I've got it somewhere.'

'I love this ice cream.'

In the lush littoral of Summertown, conversation turned again to Samir. His father had apparently taken him back to

Iran. His mother was ill. An Updark story, something cooked up with Crotty.

Someone else said, finishing her turmeric latte: 'Do you think there's going to be war in the Middle East?'

The Israeli prime minister in his most outraged attack on Iran had told the BBC that the government in Tehran posed the 'greatest threat to our world'. He repeated his promise of a fortnight before, that Israel would 'not allow Iran's regime to put a noose of terror around our neck'.

Samantha Puckey, rushing to her appointment at Cannelle Medispa, is more alarmed about the rising sea level. She is thinking of her holiday cottage on the Suffolk coast. 'Instead of shielding us,' quoting a new report by the UN Intergovernmental Panel on Climate Change, 'the world may turn around and become our enemy.'

Chapter Twenty-nine

IN THE ANXIOUS HOURS AFTER the break-in, Dyer walked down Ward Road, searching for a house number, when a black car pulled up beside him.

'You haven't been answering your phone.'

Dyer took a second to recognise the mottled face.

'I've been at the library, in fact I'm heading there now.'

'Let me give you a lift,' putting away his headphones.

'I'd prefer to walk.'

'I don't care what you want to do,' Updark said severely. 'You're going to come with me now, this minute. Get in.'

In the back of the car, Updark said forbiddingly: 'You know, John, people add up the faults of those who keep them waiting,' and slapped down a book on the seat between them.

Dyer recognised it at once. He felt his chest heave.

Updark opened the cover and rotated it so that Dyer could read the inscription.

'Your handwriting?'

'It is.' Dyer picked up the book. 'Where did you get this?'

'The headmaster. Someone found it beside the sandpit, I'm told.'

Dyer recalled the Audi parked outside Crotty's house.

Dully, he read: *To Rustum Marvar, who may have solved everything.* With his signature. And a date.

What a flat-footed inscription. Even after drinking all that sauvignon, he had been aware of what Marvar faced losing. Marvar hadn't solved anything, really.

'Notice the date?' said Updark.

'I do.'

'Which does now – officially – make you the last person to have clapped eyes on him.'

Dyer closed the book. He was conscious of Updark's gaze. 'It was a present,' he heard himself say.

'Not been in touch, I take it?'

'No,' said Dyer. He has to assume that Updark knows his every email, telephone call.

'What does it mean, "solved everything"?' Updark pulled out his cuff to cover the plaster on his wrist. 'What, like the answer to one of Slimy's fractions? Sounds like he told you something interesting, Basil.'

'It was a metaphor.'

'A metaphor,' said Updark coolly.

'He'd been having problems with his son and had sorted them out.'

'That,' Updark snorted, 'is the biggest load of rocking-horse manure. I could spread it on my allotment for a year.'

'Well, do what you like with it. That's what he said,' Dyer insisted.

'You know, John, if there was a degree for stubbornness, you'd get a double-first. You're irritatingly like Will Ladislaw. Born to trouble as the sparks fly upwards.'

Updark had been listening to *Middlemarch* on tape. The vinegary effects of those nineteenth-century conversations, like a tennis game in which the stakes were life or death, had served to remind him of the culture that his vocation was dedicated to preserve. He found that the novel nourished his journey to and from work, recalibrated him. 'It's taken me a whole year to get through. Interestingly, I've just hit the epilogue. There's a mention of you, Basil – "a plant which had flourished wonderfully on a murdered man's brains".'

Dyer derived some comfort from Updark's hostility. It suggested that Updark hadn't found out more. If his men had taken the fake post-it note, he'd be asking about that, not about the inscription, wouldn't he?

Beside him, Updark was still drawing the cork on the conundrum posed by Dyer's book. 'I mean, to leave it there, a present from you ... Couldn't have been your prose?' he said cruelly. Then: 'What do you suppose he was doing by the sandpit?'

'Building castles. Wishing he was beside the seaside. Wishing he was reading something else.' He turned, fizzing, to Updark. 'Why, what do you think he was doing?'

Updark's mouth opened like a trout sipping on a fly. 'I don't know.'

'Do you think he's been murdered?' said Dyer.

'No. At least, I'm not sure.'

'You still suspect the Iranians?'

Updark's hard watchful eyes were unreflective. 'Iran is the obvious culprit. But we're not picking up any chatter.'

'What about the threats coming out of Tehran?'

'Nothing more than hot air, steam.'

'Steam powered the "Rocket",' said Dyer.

Updark's smile was frosty. 'Do not stir up Lake Camarina, Basil. I don't need a science lesson—' He looked about to say more, but his jacket pocket all at once was playing Bach. He pulled out his phone. After identifying the caller – 'Sorry, I need to take this' – he listened to the voice at the other end, his gaze never wavering from Dyer, who had to accept that this was not perhaps the right occasion to ask advice about a dog, or even to broach the subject of his son's friendship with Updark's daughter.

After a while, Updark said: 'No, not a dickybird.' Then, in a grudging tone: 'OK, Ralph, you can have his scalp, but you'll find it covered with one of those spongy hair transplants that needs a monthly visit to the Radcliffe to get rid of the bacteria.'

He rang off. 'Friend Cubbage,' he explained. 'The Americans want to grill Professor Whitton.' Dyer did not need to know this; even so, out of some residual sentiment, Updark had confided in him.

'It was Cubbage who overruled Whitton, as no doubt you've guessed. Cubbage is adamant that information recorded by the Clarendon's cutting-edge new detector can't be faked, any more than it can be deleted – which is what Marvar, I'm told, tried to do.'

Dyer waited to see if he was going to say more. 'Could the Americans have information they're not sharing?'

Updark twisted his face. 'There is one respect in which America has changed since the 1950s. They have a great deal of trouble keeping anything secret. Their national character is to tell you everything they know. My overriding impression is that the Americans are still as much in the dark as we are about *if*, or *how*, Marvar might have achieved fusion, and also about where he might be even as we speak.'

Updark slid the phone back into his jacket and from the same pocket brought out his spiral notebook and opened it.

'Oh, I wanted to ask you about this.'

He read out: '"Ordinarily he took the train." Now what does that sentence mean? Hissop reckons it might be a code.'

This revelation confirmed what Dyer suspected. While he was eating Lorna's flapjacks in Eynsham, Updark's men had indeed been searching his house. But could it have been them also who seized the decoy that Dyer had planted in the green folder? About this, he was still undecided.

Updark looked fully at Dyer with his cold eyes. 'Why are you smiling?'

'It was a dream I had.'

'A dream,' Updark nodded. 'A dream,' he repeated, as if in another context he might like how it sounded.

Dyer gave him a nudge. 'Come on, Lionel, you must have had dreams when you imagine you've been given the answer to everything. I woke myself up and wrote it down. As you see, it was pitiful nonsense.' Like the formula based on Basil Bunting's poem 'Chomei at Toyama'. And Dyer allows himself another smile. To picture Updark, Hissop and Lorna, that roomful of code-people, crowded around a screen, their frowns.

The muscles in Updark's jaw relax. 'Speaking of dreams. That Russian mother, Katya. See much of her, do you? I gather your sons have got over their spat.'

'They have. And no, I don't see much of her.'

Updark looked out of the window as if summer had come to the Parks and he was watching a game of cricket and Dyer's reply was of no more consequence than the sound of the Audi's wheels bearing them towards St Giles. 'I can't say I'm surprised. "It's quite hard to trust a nation that is prepared to cheat at mixed curling,"' which sounded familiar, until Dyer realised that Updark was quoting Dyer's own words back at him, not from a previous conversation they'd had, but from a text that Dyer had sent to Leandro after the bullying resolution. 'Little piece of Moroccan advice, Basil, that our American friends feel Professor Whitton might also benefit from. He who has fire in his heart has smoke in his head.' He let the silence linger. 'And here's another. A poor man is never believed.'

The car had stopped. They were outside the Taylorian.

'Off you go to your library,' Updark said, snapping shut his notebook. 'Just don't go planning a trip up the Amazon, that's all. We need to keep in touch.'

Dyer's hand was already on the door handle. He got out, shaken. Why was Updark referring to his Brazilian research? Was Dyer wrong to have put his trust in the librarian, her guarantee? Had Updark discovered Madrugada's book?

He closed the car door, and was about to walk away when he stopped and tapped the polarised window.

Updark's features unscrolled into view. He pushed his pink face to the light. It appeared still to be suffering from what Dyer's book dealer in Rio had once referred to as scattered insect damage.

'Thought of something?'

'I forgot to ask,' said Dyer. 'How's the patch-testing? Have they found any suspect agents?'

Updark, disregarding his tone, answered in a deadpan voice. 'They wondered if it might be an eczema. They've given me a steroid, but as you can see it hasn't solved it.'

Chapter Thirty

OBSERVED ONLY BY THE COUPLE in the painting, Dyer sits down in the French and German reading room, and opens the book. The plunk of his heart.

Still there.

Dyer puts Madrugada's monograph back in the stacks, his faith immediately restored in the system which has promised to look after it for five more days, and returns to Ward Road.

He walks past the house where he was standing when Updark's car drew up, as if catching him red-handed with Rougetel on one of their illicit outings into town, until he finds the front door with 'No. 8' on it, and rings the bell. He waits, rings again. No answer.

Desperate to remove Leandro from Oxford, Dyer went home and spent the morning making plans for the exeat. He was not going to let his son out of his sight. He had taken him to school, and was there waiting for him when the bell sounded, signalling the end of lessons.

The first moments inside the gate were like the first moments in the *favela*. Dyer noted the activity, of which he was always on the edge, the boys and girls flowing out of their classrooms. The playground acted as a sound-box. Shouts reached his ears, then words – about teachers, prep, games, bun-break. They were exchanges that Dyer knew by heart, like lines from the *Phoenix Book of Verse*. He was formed in this echo chamber, now it had received him back.

On this Thursday afternoon, he felt that he was walking into a dream. He saw it and he did not see it. Time passed in a strange way. He noticed details that he never normally recognised, alert to see if whoever had taken the false post-it note had swallowed the lure – and therefore had no need to harass Dyer further about it.

The head girl was pulling the rope. On the roof of the Rink, the bell rang, ding dong.

Dyer cast his eyes about for his son. He couldn't pick him out, and then the crowd thinned, and he saw Leandro standing beside a boy in his class. They were talking to an adult, who lifted his head at Dyer's approach: a lean Asian man in an ochre suit, with the chiselled features of a minor actor.

'Who's that?' taking Leandro by the hand. He glanced back. Something about that face. In a dashboard light.

'Oh, that's Hui's bodyguard.'

Hui was Chinese, a plump, polite boy with the slightly glazed look of someone who is good at maths. Leandro had once brought him back to St Barnabas Street.

'Hui's invited me to go paintballing.'

'When?'

'Tomorrow.'

'Well, that's too bad,' Dyer said in a firm voice. 'I've made other plans.' He had a sudden, chest-tightening recollection that Hui's father worked for a telecoms giant in Beijing.

Leandro climbs into the car and says nothing until Dyer turns right on Bardwell Road.

'Why are you going this way?'

'I was trying a shortcut to see whether this is quicker.' And to shake off the white Renault Clio that might have been tailing them.

He turns left into St Margaret's Road, and the car shoots past.

His shortcut brings them out near Jamaica Road. Dyer slows down behind a bus. He puts the car into neutral, waiting for the passengers to board, and glances over at Leandro.

Beside him, his son looks as lost as a dog that runs after birds.

'What?' says Dyer.

'Dad ... you know how you changed your telephone number? I wonder if I should change my password at school ...' And out it comes, how Mr Tanner had sent an email with an attachment, asking Leandro to look at his report, but when Leandro clicked on the attachment it wasn't what he expected. 'I've been getting messages ever since.'

'What sort of messages?'

'Weird stuff, telling me my device has been hacked, they can see everything on my screen ...'

'It must be a malware,' Dyer tries to reassure him. A similar email had arrived on his laptop from someone claiming to have infected Dyer's router with a program called Spyware, but he'd ignored it.

'No, no, Dad, you don't get it. They know the last game I played on Xbox, what I have on my wall, they even ... Dad, has someone been using my room?'

Dyer had not told him about Marvar staying the night. At the time, Leandro hadn't seemed to notice, all his focus trained on Trafalgar.

'Why do you ask?'

'It's crazy. They want to get hold of this person. They'll leave me alone if I tell them how. I literally have no idea what they're talking about.'

Ahead of them, the bus juddered off.

'It's just some nerd,' said Dyer, putting the car into gear. 'Some sick nerd.' Yet it was he who felt sick. 'I'll ring Mr Tanner when we get home,' he promised. 'We'll ask him to change your password.'

As Dyer turned left into Jamaica Road, Vasily sprang into view, spinning a yellow football on his finger while he waited for the security gate to open.

They both spotted him at once. Leandro's instinct was to slide down in his seat, so that when Vasily looked over he saw only Dyer – who was thinking: *Where's your mother?*

'Hey, I thought you guys were getting on better,' said Dyer, after they had driven past.

'We are,' from his reclining position.

'Leandro—'

'Scrape out.'

'Scrape?'

Leandro laughed at Dyer's expression. 'You don't understand, do you?' sitting up. 'Everything's fine, Dad.'

Dyer had hoped the bullying incident was behind them. The airing of it had brought the matter to a head and popped it, yet the possibility of re-infection was always there. But maybe that defined parenthood. Dyer couldn't protect his son from everything, and at this moment Vasily ranked low on the list of imminent threats.

About Vasily's mother, Dyer felt a haphazard contrition.

His remorse was merely lust's dessert, his aunt would have joined Updark in reminding him. He was able to recognise that now. Whatever had fogged up his view of Katya Petroshenko was gone.

Even so, Katya had exerted a sort of hold on Dyer. When he saw her next day, he didn't have much time to go through complicated contortions to avoid her. She was shepherding Vasily from the playground. He looked at her in her lavender cashmere (did she wear any other kind of jersey?) and recalled with a shudder how she had potentially tried to poison him. She showed no curiosity on recognising Dyer. She gave him a quenched look, then opened wide her large grey eyes at Mr Tanner, ostensibly fascinated by his plans for the upcoming long weekend.

PART THREE

Chapter Thirty-one

A SPRAWLING COUNTRY HOUSE IN Lancashire outside the village of Browsholme. Posters of the Great Northern Railway on striped wallpaper. Logs burning inside a marble fireplace, and the River Hodder murmuring over stones in the darkness below.

Tonight's dinner is smoked trout, lamb and Argentine merlot, and a lemonade for Leandro.

A cancellation has brought them to this warm dining room. Dyer had borrowed Paula's mobile to make the booking. To begin with, he was told that the hotel was full for a wedding party. Then, on Thursday afternoon, Paula rang his doorbell. 'They've called back.' A room had come free. Plus she had four Amazon packages for him.

He was careful not to inform anyone. Updark had never said to him that he couldn't leave Oxford. Dyer had trusted Paula alone with the secret of where he was taking Leandro in fulfilment of a long-standing promise made on a yellow sandy beach nearly six thousand miles way.

They departed on Friday afternoon, four hours up the M6 and over the fells through the Trough of Bowland, between unfenced green hillsides and sheep grazing beside a stream. Dyer worried that the Beetle might not complete the journey after an orange light beneath the mileometer started flashing. Leandro leafed in vain through the manual, but the light went off after Dunsop Bridge, and shortly before eight they arrived at the Inn at Browsholme.

He had to be patient, and the fishing would be good for that. The Hodder was one of the rivers on which Dyer had learned to cast a fly – when two years older than Leandro. As well, he was familiar with the inn.

Dyer's surge of relief mingled with nostalgia lasts through the meal. Gold flames dance in the grate as though the fire has never gone out.

Thirty years before, on one of their last outings together, Dyer had sat in this dining room opposite his grief-stricken father, in an unspoken truce not to talk about his mother – who had been born near here, in Clitheroe, and a portion of whose cremated remains they had brought with them in a marmalade jar. The atmosphere, like the decor, had not changed. Blink and it could be the same tea arriving in a heavy silver pot with a scalding handle. Only the absence of an ashtray would have made his chain-smoking father twist in his seat.

No other anglers are staying. Aside from Dyer and Lean-dro, a subdued group at the far end are the only ones dining.

After finishing his tea, Dyer sees his son to their riverside room on the second floor, and then comes back downstairs for a nightcap.

In the bar, a grizzled local with a brackeny beard was talk-ing to one of the group – distracted-looking, clean-shaven, from his accent an American – about how to preserve the grouse moor against hen harriers.

In memory of his father, Dyer ordered an Armagnac. The young barman who poured it had washed his hands, and the ends of his cuffs were dark with dampness.

Dyer took his glass into the deserted dining room and sat by the fire. An unrecognisable odour that was familiar came off the walls and blended with the woodsmoke and the smell of Armagnac. Being here with Leandro returned him to boy-hood. He stared into the flames.

A light rain was falling when they set out next morning, cov-ering with a grey veil the sun that was shining that moment over Rio. The meadow hadn't been mown and was a struggle to walk through in new wellingtons. Butterbur like dock leaves, and tall grass on the bank.

Their destination was the weir – a calm elbow of river in a dip, with a flat shore of brown pebbles narrowing into a patch of ruffled water, and stepping stones beyond.

'We'll start you off on grayling,' he told Leandro. The Hodder was a good river for grayling.

Earlier in the rain, they had practised casting on the narrow front lawn. Along with his new boots, Dyer had forked out to buy Leandro a two-piece monofilament rod. Leandro was boyishly delighted with it, but for his induction Dyer insisted that Leandro try out his father's longer split cane.

He stood in the top of the pool at Leandro's side and reminded him to treat the rod as a lever. 'See how there's a sweetness to it, the way the line blossoms back...' It was a load off his mind that Marvar had not damaged the seventy-year-old bamboo when tripping over it.

Once Leandro had attempted a few casts, Dyer tied on a Kite's Imperial size 14.

'To catch a grayling, you use a small fly and bend it out.' Dyer heard his father's tobacco-scented voice in his as he explained to Leandro how grayling had their own way of feeding. 'They come up from the river bed and seize the fly in a different motion to trout, who attack it parallel and turn their head.' He handed the rod to his son.

Leandro made a number of false casts before letting the line out with a splash. He snagged his next cast in weeds. Dyer waded out to retrieve it. 'Don't despair, be patient, you can't learn it all in a day,' and reminded Leandro of the tangles he'd got into on the rugby pitch.

'Try over there at forty-five degrees. Remember to strip in fast – and strike as soon as you feel something.'

Hours passed. By the time the rain had stopped, Leandro was casting better. He was fairly positive that he had felt two tugs.

They ate a late lunch on the bank, sandwiches provided by the hotel. It was already mid-afternoon, a breeze was stirring the tall damp grass. A flock of doves settled on the top of a tree and flew off, flapping like pages in the wind.

Lunch over, Leandro leaped to his feet – impatient to try out his carbon rod. Dyer set this up. Then, after watching his son, he left him by the stepping stones and walked upstream with the split cane, to a long beat in shadow under the trees, just far enough away to still have Leandro in sight. He wanted to be on his own for a while, take stock.

After a morning on the river, Dyer no longer had the insidious sense of being watched which had oppressed him continually since Rustum Marvar stayed the night. Leandro, too, seemed calmer. Mr Tanner had acted fast in letting him choose a new password to access the school's computer system; on Dyer's advice, Leandro took a line from "The Prelude", and the menacing emails had immediately stopped.

Away from Oxford, Dyer was able to focus with greater clarity – in a manner not possible before – and think about what to do with Marvar's post-it note.

Three more days, was the deadline he had set himself. The library book was reserved until the following Tuesday, and then Dyer needed to make a decision. Did he leave the algorithm folded inside the last chapter for an unknown researcher to find – and inevitably throw away? Did he choose a new book to slip Marvar's information into, and then another, until he ran out of books? Or did he find some other person and press it into their palm?

The deadline was utterly subjective, of course, a contrived zero hour of no more significance than one of the cracks in the pavement that Dyer hopped over, yet that superstitious side of him was treating it as one of the most vital assignments of his life.

Dyer looked to the Hodder to provide an answer.

Trapped behind rocks and fallen branches on the water's edge was a band of detritus and foam. Dyer shifted his gaze to the middle of the wide stream and followed it towards the hills. The river had wound through this valley for as long as there were people in it. From its bank, he and his father had tumbled his mother's ashes into the ripples. For an intense moment, he experienced the thrill of being absorbed into this landscape, tethered.

A goosander exploded from the reeds, dripping water onto the surface. Dyer waited, deciding what lure to tie on. More of his father's words came back as he leafed through his fly book that one of Updark's men had turned upside down. '*All you need is a piece of pheasant's tail and some copper wire, preferably plum brown in colour from an old transistor radio, and some ochre strands of wool.* His father hadn't been living in the days of laptops and mobile phones, or data sniffers.

Anywhere else, he can't picture his father so clearly. Only on the riverbank does he return, in the dogdays after his mother's death, cross-legged in the grass in a blue felt hat, smoking a cigarette lit with another, his watery green eyes and index finger raised at the sound of martins swooping in the clear sky above, talking in a rheumy voice about male songbirds.

From his father, Dyer had discovered how to fish. How to tie a knot and lick the line, what fly to use, where to look. The trick of how to cast by tucking a bible under his arm. On the Hodder and then on other rivers and lakes – the Itchen, Ullswater, the Lune, the Nadder – his father taught him patience and respect, and that the only way to succeed in the water was to be unnoticeable. To have any chance of catching a fish so alarmable as the trout, his father had impressed on him, you had to blend in with your surroundings, take on their pace, distil yourself into a still and silent shadow until you were indistinguishable from the trout.

It was a lesson that Dyer had tried to apply to his present situation in order to throw his hunters off his scent.

Catching the trout was only part of it, though. Fishing sharpened your memory and perception, and allowed you to see connections that might otherwise have drifted by unnoticed. Later, Dyer carried its lessons into journalism. As a cub reporter, he discovered that almost everything about fly fishing, from his selection of a fly to his method of casting the line, had this in common with a line of prose: it could not hide his character – although, paradoxically, everything condensed towards trying to suppress that character.

Above all, he learned that even the smallest grayling lifted flashing from the water could stand as a true image, a true sentence, the scrap, as it were, of a greater truth. A muscle of light and agitated life that connected the angler to the universe.

Athough he kept his father's rod in the hall as a standing reminder of something he intended to do, Dyer had not fished in England for years. He had fished the Piabanha near Petrópolis, the Paraná further north, and the Amazon – from sturgeon-sized *peixe*, whose each pearly scale was the size of a woman's purse, to tiny blue hatchet fish, as if a kingfisher had dived underwater and shattered. But he had hardly picked up a rod since Astrud's death, and not once to fish with a fly.

He hesitated over an elk-hair caddis before selecting a white Klinkhammer, and tied it on. As on his last outing to the Hodder, he squirmed along the bank: this impatient, messy, blind, noisy form a crushing argument in his own person against the qualities needed to catch a fish. His aim this afternoon was simple, as when he first came here as a teenager. To untangle himself into becoming what normally he was not. And so achieve that meditative state in which his mind was carried forward by the flow of the stream – until it was both cleansed and primed to make connections; to strike, to hook.

He stood on a rock and cast upstream. It was difficult to distinguish his white Klinkhammer from the bubbles and foam. He had to raise the rod and drag the fly back so that it lay on the surface. *'The secret is concentration. Brain, muscle, ear, eye have to have coordination. You can't teach that.'* Among the superstitions that his father had passed down was his belief that fishing was about concentrating on the fly until it took you into another world.

Dyer cast again, like a prayer. With every cast he was dropping a line into the unknown in order to reach out and connect. Until the moment arrived when, instead of a white dot bobbing between chevrons of rippling water, he is conscious of an eye measuring him.

He stares back. This eye – impassive, matter-of-fact – evaluates him for what he is, and not for any secret he might have concealed in a library book. Rougetel lifts the candle to her face.

Dyer goes on staring as one memory lights up another.

The Greek island of Kythera. His first long vacation. Their meeting outside Molesey Boat Club is still a year in the future.

This encounter takes place in the cobbled town square at Banda Landra, and has been planned in advance on discovering that both of them will be in Greece that August.

Dyer hears his name and turns to see a motorcylist waving. The helmet lifts to reveal a freckled white face with a dented chin. Rougetel.

He's in his gap year, teaching at the local school, and on his way to visit a small chapel, ordinarily locked, which contains Byzantine frescoes. The priest – his niece is one of Rougetel's pupils – has lent him the key. 'Why don't you hop on the back?' he says to Dyer.

A short ride through rocky scrub brings them down a bumpy track to a jumble of mushroom-coloured roofs. Inside, low barrel-vaulted ceilings and blistered walls with saints painted in faded reds and blues. Rougetel lights a candle to examine their crumbling features. Irresistibly, he is drawn to a mildewed fresco of the Madonna. This strikes Dyer as disconcertingly crude, little more than flat patches of colour arranged in the simplistic form of a young woman. But Rougetel views her differently. Dyer is approaching the Madonna in quite the wrong way, he needs to cast himself back into the mind of a thirteenth-century John Dyer, a young man who would not have perceived the Virgin purely as a figurative representation; rather, as a two-way mirror – with her eyes operating as a peephole into, but also from, another dimension. Inside that chapel, Rougetel is telling him in a reverent voice from which he cannot keep his excitement, he and Dyer are as much the watched as the watchers. 'You might think you're looking at her. Actually,' holding the flame higher, to show how the whites in her eyes – a compound of crushed chicken bones and purified fish glue – are raised to catch the light, 'she's also looking at you.'

The wind was walking on his line. He drew it in. Six hours on the riverbank have rinsed everything out of his head. What he most loved about fishing was another property that it shared with reading and writing: it concentrated the mind, while at the same time liberating it. It was much less about catching a fish than releasing the fisherman.

On this stretch of the Hodder, no one was watching him. Here, he was the hunter. For the first time in several days, Dyer felt in his own dimension.

He cast again, and a trout went for his lure, but he had been grayling-fishing, and struck too early.

At last he caught a small brown trout blotched with fungus, as if he had got his hook in the bony mouth and stiff upper lip of Updark.

He let it go and was preparing to rejoin Leandro when the farmer came by and chatted: toothy like a fairy-tale witch, but friendly. He had observed Dyer teaching his boy. 'Yer catchin' 'im in gude time,' he grinned. He had watched king-fishers on those steps training their young to catch fish and bash their heads out on the stones.

*

Leandro had felt a further three tugs, but caught nothing. Dyer was pleased to see that the experience had not made him downhearted, the opposite in fact. They ate an early dinner in the bar and went out again.

In the vanishing light Dyer led his son to a large basin of water below the inn. They heard a fish splash back into the pool, creating ripples in the shape of a widening eye, and leaving bubbles on the surface.

Sea trout didn't run until May or June. It was probably a salmon kelt, or a slob trout that had not swum to sea, he told Leandro in a low voice. They stood still, listening out for another splash, the shivering noise that a fish makes when it jumps, not speaking.

Between the steep banks the Hodder, flowing with dark water like cold black coffee, resembled a river from which a hand might emerge to catch a sword.

Not seeing any more disturbance, they waded across and walked one behind the other along the far bank, holding their rods behind them parallel to the ground. The sounds were amplified at night, the pad of feet, the rustle of a water vole emerging from its burrow. Upstream, a silver flash and *spladoosh!* was the same fish erupting and crashing back into the pool.

Leandro instantly wanted to cast for it, but Dyer cautioned him. 'When you hear that splash of a sea trout, you need to wait five minutes. You won't catch it if you cast too soon.'

Once again, they stood in the river not moving. In the middle of the basin, rocks rose up above the surface, shimmering with the water that swirled over and around them. After an interval, Dyer nodded. Step by slow step, they inched closer to where they had observed the splash.

Ever so careful, Leandro waded further in. Dyer whispered to him how to fish at night. 'You don't need to move from there. Just be patient.'

The sky above was virtually pitch dark. The overhanging sycamores and the high banks formed by the gorge blocked out most of the starlight. Leandro began casting, the sound of his fly line swishing to and fro.

Then a glow began to appear in the sky. Dyer watched the nearly full moon climb free of the trees. Moonlight on the water, flash of phosphorescence on the line. The currents made shadows on the surface like the lattice in the confessional box in Nossa Senhora da Candelária. On these banks, he felt that he could tell Leandro how much he loved him, how he would protect him to the death

A small tug. Leandro had something. He reeled it in, too quickly, but still on the line, the rod tip bent and quivering, and Leandro shouting: 'I've got one!' – and then Dyer noticed a bow wave on the water. The moonlit surface dimpled with the flight of small frightened fish. There was a jarring pull and the rod straightened and the line went slack.

Dejected, Leandro reeled it in over the stones, a small severed parr trailing its spinal cord.

Dyer switched off his torch. 'A salmon – or a chub, or maybe a wild brown trout ...' he said of whatever parasitic creature had lunged from the dark depths to bite the parr in half. 'The favourite food of a big trout is a little one.'

But he knew what his son was feeling, and tried to console Leandro by telling of his own despondency after he lost a two-pound trout in the barn pool upstream. How he had brought it in and up over a rock face – 'I can take you to that bank right now, thirty-five years on' – and how the line snapped, and he watched the trout slide and judder back down the rock and into the river.

Leandro was not to be consoled.

In silence, they returned to the inn. The lights of the rooms swam weightless through the trees. From the copse above the front lawn came a hoot.

Dyer stopped. He cupped his hand and hooted back. He was never able to imitate a hare in distress, like his father, but once upon a time he could pass muster as an owl.

Soon afterwards, to Leandro's unlooked-for delight, they heard an answering hoot from deep within the wood. Dyer repeated his call. The other responded, closer now.

Dyer walked, hooting, up the lawn until, with a sudden flutter of leaves, there appeared a large and furious-looking barn owl on a branch twenty yards off, quickly followed by the arrival of another two owls and a chick, all solemnly gazing down on this territorial impostor. At this point Dyer lost his puff and Leandro started giggling.

Not until late on Sunday afternoon did Leandro catch a fish.

He stood in the Hodder beneath the inn, trying for the spring salmon or slob trout that they had heard jumping there the night before.

After forty minutes, Leandro waded ashore, moving further along the bank to where a drainpipe fed into the river. He stood on the grass ledge above the pipe and gave a speculative cast. At once he felt an imperceptible bite.

Something trembled.

The line started to vibrate and slide.

'Dad!'

'Keep the tension on the line.'

It was emptying his reel.

'Hold the rod up.'

He stood by his son's side.

'Now bring it in.'

Leandro's fingers gripped the cork handle. With his left hand, he began turning the reel. On his face, the involuntary expression a child makes when playing the cello.

'That's it.'

With tremendous concentration, Leandro wound it in.

Dyer, stumbling over a submerged tree trunk, crouched forward, extending the net. He scooped it over the tail, lifted it sharply up.

'Got him!'

Not a salmon, but a wild brown trout. And a big one.

Straightening, Dyer stepped out of the water, placed the net on the ground, and reached into it. His fingers under-cupped the fish, holding it in his palms as he had held Leandro. Bits of grass and water lily and the smell of protective mucus.

He laid it upside down on the bank to remove the fly. The trout seemed to have grown in the net. It was even larger than he had first thought – about three or four pounds, with a lovely gold belly.

Leandro leaned over. Dyer put an arm around his shoulder and hugged him, wishing that Leandro's grandfather could have seen this moment. 'That's a good fish. You could go your whole life without catching a fish like that.' He had no idea what he was saying, his voice came from another level of sound. He felt an exultation, for himself, for his eleven-year-old son. 'I bet if we slit open its belly, you'll find the rest of your parr inside.'

The expression on Leandro's face, he doesn't know whether to smile or burst into tears.

'What should I do with it?' he asks in a sheared voice. In Portuguese. His first fish.

'You can take it back – have it for breakfast, if you like.'

'What would you do?'

'What would *I* do?' Dyer remembered his father saying, without quite understanding at the time: '*The first best fishing* experience is catching a fish. *The second best is letting a fish go free.*' He went on looking at the trout. It was spotted like a leopard, with its gold belly and fins. On the towpath he sometimes stopped and talked to the tench fishermen. Once he had wanted to catch anything. Then he had wanted to catch only the biggest. Now he was like his father. He wanted to release everything, as a proxy, perhaps, for himself.

He said after a pause, 'What I'd do now is not what I'd have done at your age.'

In rapturous silence, Leandro picked the fish up with both hands, a flashing blade drawn out of the stone. He caressed it, and for a moment Dyer was convinced that his son would opt to keep the trout, but all at once Leandro turned and bent down to the water.

There's a righting of the tail, a shiver and a kick, and then it flicks off over the stones into the river.

Down the river. A *spladoosh*! The salmon kelt, or whatever it was, still out there.

Chapter Thirty-two

DARKNESS WAS FALLING AS THEY returned to the inn. Across the river a car's headlights swept over the trees, painting the topmost branches orange, dipped, and switched off.

Leandro walked beside him, excited to relive the last hour. Catching the trout, letting it go. It was up there with his goal against Horris Hill, suspending all talk of a dog.

A large silver Mercedes was parked on the lawn. They stepped around it, into the lobby, and propped up their rods behind the big oak front door. While Leandro raced upstairs to have a bath, Dyer paused in the hallway to look at the newspapers.

The word Iran was repeated in all the headlines. Haunted as he was by that subject, Dyer took a copy of *The Times* into the bar. He was about to order a drink when he heard a familiar laugh.

Elongated head, slate-grey hair, jutting jaw. He sat on a stool, dressed in a bottle-green polo-neck, talking to the bearded man.

Dyer hesitated – should he retreat? – when the eyes of 'our resident predator', as he remembered Miranda calling him, swivelled in his direction.

'Jean Dyer.'

'Gilles Asselin.'

How had Gilles found him? Only Paula knew his whereabouts.

Any pleasure that Dyer had been feeling was numbed by a premonition this was no fluke.

Gilles released himself from the embrace that he had initiated. 'Craig here has been telling me how to catch hen harriers with a night-vision camera…'

'You'd better watch out for the RSPB,' Dyer warned. 'They're a powerful lobby.' He drew up a stool. 'Silvi and Pierre?'

'In Oxford.'

'What brings you to Browsholme – aside from raptor politics?'

Gilles fluttered his fingers as if touching ice. 'Business interests.'

'I tried to ring you.'

'Silvi said. I've been away.'

'You've been gone a while.'

'I have a little problem. Bit of an issue. Hey, what are you drinking?'

Dyer felt at once self-conscious. 'I was going to order a ginger-beer shandy.'

Gilles nodded to the barman, who snapped to attention with a servility not previously on display. Reflectively, Gilles watched him pour the spicy ginger beer slowly into the bitter. 'You know, I've never tasted one of those.'

'It's what I drank last time.'

He looked at Dyer. 'You've been to this hotel before?'

'My father used to bring me here.'

Gilles said to the barman: 'Make that two.' Then, after paying for the drinks, and leaving his malt whisky on the counter unfinished, he sprang to his feet straight to his full height: 'Why don't we go through there, it's warmer.'

They stepped up into a side room hung with framed photographs of the local cricket team taken in the 1950s. A fire burning, tables laid for dinner.

Settled in at a small corner table, Gilles did not pick up where they had left off.

'You were lucky to get a room. Craig said they were booked for a wedding.'

'Then he'll have told you the bride's aunt died on the ferry over from Ireland, and so it was decided to cancel the party, but to go ahead with a small ceremony.'

Gilles nodded. He would like to have stayed here tonight if he wasn't taking Pierre next morning to a football match.

'I must say,' giving an approving look around, 'this is a magical place to invite someone special. I must bring Silvi,' his smiling gaze coming to rest on Dyer. 'And you. *Comment va ta petite amour?*'

'With who?'

Dyer sensed a predatory swirl on the surface.

'Come on, Jean. You needn't be shy with me. Let's start with Miranda, *pourquoi pas?*'

Dyer's laugh is that of a man who has thought of something else while he is removing the fly from a wild brown trout. 'I haven't set eyes on Miranda since your dinner party.'

'I'm disappointed. That's too bad.'

'Though I did send her a list of books.' Silvi would have told him this anyway.

'*Tiens*, is that all?' Gilles shook his head. 'You should ask her out. I said to Silvi she was your type. I can see you two getting on. She's not so, so ...' flicking his fingers.

'Not so what?'

'Russian,' said Gilles, with an unexplained chuckle.

Clever Gilles. But Dyer had to be cleverer.

'No,' he agreed, 'I don't imagine she is.'

Is that all? Did Gilles know about the package? Dyer pushed back the thought. Gilles was doing what he did instinctively. He was no different from your average witch-doctor, making you believe that he knew everything about you.

Gilles looked at him carnivorously. 'In Russia, they say if someone smiles, they are either stupid or telling lies.'

'I've not been to Russia.'

They were circling each other.

One evening, Dyer's father had played a game in which he studied the faces at the bar and imagined if they'd been fish to what species they belonged. Up until this moment, the playing fields of North Oxford had served to camouflage Gilles. A gagged voice somewhere in Dyer had kept trying to tell him: *Never trust a grown man who shows pictures of himself on a podium.* Yet Pierre's father for the most part had blended in successfully with the other touchline dads; he was merely one of a shoal of undifferentiated scavengers.

Now in this river valley, Gilles Asselin had swum into view: he had the sharpened head and coiled aggression of *Esox lucius.* His type was durable, with jaws developed in the Cretacean period. Like the northern pike, he had survived a score of Ice Ages, travelling up becks and streams, from Oxford to Moscow, across the Himalayas to Beijing, and over the oceans to New York and Montreal.

He was looking at Dyer with his pikey eyes. 'You know, Jean, I wouldn't go too near the Russians right now.'

Dyer said evenly: 'Who would you go near – aside from Estonians, naturally?'

Gilles took a sip of shandy and, without commenting on it, put down his glass. 'Being French-Canadian, the Americans maybe.'

'What, like Bonnie Cubbage?'

'Dear Bonnie.'

'I'm not overly keen on evangelists.'

'That rules out an Arab then.'

'An Israeli, too, probably.'

'Pity. They're so attractive, straight-backed. All that military service. How about a Persian?' and kicked his feet together, waiting for Dyer's reply.

'What, like Scheherazade?'

'*Peut-être. Peut-être.*' A merciless look had come into his eyes. 'Or Shula Marvar.'

'By the way,' said Dyer undaunted, 'it was her husband I was ringing you about. I may have been the last person to see him.'

'Not quite.'

Dyer glanced at Gilles.

'Silvi didn't tell you? Someone else saw Marvar after you.'

'Who was that?'

Gilles picked up a ceramic salt cellar from the table and toyed with it. '*Moi.*'

His morning jog on that Sunday had taken him past the Phoenix. He noticed Marvar sitting by the edge of the sand-pit, holding a book. 'He was wearing a suit, like he might have been going to the service in Hall.' At the sight of Gilles, Marvar scrambled to his feet and gave a reluctant wave.

Gilles couldn't say if this had any connection with Marvar's unannounced arrival, three hours later, at the Asselins'

315

house. Gilles was not at home, he had stepped out to the Covered Market to buy cheese. Marvar, as Dyer was bound to know, had turned up – unexpectedly early – to collect Samir. 'He seems to have been in a mighty haste to get to wherever he was going.'

'What do you think has happened to him?'

Gilles replaced the salt cellar. He stretched out his right hand, and one by one bent back the fingers. 'The truth is, I don't have any more idea than you. But I would like to find out. Believe me, Jean, I would like to find out.'

He was not going to insult Dyer by beating around the bush. Friends in the intelligence community, whose investments he looked after, had alerted Gilles to the possibility that Marvar had in his possession information that could benefit Gilles – benefit them all, if Marvar was alive.

'Business respects no borders, any more than GCHQ.'

The irresistible rumour swirling through safe rooms from Millbank to Riyadh: an unknown young Iranian physicist at the Clarendon had conducted an experiment which stood to recast the future of energy.

'The dinner party you came to with Miranda. Remember Ralph Cubbage? Well, after you had gone he stayed on, I naturally assumed for my fine old Cuban rum, but no, it was to tell me a story that I found most interesting. I would be curious, Jean, to know if you think it as interesting as I do.'

*

The incident which Cubbage described had taken place on the day of the Asselins' dinner party, early in the morning. 'He couldn't get it out of his mind,' Gilles said.

As was his energetic habit, Cubbage had arrived first thing at the Clarendon. He unlocked the door into the laboratory, and immediately was on the alert. 'It was obvious to his vigilant eyes that someone had carried out an experiment, and left in a hurry.'

Strange particles of sand in the target chamber. A single loose zirconium sample – tiny, white – staring up from the concrete floor.

'Even as Ralph retrieves the sample, his suspicion is falling on which one of the eight has dropped it. The night before, Professor Whitton had treated the team to dinner at the Magdalen Arms, but the student from Tehran had excused himself.

'Ralph logs in to the cameras, and sees that they were last operated at 7.32 the previous evening. The details are important.

'But here's the intriguing thing. The experimental data has been removed from both.

'He is suspicious. He switches on the new neutron activation detector, installed at considerable expense only in January, thanks to a last-minute donation from Berkeley. Ralph had set the biometric access code himself, shortly after his arrival here – he has not a big amount of faith in the Clarendon's security, he tells me.

'The results are so strange that he examines the system logs. They show a denied attempt to delete files. The unauthorised user did not possess the administrator privilege to do this.

'I think we can picture the intruder's face. Unshaven, panicked – pushing buttons, keys, frenetic to cover up records of his test. Ray's first thought: "He's jammed the motherboard – that's why he took off." But sorry, it's not jammed.

'Ralph takes a longer look at the display panel, the number on it, and his anger is mingled now with a confusion *énorme*. Because whichever way he tries to explain it, the explanation is the same, and it has preoccupied him ever since.

'The number gives the count of the radioactive decay, but what the count suggests is impossible, it doesn't make sense. It does not make sense. "Unless," Ralph tells me, "the oaf has revised the laws of physics."'

'I have only Ralph's word,' said Gilles austerely, 'but I trust him. If it is true what I suspect Ralph is beginning to think, then it would at once render obsolete a number of things in this room – that lamp, that fire, that radiator ... and not only in this room.

'Speaking commercially – my native tongue, you told me once,' he was counting again on his fingers, 'it could be worth more than Amazon and Google and Facebook and Apple put together and multiplied by at least a million.'

Gilles had spent the past days urgently trying to get hold of Marvar. First, to ascertain if the story of his experiment was true; second, if it was, to offer him a proposal concerning the development of his invention. But despite all his efforts, Gilles had not managed to find him.

'What is Marvar supposed to have invented?'

Gilles's laugh floated back. 'Ah, Jean, ever the curious innocent. The most dangerous challenge to the ambitious businessman is an honest man. Perhaps that is why I am drawn to you. It seems to exist at this moment only in the form of information. But information, from what I understand – *pour faire une histoire courte* – which could allow its owner to repeat the experiment again and again, and make them rich and powerful. No, no, let me rephrase that. The richest and most powerful person you can imagine.'

'How so?'

Gilles contemplated him judicially. 'I tell you this not because it interests you, which I know it doesn't, but because it's easy to find out.'

In a voice which led its owner back to the boardroom, Gilles went on: 'History does repeat itself. Why? Because we don't evolve much. If you had discovered a revolutionary, super-efficient way of reducing the energy price to two pence per kilowatt and that could be put cheaply into production in, say, China, what would be the best way to play it? You'd short Brent Crude and WTI futures with a seven-day duration, and then you'd leak to a known industry source, let the ripple start impacting energy price volatility every-where, and sit back and watch the wisdom of the crowd take over. Because as soon as this invention is out there, everyone will want to get in on it. Two plus two still equals four, Jean, even today. The tidal wave of panic would cause mayhem in energy securities as the hedgies unwound positions in conventional oil and gas. The leverage through futures alone could be way more than a hundred to one.'

Gilles was right. This talk of money and power, it was a foreign currency to Dyer, like the notes on the Bookbinder's ceiling. Marvar had probed the mystery of the depths, seen stars on the river bed. What had Gilles seen? Vaz de Caminha related how one Portuguese captain had listened patiently to a Tupi elder speaking 'without anyone ever being able to understand him, or he us'. As so often when conversing with Gilles, Dyer felt much the same incomprehension.

'What do you think of this shandy?' he asked.

Gilles surged on. He knew he was boring Dyer, but he wouldn't be deflected. He was addressing an international audience of bankers and patent brokers, and not Dyer across a rickety teak table laid for a meal that neither of them intended to eat.

'What I'd like to know from you, Jean, is this: has Marvar made such a discovery? If so, where is the proof? You see, I need proof. Concrete proof,' his fingers tightening again around the salt cellar.

'*Mon cher* Ralph is convinced that Marvar, being Iran-ian, will have given his information to Iran. But Ralph is CIA, as doubtless you have realised, and like many intelli-gence officers his understanding of human nature is, let us say, *pas trop intelligent*. You have only to speak to Marvar for two minutes to realise his hostile attitude to the Mul-lahs. He wears that big coat, hoping it covers up everything, what he's thinking, his amazing leap forward, his anxieties, but he can't help it! He is naked in his heart. A bit like you, Jean, eh?

'*Non*. Contrary to what Ralph and those in your old profession might want us to think –' tapping the news-paper that Dyer had laid on the table – 'I have yet to be convinced that we should finger Iran for Marvar's vanish-ing act. They have taken his wife and daughter, yes. Without doubt, the Mullahs would welcome Marvar's information, and even go many lengths to secure this. Yet from what my contacts are saying – and my sources are the best, Jean, trust me, the *very* best – there is no more reason to believe the Iranians have kidnapped Marvar than have the Russians or the Israelis. And, yes, in case you are wondering – and after your unfortunate experi-ence outside the Randolph, why wouldn't you wonder, *mon dieu*? – the same holds true for the Saudis, the Chi-nese *et comme ça*.

'But nor, on the other hand, do I have the strong impres-sion that Marvar would willingly sell out to Iran's enemies.

This doesn't suit his character either, from what I have been learning of him.

'So, I ask myself, who does that leave?'

He was thinking his own thoughts, swishing his tail. '*If* Marvar *has* voluntarily given his information to someone – and it's not merely Ralph who thinks this, mind – then *who* could that person be? The kind of man Marvar is – or, if one has to be pessimistic, was – it stands to reason he would seek out an honest broker. I see him as clearly as I see you, Jean. He's in danger, he's afraid. He doesn't trust his regime. He doesn't trust the West. What he's in search of – desperately – is someone he *can* trust. But who? I considered all the people he might approach, and one after another I dismissed them.'

His brows came together and he looked at Dyer from far away, a hen harrier who had espied a little sparrow far below.

'Then I kept thinking, for some reason, Jean, of you.'

'*Moi?*' said Dyer, taking another sip. They had been fencing. Time to stop parrying.

'I said to myself: didn't Marvar spend the night at Jean's house before he disappeared? Then I heard something most peculiar. You were observed wearing Marvar's coat soon afterwards. How very odd, I thought. And then I remembered that I had seen you both talking at the match against Horris Hill – and also, now it came back to me, one evening at the school sandpit, yes, the very sandpit where on Sunday

I interrupted Marvar reading, or whatever he was doing before he leaped up in such a terrible hurry. I could see you sitting there as I ran past, heads together in conversation, like we are now, and I wondered if he might have spoken to you of his exciting development, what he was planning to do with it, given you something even?'

Gilles made a motion with his lip, linked to a smile but not a smile.

'Before you answer, I have a hunch – it is only a hunch, yet Silvi will tell you my hunches have a tiresome habit ... I won't go on ... but this hunch is whispering in my ear that Marvar may indeed have given you something. You might not think it's important, you might not understand it, you might not even realise what it is, that it means anything. It might be, as you like to say, pure gobbledygook, but as we know – it's what the Phoenix teaches our children, *mon dieu*! – one person's goobledygook can be the answer to some-body else's prayers.'

There was no mistaking the menace behind his words, or the iron look that followed, but he spoke in a sympathetic tone, as if he was offering Dyer not a hypothesis so much as a chance to save himself.

Dyer refused to offer his neck to the blow. 'I didn't know you were religious, Gilles.'

Opposite, Gilles's face erupted into a smile.

'Hey, Leandro! Over here.'

Dyer turned, and uttered a parental sound.

Leandro hovered in the doorway, looking for him. His eyes grew enormous when he saw Gilles.

'Hi!'

Gilles leaped to his feet, stood up, and shook Leandro's hand like an adult. 'Silvi and I really appreciated getting your letter.'

'Thank you so much. I had an amazing time.' At Dyer's urging, Leandro had written to the Asselins following his sleepover. He had returned from their house in Ward Road in something of a daze. The gym, the games room, the TV screen, the double cheeseburgers, the photos of Gilles with his medals – were a far cry from lamb chops past their sell-by in a small rented kitchen in Jericho, and pictures of an absent mother on his bedroom wall.

Gilles gave his shoulder a simulated punch. 'Ring me and we'll have lunch sometime.' Then: 'I hear you've been on the river.'

Leandro told him about his trout – which Gilles asked to see, affecting incredulity when Leandro said that he had released it.

'Now why would you do that? Isn't that, what's the word …' flicking his fingers. His eyes glanced to Dyer and back. 'Hey, what are your plans tomorrow? Do you guys want to see Chelsea play Arsenal? I've got a box. Come with Pierre and me.'

Leandro gasped. Before he could reply, Dyer broke in to say that they were booked for one more day's fishing.

'*Tant pis.*' But not to worry. Another time.

Speaking in Portuguese, Dyer said to Leandro: 'Darling, please go and wait for me in the dining room. I need to finish talking to Gilles.'

'And I must be on my way soon,' said Gilles, patting his trousers for his keys.

He waited until Leandro had left the room, and sat down.

'Lovely boy you've got there,' tossing the keys from one hand to another. 'He reminds me so much of Samir.'

Dyer suddenly saw Gilles peering up from the depths, fanged. Perhaps it was his name. The only place to grab a pike without getting your fingers severed off was under the gill plate into the lower jaw.

'Oh, I think he has more in common with Pierre. He's a great fan of your son. He says Pierre could easily be goalie for the Oxford Schools team.'

But Gilles wasn't to be caught like that. He said with sinister emphasis: 'I have been wondering if perhaps, Jean, you know more than I know.'

'About Oxford Schools?'

'About Rustum Marvar.'

The only sound in the room, the portentous jingle of his keys.

'Perhaps I do.'

Gilles sat back, hands quiet, waiting to hear what Dyer had to say.

Dyer raised his eyes. 'I did in fact come into possession of a Ziploc sandwich bag of Marvar's – but only for a short time. I lost it, unfortunately.'

'What was in it?'

'A post-it note.'

He waited for his answer to sink in. It sounded so silly. But Gilles did not think so.

'Just one?' His voice was shrill with a businessman's impatience.

'That's right.' Dyer saw no need to mention the two extra blank notes. 'With some kind of mathematical formula written on it.'

'And before you lost it, you made a copy?'

'I didn't.'

'You didn't have time?'

'Not that. It's hard to explain, but I felt it wasn't something Marvar would have wanted me to do. He told me he had very deliberately made one copy only, and this, I presumed, was it.'

'Did you believe him?'

Dyer chose his words with care, like biting off the right length of nylon for a fly. 'I believe that he believed he had achieved something remarkable.'

Gilles was looking at him as Katya had. 'No, do you believe he only made one copy?'

Dyer intuited that an awful amount depended upon his answer. Not only that, but none of his answers so far had come as a surprise to Gilles. The feeling overwhelmed him that Gilles was involved with the second break-in, and he had read the substitute post-it note inspired by Basil Bunting's poem. Or if he hadn't read it, then he was in contact with others who had, and was coming to the conclusion that it was the ravings of a madman. But first he needed to be convinced beyond doubt.

'Yes, I do believe him,' Dyer said.

'This post-it note, can you remember what was written on it?'

'God, no! It was an immensely long algorithm – ten, eleven lines of figures, covering both sides.'

'Just figures?'

'Plus some letters. Oh, and a quote from a German scientist.'

Gilles was not interested in Otto Hahn. 'Could Marvar have remembered the algorithm by heart?'

'I doubt it. Or he wouldn't have needed to write it down. As I said, it took up the whole post-it note. No one but a nuclear physicist would be able to make head or tail of it.'

Gilles said with a bitter laugh: 'Some things can't be understood no matter how much one studies them.'

Dyer paused before making his next cast. 'A lot of poetry is like that.'

'Not only poetry! I started reading your book...'

It hadn't been meant unkindly, and Dyer's tone in response was light. 'I bet you didn't get any further into it than Marvar. Incidentally, I gave him my last copy.'

'So I understand. With a most touching dedication.'

'He may have been reading it when you saw him,' said Dyer, wondering how Gilles knew this – from Updark? Crotty? Or was it Gilles himself who had handed in Dyer's book to the headmaster?

But Gilles's mind seemed to be on what Marvar – not on what Dyer – had written. He was reassuring himself. Marvar was like every scientist who claimed to have discovered the St Graal of nuclear fusion. He would end his days, if they hadn't been terminated already, like that German in Bariloche, a forgotten laughing stock with a changed name.

He was playing with the ceramic container again. The sound of a man rapping the table to loosen the salt.

'Jean, I know wealth means nothing to you, but if you do have information ...'

Dyer held his gaze. He made sure that what he said was so close to the truth that Gilles and whoever else had their skin in this wretched game would be certain to believe him – and then leave Dyer and Leandro alone. They had the room to themselves, but he spoke to Gilles as though addressing a boardroom crammed with every interested party that he could think of to summon: every hedge-fund manager, banker, spy, kidnapper, assassin, telecoms magnate, revolutionary, nuclear physicist, news reporter, father.

'I swear I do not have anything of Marvar's in my possession. Marvar left his overcoat – and I haven't even got that. Someone broke into our house and stole it along with the sandwich bag.'

Gilles smiles like a man who is shocked and sad to get what he asked for. 'Another shandy? The ginger beer is very good here.'

Chapter Thirty-three

HE WAS LEFT WITH A cutlass, a knife, perhaps a match-lock and some pinches of powder in his sabretache. His few metal pieces had bewitched the Indians. These were his passport and his shield, regarded by the Tupi as creations from another world, totemic, beyond anything in their experience, like the chicken that had astonished two of them in Cabral's cabin. For his modest collection of iron, Ribeiro was offered brazilwood, beautiful bows and arrows, his choice of woman, anything. A local chieftain took him in. He had a child with one of the chieftain's daughters. He was feared, respected. How he lost his precious talismans is not known. But a legend passed from tribe to tribe, from visitor to visitor, how the Tupi had expelled him, indifferent to his presence once he was deprived of his iron, until one day a man stumbled into the campsite of some French timber merchants four hundred miles north, another exiled

European, with the ribs of his midriff showing between two sections of his shirt pinned with one remaining button. He could babble a few words in Portuguese.

The story of how a young Portuguese sailor survived in Brazil having been cast ashore on a beach south of Bahia was Dyer's chief distraction on Tuesday, following his return from Lancashire.

Tuesday was the deadline that Dyer had imposed on himself. Yet when he entered the Taylorian and his eyes once again saw Marvar's post-it note folded inside Madrugada's book, yellow as virgin sand, untouched, safe, he relaxed. Oxford with its red-brick houses and bus shelters stepped into the sunlight.

Dyer's relief lulled him into questioning his deadline. He looked around, savouring the silence. Unhurried as before, the couple in the painting went on with their private business undisturbed. The kneeling shepherd continued to hold tenderly in his palm the injured heel of the woman, who gazed down at him with dilated nostrils, swelling breasts, smiling. They looked as if they had all the time in the world to deal with a mere splinter or scratch. Why not take his cue from them, borrow the skills that fishing had taught, and which Dyer's three days in Lancashire had refreshed. Be patient and still – wasn't that the way?

Am I being too hasty? Do I need to decide today? The deadline was artificial anyway.

All his previous apprehensions seem suddenly ridiculous to him, like a fear of stone lions.

This is what he is thinking when, hours later, he attempts to renew online the book featuring Afonso Ribeiro that he had started a fortnight before, and was near to finishing, and the library's Solo system won't let him.

Puzzled, but with a stab of worry, he went and talked to the peroxide librarian. She consulted her screen. What she said next cramped his chest. 'I see here someone has requested it.'

The air in the room was unbreathable.

'Who?'

'You know I can't tell you that.' The book would be collected from the stacks at 9 a.m. next day. 'You may re-request it for yourself, and they can have it for one week. You'll get it back on the morning of the eighth day.'

His fingers clenched the red spine. Back in the domed reading room, he darted his eyes around. Not since its publication had another person requested *Uma Nova Luz Num Litoral Antigo*. Now out of the blue someone wanted to read it.

A male assistant in a maroon cardigan pushed a loaded trolley across the carpet like a sleepwalker.

The drumming in his heart. The heels of his pursuers. Whoever had ordered up the book, they were not interested in Madrugada's scholarship – of this he was sure – but in Marvar's scrap of paper that Dyer had reinserted, moments before, between pages 223 and 224.

How quickly a man's beard grows when he's dead. Marvar's algorithm was like that, it had taken on a supernatural life of its own. Dyer couldn't leave it there.

Heavy-hearted, he returns to his chair with the book. Unlike the couple in the painting, he has no time, he has to act now. His fingers shake as he takes out and starts to reread the figures and letters, in the hand that wrote 'BOOM-ERANG' on his fridge.

Was any real purpose served by this yellow post-it note – beyond its use as a bookmark? Far simpler to rip it into a thousand pieces and scatter them on Port Meadow. It would remove the hazard of the note being found in his possession. Besides, who would know? He hadn't admitted to anyone that he has this. And if he did remain under suspicion that he might be hiding something, it wouldn't be for long; enough time would pass for everyone to forget about it. He would be free, safe.

The temptation to obliterate, as Marvar had obliterated his marks in the sand, was fierce. But even as Dyer yielded to it, he remembered Marvar's searching eyes. Those eyes had taken Dyer out of himself into a world where suddenly nothing seemed impossible if it was to be done for another person in trouble. Irrespective of whether he believed in Marvar's abracadabra, Dyer was bound by his obtuse sense of duty to a man who for some reason had touched him.

If Dyer was not to erase Marvar's calculations, then the only alternative was to preserve them. He couldn't risk putting the note back into his shoulder bag. Recent days had spelled out the very clear danger of having it on his person or in his house.

The most obvious immediate hiding place – until he reached a settled decision about what to do with it – was another book.

He returned to the main reading room.

Never more had the identical galleries beneath the dome reminded him of one of Borges's infinite libraries. A story came back to Dyer of a librarian in dark glasses who had grown blind looking for God in one of the letters on one of the pages of one of the four hundred thousand volumes.

Of course, anyone could come in and search the stacks, but they would have to know what title they were looking for.

Surreptitiously, before sliding the note inside, Dyer opened a volume lower down on his pile; a calf-bound facsimile of manuscripts written by seven eyewitnesses who had accompanied the admiral in charge of the Portuguese fleet, Pedro Álvares Cabral, on his voyage to Brazil.

Dyer had no difficulty in reserving this for a further week.

He was passing the front counter on his way out, having left both books in the stacks, when he caught the librarian's eye, and stopped to ask if she might check the availability of one other title.

She called it up, seeing his face. 'J. W. Dyer, did you say? Here we are. *A Social and Cultural History of the Lower Amazon Basin.*'

His shoes on the grey stone steps have the sound of some-one in an empty hall slowly clapping. He hadn't grasped how on edge he has been since returning from Browsholme, uncertain if Gilles had swallowed his denial. What the librar-ian tells him: no one is swallowing it.

Lips pressed tightly: 'I'm sorry, that's also been requested.'

Jolted by the anonymous requests, all Dyer's fears writhe up like maggots in a bait tin. He walks down the stairs as if each step is taking him nearer to an incomprehensible menace.

Leaving the Taylorian behind him, Dyer made his way up St Giles. As if carried there by an invisible thread, he crossed Parks Road into Norham Gardens and turned right, into Ward Road, past the Asselins' imposing house, to the end of the street, and unlatched the low wooden gate to number 8, and rang the doorbell. Once again, no answer. He peered through the curtained front window. Where was she?

Three-forty. Leandro would be at a football training ses-sion. Dyer had promised to collect him at six.

On the way to the Co-op to buy dinner, Dyer stopped off in a cocktail bar to taste the cachaça in a bad caipirinha. Barico was the place's name. He had never noticed it before. He recognised the barman from his stall in the Broad: it was the purveyor of panama hats.

There were newspapers on the zinc counter. Dyer's eyes picked out a report on Iran. The BBC office was being shut down for 'conspiracy against national security'. He thought of how Basil Bunting was expelled as Tehran correspondent for *The Times* in 1952, and how he had joined the masses ululating for his own extinction. *'I walked into the crowd and stood amongst them and shouted DEATH TO MR BUNTING! with the best of them, and nobody took the slightest notice of me.'* Dyer hadn't needed to go to the Middle East to find himself in the same pickle. He'd first been drawn to Bunting because of his name – to come across a bracingly good poet also called Basil was a huge comfort. But there was this crucial difference between them: Dyer had been noticed.

No mention of Rustum Marvar, or his wife.

He drank his over-sugared caipirinha, feeling a renewed sense of isolation. Who had ordered those two books? Conscious of being under surveillance, and now of being read, he felt as if he was being crowded simultaneously from all sides by men of different skin colours, religions, politics, a scrum of Phoenix fathers hunting after the same information who had more than a sneaking suspicion that Dyer was in possession of this, and were charging hell for leather down the pitch to tackle him.

It shocked Dyer to realise how connected these people were. Gilles Asselin had a box at Chelsea because – of course! – Katya's husband was a shareholder of the club. Ralph Cubbage and Lionel Updark were clients of Gilles – and Gilles had boasted to Dyer of his links with high flyers in foreign intelligence services. ('The intelligence community is a broad church that worships different gods.') They probably had children at the Phoenix, too.

He ordered another caipirinha with the panic of a man on a foreign shore, surrounded by once-welcoming tribes who had turned hostile. His only salvation, a post-it note covered with impenetrable scribbles. Eight days since it first came into his possession, and he still hadn't been able to decide whether Marvar had written nonsense on it – like Dyer's dream – or the answer to everything, like the 'total book' in Borges's story, which was 'the formula and perfect compendium of all the rest'. Dyer saw no nuances, he was bad at nuances, he was bad at so many things.

He liked to think he had become wiser, but how little his character had matured. *Nosce te ipsum*. That was the wisdom he had been educated to seek at Leandro's age. Nearly half a century on, he was a world away from understanding himself. Nuclear fusion was an easier nut to crack.

Even so, the problem remained. What to do with the small square of paper currently sandwiched inside the back flap of *Os sete únicos documents de 1500, conservados em Lisboa, referentes a viagem de Pedro Álvares Cabral* (Lisbon, 1940). That part of his brain which should have solved it wasn't working.

He had rehearsed all the options: Updark, Cubbage, Euratom, Wikileaks, his old newspaper. But these were Marvar's thoughts, not his. He had to come up with ideas of his own. He had tumbled it over and over till he was weary, and he couldn't put an answer together. *What if there is no right person?*

And what the hell had happened to Marvar?

His head felt as though it was buried in sand. Tumultuous thoughts coursed through it. He went on playing the scenarios in his mind. They hadn't changed. Nearly a fortnight after Marvar's disappearance, nothing had changed. But dead or alive or wherever he was, it didn't matter. Marvar had wanted Dyer to decide for him.

Initially, Dyer had relished the challenge. His self-esteem had rotted and he saw a chance to earn it back. But the past days had educated him, he recognised that he wasn't the right person. He was a conduit, a middle man, a quondam journalist with yet another story that he couldn't tell and had no idea what to do with.

Edit yourself out of the story, the caipirinha is telling him. *Spike your interview. Rub the blue pencil over anything connecting you to Marvar. Remember Bunting: 'Notes are a confession of failure.'*

Before Dyer went to collect Leandro, he made another detour to Ward Road. Still, the house lay in darkness. The drawn curtains reminded him of the flat above Yolanda's dance studio in the Surquillo district of Lima, in which Ezequiel had hidden out even as he choreographed his world revolution. Gilles was pursuing the same kind of dream, and with no less ruthlessness. For the first time, Dyer worried about Miranda. What danger had he placed her in by sending her his notes? Gilles was aware that Dyer was connected with Miranda, from the knowing way that he had referred to her in Browsholme – did this now mean that Gilles connected Miranda with Marvar?

Oxford in the evening and Dyer's face lit by the windows along North Parade. Gaudy lights from Gee's restaurant, the night-neon of florists. He walked as if an old dog was following him, his heels clacking on the pavement like the slow *tok* of a *berimbau*.

Chapter Thirty-four

LATE NEXT MORNING, DYER PRESSED the buzzer outside number 8 Ward Road and inclined his head to the
perforated speaker. This time a female voice answered.

He waited for her to open the door.

She wore an apron over a pale yellow linen dress.

'I'll be scrubbed!' She pushed her hair back, a twinkle in
her eyes. They assessed him through a new pair of polka-dot-
framed glasses. 'God, your face.'

He had forgotten her slight lisp. 'What do you mean?'

'You look like a moping cod fed on phytoplankton.'

Before he could answer: 'I know what you're here for.
Come.'

She led the way, limping slightly, down a passage and
into a drawing room. The room is large and untidy, with
high ceilings and tall windows onto a garden – and at once
feels well-heated compared with Dyer's in Jericho. On the

right, beside the entrance to a conservatory, is a long comfortable-looking sofa with a torn arm. Photograph albums are scattered, open, on the lumpy cushions. There is a green baize-covered card table with a silver hand mirror and books on it, and a tapestry and paintings on the wall. To the left, the room opens into a kitchen area. A radio on the counter is playing classical music, and a long-haired black-and-white dog bounds about, a streak of mud on one of its ears.

'Apologies for the mess, I only got back last night.'

From a package holiday to Paguera, reduced, at the last minute, to one third of the original price – 'a hideous resort with quite a nice view from my balcony'.

She always became depressed in Oxford in February, she said.

Having sat under a Mediterranean sky and read for four days, Miranda had returned home tanned, with dappled brushstrokes on her cheeks from where the sun had coloured her face through a straw hat. The hat – battered-looking, with a yellow-and-red college band – hung on an antler above a wooden armchair on which she gestured for him to leave his shoulder bag.

'You got my parcel?' he said.

'I did.'

'Thanks for keeping mum.'

'Who's that?' came a voice from the conservatory.

'Speaking of which . . .' she laughed.

A white-haired old woman with grey eyes pushed into the light, her hands gripping a metal frame on wheels. Her round cross face had the texture of an abalone shell, with smooth pink patches between wrinkles.

'Mummy, this is John.'

'Of course it is. Nothing wrong with me,' and fixed him. Her eyes were two glasses that needed to be rinsed. She held out her arms. 'Is Miranda treating you well?'

'Very well.'

'She's a good girl at heart.' Her hold was clammy for such thin hands.

'Mum, why don't you go and sit down, and I'll bring it to you.'

He had interrupted Miranda as she was making an omelette.

'Wait till I've done this,' she said to him as her mother shuffled and squeaked towards the card table, 'then I'll find your envelope.'

A pan was heating on the stove. She turned the gas back up. 'I must say, it was exciting to be treated as a poste restante. It's something earth-shattering, I hope.'

'Oh, yes,' he said, failing to smile.

'I was grateful for your reading list, incidentally.'

Dyer looked blank, before he remembered. 'That was no trouble.'

'Unlike the rest, you mean?' Then quickly: 'Shut up, mouth. Sorry, but I was always taught that the wise read a letter backwards.'

He smiled. 'I haven't heard that phrase since ...'

'University?' She was breaking an egg into a bowl.

'I expect.'

'Were you at this place?'

'I was.'

'Studying?'

'English.'

'Ditto.' She had stayed on to do a doctorate, on English Linguistics from 1900 to 1940.

'I stayed on, too,' he said, 'for a while.'

She licked her finger. 'Talk to me – if I start I won't stop.'

It was only for a year, before he joined the newspaper. He tells her about it as she prepares the omelette ('one of my specialities'). His dissertation on the one hundred and nine claimants to the authorship of the plays in the First Folio. He had used Francis Bacon's code to prove that P. G. Wodehouse had written *Love's Labour's Lost*.

He said: 'You can prove anyone is anyone. Is what I learned.'

She laughed. 'Marriage taught me that. No, what am I talking about. I'm talking bollocks. Hey, Thor, down from there!'

She shooed the dog off the photographs which her young nieces had jumbled up when they came by last night; she had deposited her mother for the time she was away with her sister in Streatley, Thor with a neighbour up the road.

Photographs had spilled onto the carpet. Dyer stooped to retrieve them. One showed Miranda in a white gauze dress with a not very tall sturdy man in a suit.

'Is that him?'

'You monster of curiosity. Yes.' She looked over his shoulder to refresh her memory.

Dark receding hairline, strong jaw, direct crinkly gaze. 'He was a great flirt. He had superb eyes, they came out of his head whenever he saw a pretty woman. He left a lot of long faces when he married me.' She hobbled back into the kitchen area. Earlier, she had kicked her suitcase under a bed, splintering a toenail.

'Pinot?' lifting a bottle.

'Yes.'

'Good. I don't trust people who don't drink red wine.' She unscrewed the cap and looked for two glasses.

For seventeen years, she had ironed his shirts and made sure no dandruff was on his collar. 'After he left, I thought I'd never be happy, but sometimes I realise when I read a book or see a sunset or hear music I am absolutely content.'

She poured the omelette mix into the heated pan. 'Ah, that is a nice sound, that's how it should sound, and we'll have to eat it right away. You will stay for a bite, won't you?'

She apologised for eating at a nursery hour. She leaned forward to sample the omelette so that it wouldn't dribble over her dress. Something in her eyes was bright and full of life as she bustled around.

She asked him to smell whether a dressing she had opened last night was off – 'No, I don't think so.'

She urged him to help himself from a bowl filled with small tomatoes.

'Tomaters!' erupted a voice from the card table. 'Ain't seen a tomater since pussy pulled the fevvers out o' the frush's froat.'

Miranda rolled her eyes. 'Thank you, Mother.'

She told him in a new voice, running a spatula around the rim of the pan: 'She's eighty-seven and has been like this for two years. She listens all day to the radio and then regurgitates some of the things she's heard. My sister stomps off furious, trailing vapours.'

Last night, her small nieces had insisted on looking at Miranda's wedding photographs. Her mother had flicked through them and then asked: 'Who's the woman in white?'

'You just wonder what world she's in,' she said rather hoarsely. 'I used to say "Basingstoke" when she repeated a story, but the train's got stuck in the station. After not seeing Thor for a week, she didn't remember him, and the odd thing is, nor did Thor recognise her. I'm worried she's just circling the plughole.'

Dyer grimaced. 'I'm sorry.' The old lady's reaction was similar to those his mother would give, he said.

'Did your mother have dementia?'

'If not, something like it.'

It had started out as Charles Bonnet syndrome, affecting her peripheral vision. 'She'd see little fairies in the corners of her eyes, little wee people all running around through the air, and tell them to go away.' Near the end, she behaved like this towards Dyer.

He had images of his mother, opening drawers and leaving the contents on the floor. Her lengthening ash. The glass potty under her bed. Her memories divided by flimsy partitions through which they eavesdropped on each other. She eventually was given electroconvulsive shock therapy for her depression. Close after that trotted cancer and chemo. They had kept her in hospital; Dyer visited twice a week with his father. He thought of the last occasion he saw her. Shapeless like a chair covered with a dustsheet. There were burns on her leg from a cigarette that his father had lit and which she had forgotten she was smoking. Make-up had run over her dress. She had taught French and German for twenty-seven years, and Dyer to teach himself.

Afterwards, Dyer watched his father wordlessly climb into the car. He knew that he was going home straight to his study. Dyer followed him in his mind through the veil of Turkish cigarette smoke. He opens the whisky bottle, pours the glass to the top, drains it, pours another, drains, covers his forehead with his arm. His father was a naval historian, an expert on seventeenth-century Dutch shipping laws. He had told Dyer: 'I can't teach you anything.'

346

Her father had been a philosopher. He had left them this house in Ward Road. It was where she'd grown up.

She was flipping the omelette. 'I hope you like it runny.'

They carried their plates over to the card table.

'You've got long legs, so sit there.'

Miranda's mother was lost in her thoughts. Thor avoided her, instead slinking under the table to Dyer's chair. He looked plaintively at Dyer's omelette, and pawed his knee.

'Thor! Off! I'm sorry, he's more promiscuous than my ex. Just smack his nose.'

'He's gorgeous. What is he?'

Miranda laughed, a kind and appreciative laugh, full of pride and affection. 'A Welsh border collie crossed with whatever mutt his mother ran into on the Malvern Hills. But before you get carried away, he wags his tail like that to Ralph Cubbage – even, Lord love a duck, to Gilles Asselin.'

Her giggle: 'Oh, you'd have relished the scene this morning! There I was in the Parks, minding my own, when Gilles jogs past, in the middle of a conference call which I have to say does sound awfully urgent, and Thor – I don't think he can have been exercised enough – shoots off after him, barking merrily. I follow in super-hot pursuit, blowing the dog whistle, and finally catch up with them by the bridge, where I find Gilles battling to shoo away my slobbering hound, all the while clearly frantic to continue his conversation, which as far as I could tell – and this is so off the record – was nothing less

347

than Gilles trying, in between excited barks, to organise a massive buying spree. I knew that if I hung around long enough he'd tell me what to do with my ISAs, but this is where Thor and I are not on the same page. Gilles gives me the creeps, he reminds me of one of those golems in the Pitt Rivers sculpted from mud. I always feel talking to him is like being whipped by dervishes, or something. So I dragged Thor away by his ear and gave you a sound ticking-off, didn't I?'

After they had eaten, Miranda's mother touched his arm. 'Let's go, then. We're ready, aren't we?'

While Dyer considered his reply, her hand rose to her throat and toyed, as if to see it was still there, with a thin silver chain around her neck, like his mother's necklace that brushed his cheek when she bent to kiss him goodnight. Like Katya's. What a disaster that had been.

'I'll fetch your tickets,' said Miranda, playing along. She got up from the table and disappeared. When she came back, she was clutching the brown envelope that Dyer had addressed to himself, containing the eleven pages of his conversation with Marvar.

The old lady was combing her hair in silence.

'It's all right, you don't have to tell me,' Miranda said, ignoring her.

But he wanted to. 'It's the explanation to a problem, the background to it.'

She looked at him diagnostically. 'A big problem?'

'You could say that.'

'An explanation that others would itch to get their hands on?'

'More or less.'

'Without which the problem stays a problem?'

'Yes.'

That was it, he realised. No one would understand the significance of Marvar's algorithm without reading Dyer's notes. The one depended on the other. The two documents were bound inextricably. Like Dyer and Marvar.

'And who's it for?' she asked. 'This explanation?'

'I still haven't made up my mind. I first wanted to check it was safe.'

It was pitiable, he was backtracking already. Just when he'd hoped to disentangle himself by destroying his notes, Miranda showed him that this was impossible. For Dyer to wash his hands of what he had written would be to flush Marvar's algorithm down the same sink. He would have to destroy them both. Or neither.

She nodded at his dilemma, she saw it in his moping cod expression.

'You can leave it here if you like. Until you've decided.'

He was regarding her. Her tanned face was in profile. She had seemed a little dowdy, perhaps it was her hair. He was thrown off balance by her without knowing why.

Her mother was still combing. She did not glance up or say anything when Dyer rose from the table, gathered his shoulder bag.

Miranda opened the front door. She held his envelope in her other hand. 'It's here whenever you want it … *Ixé oka pupé aikó*' – and after he arched an eyebrow: 'That's Tupi for "I am inside the house."' She had tracked down one of the titles on his list: 'Rather impressively, they had it in the Oxfam bookshop.' She had read it on her hideous balcony in Paguera. Her quick honest eyes looked at him through their polka-dot frames. When she smiled, she tilted her chin downwards slightly, giving evidence of her shyness. 'I learned a lot. I was interested that they couldn't pronounce the Portuguese words for "faith" or "law", and that there's no future tense – all Tupi sentences are either in the past or the present. But you'd know that.'

Dyer walked away in a thoughtful, calmer mood. He had arrived an hour earlier to retrieve and rip up his interview with Marvar. He didn't have to leave it with Miranda; it was not what he had intended.

Chapter Thirty-five

IT SOUNDS LIKE AN OWL calling.

Dyer woke in the middle of the night overcome with fear, not knowing where he was, caught up in a dreadful flux of monstrous animal and human shapes. In bed with Astrud or Nissa, he didn't have time to worry about himself. Alone, his fears gnawed vulturously on each other.

He tensed, waiting for the call to come again, but it didn't.

Eyes shut, he saw letters and figures, pluses and minuses, brackets of long division, as if he were back in Slimy's class.

A car, driving slowly, crept along the street. He thought he heard voices speaking. With that animal impulse to seek shadow, he wanted to disappear into another world, crawl into the back of a cupboard and reappear in a third dimension, on a beach somewhere in Brazil where no European had been, no cars. There was always sun in Brazil; it fell through his window that faced the sea.

But he couldn't disappear. He had Leandro. They knew where he lived. They knew where he worked. They knew where he was each day at 8.30 a.m. and again at 3.30 p.m., where he took his coffee breaks. He was steeled for them to finish him off at any moment, shoot him like a kid in Rio.

Dyer jumped out of bed and went downstairs into the kitchen, in the darkness knocking over a chair. He double-checked the front door, the locks on the French window. Then he returned upstairs, rubbing his shin.

His head sank back, but sleep doesn't come. He is scared, he feels his body tapping inside. He doesn't want Leandro to hear his fear. He lies in the dark and listens to the overnight train – the sounds in the distance taking him away. He was not there. He was travelling south. He was coming into Petrópolis.

A need to escape from himself sent Dyer back to the Taylorian next morning. This circuit to the library was his rosary, he had become locked into his telling of it.

After his sleepless night, he felt weak, nauseated even. Continually circling and never moving forward, he trod the grey stone staircase, cold step by cold step, not noticing his surroundings.

But he senses it like a stare from the back. He knows something is going to happen.

In the centre of the room beneath the dome was a round table. Dyer passed the chairs of two people reading, and looked over their shoulders. The gull-faced girl, the bearded man, neither immersed in a book with wine-red covers.

Madrugada's monograph had disappeared from the stacks, already on its way to whoever had requested it. Conscious now of feeling paranoid, Dyer collected the calf-bound edition of facsimiles relating to Pedro Álvares Cabral's voyage, and took it into the French and German reading room. No one had switched on the lights, but his tired eyes were grateful for the dull daylight falling through the windows. The only presences in the room were the crouching shepherd and the wounded goddess on the wall.

In the feeble light he sees a movement in the painting, or thinks he does. *They look as if they're about to fall in love*, it strikes him for the first time. *That's what they look like.*

With pounding heart, he opened the back cover to check if Marvar's note was where he'd left it – inside a pocket sewn into the endpapers, containing a map of the Brazilian coast.

A part of Dyer buckled to see the yellow scrap of paper. The writing on it stood out. The ink had the dark glare of something that had fallen hissing to earth. He could imagine it burning a hole in the hull of Cabral's flagship.

How Dyer wished – for the first time – that he had not responded to the lure of the word 'BOOMERANG'.

Doors opened and closed. Cars hooted. The window-fan whirred. Someone switched on the lights. He swung round; it was the gull-faced girl. He shielded his eyes. He was drowning in the brilliance, as though a hand holding a gigantic magnifying glass had focused all the sun's beams on him and he was a bright spot curling into flame. His fingers folded the note back into the pocket and flicked through the pages to the first chapter. Dyer tried to concentrate on the words in front of him, about the admiral's reaction to the Tupi Indians gathering on the beach, how they approached in friendliness and innocence, but when he looked at the words they went blank, until he had the impression that he was gazing through a smouldering cavity at a world that was on the verge of extinction.

It was not yet eleven when Dyer broke his routine and left the Taylorian. The cobbles outside were dark from an earlier rain. After a warm snap, the cold weather had returned.

He was walking along Walton Street when he sensed that someone was following him. He dashed into the Dragon Cinema, and bought a ticket to a film that had already begun. He fell asleep after ten minutes, and when he wakes up the three people in the cinema are leaving. It's the middle of the day as he emerges. He has no memory of what he's watched. He feels in another time zone, another country.

In slow steps, he headed back towards the town centre, plunged into a canal of images. The asthmatic misfire of an exhaust made his hair stiffen. His eye played tricks. He thought he saw Lorna coming out of Boswell's, carrying a saucepan. When he looked again, she had transformed into a grey-haired old lady holding a Sainsbury's bag.

His fears nipping at his heels, he stumbled, caught himself, and continued walking down George Street to Gloucester Green. There was a market in the square. Cloudily, he ordered a hamburger from a van. The chips made him think longingly of cassava fries; the stalls, of the market in Belém – boxes of old comics and blue-and-white patterned teacups of the sort that his parents sipped from. He wolfed down the hamburger. He needed an astrolabe to find his bearings.

Hunger assuaged, he struck out across the cobbles. He was letting his instincts lead him, following one of the goat paths that he had carved out with Rougetel, and behaving with the same furtive watchfulness.

Checking over his shoulder, he left Gloucester Green, and made his way through Wellington Square to Claridge Street, in through the black-glazed door of Barico's.

This time, he didn't look at the papers on the counter. The news about Iran no longer touched Dyer. His own drama consumed him.

He ordered a caipirinha, then another, the only customer, a solitary tapir coming to drink. It wasn't hard to imagine that he was back in Brazil. Looking out from his flaking windowsill. He felt like a car on sugar-cane alcohol. Putter putter putter. The condensation on the glass was the rain on the windscreen of the yellow Beetle taxi taking him to her funeral in Petrópolis.

Dyer hadn't thought about the ceremony for years, and goodness knows what prompted him to recall it now. How it came back, that humid day, and the smell of rotten mango and the spasm in his foot, and Vivien, who had flown in from Lima with Hugo. He sat by Astrud's body for some time, and then Vivien handed him a large glass of cachaça.

He had cast and recast over that pool in his memory. It was emptier than the flat to which he had returned in Joaquim Nabuco. Every article of clothing, every ornament and painting they had bought together, was drained of her existence. The flat reminded Vivien of a lodge in the jungle; you needed to shout and knock before a light came on. As the sun rose on Leblon, small waves broke on the sand like a cat gently rolling over a dead bird.

Astrud would have told him what to do.

The memory was choking him. He sat in a dazed paralysis. It infected his every bone. He couldn't lift his glass without it trembling. The cold had finally got to him, it was in his marrow. Like Marvar.

The Iranian scientist wasn't someone he had met only three times; he was an illness who had come in through the cracks, to nest.

Dyer got up from the zinc counter and went into the reeking urinal. Washing his hands, he couldn't avoid his reflection in the mirror, with graffiti on the wall behind and a poster for an exhibition of Cézanne portraits at the Ashmolean.

The stale cast to his face. It explains Miranda's reaction the day before. Grey stubble ashes his cheeks. His eyes are vacant. He looks like one of his street kids, like that accordionist outside the Oxfam bookshop. He feels himself vanishing.

A wave of panic swept through him, he was frightened by its force. He couldn't keep his thoughts upright in his head. He had a moment of realising what a mental collapse was, the impossibility of making a decision.

A mathematical equation is true for ever, Marvar had said. But only if you knew the equation. If, however, you got rid of it before anyone else found out, who then would know it had existed – save for the person who had come up with the equation in the first place?

If Marvar was alive, he would be able, surely, to replicate his knowledge.

Leaving Barico's, Dyer turned right onto St Giles. A little dog ran up to the bars of a gate and watched him pass by. He moved as if he were taking his last steps in chains, like someone about to commit a crime. His gestures were mechanical, his strength had leeched from him. But in the urinal he had reached a decision, and his face is oddly composed as he walks past the Oxfam bookshop towards Blackfriars, in the direction of the Taylorian, once again.

He had bottled out yesterday at Miranda's. He is determined, this time, to see it through.

Chapter Thirty-six

THE OUTSIDE OF BLACKFRIARS HAD the look of a prison. The pavement was wider here, with benches. It was a spot favoured by Oxford's homeless, a place for them to stretch out their legs like starfish, trip up consciences.

On a bench near the entrance to the priory, staring ahead with an opaque expression, a smiling young woman of about twenty, frizzed blonde hair wound in plaits, sat chattering on her phone.

Down on the damp pavement beside her, back against the railings, a man lay in a sleeping bag of a strange winter blue. He wore a sweatshirt with 'Cambridge University' on it, and had close-cropped sparrow-coloured hair with the glint of a tonsure. Quite unperturbed by the world rushing by, he read the *New Scientist*.

Dyer flicked his eyes over him, thinking at first it was the accordionist, and feeling a pang of empathy. In the space defined by his belongings, he had distributed a Kathmandu backpack; a shallow black hat, upside down, to attract coins; a grey felt blanket with an Inca pattern on it; a KitKat wrapper; two paper cups; and a white metal rod. These were the objects that furnished his world, like the photos that lived beside Dyer's bed. Dyer skirted past dismal stage sets of this kind every day. Not even the pile of *Science et Vie* magazines marked him out. To Dyer, this was standard decoy material, like the man's sweatshirt; designed to manipulate Dyer into mistaking him for a former graduate down on his luck.

Without knowing why, Dyer stops. It's about his concentration. That, and the absence of a carrion smell and a bottle. He doesn't have the sadness of a homeless person. He doesn't look like someone who hates waking up, worrying what the day will bring, caged inside the same inescapable tune. He looks different, somehow.

Dyer has the distraction of a man searching his pockets for money. 'Are you enjoying that?'

The article that he reads so attentively is headlined 'The Dark Side of Meditation'. He finishes his paragraph and then glances up, as if Dyer were a policeman looming out of the sky to move him on.

Their eyes clash.

Dark, glowing out of a narrow bearded face. They pin Dyer down with the mesmerised absorption of a precocious child. Dyer has the sudden sharp sense of having met him before.

He's a man of about the same age, but his brown, pupil-less eyes are those of a person rising up from an immense depth. Dyer wonders for a moment if he's blind, but he realises when the light catches the irises that they are a very deep brown. He has never seen such dark eyes, and they pull him in.

He is gazing at Dyer as if through binoculars at a shape he isn't quite sure of, a spectral presence.

Then he sees who it is, and he smiles. 'Basil?'

Dyer's heart thumps like a man stamping sand from his shoes. He feels the blood rushing from his face. He's aware of how bewildered he looks, with a £5 note in his hand, how exposed, as if he's trying to cover himself with a flannel.

'Do I know you?'

'You are John Dyer. Aren't you?'

Dyer stares at him. Bearded, older, with a dent in his chin. 'Rougetel?' is all he can stammer.

PART FOUR

Chapter Thirty-seven

THE FRIZZY BLONDE YAKS AWAY on her phone as Rouge-tel emerges from his sleeping bag.

Before her unseeing eyes, he stood up, rain on his shoulder, his legs thin as saplings in his black jeans. He remained invisible to her while he slipped his sockless feet into a pair of worn trainers. Nor was she distracted when he bent to roll up the sleeping bag, and strapped it – with the grey felt Inca blanket – to the underside of his backpack.

He stuffed the *New Scientist* he had been reading into a side pocket, scooped up the remaining magazines, cups, chocolate wrapper, and carried these over to a dustbin, dropping them in. Then he emptied into a pocket the coins from his hat and put it on.

The only trace that he has left behind is his dry outline on the pavement.

To Dyer, the sight of the friend he last glimpsed when he was twenty is overwhelming, a phenomenon so extraordinary that it drives all else from his mind. One look at Rougetel, he forgets Marvar's post-it note, his scheme to eliminate it from the face of the earth.

'Are you hungry?' he asks after a silence.

He was struggling to find Rougetel – his freckled pale face – in the dark deep-set eyes, steady and direct; the aquiline nose; the beard, one side trimmed tidier than the other. Lean, fit-looking, he wasn't a shambles. He was quiet and watchful. They were the same height.

Rougetel nodded. He hoisted his backpack onto his shoulders, and the two of them set off together without a word.

They crossed the pavement where Dyer had avoided kidnap, and picked their way through the lunchtime throng of released students, who parted to let Rougetel by, gripping the white steel rod in his right hand, as if he were a blind man. His gait was loping and slow, pigeon-toed a little; his face half hidden by his shallow-brimmed hat. In the direction they were going, they walked as if on a predetermined route, up Cornmarket, through the Covered Market, past slabs heaped with whelks, into the Café Lisboa.

The seats by the window were taken. Miguel showed them to a table set against the back wall.

Rougetel unhitched his backpack, placed the white rod on the shiny tablecloth, and sat down.

'I remember this place.' His voice was low-pitched and flat, sanded of the middle-class accent which Dyer had largely retained. 'It was strictly out of bounds.'

He took off his hat and looked briefly around, his expression serious as a bird. He was struggling to tally the café with his recollection.

Dyer reminded him: 'We used to sit against this wall in case Slimy spotted us.'

Rougetel flicked his glance through the glass pane to the passage.

'But he never caught us, did he, Slimy?' he murmured with a note of pride. 'He'd have whacked us for sure.'

He went on staring at the window with a concentrated gaze as if it reflected back those years and the shadow of his younger head, the smells of Player's cigarettes and fried bread. He smiled as if he was no longer afraid.

Those boundaries they had crossed at school, his smile seemed to say, they were rehearsals for future transgressions and explorations. Once you had played truant by going to the Lisboa or the St Giles Café, no place would ever feel off-limits again.

'What do you want to eat?' said Dyer.

Rougetel read his menu, but he was not seeing the dishes. The food had changed since he last sat opposite Dyer, possibly at this table, devouring a forbidden egg on toast (while explaining with a waxy face why he had taken the train on his own to Paddington). It wasn't what he was used to.

'Why don't you choose for me?' he said, and closed the menu.

Miguel returned. Dyer ordered two dishes of the day. The slow roast pork for himself, a vegetarian falafel for Rougetel, and apple juices for both.

Scraping forward his chair, Dyer bumped his knees against the table, dislodging the rod.

'What's this for?' retrieving it from the floor.

Rougetel tipped his head. 'In case I'm attacked.'

In a convulsive movement, he brought his arms up from his lap, stretched them out.

Dyer had forgotten how unexpected he could be.

He looked at the backs of Rougetel's hands and saw that they were bruised: the mauve marks – like Ribena stains – still angry from where some drunks had stamped on his wrists two nights before, snarling 'Vagrant!' while he lay on the pavement outside Balliol, having fallen asleep. This was the first time he'd been assaulted. He normally slept in Iffley, he said.

Dyer fell silent. He didn't know how Rougetel wanted him to react. There was a curious pleading expression in his face. It threaded Dyer's glance back to the bathroom mirror in which their eyes had met, a floor that stank of disinfectant, a dormitory of pinch-faced boys who had buried Dyer's model aeroplane in the sandpit, and the occasion when Rougetel, in a quiet serious voice, after Dyer thanked him for saying where the Boomerang was hidden, revealed that he came from Pluto, and Dyer wasn't to tell.

La Paz is what Dyer understood Rougetel to have meant, but when Dyer thought about it later he was not so certain. Rougetel wasn't a joker. Maybe his mind had slipped. Maybe he was an unstable fantasist. Or maybe he had been telling the truth, he did come from outer space, and all other people on earth were the aliens.

At any rate, he still had a look of great sincerity, he hadn't lost that. His need to know what was true, what was not, had been a permanent crease in his character, like the dent in his chin. Rougetel's hankering to get to the nub was the quality that had attracted Dyer and soldered their friendship. They had forged something between them at the Phoenix, an understanding, the kind that trained its compass points on worlds yet to be encountered.

Their meals arrived, and Dyer lost what he was going to say.

Across the table, Rougetel ate with his fingers, in haste. He was not ashamed of his hunger. His teeth were yellow, uneven.

Dyer felt self-conscious, picking up a knife and fork. He had become aware of a queer smell – not urine or body odour, but musty, vegetably, and overlaid with a powerful lemony scent. It was the smell, he realised abruptly, of someone who slept in the open.

He lifted his head very slightly to observe Rougetel swallowing down his food. He wasn't dressed like other homeless men in Oxford, as though in the uniform of a defeated army. His clothes were clean; not ironed, but clean. Even so, he looked grindingly poor.

The canvas oilcloth stretched tight over the table.

Dyer said: 'I last saw you—'

'On the river bank near Hampton Court,' said Rougetel. His tongue was creamy with falafel. 'You'd been rowing.'

'I used to row with the Molesey Boat Club in the long vac.'

In the slightly guarded and watchful way that was part of his character now, Rougetel peered into Dyer's face.

'What did you do after university?'

Dyer wanted to tell him: how he had abandoned a doctorate, become a cub reporter, then a special foreign correspondent in Latin America, back in the day when Rio was still. His decision to take the job in Brazil, at the time warmly supported by Vivien, was the fruit of a wild seed that Rougetel himself might have planted, with his vivid schoolboy descriptions, spiced with Spanish and Aymara, of the Andes, the native communities on the Altiplano, and the orange-roofed villa in the Achumani district of La Paz where the Rougetels lived.

'I did try and look you up,' Dyer needed him to know. In his second year in Brazil, his newspaper had sent Dyer to the Bolivian capital for an article on the Dia de los Muertos. Yet no Rougetel was listed in the telephone directory. 'No one at the Embassy had an address for you.'

Rougetel's fingers closed around his glass. 'What kind of stuff did you write?'

'News items, features.'

'About?'

'Politicians, revolutionaries, current affairs. Their impact on people.'

A man at the table next to them yawned.

'And what makes an impact ... in your opinion?'

'Well, no doubt if I was to do a story right now, you'd be reading me on the Iran nuclear deal.'

Rougetel looked puzzled, as if he had been told his jersey was on back to front. Dyer could immediately see in his expression that he wasn't involved or concerned about Iran.

'This nuclear deal ... you're not writing about it then?'

'I gave up journalism long ago.'

'Why?'

'Oh, there was a story – my best, I feel – which I decided not to file.'

Rougetel nodded. He didn't ask why Dyer might have spiked it or what the story had been about. Instead, he wanted to know, 'Was that a crashing point for you?'

Dyer considered before answering. The last person who made him reflect in this way was Rustum Marvar. 'One of them, I suppose.'

The door opened, bringing in a smell of fresh-ground coffee from Cardew's. It triggered an instinctive memory. And another and another. Dyer in Rio in a newspaper office, Dyer in the *favela*, Dyer the husband, the widower, the father, the author.

He glanced once again at Rougetel. His reappearance, wildly unexpected, but also natural somehow, even inevitable, had come as a colossal relief. Rougetel was so much more than a distraction from what preoccupied Dyer. He was a lightning rod that took Dyer back to his schooldays, and also, by dint of Rougetel's upbringing in Latin America, to the years in between.

Dyer had an urge to tell Rougetel about Astrud. How if their daughter had lived, they'd have called her Xuxa. He longed to tell him about Nissa, Leandro, the book he was writing, Marvar and the post-it note – he kept thinking of Marvar, although he would rather not – but it was too soon to begin that sort of conversation, and anyway nothing insisted on being talked about more than the crashing points, as he had called them, of the person seated opposite.

He hadn't heard anything of Rougetel, not since Trundle's putative sighting in Benin.

'And you, what became of you?' Dyer asked. 'When I met you in Greece, you were about to go up to Cambridge.'

There was a tension in the hand which picked up his glass.

'What became of me?' his voice tightening. Something was frostbitten in the numbed way his throat closed on the words. He wiped his mouth with the back of his other hand and gulped his apple juice.

Until that moment, Dyer had failed to appreciate how disturbing it was for Rougetel to be recognised or asked about himself. It was only with a deliberate effort that he had enquired into Dyer's life. Already, his eyes were blurred with the memories stirred up.

'Yes,' Dyer insisted, 'what on earth happened to you?' His surprise was there in his question, as pointed and sharp as the white steel rod. How Rougetel had changed, how he had adapted himself to a different life, and lost the canon of his background and class, and discovered other aspirations and beliefs, perhaps.

Thrust into seeing himself through Dyer's eyes, Rougetel said nothing. He was having to unthaw memories that he had put into cold storage, and it wasn't comfortable. The table, his empty plate, the chat of Miguel behind them – these seemed to be answering for him.

He scratched his thin ankle. He opened his mouth. He tried to speak, stopped, then tried to speak again.

Rougetel began so hesitantly that Dyer had to crane forward. At first, he sounded like someone braced for the majority voice to stamp on his wrists and laugh at him with derision. He wasn't so self-absorbed that he couldn't see how his story might strike the ear of a former foreign correspondent. But once he observed the intent way that Dyer was drinking in his every quiet word, he spoke with less reticence, no longer like a man trying to read without his glasses.

He had always been honest, and nothing had changed. They had known one another before their characters solidified. It was to this person – trustworthy, unjudgemental, his first real friend – that Dyer listened with total concentration.

The years were gone and they were back at the same table, as Rougetel explained what had launched him on a path that diverged in such a radical way from Dyer's, and from the trajectories of virtually everyone else with whom they'd been at school.

This time he didn't stop.

Chapter Thirty-eight

IN SUBSTANCE, IF NOT IN these words, this was the story that Rougetel told:

'If you were to take a Ladybird Book look at my life, you'd start on December the 3rd, 1980.'

Rougetel was in his first term at Cambridge when there arrived in his cubbyhole a telegram from his father's telephone company in La Paz to say that his parents had died in a road accident. Driving at night from Cochabamba along a narrow mountain pass, their car had rounded a corner and met a local bus with a defective headlight. It had begun to rain. The dirt track was not cantilevered. The valley lay five thousand feet below. Rougetel's father pumped his foot on the brake, but his white Range Rover continued on its inexorable slide. The police laid a felt blanket over the couple's faces. Rougetel had been their only child.

When your parents vanish like that, nothing else is very serious. About six weeks after receiving the telegram, hungover and without a family, save for a grandmother in Scotland, Rougetel was walking beside the Cam to a lecture when he fell into conversation with a smiling Frenchman with a long grey motorcyclist's beard. Henri Lemoine was a missionary who had lived in India and had found 'realisation' using Eastern contemplative practices. Long before they reached the Sidgwick Site, Lemoine had gauged Rougetel's terrible loneliness, and recognised in the heartbroken young fresher someone who might benefit from his heterodox 'fusion religion'. On the banks of the Cam, he introduced Rougetel to its four noble truths:

Nothing is
Nothing is not
Nor is it neither
Nor is it both

Lemoine was a disciple of the French swami Marc Chaduc, and had come to Cambridge on a visiting fellowship after Chaduc, or Saraswati as he became known, disappeared from his hut in Kaudiyala in April 1977. Chaduc's glasses without which he was blind were discovered in the hut, but no one had seen him since; Lemoine believed that he had given himself up to the Holy Ganges.

'I am not here!' Rougetel cried when Lemoine knocked at his door next day. Another week passed before he accepted an invitation to Lemoine's second-floor rooms at Westcott House. The French priest sat Rougetel cross-legged on a purple foam mat and instructed him to close his eyes and hum, and then to breathe in and out from the pit of his chest.

To begin with, Lemoine's Buddhist-based meditation eased Rougetel's depression. It reduced his anxiety and stress, he felt more energetic. He was not seeking any mysterious communion with the depths of his soul; he wanted to lose himself, that was all. His application of Lemoine's methods to access his 'inner sound and light' by pressing his eyeballs hard and inserting his thumbs in his ears had no effect other than to give Rougetel spells of dizziness and a blocked ear-duct.

Then two months later, it happened; inside his head something snapped. Suddenly, the whole of him was flowing out in a constant stream, not diminishing, but surging through him in a tremendous rush of energy with a sense of unending expansion, stretching into infinity as far as light and words could reach.

The very nature of language is linear and follows a straight line to a destination. Rougetel's mystical revelation was as hard to describe as to follow. But language was the only tool that Rougetel possessed. What transformative experience Rougetel passed through in his badly heated room in Thompson's Lane – the radiance that engulfed him, his unparalleled exhilaration – Dyer had to approximate rather than comprehend.

Already several times at Cambridge, Rougetel had got drunk, and was repelled by the conceited and scornful person alcohol turned him into.

This was the opposite.

He had been subsumed into an oval of light, white, brilliant. It was like an internal sun glowing in his head, very clear and bright, without proportion or edge. He felt an effortless stillness, as if he were at the centre of the cosmos, inseparable from it, a child back in the proverbial womb, in a peaceful bliss of nothingness that extended out into the actual sun and stars.

'If someone shines a torch in your eye, you look into the dazzle and see light and colours, and then, if you go on staring, you can start to penetrate into a cascade of thoughts and feelings, like superfast broadband.'

In that brief intense flash, the future didn't exist, nor the past. He was fully sober to the moment. He felt as if he had located his heart, mind, character in the source of all nature. He was composed of the energy which is the essence of life, his brain made up of the atoms and neutrons that generated the sun, part of the same infinite process.

Superfast broadband, an absolute whiteness – Rougetel had tumbled in language, but this was the best he could do. Dyer had to stamp on the same strong urge to laugh in an embarrassed way that he had felt with Marvar.

Rougetel looked at him with his startling pupils. He said that before the whiteness dissolved there appeared at its centre a dark disc like an eye. The sole occasion that he had seen something comparable was in the Byzantine chapel on Kythera when, observed by Dyer, he had held a candle to a blistered wall and touched a white mark painted on it.

In common with Dyer, Rougetel had been raised in the Church of England. His dramatic experience now made him take seriously the existence of another world view. All religions, it appeared to Rougetel, whether Protestant, Catholic, Byzantine, Eastern, Andean or Amazonian, were a quest for matches with different-coloured heads, when the flame was the thing. They were imperfect constructions of the human intellect in its search for what transcended it. They formed different paths up the same mountain, towards a summit which towered beyond any man-made religion.

That inner sun was the entrance to his path. He never achieved a further vision of it, but he had felt the intimacy of its embrace, and it was very powerful, nothing could displace it. He missed it with an intensity that astonished him and had never abandoned him. He believed that he had glimpsed the best of himself, of what he could be. From this moment on, he wanted to be that person as often as it was possible, a receptive void disengaged from the intricacies of living.

Outstanding at mathematics as at English, Rougetel might have pursued a prodigious career as an academic or as a communications whizz-kid, or made his mark in government. But at the end of his first year at Cambridge, less than a month after he encountered Dyer on the towpath outside the Molesey Boat Club, he went on his long vac to Bolivia and failed to return. In his parents' empty bedroom in La Paz, he lay with his eyes wide open in the dark and realised he had made his decision. That autumn, living off the proceeds from the sale of their house in Achumani, and off the rind of an insurance policy, he set out on the road that he had been treading ever since.

'How to describe it? You could say it began as a Western interpretation of Eastern religions – the world is in yourself and also a reflection of what is in you.' But quite a lot of it, Rougetel had come to realise, speaking now to Dyer, was a continuation of what they had been taught at the Phoenix.

Rougetel sucked his fingers clean. He was still hungry. Dyer ordered two rice cakes. Despite all the questions that he itched to ask, he said nothing else, he wanted Rougetel to continue, as once he had longed for Rejas to go on speaking, and more recently, Marvar. To interrupt at this point would be fatal.

The cakes arrived on a tray as Rougetel filled in the years:

The start of the Michaelmas term found him in the Arctic Archipelago. 'I wanted to go as far as possible from everything I knew.' Yielding to a similar impulse, he had run away from the Phoenix in his first term, disappearing on himself like an anorexic girl.

If you wish to look hard at your life, Father Lemoine had said, you must vacate it. Through a contact of Lemoine's in the Oblate Fathers, who had a mission on King William Island, Rougetel lived two winters in a rancid-smelling igloo with Netsilik seal-hunters. Here he was released from the complications of the world that he had grown up in. The horizonless topography spoke to him of the early simplicity of the universe. He was shorn of possessions, not even the cut snow that formed his home of ice was his own. His deprivations taught him the skills which allowed him to survive on any roadside thereafter. No night had a chill after the extreme temperatures of the glacial ocean. No taste was too revolting after he drank tepid seal blood out of a caribou skull. He would rarely again experience anything quite so extreme.

Astonishing to Dyer was how many times a face could change in an hour. It animated Rougetel to recall his months in the north, the hours he spent crouched over the ice, searching for a seal's hidden breathing hole. He half-rose out of his chair, his face filled with glee. His right hand was the sled he had pushed across the frozen sea, his left was the moving wave he had watched petrify into a scroll, and the uneaten rice cake was a whirling wall of snow in which his feet stood invisible. By the glow of a seal-oil lamp inside his fetid igloo, he worked his way, page by page, through a dictionary spotted with fat – the white steel rod – in which, recognising the condition to which he aspired, he had underlined the Netsilik word for polar bear, *tara-i-tua-luk* = he who is without shadow.

From the clean white crucible of Nunavut, his true features emerged. He reflected: 'To be adult at such a young age, it splits you open.' After fourteen months, he was ready to strike out on his own, make sense of the world for himself.

In the spring the ice melted. He left the snow and the seals, headed south. Summer found him in Cochin studying the Upanishads. To his Spanish and his smatterings of Aymara and Inuktitut, he now added Sanskrit. The research suited him. He discovered that he loved it. Languages led to linguistics, linguistics to artificial intelligence. The more he read, the more he hungered to read. 'I wanted to know everything.'

The effort he might have dedicated to a thesis, had he stayed on at Cambridge, he ploughed into his life's project: a careful study and sustained meditation on the meaning of the texts to which intuition, curiosity or blind chance would lead him.

His practice was to take one subject at a time and master it. He sought out the acknowledged authorities, read their works with stubborn interest, clarified his thoughts. He devoted his next winter to the Theosophists; the winter after that to the rise and fall of the Nabateans. Since then, he had immersed himself in – counted on his crushed fingers – philosophy, history, science, biology, mathematics, economics, medicine, psychology, astronomy, anatomy, archaeology, politics, physiology. Seeking the interconnectedness that lay in everything, he meandered from subject to subject, one fertilising another, to investigate how it fitted into the universal puzzle.

He swallowed his rice cake in quick gulps. He was grinning now. For the first time, he was telling someone who had known him, who might possibly understand, the extent of his journey.

To cram nearly forty years into a conversation over lunch is not easy. Dyer's sense of Rougetel's life was riddled with gaps. What did he do for money, sex? Had he been in love? What did he regret? Most of all, was he ill, on drugs?

These were questions Dyer kept to himself. He hoped they didn't show on his face.

But his thoughts were all tangled. Rougetel's story hardly seemed possible. Dyer would have found so much of it difficult to believe if he hadn't known what Rougetel was capable of.

He wondered about 'crashing points'. There was Rougetel's grief after the death of his parents. Had there been other crises? If so, they didn't feature in his 'Ladybird' autobiography.

Dyer took in that Rougetel had passed his twenties and thirties abroad. He had not returned to Latin America. He avoided big cities. All the time that Dyer had worked as a journalist in Rio, Rougetel's incessant reading was guiding him, in intense bursts of travel, to oblique parts. In book-lined rooms – dusty, deserted – he had steadily augmented his knowledge.

At Dyer's encouragement, Rougetel traced a map with his forefinger on the tablecloth, moving between places where he had halted in order to study. Djibouti, Ceuta, Niamey, Al-Ula, Tromsø, Royal George, Akureyri, Darovoye, Jotogh, Sihanoukville.

But he hadn't always stayed abroad. For more than twenty years he had been in England, and for the past two years in Oxford. His new focus of interest, what had brought him back here, was the human brain, and the differing world views of the left and the right hemispheres. He had been inspired by a 608-page book, the fruit of two decades of research, written by a Prize Fellow of All Souls, a scholar in English Literature who had returned to the college to retrain in medicine.

Excited, Rougetel unfastened the straps of his backpack and brandished the thumbed volume for Dyer to see. It looked waterlogged, as if he had dropped it in the Cherwell – until Dyer realised why the pages appeared so bulged-out and yellow: because of all the post-it notes that Rougetel had inserted.

Rougetel had almost finished digesting the book, the implications of which he found inordinately interesting. He had obtained a Reader card for the Bodleian, and had used the library for his background reading, steadily making his way through the author's bibliography. In a day or so, he would be leaving Oxford.

He glanced across at Dyer, who was still looking at the yellow markers, and gave him a sympathetic smile. 'It's lucky we bumped into each other. Next week, I might not have been here.'

Mutely, Dyer watched him tuck the book back. All these months, he and Rougetel had been living in the same city. How many times had Dyer stepped past him?

A line of Horace came to Dyer. Never be amazed by anything.

Chapter Thirty-nine

DYER'S FIRST WILD THOUGHTS WERE tinged with pity. Rougetel's story could be ascribed to one word: cannabis. Dyer had known several casualties among his university contemporaries, and plenty more in Rio. Freelance mendicants were a common sight up and down the back trails of Latin America. It's one of the things you can do if you're damaged or if you've experienced heartbreak: you can roam.

He had a quick vision of a wandering singer who haunted the bus stop below the *favela*, delivering serenades to the queue in a despairing or ecstatic tenor. Rougetel offered up harmonious snatches of knowledge: he was an intellectual and spiritual nomad, reclusive, who had renounced the ordinary agitations of life to live in libraries and books.

But Rougetel didn't have the manner of an addict, or the air of someone whose experiences had broken him. If he was on drugs or suffering a breakdown, there was no outward sign of it. On the contrary, he seemed, to Dyer, unnaturally coherent. He could smile at himself. At Dyer. He had the lucidity of someone with a clear conscience. He seemed incisive, open, aware. Not out of his wits at all.

Dyer asked for the bill. He had lost his time sense. They'd been talking for more than two hours. 'I have to collect my son.'

'You have a son?'

'Come with me, why don't you? He's at the Phoenix.'

Rougetel's deep-set eyes with their dark brown irises looked at him. 'All right.' He reached for his hat and his rod. 'I'd like that.'

Across the café, his coat on a chair, was a research fellow from Lincoln. Dyer couldn't remember his name. He eyed Rougetel in a curious way that made Dyer feel protective.

Dyer, after paying Miguel, picked up the backpack for Rougetel to put on. It surprised him how little it weighed.

He opened the door for his old friend and they stepped out into Market Street.

Inside the Lisboa, Dyer had been a silent listener. Here in the street, his questions tumbled out. It fascinated him to know where Rougetel ate, slept, how he funded himself, filled the day.

They walked down Cornmarket into St Giles, as Rougetel described his circuit.

'It would only take you a week to get used to,' he said in his sincere, serious voice.

His morning today had begun in Iffley. He had caught a few hours' sleep inside the porch of St Mary the Virgin. He had risen at 4 a.m. before the lights in the vicarage switched on, brushed his teeth, picked out what to wear. He kept in his backpack, wrapping the one or two sacred texts on the subjects he was winnowing: a pair of Primark swimming trunks with a net layer that was easy to wash, three pairs of socks, a shirt, a pullover, plus a toothbrush/toothpaste, a comb, a water bottle, a torch, a penknife, and a bar of L'Occitane verbena-scented soap.

After completing his exercises on the grass, he had jogged, backpack on, along the towpath to the train station, which opened at 4.30 a.m., and sat on a bench. No one threw him out ever, or talked to him; he had no conversations with anyone – 'I try not to draw attention to myself.' Dyer wouldn't have noticed him, necessarily. In his parallel dimension, he fitted like a trout into his surroundings.

At 6 a.m. he walked from the station to McDonald's in Cornmarket. There he ate an egg and cheese McMuffin.

At 9 a.m., he entered one of the university libraries, producing his Bodleian Reader card. He had yet to climb the art-deco staircase to the Taylorian. His three favourites: the Vere Harmsworth Library in Parks Road, the Sackler Library in St John's Street, and the Social Science Library in Manor Road.

Invariably, he spent his day in one of these reading rooms, studying or napping. Twice a week for several months he would wash his clothes in the men's toilet of the Social Science Library, hanging his socks and pants out of the window to dry, or on sunny days spreading them on the hedge beneath, while taking his lunch on the grass strip beside St Catherine's. But George, the doorman, had recently grown suspicious. He had approached Rougetel while he was reading a biography of Max Weber, and warned: 'We've been watching you for some time.' Rougetel had since found an alternative wash basin, in a steam-room on the top floor of the Westgate shopping centre; the door was locked, but he could prise it open with his penknife.

The pattern of his life emerged like a brass rubbing with each loping step.

In the afternoons, he slept for an hour or two in a leather armchair in the Oxford Union – his radical grandmother had given him a lifetime's membership. His eyes became glinty when Dyer asked what he did to stay afloat, as if the subject bored him. 'Money? That's just numbers.'

For his daily expenses, he stretched out on the pavement outside Balliol or Blackfriars, and dozed or read while waiting for money to collect in his hat. On a good day, he funnelled £30 worth of coins into his trouser pocket, concealing any notes in his trainers. A lifetime on the road had taught him how to economise. At lunchtime, he bought a 'meal deal' at Tesco for £4.50; on alternate afternoons, a latte from the stall beneath the Saxon Tower for £2.60. If it was raining hard, he forked out £22.50 to spend the night in a shelter for the homeless. Generally, though, he shunned hostels; the inmates were drug addicts or alcoholics who perceived Rougetel in terms of what materially could be begged, borrowed or filched off him.

Most nights, he walked back along the canal to St Mary's, Iffley, after eating a second egg bap before McDonald's closed at 2 a.m.

He lay down beneath the dog-tooth arch, sometimes on the bench in the porch, sometimes on the stone step – 'surprisingly comfortable' – and always a little nervous in case the vicar should discover him. It calmed something in Rougetel to know that an anchoress had lived here in the thirteenth century, Annora of Iffley, a widow who had holed herself up for nine years beside the church, in a timbered cell with a curtained window, surrounded only by religious books and writing materials, never stepping out into the world. On cold nights, under his tattered Bolivian blanket, reclining against his rucksack, Rougetel recalled his experiences on the road, and felt unexpectedly close to her.

The sun had come out. They crossed Norham Gardens at the entrance to the Parks. Flat bandages of cloud stretched over the trees. Near here a week before, Updark's car had stopped to pick up Dyer.

The sob of a siren sucked Dyer back into the present. He wanted to ask Rougetel his opinion of America and Iran, but then recalled the bafflement in his eyes when Dyer had mentioned the nuclear deal. Dyer predicted that Rougetel would perceive the latest stand-off as not all that important in the great scheme: merely part of a continuity that stretched back, before Annora of Iffley even, to a period when Iran was the Achaemenid Empire and ruled the world – in its way so much larger than now – as the American president strove to dominate today.

Dyer's bewilderment had increased on discovering how Rougetel occupied his days in Oxford. His abnegation was something that Dyer didn't pretend to understand. It was as if they stood facing each other on opposite banks, and there floated between them a dark canal that was unbridgeable.

While it was hard for Dyer, walking on the broad pavement beside him, to think of Rougetel as a neurotic fantasist, his story was so picaresque and unusual that it crossed over into the implausible. He had the childish traits of someone who had sat far too long among books, for whom reading had become a stand-in for life.

Dyer pressed Rougetel further as they walked down Bradmore Road. What was he looking for? What had he found? Had his life travelled the questions he had asked of it into a resolution? In the boundless expanse of his reading and meditating had he come across one entry point, like a seal's breathing hole in the ice, which led him to the core?

Rougetel's response was a shy smile. He had not yet synchronised his experiences into something tangible, a fusion of his knowledge in which he saw everything together and all at once – at least, not in a way that Dyer might easily understand. He was carrying it in his head, references, footnotes, conclusions, until he was ready to write it down. He was close to that point, but in no hurry. It didn't need to be finished by a particular date, it was not an article for a newspaper or a linear journey; it was open-ended, ongoing.

'Do you get depressed ever?' Dyer wanted to know.

Rougetel looked steadily at him. The skin around his eyes had the transparency of an ascetic. 'No.'

'Do you never feel self-pitying in the rain under the porch?'

'No.'

'So it's been a success then, your life?'

He couldn't say it had been a waste. To think in these terms didn't fit in with his philosophy. Justifications were for others. For Rougetel, there was no such a thing as a false trail, a dead end, a phoney prophet, a bad book. It was all learning. At the same time, his life, the purpose of it, still awaited an explanation.

Meanwhile, only the present moment exists, is what he'd learned.

His steady, self-contained gaze intimidated Dyer who, being one himself, recognised the solipsism of an only child. Rougetel had had none of the counterbalance of a sibling to hold up a corrective mirror, or a son like Leandro. He had lived, emotionally and intellectually, on his own resources, without the encumbrance of family or belongings, so that to all intents he might have come from Pluto. He had no partner, dependants, domicile, job, yet something mysterious had taken their place, a spiritual life stripped of egoism, full of revelations that he sensed but had yet to articulate, and it was childish of Dyer to want Rougetel to join him on the same bank.

Rougetel, it penetrated Dyer, as they entered Phoenix Lane, was not looking to be rescued or understood; he was too involved in trying to understand. He was content with his life, its arrangement suited him. Not for an empire would he be in Dyer's trainers.

Every instinct in Dyer had prompted compassion for this poor creature, but it was Rougetel who pitied him, who saw Dyer as benighted.

Dyer said quickly in a new voice, overtaking any note of disbelief: 'At least you had a real go, probably the only one of us who did. You took a journey none of us dared to do.'

After all that, they had arrived early at the Phoenix. There was no one else in the playground. Side by side, like brothers who have never quarrelled, they walked towards the Rink.

Rougetel looked up to the bell on the roof.

'I remember ringing that,' in a slow voice.

'Why?'

'I don't know, I was head of something.'

'School?'

'Something like that.'

He lowered his eyes to the team notices. Leandro's name was posted for the final match of term, against the Dragon School.

'Your son?'

'That's right.'

Rougetel went on staring. '"Parents are welcome to the match tea ..."' His mouth was open. 'Do they serve scones still?'

'They do.'

'Custard creams?' The tip of his tongue. Seeking the taste.

'As well.'

More memories resurfaced. He had been wicket-keeper for the first XI. Also, captain of swimming – although this hadn't stopped Slimy from beating him.

Dyer turned. He was still processing the image of Rougetel keeping wicket. 'Slimy beat you? Whatever for?'

Rougetel screwed up his eyes to the window above the white clock – Slimy's study.

'I'd gone to the barge ...'

The graininess of memory. The scene unreeled in his mind with the haphazard continuity of the films they would watch in Hall on Sunday nights. The rain belting down. A notice with the words: 'Fields out of bounds'. Behind the window, a man with thin lips adjusts a lens.

On certain wet afternoons, Slimy spied on boys who trespassed onto the waterlogged pitches. 'He wrote down our names,' said Rougetel, as if he could see the outline of a telescope afloat on the glass, 'then summoned us to his room one by one.'

If anything, the punishment – ten whacks with a gymshoe of Rougetel's choice, and much less painful than symbolic – had served to make the barge a destination yet more tantalising. Not long afterwards, Rougetel had spent the night in its hold. In defiance of every rule, he had stolen out of his dormitory carrying a punnet of raspberries, hoarded over from Sunday tea, in case he got hungry, and a towel to dry himself following a midnight dip.

Visible from the playground until its demolition, the blue oblong hull had loomed on Rougetel's boyhood horizon as the archetypal frontier post, like the two or three cafés in town that it thrilled him to visit with Dyer. A quarterdeck from which to espy, not merely the far riverbank, but, with that divine intoxication Emily Dickinson had flagged in their English class, 'the first league out from land'.

He was looking across the playing fields. Without speaking, he stepped away from the Rink and took some of his lolloping strides out over the Hard Court. Dyer caught up with him on the football pitch, and they continued walking towards the river.

The blue barge had been on Rougetel's mind when he climbed over the fence on a cold September evening shortly after arriving in Oxford eighteen months earlier. Never before then had he returned to the Phoenix, but compelled by a desire to revisit the site, he spent that night on the river-bank where the barge used to be. Inside its converted hold during his last summer term, he had changed into his swimming trunks, hopping on one leg like a stork, before diving into the Cherwell to compete against local schools. Yet this time he had found it hard to sleep when he lay down on the wet grass and recalled his races back and forth across the muddy water. 'I felt I was swimming through these strong dark currents, cold, warm, sometimes clear, and sometimes with my feet in the slime.'

His serious brown eyes drifted to the far bank. They touched the rushes, then swept back over the War Memorial, the cricket pavilion, the playing fields, to the familiar brick buildings, the toothpick mast of the flagpole, and the playground where the two of them had stood but moments before. It had been blacker than tar on that chill September night, and Rougetel had crept away before sunrise.

Now, for the first time as an adult, he was seeing the whole of the Phoenix set out before him in conditions of daylight. It was almost too big to absorb.

'We followed the path laid by our parents, leaving home, feeling sick at having to come back to school, with no one to talk to about our feelings, not daring to utter them in case we were struck down or mocked ...'

A boy was speaking from the years before. The unaccompanied minor from La Paz being led away by the stewardess after kissing goodbye to his mother and father, neither of whom had ever sat Rougetel down and said to him: '*This is what the deal is.*'

His gaze pulled back over the sandpit to the swimming pool erected in Dyer's last year as a substitute for the Cherwell. His eyes sought the low Nissen hut where he and Dyer had nailed together their wooden weapons. He was hearing the war cries of boys in faded blue corduroys, the splutter of make-believe machine guns.

He was still reflecting. 'I felt we were being trained to go into battle like my grandparents, and now I'm nearly sixty and there's been no battle, I wonder if actually the battle was fought here when I was eight, and that it was about learning to cope.'

The bell was ringing. Mr Tanner could be observed in the distance, crossing the playground in purposeful strides to take up his newly adopted position by the gate. Parents had begun trickling through it, assembling in clots outside the Rink. Soon Katya would stand there, and Silvi, and Updark's overscented wife.

'Let's go and find my son,' said Dyer.

Rougetel gave a last glance at the riverbank. He fell in step as they walked across the grass in the weakening sunlight. His gait much lighter somehow, as if a load had lifted.

As they approached the Hard Court, a boy advanced towards them.

Dyer called out: 'Leandro, come and meet someone.'

It was hard to talk against the sound of other conversations, with mothers and children hurrying past, and Dyer unable to give Leandro a background to the lean, bearded figure whom he introduced, other than to say: 'We were at the Phoenix together.'

Following a polite exchange – he didn't say twenty words – Rougetel excused himself.

The strange light in his eyes told Dyer that he was still on his path, and was impatient to be off again.

Under the keen scrutiny of Mr Tanner, Dyer escorted him through the gate. It was clear from Rougetel's hesitation, the way that his gaze roamed up and down the street, that he intended to leave in a direction opposite to Dyer. He had a mission to fulfil, more nets to set under the ice, and Dyer was not going to detain him.

'Where will you go?' Dyer asked.

'The Hebrides, most likely.' His grandmother had left him a croft – a good place to mull over his next subject. Already, his mind was turning to what he might study.

He stood with his heels on the edge of the pavement, working out his farewell. He repeated how lucky it was that they had bumped into each other. Providence had put Dyer in his path. He was grateful for their catch-up. He took Dyer's hands. 'It's done me good to see you, it's refreshed me. I'm reminded of so many things, and I'll be the stronger for it.'

'It's done me good too,' said Dyer, and rarely had he meant words more.

After a verbena-scented embrace, and a nod and a smile to Leandro, Rougetel set off down Bardwell Road. He had gone a few paces when he stopped and turned. He raised his arm in a half-completed gesture like a child reaching up to hold his mother's hand. Then he continued walking, and this time he did not look back.

Thinking afterwards of his wonderful old maniac of a friend, Dyer said to himself that he would be entitled to believe their whole afternoon together had been a dream. If he had been in the Andes, climbing Mount Ausangate, he would be asking himself if he had seen Rougetel, or was it the altitude?

'Has he changed?' Leandro wanted to know.

In spite of everything that had happened in between, some vital part of him had remained untouched. He still wanted to get to the nub.

'I'd say hardly at all.'

Chapter Forty

'A TROUT FLY CAN'T BE *withdrawn the way it has entered,'* said his father. *'It must be pushed right through.'*

So with Marvar's post-it note. Dyer could not rebury it in the sandpit, he couldn't leave it folded in limbo inside a library book. He had to pull it up, out, away.

Next morning, Dyer resolved to finish what his encounter with Rougetel had interrupted. To avoid arousing any further suspicion, he had had to persuade himself that his solution lay in plucking out Marvar's algorithm and destroying it. The sooner he accomplished this the better; no one must know it had existed. He no longer saw it in terms of the gains or dangers to humanity, only its impact on him. It had to be destroyed so that he did not die, and so that he and Leandro could live. He wasn't brave. He wanted to be safe and his son to be safe. Simple.

From near the bottom of his reserved pile, Dyer prised loose the calf-bound volume and took it next door. As soon as he opened the back cover and his eyes fell on the folded piece of paper floating around the map of Brazil, he felt the tension subside that had been growing as he climbed the staircase.

He lifted his eyes to the wall opposite, and his obliterating impulse receded, and he was overtaken by a warm, inexplicable calm, as if a blue haze has enveloped him.

He is back in the Café Lisboa. Rougetel is riffling through the book he has produced from his rucksack. Its pages flutter like a kaleidoscope of butterflies with yellow post-it notes to mark the passages which had captivated him.

Even as Dyer detaches Marvar's note, Rougetel's voice is knocking on his thoughts.

It's almost the last thing Rougetel says to him. They're standing at the school gate, Rougetel is talking about how close he is to wrapping up his research into the human brain, and looking forward to immersing himself in something quite new, although he has yet to decide what this will be.

There's a moment in the middle of a hangover when you have a sudden penetration and you see the world with complete clarity. You have it seldom, but when this flash comes it seems as if it's calculated, like an oracle. Dyer had experienced it once or twice when he rowed. Instincts take charge and you see what is important, what not, and how to plunge ahead. The Buddhists probably had a word for it. Thinking too much was the problem. The answer came to him when he let his body and instincts do the reacting, with not too much brain.

Like a man smoothing out something he had crumpled, Dyer saw what he must do.

'That can go back,' he said to the librarian. He handed her the collection of first-hand accounts describing Cabral's voyage to Brazil.

She took it without glancing up.

'You don't want to renew this?'

He looked down at her white head. 'No.'

The way she diverted her gaze to hide that she'd been watching him. She walked as though she wore velvet slippers, her dark hair in a Suebian knot.

A sporty-looking woman he had not seen before descended in quick silent steps behind him. He reached the bottom of the staircase and pushed out into the street through the open glass door. Then something made Dyer turn and pull it shut.

In the ferment of knowing how he was going to dispose of Marvar's algorithm, Dyer had let go the danger of carrying it on his person. But he had learned to trust his presentiments. After a moment of imbalance, he was wide awake.

At an unswerving pace he set off, as though heading in the direction of the Martyrs' Memorial. Crossing the road at a diagonal, he waited for a taxi to go by, before cutting between it and a Waitrose van. As the van moved slowly forward, shielding him momentarily from the Taylorian, he ducked left behind it.

Yards away – about to pull out – was a red double-decker Citysightseeing bus. Dyer ran towards it, keeping his head low. He jumped on board as the doors hissed shut, and then thrust his way past seats occupied by smiling Chinese tourists, taking cover behind a broad-faced man who stood in the aisle holding a microphone.

Through the rear window, Dyer watched the woman hurry from the library. He shrank back, out of her line of vision. When he next risked a look, she had stopped on the pavement, and was searching up and down St Giles, peering intently at the van, the passing cars, the receding bus, before reaching into her tight-fitting anorak and, after a flicker of hesitation, jogging off in the opposite direction.

'Well, hello, again,' said the man, who wore a black blazer with brass buttons on it and a familiar striped tie. 'Come to join my tour? Let me introduce you to this vibrant and cultured city.'

Overcome with relief and gratitude, Dyer purchased a ticket.

Minutes later, the guide's educated voice poured out of the speakers in a soothing rhythm. 'Our first stop is the University Parks. Many of you may have heard of Mesopotamia ...'

Dyer hopped off. To reach Ward Road, he took a strange route through the Parks until he could be sure that no one was on his trail. The bridge where Thor had slobbered over Gilles. The cricket pavilion that Updark had eyed with nostalgia. At one point in his circuit, Dyer left the path and stood for several moments concealed beneath the low-hanging branches of a conifer. The tree had grown since the afternoon when he climbed it with Rougetel, and where, high up, tucked in a cleft between the trunk and the bough on which they had managed to perch, they found, neatly folded, a page torn from a magazine, and opened it to see, ineradicable, their first naked woman.

She opens the door and stares at him. 'You've decided?'

'I have.'

Her face in the morning light. Already she is losing her tan. She pulls down her dress to get rid of the crease.

'Go and wait in the drawing room, and I'll fetch it. You can talk to my memory, she'll be pleased to see you.'

He walked to the end of the corridor, towards the sound of a Brahms clarinet quintet.

Thor bounded off the sofa to greet him. There was the squeal of farm machinery, and then Miranda's mother shuffled out of the conservatory on her walking frame. A sudden warmth filled her unsmiling face when she saw it was Dyer.

'There you are!'

He took her hands, her fingers grey and shiny like cake paper.

She looked severely at him. 'Why haven't we seen you?'

'I've been travelling,' he said. It was only the previous day that they had stood in the middle of the room like this, the radio playing.

She frowned at him, but changed her mind. 'Miranda has missed you.'

It was a novel feeling for Dyer to sense that someone cared for him. She must have known it would take him a second to answer, because she leaned across and fixed Dyer with one eye like a chicken. 'She can be peppery as a single woman. Marriage made her the salt of the earth. Her life has been tasteless since he went.'

'Talking about yourself, Mother?' said Miranda, entering and turning the radio down. She laid Dyer's envelope on the counter. It was the same colour as her dress. 'Coffee?'

What meaning was held in her glance, he couldn't tell. 'If it's not any trouble ...'

'Trouble, trouble, trouble, trouble,' tutted Miranda's mother in a high raspy voice as if she had swallowed Thor's whistle. 'Trouble been doggin' my soul since the day I was born,' and began navigating her frame towards the card table.

Miranda met his eyes and gave a see-what-I-put-up-with shrug. 'This morning, she had all her suitcases stacked in the hall. I asked why on earth hadn't she let me bring them downstairs, to which she replied: "I just chucked them down the stairs in front of me as I can't possibly manage the steps carrying anything." But it's good to see her talking,' she said bravely.

Her mother had been ill, her voice had only just come back. Miranda very nearly had had to return early from Paguera.

'She's still complaining of the cold.'

'She doesn't look ill,' observed Dyer.

'When she gets unwell she looks very well because she gets these lovely rosy cheeks,' and went to fill the kettle.

It was no use thinking old age might be different, Miranda continued. However prepared you thought you were. One thing her mother had taught: 'We learn nothing, it all has to be re-learned.' Not even if you were an expert did it help. 'Have you noticed? All hair surgeons are bald, no coach plays tennis, no critic can write.'

'You sound like my aunt.'

'What do you think, Mummy? Could we have done this better?'

Seated at the card table, her mother was combing her hair in a silver hand mirror.

'Mother?'

No answer.

He thought of his mother brushing her thinning hair, not out of vanity, but so as not to frighten others; not to see reflected in their faces the brown bloated features of chemo.

'Let me plump some life into the old cushion. Stay there.'

Miranda leaned over her, saying in a comforting voice: 'I'll keep the heating going. I won't switch that off. You're in a safe place, darling.'

Dyer could not help admiring her, the concerned and patient way she treated the old lady. Her energy was unexpected, homely but with something grand about it, like an apron worn over a ballgown. He had a sudden vision of the fury of other women at the modest one who wins the prince.

She came back to finish making their coffee.

'How's your toe?' he asked.

'Getting better, thank you.' And flexed out her foot.

There was a simple sensual confidence in the movement. Unhurried, she turned her slender neck, her face. It was a lovely face. Pale and oval. The face of a woman in a classical painting.

He looks at her for a fraction of a second longer than is normal, not seeming to notice the dog that has come between them. She lowers her foot, raises her head. Their eyes meet over the counter in an unspoken recognition that he related afterwards to a shared sense of humour, an involuntary start at a beautiful view. She looked at him and she knew him.

'Thor! Off!'

Dyer stooped to stroke him and a soft muzzle brushed his heart.

'I need some advice,' he said, straightening.

In the corner, Miranda's mother was chanting to herself in the mirror: 'She's got hair on her pussy that sweep the floor, she's got knobs on her titties that open the door.'

Miranda, disregarding her, poured the hot water over the coffee. 'My favourite sentence in the world is: "Can I ask your opinion on this?"'

A while later, Dyer paused in the doorway. He stared at the envelope that he had addressed to himself, like one of those brown envelopes he opened at the last moment, and then up at her.

'I must give you my new number.'

He watched Miranda enter it into her phone, feeling the tight pull in his chest now that he had decided to trust her. 'I know we've just begun to get to know each other. Would you … I don't want …'

She hears the catch in his voice, puts a finger to her lip. 'Xasó putár neirúm.'

The next time they meet, she will tell him: 'My father taught me that beginning is more precious than money.'

Chapter Forty-one

THEY CAME OUT OF THE throat of the dawn, three of them, rearing up from behind a parked car as Dyer inserted his key in the lock. They were efficient, well trained, wearing balaclavas. They did not speak as they pinned him up against the boatyard's wooden entrance and roughly searched him as he stood there. He couldn't see their faces, they were like beings from another place. Their gloved fingers quickly picked through his coat, jacket, trousers, wallet. Then they pushed him onto the ground and took off his trainers and socks. They must have suspected him of having Marvar's algorithm on his person after removing it from the library. They had already combed his house, and knew it wasn't there. If it existed at all, then he must be carrying it. He wished he had a gun so that he could shoot them one by one between the eyes, instead of lying supinely recumbent on the pavement where Paula had spilled her tins of pineapple chunks. He lay there rigid, as if in a coffin the lid of which they were on the point of nailing down, not resisting, not moving, not saying a word, seeing in their black woollen faces the pointy features of Gilles Asselin streaked with war-paint, and for some reason recalling a story that Gilles had told at his dinner party before leading his guests downstairs to eat, how the African king of Kitara was fed by his cook with a fork, but if the fork accidentally touched the king's teeth he was executed, until a noise disturbed them – Paula opening her front door – and they stood up, tossed his wallet back at him and calmly walked off, abandoning Dyer by the side of the road, his clothes strewn around him, with his heart thumping like a tennis ball, and feeling as if he had come to the end of his ordeal.

Chapter Forty-two

DOWN THE STRAIGHT NIGHT-TIME street in the cold, at the hour when curtains are still drawn and the only thing that tells you which decade it is are the posters on the windows saying 'Brexit means Brexit!' and 'Stick to the Iran deal!', Dyer had two hours earlier walked to Iffley.

He had followed the route they took as schoolboys when they wanted not to be noticed. Remarkable how it came back, the strategy they'd devised to enable them to melt into their surroundings. It had been learned in the playground as they chased each other around the Rink yelling: 'Uh-uh-uh-uh,' and enacting out war games derived from comic books in which there was a lot about Rommel in the desert, and all Germans went: 'Aaagh ...' or 'Achtung!'

Fork right at the bridge. Dash through the trees. A five-minute crouch between two barges to ascertain if anyone was on his heels. He had climbed out over Paula's fence, and clung to the shadows as he crossed the deserted boatyard. Anyone watching him would be waiting in St Barnabas Street, on the other side of the big wooden gate.

Satisfied that he has not been seen and no one is following, Dyer stands up, steps back onto the tinder track.

His hard knuckle of obtuseness leads him along the towpath. His mind is focused and steady, he has stumbled out of his plasma. He'd been breathing on a mirror, and wasn't able to see himself until Rougetel rubbed a thick book about the brain over this patch of mist and it was clear again.

After leaving Miranda's house, Dyer had spent the afternoon searching the streets and libraries of Oxford. He had visited in turn the Vere Harmsworth Library, the Sackler Library, the Social Science Library. Rougetel wasn't in any of the reading rooms. Dyer had poked his head into the Union library, but the sole dozing figure was a stoutish young undergraduate, blond, in a green tweed suit. He had checked the pavements outside Balliol and Blackfriars, the train station, McDonald's, Tesco. Nowhere could he spot a lean, bearded figure in black jeans, like Atlas, carrying a Kathmandu rucksack.

The church at Iffley really was his last hope.

He needed to get to him quick. Like all nomads, Rougetel would strike camp in a flash. Fearful that he might even now be on his way to the Scottish isles, Dyer took such large steps that he was practically running.

In the motionless dark of the Oxford dawn, he thought of his honest-eyed friend. How he had followed his path, withstood blows, and acted with courage, perseverance, integrity. Rougetel contained multitudes. He was not sectarian, not an ideologue. He was so much more superior to Dyer. The road had taught him to discard as dross the wasteful emotions that continued to consume Dyer – impatience, anxiety, selfishness, self-doubt, fear, envy, lust.

Plus, hadn't he said he was ripe for a new project, a fresh text?

It had struck Dyer in the Taylorian, as he was taking out Marvar's post-it note with the firm resolve to destroy it, how similar at superficial glance was the process that Marvar had described to that experienced by Rougetel. The ever-expanding energy, the white light, the close connection between atoms in the brain and the nuclear forces in the sun.

Dyer had been looking for distraction at the painting – envying the couple in it, how they existed beyond the pressures of Dyer's world in a landscape much like the Lake District, now he came to think of it; and how tempted he was to climb the red rolling library ladder to join them – when the idea burst on him.

Rougetel would make sense of it if anyone could. He was a free spirit, he had no dependants, no allegiances save to what his instinct told him was true. Marvar's breakthrough wouldn't be lost. It would be considered, assimilated, added to the synthesis of Rougetel's worldly knowledge. And if his algorithm was everything that Marvar claimed, Rougetel, out of all the talented people Dyer had met in his life, could be trusted to make an objective decision about who to give it to in order for it to be exploited for good.

Dyer turns his head, checking again.

A further factor in Rougetel's favour: he doesn't possess a phone or a laptop, so no GPS will be able to track him. Beyond everything, there had to be no risk to his person; no one must know what Dyer is about to do.

Not a thing moves in the street, in the windows.

A light breeze blew up as Dyer approached the entrance to St Mary's. Leaves from the trees overlooking the cemetery whirled across the paving stones. The porch lay in shadow. Dyer thought it was empty. Then his eyes readjusted to the shadows, and he made out a figure stretched on the bench.

In silence, Dyer stepped up to him. Rougetel lay on his back, asleep with a slight smile. His head rested on his rolled-up blue sleeping bag. He had wrapped himself in his Inca blanket, and his pigeon toes protruded from under it with their socks still on. In these surroundings, his hat like a sombrero, his white rod, his backpack seem excessive luxuries. The dawn light makes him Christ-like, but it gives to him other faces as well. A boy who lies on a riverbank with his eyes half-closed. A voyager from another world who will rise in a short while on the strand of a new continent.

Careful to make no noise, Dyer took the envelope from his coat pocket. It was the brown envelope that he had posted to Miranda, containing his detailed account of all that Marvar had told him on Port Meadow. Dyer had stuck Marvar's post-it note to the first page, with an explanatory letter.

Rougetel scratches his ankle in sleep. As vulnerable and exposed as the corner of a book.

Dyer unfastens the rucksack, slips in the envelope, and does up the buckle.

He stands for a moment in a kind of benison. Then he takes a step back and turns and quietly leaves.

His earlier panic has left him. He feels reinvigorated, as if he has let a great fish go free. Walking home, the sound of birds, a roseate glow in the sky, suddenly all the irritations of Oxford seem precious.

Chapter Forty-three

ON SATURDAY MORNING, MR TANNER hoisted up the flagpole a square of yellow cloth stitched with the blue emblem of a phoenix.

That afternoon, the Phoenix were playing the Dragon. The schools had been rivals for years. A big turnout was expected.

Traditionally, both schools fielded their first and second XIs. The touchlines thronged with parents who had children in the teams. The largest group of spectators was made up of Phoenix parents and teachers. A victory against the Dragon had a taste of its own.

Dyer arrived in good time for once. He waved to Leandro as the teams filed out. The clock chimed two, and the games kicked off.

Leandro's team very nearly conceded a goal in the opening minute. Only a desperate punch from Pierre Asselin diverted the ball. He saved two more strikes in quick succession, his teammates clustering into the goalmouth to congratulate him. They looked nervous, outclassed.

The Dragon continued to dominate. Time and again, the Phoenix defence failed to push the game into their opponents' half. Leandro, at centre forward, was unemployed for long stretches. He burst unchecked into an empty space, called for the ball, and when it was intercepted ran back.

Pierre stopped a fourth near-goal with his knees. This unconventional save somehow galvanised the team, and the Phoenix started to rally. They played better, more fluently.

Leandro raced up and down. Dyer's eyes followed his son until he wasn't looking at him. He was watching him, but he wasn't looking at him.

Dyer glanced, at last, over to the other pitch.

Katya stood talking to the father in the black beret. Her profile was haughty now. Entrenched in her superior passivity.

The two were watching the second XI. In the event, neither of their sons had been promoted to replace Samir. That honour had gone, instead, to Henry Puckey.

A baseball cap all of a sudden blocked Dyer's view. Shuttling between both games, with his carroty hair and insatiable smile, Ralph Cubbage had no child playing in either team.

Already, Dyer had registered the coded manner in which the cellist's father had greeted Updark. Not long after that, Cubbage had paused to speak to Gilles in earnest, nothing-to-do-with-football tones. Now, he monitored Katya and her wild-haired companion, who, it had dawned on Dyer somewhat late in the day, was none other than Marvar's professor at the Clarendon, Bruce Whitton.

Dyer's eye was caught by a figure approaching in a fur hat and a long white-and-blue scarf. He looked like a Brazilian construction boss, stumpy and round-stomached, his leather jacket dark and shiny as the Chevrolet that Vasily boasted his father had imported from Havana. His shoes with chains across the toecap lent a dapper touch.

He was marching over the grass towards Katya. Cubbage, noticing him before she did, lowered his head and nonchalantly rotated his cap.

Gennady had appeared, late, like the ominous stranger Dyer once witnessed descend on a Brazilian film set. When Dyer had enquired who this was, he was informed that the man represented the film's backers – invested with their absolute authority, should the production run over budget, to say: 'OK, that's a wrap.'

Cut free of Katya's gravitational sway, Dyer created the details. He knew how it would be. In the apartment off Jamaica Road, after the match. She waits for him, he has come with a box of salmon for Vasily, a cashmere sweater for her; they go out to dinner at Gee's. He touches her face, the lights glint on his leather jacket.

'He doesn't know,' she says to Gennady. *'For a while, I had this suspicion, but – truly – he doesn't know anything, unless it is about some Brazilian tribe,'* and counterfeits his voice: *'"My subject is sixteenth-century Brazil. The twenty-first century can go screw itself."'*

To Dyer's relief, neither Gennady nor Katya nor Whitton nor Cubbage, nor even Hui's bodyguard, who has popped up wearing a brand new Phoenix scarf, once turn their face in his direction. They display all the indifference of the Tupi to Afonso Ribeiro, after Ribeiro relinquished his one or two metal objects which had so mesmerised the tribe. They have looked into Dyer long and thoroughly enough to be satisfied that he doesn't know anything useful. He's been questioned, followed, intimidated, bribed, his house searched, his communications investigated, his research checked. They have run through all their options, and feel confident that he would have cracked by now. With nothing solid to connect him to Rustum Marvar, Dyer is not any longer a target of interest. He has reverted to what Updark always took him to be: an under-employed ex-journalist who likes to stir things up, perverse, stubborn, but not a troublemaker, not a dangerous subversive. A bit player caught, for the briefest of flashes, cringing in the headlights of a juggernaut that has since roared by.

*

A bark drew him back to the game. Beatrice Updark teetered on the touchline, doing her best to restrain Spassky.

The first time Dyer saw Spassky, he had thought of savage-eyed dogs snapping at him, the metal entrails of unfinished floors rusting upwards to a blue, vulture-specked sky. But Spassky was not like that, with his eyebrows like 'caramel waterfalls' as Leandro put it; he wanted to drool over Dyer's hand, not tear it into shreds as Dyer until very recently had wanted to rip up Marvar's post-it note.

Held back by his collar, Spassky craned to watch the Phoenix players dash forward. It was a moment before Dyer realised that the dog's eyes – like Beatrice's ... and now his – were trained on one boy: arm in the air, long legs, sand-coloured hair. His part-Tupi son. He was gesturing to Puckey, who suddenly had possession.

Leandro spun, unmarked, into the Dragon half, and was again denied the ball. Control, pass, control, pass, the Dragon forwards kept it out of his stretch – thundering down on him when he did force an interception. He floated over one pass, wasted another.

Even now, Dyer was plotting his next progress report that he had undertaken to write to Nissa at the end of each term. He would tell her that their son had ended this term on a high. Dyer saw no gain in mentioning Vasily's bullying earlier. Aside from being selected for the school football team, Leandro had improved in his academic work, history in particular. Commended for his test on Trafalgar, Leandro had climbed over Paula's fence to thank her. He liked a bit of a fuss so that he could flaunt his modesty, admitting to his father only late in the day that he had received assistance as well from Beatrice. Who would have thought this at the start of term?

The whistle blew at half-time with neither side having scored.

While the teams changed ends, a group of Dragon parents standing beside Dyer moved away ... exposing Gilles Asselin.

He was talking in a frantic voice on his phone.

'I'm ringing totally the wrong number. It's Gilles, I thought you were someone else. Sorry about that. Take care. Bye.'

He saw Dyer, and stiffened like someone about to be photographed.

'Jean ...' crushing his gloves.

One look at his face.

No longer a pike sizing up a parr. No longer on any podium.

Out of his throat rumbled the words: 'Do you have it?'

'No.'

'I thought you did,' with a sad gulp. 'I got you wrong.'

He had not believed Dyer. His hunches which, until now, had profited him so acutely had whispered into his over-receptive ear that Dyer *was* sitting on Marvar's epoch-defining information – why else would Dyer have made that dedication in his book: *To Rustum Marvar, who may have solved everything*? Why else would the waiter in the St Giles Café have overheard Marvar rise abruptly from the table where he had been scribbling on his fourth paper napkin, muttering: *'I've done it, I've done it ...'* Why else would Marvar have texted his wife: *Now I may have done something!*

Calculating that even if Marvar didn't capitalise on what it was that he had done, then Dyer was bound to, and therefore would need to act on it as soon as possible, Gilles had asked himself: 'Who's going to be affected by nuclear fusion? Let's short them. Big governments that rely on hydrocarbonates. Companies like BP, Exxon. Venezuelan debt.'

Gambler that he was, Gilles had shorted everything that lay within his global financial compass to short, borrowing 'right up my Wazoo', he admitted to Dyer with a ruined smile. 'I poured shitloads into speculation about where next.' He had sold out of coal mines, bought up deserts ... He was heading south fast.

He looked haggard.

Dyer stayed obstinately silent.

Arms crossed, with her back to them, Silvi squinted at the football game, which had resumed.

'Pierre's had a good first half,' said Dyer, stepping out, he hoped, on a safe path.

There was something wrong and uncorrected in her posture, like a picture hung upside down.

*

'Basil!'

His name was being called by a man in a faded yellow-and-blue striped scarf.

Further along the touchline were Lionel Updark and his wife.

Dyer had not spoken to Audrey Updark since her house-warming party in January. He kissed her on the cheek. This afternoon there was a change about her that he couldn't put his finger on. Her hair? Then it came to him. She smelled different.

Something miraculous meanwhile had happened to Updark: his face had cleared up, and with it his outward hostility. He stood there spotless, not interested at all in discussing the game's first half, but grinningly eager to talk about what had caused his skin to come out like a red *cruzeiro* banknote, and how the problem had been traced. It was his wife's perfume!

'They forgot to look at Audrey. No one thinks: "What's the wife wearing?" Turns out I had an allergy to a scent she bought in Morocco.' The cologne contained a psoriasitic chemical, musk ambrette, that was banned in the EU. Every time Updark walked into the bathroom after Audrey had sprayed herself, he had a facial reaction. "Allergic contact dermatisis" is what the cuckoos in Milton Keynes had diagnosed. He patted his cheeks as though applying aftershave. 'The rashes disappeared seventy-two hours after they discovered the cause!'

Of course, Audrey had had to bin the perfume, but he'd bought her some Jo Malone Pomegranate Noir at Heathrow while on a reconnaissance trip to his next post. He wouldn't tell Dyer where this was, although he did say that Lorna, who had been appointed his successor in Eynsham, had enquired fondly after him.

Inevitably, it was Leandro who scored the winning goal with seven minutes to spare. His Pelé-like kick from inside his own half was unexpected, completely. A divinely aided bolt that made Dyer think straight away of Samir and Marvar and the trigger for Marvar's spherical laser. Fusion, football, a sudden wind from the south ... it had the temporary effect of stunning everyone on the pitch. The Dragon never recovered.

'I had no intention of scoring,' Leandro blurted after the final whistle when Dyer came over to embrace him. 'It was a total accident. I wanted to clear it, to send it to someone else. I thought I was going to cross it forward, and ... oh, my gosh, is it going towards the goal? ... and I stopped for a second and I saw it go into the goal and I saw the Dragon goalie reach for it and I saw it hit the back of the net – what?!'

All around them, parents were leaving the pitch and heading across the playground to the dining room.

'I'll see you in there,' he said to Leandro.

It would be unsporting not to join them for the match tea, Dyer decided. He would eat a scone for Rougetel, the wicket-keeper. And a custard cream.

He'd be on his way by now, walking out along the cinder towpath on his long loping legs, his pack on his bony shoulders, seeing what the universe would bring. Locked in his meditative trance from which he would return one day to fetch the souls of others into the light.

Chapter Forty-four

LOVE HAD MADE HIM A child again.

He slept much better

He had begun writing.

The New World acted as a Black Spot for the men who set eyes on it for the first time. Pêro Vaz de Caminha, after sending his account to Lisbon on a special ship, perished within months, killed in Calicut. Pedro Álvares Cabral, the leader of the expedition, died in obscurity, as did two of the three convicts left behind as breeding stock on the dazzling strand at Porto Seguro. Only Afonso Ribeiro of this initial landing party survived to learn the customs of the Tupi and to speak their language, starting a family whose descendants are today dotted over north-east Brazil.

In Summertown, the freshest bread from the rumour mill was that Gilles Asselin had lost his shirt.

'I hear their house may soon be on the market.'

'All the contents, too, Silvi told me.'

'The private jet will have to go ...'

'And the chateau in France.'

'Poor Silvi. She's just joined our reading club.'

Conversation turned to Beatrice Updark's father. He had been appointed Ambassador to Portugal. 'He says that Lisbon is not Paris, but it's still a most desirable post. There's an excellent chance of a royal visit, and with that a knighthood.'

In charge of a collection to buy the headmaster a leaving present, Samantha Puckey had raised £92.

In the Café Lisboa, the faces absorbed in the newspapers were a little less grave. Iran and America had reached a stalemate. The American president had taken a hard look at war in the Middle East, and, like something you are anxious to have and a moment later decide you don't want, had turned his attention back to Canada.

In a bay on Tasmania's west coast, the mathematician Todd Angle had been found alive, having lived on berries for forty-seven days.

About the fate of a missing Iranian scientist, his family, nothing.

Dyer glimpsed Marvar in scraps of conversation. At High Table in Trinity, from a Fellow who was a brain surgeon, Dyer heard the story of a terribly sick man who had been delivered unconscious in a military ambulance to the John Radcliffe, and carried to his own room in the John Warin ward, where he was guarded by two armed soldiers who conveyed to doctors and nurses that they must not comment on or remember anything the man might say in his ravings. Not one of his friends or relatives was allowed to be with him during his last hours. The surgeon had seen the body. He started to describe someone bearing no resemblance to Marvar – short, slight, grey hair – and was surprised when Dyer laughed suddenly.

In a story of 'rickety authority' – i.e. Cubbage – Updark had heard that 'oil men' might be involved, and that operatives working for Exxon or Chevron had abducted Marvar. 'The rumour is – and I underline rumour – he may be in Houston.'

Hissop, meanwhile, was following a lead that the weapons industry lay behind Marvar's disappearance.

Dyer detested these scenarios. Against the vacuum of hard, verifiable fact, he elaborated another theory, one that his most superstitious and stubborn self held to be no more rickety: from his safe place of refuge near Howtown, Marvar had contacted General Damghani of the Revolutionary Guard, and they had hammered out a deal – as once upon a time Rejas had made a pact with Calderón in order to see Yolanda again.

In Dyer's alternative fictional version, Marvar had said to himself something like this. The whole universe came into being by fusion, built up from a pea soup of hydrogen, with a cosmic explosion; its moment had arrived, no army in the world could stop it; whatever human beings were capable of, nuclear fusion was a factor we were all going to have to live with, for good or bad, and if that was the case then what did it matter who had it first, whether it was the Iranians or the Americans or the British, because everyone would have it in the end, and that included Israelis, Saudis, Chinese, North Koreans, even tribes on the Amazon; but personally Marvar could not, in the end, exist one further moment without Shula.

'*There's always a woman.*'

Dyer had a persistent vision of Marvar peering down at a narrow country lane, straining his eyes.

It was already afternoon, the wind was stirring the grass. Dyer could see them on the skyline, near the grazed peak. The wind was flogging Marvar's hair into his eyes. He was still climbing.

Again, he turns. The view to the lake. The conifers outlined against Martindale church. But not a stir in the valley below.

Then he spots it, a white dot moving through the bracken.

The van trundles up the winding lane, over a cattle grid, coming to a halt in a passing point beside a cairn. There's a moment of stillness. The doors open. Two men step out, then a dark-haired woman. They stand, looking up. The woman is cradling something.

'Shula!' he calls. 'Samir! Look! It's Shula – and Jamileh.'

He is hopping from hillock to hillock – shouting aloud – in a dirge.

'Shula!' through the hair that flops over his face. 'Jamileh!'

It was the last day of term. Tripping out of the Taylorian to collect Leandro, Dyer realised that winter was over. He had come to life. His focus was abnormally sharp, as if he'd slept on his arm and the blood was flowing into it again. Suddenly, he saw blue in the sky.

He wanted to roll on his back in the mud. He wanted to chase pigeons and bark at swans.

They would get a dog, even though his son was admitting to second thoughts about a cockadoodle. 'I like Spassky...'

'But what?'

'What if it's not like Spassky? And doodles are *their* thing. Anyway, they're a bit too curly.'

'What would you say to a border collie crossed with a mutt?'

He had longed for his loss to recede, until with a gentle last push, he could say goodbye to it, and face a desired future, alive.

There were complications, like her mother, like the fact that they had not kissed even, like the fact that Leandro had not met her, that Dyer had yet to speak his flame; but these were the loose strands out of which any life was stitched.

He still had left in his wallet one blank post-it note of Marvar's. To write on it what complicated equation he, John William Dyer, chose.

Spring was not far off. Everything seemed to be aware of it. The branches trembled, the sun appeared for longer. On the other side of the canal, bicyclists tinkled their bells. In the patio, in the tub, a snail crept further up the magnolia. A bird had pecked at its shell.

Gilberto Gil is playing. The cool of the evening. The sky red above the terrace.

Acknowledgements

THIS NOVEL MAY BE READ on its own or as a sequel to *The Dancer Upstairs*. It is a work of fiction, no one is drawn from anyone in life. Although it shares a superficial geographical proximity to another prep school in Oxford, where I spent five happy years, the Phoenix School is an imagined place.

I am indebted to the following for their help: Charles Alexander, Clare Alexander, Jonathan Beswick, Charlie Bowman, Justin and Jane Byam-Shaw, Mary Chamberlain, Jonathan Colchester, Steven Cowley, John Davies, Matthew Dodd, Mark Evans, Miguel Farias, Vernon Flynn, Liz Foley, Mike Forrest, Peter and Jessica Frankopan, Sheru George, Barry Green, John Hatt, Gillian and Jo-Ann Johnson, Peter and Juliet Johnson, Ian Kellas, Craig Kendall, Matthew Kidd, David Kingham, Piers Litherland, Nigel McGilchrist, Kate McIlwain, Brian Menell, Alain and Max Michaelis, Philip Norman, Jean and Marie de Portales, Henry Porter, Harry F. Robey, Nick Robinson, Ben and Max Shakespeare, Christopher and Francesca Shakespeare, Kasia Starega, Yiannis Takitos; the staff of the Taylorian Library.

I would like to pay tribute to *A Death in Brazil*, by Peter Robb (Bloomsbury, 2004); *Brighter than a Thousand Suns*, by Robert Jungk (Harcourt, 1970); *The Master and His Emissary*, by Iain McGilchrist (Yale, 2009); *The Old Man and the Sand Eel*, by Will Millard (Viking, 2018); *Losing an Enemy*, by Trita Parsi (Yale, 2017); *Kabloona*, by Gontran De Poncins (Reynal & Hitchcock, 1941); the Iran Human Rights Documentation Center.

The lines *'Trouble, trouble, trouble, trouble/Trouble been dogging my soul since the day I was born'* are taken from the album 'Trouble', by Ray LaMontagne, 2004.

The lines from 'Chomei at Toyama' are from Basil Bunting's *Complete Poems* ed. Richard Caddell © Bloodaxe Books 2000. Reproduced by kind permission of Bloodaxe Books.